For every Tommy, sailor and airman who
went to fight in the Great War.

Also for the people who staffed the
hospitals, casualty clearing stations,
ambulance stations and other medical
outposts in France and elsewhere.

For Grant and Mark with much love always.

# 1

Wood Green, North London, Summer 1916

'Mum would really appreciate you coming back from France especially for her funeral, you know.'

Olivia Bone knew nothing of the sort. It wasn't as though she and the deceased had got on. But as the woman had been her aunt, and also her father's dirty little secret, Olivia had felt that she owed Sybil Wright something. During his lifetime Tommy Bone had shown his lover little respect, and for that alone his eldest daughter believed there was a final debt to be paid.

Once their astonishing deceit had finally come to light, Olivia had thought she hated her father. That was before she joined the Voluntary Aid Detachment. As a junior nurse serving in a military hospital on the Western Front, she had seen things that had given her better reasons to rail at life's vile injustices.

Olivia's mother Aggie Bone had never known about her husband's cheating. She had died in her prime, giving birth to her only son. Thereafter, Tommy had carried on sneaking about with his wife's sister even though he was free to marry.

Now the adulterers were dead too, Olivia sincerely wished them both peace. Her mother had had the last laugh, after all. Aggie had been of a beautifully sunny disposition, popular with all. Her guilt-ridden husband had sunk into bitterness after she'd passed away and had eventually met with a violent end. As for Sybil, she might have managed to seduce her brother-in-law but she had never captured Tommy Bone's heart. He'd loved his wife until the day he was murdered.

Olivia's pensive mood was cut short by her cousin Ruby shaking a plate of fishpaste sandwiches beneath her nose. To be polite Olivia took one although the smell of bloater was making her feel queasy.

It was a stifling hot summer day and the windows and curtains had been closed in the small terraced house in Wood Green. The wake had been hastily arranged after Olivia had agreed to stump up the cost of a modest do. Ruby might have been the deceased's daughter but she'd baulked at the idea of laying out for a few plates of food to give her own mother a send-off. She had reminded her cousin Olivia — as she often resentfully did — that as the best off amongst them, she could afford to pay for things like funeral teas. Olivia knew she'd been fortunate to inherit her fiancé's house after he'd perished at Ypres. Nevertheless, she would far sooner have had her beloved Joe safe at home and was growing fed up of being put upon financially by family members.

Olivia was itching to leave the wake, or at least escape into the garden for a breath of air. After another ten minutes or so she and her brother and sisters would have stayed for a decent enough time and could catch the bus back to Islington where they all lived.

As Ruby wandered off to thrust the plate of sandwiches under other noses, Olivia's younger sister sidled up to her to hiss, 'Bleedin' stinks in here!' Maggie wrinkled her nose in distaste. 'Let's go home, Livvie.'

'In a little while.' She gave Maggie a sympathetic smile. 'Coming out the back for a breather?' she suggested, glancing about for somewhere to dispose of her half-eaten sandwich. She finally decided to take it with her and feed it to the sparrows in the garden.

'So what did the inquest make of your aunt's sudden passing, love?'

Before the girls had made it out of the parlour they were brought to a halt by a neighbour's question. Mrs Cook was clutching a cup and saucer in one hand and Olivia's elbow in the other. She inclined her head expectantly, hoping to hear some juicy gossip. All she got was a couple of neutral smiles, so she tried a different tack. 'Such a shock it was to hear what happened to the poor cow.' Ethel sucked her teeth. 'She looked right as rain just the week before when I bumped into her up the road . . .'

'It was her nerves made her giddy. Me mum suffered something chronic with 'em,' Ruby rudely butted in, making Ethel jut her chin defensively. 'She must've fainted and hit her head. Doctor said so.' Ruby pursed her lips as her next-door neighbour stalked off with an affronted sniff. 'Nosy old bag. Anybody asks

3

what happened to me mum, just say she come over funny and fell off a chair while cleaning the pitcher rail.'

Olivia and Maggie exchanged a glance, murmuring agreement to the yarn. The family, and no doubt the neighbours too, knew that Sybil Wright had never bothered keeping anything clean, even herself. Their aunt had been a slattern and a drunkard; the parlour of her home held an unpleasant colour of ground-in dirt and stale alcohol. She'd had her accident after she'd been drinking. She *had* tumbled off a chair, fracturing her skull on the hearth. But it had happened while she'd been reaching for another bottle of gin, stashed on top of the wardrobe. The sisters understood that Ruby didn't want that broadcast. Neither did they. Family stuck together even if it meant bending the truth. Olivia pitied her young cousin Mickey; he had found his mother lying dead on the floor when he came in from school that day. The kitty kept in the jar on the shelf had been missing, but Sybil had been known to raid the rent money for booze. A full bottle of gin had been found smashed on the floor beside her. Ruby had bleakly joked that the sight of that going to waste would have given her mother a heart attack even had she survived the fall.

A pretty young woman had entered the parlour and was craning her neck to catch Ruby's eye. 'Connie Whitton's turned up after all. She told me she couldn't make it.' Ruby waved at the newcomer. 'Offer these around, will you, Livvie?' The sandwich plate was shoved at

4

her cousin. 'They're already curling.' Ruby glanced at her neighbours, grouped together on the sofa. 'If you and Maggie could just lend a hand collecting up the used crockery and doing the washing up, that'd be a help.' Ruby sidled away to speak to her friend.

'Yes, sir, no, sir, three bloody bags full, sir,' Maggie muttered sourly, watching the two peroxide blondes nattering together.

'Come on, we did say we'd help out. Sooner it's done, the sooner we can head home.' Olivia passed the plate of sandwiches to her sister. 'Nancy can pitch in too.' She beckoned the youngest Bone girl with a jerk of her head. Nancy stopped staring morosely into her empty teacup and got to her feet.

'Alfie's in the street kicking a ball up against the alley wall with Cousin Mickey,' she said in answer to Olivia's question about their younger brother's whereabouts.

Alfie got on well with Mickey. The boys were both nearly ten years old and enjoyed a game of football. Just then Olivia's attention was diverted to a quiet commotion on the other side of the room. Ruby and Connie appeared to be bickering; a moment later they disappeared into the corridor as though to keep their differences private.

'You'll never guess what, Livvie?' Ruby had come up behind Olivia as she was flicking washing-up water off her fingers.

'What?' She turned about, drying her hands on a towel. She'd been expecting to hear something unfavourable after witnessing that scene but was nonetheless surprised to see her cousin's pallor. 'What is it?' she asked quickly. 'I saw you having words with Connie.'

'She's brought me dad with her. He turned up looking for us in the Bunk 'cos he thought we still lived there. He's waiting outside.'

Olivia was speechless. Edward Wright had disappeared a decade ago following a huge bust up when he discovered his wife and Tommy Bone were having an affair. Sybil and her kids had then moved into a slum in Islington known as the Bunk. 'Your *dad*?' Olivia exclaimed in an astonished squeak.

'He's outside by the gate. Ain't seen him in so long that I'd forgot I had one. Mickey was still in his pram when Dad run out on us. Perhaps I should just ignore him. 'S'pect he'll go away.' Ruby was keeping her voice low, shooting glances here and there to detect any eavesdroppers.

'Don't think he will.' Olivia gave a discreet nod of her head. But for Ruby giving her a clue to the stranger's identity, she would never have recognised the grey-haired individual who had just appeared in the doorway. She remembered her uncle Ed as a mild-mannered man with fair colouring; now he looked careworn and close to seventy. He wasn't that old. Her aunt had died at the age of fifty-one, just a couple of years younger than her estranged husband.

'Gawd's sake!' Ruby exclaimed under her breath. 'Why couldn't he wait outside? This'll start the old biddies off.' She looked flustered. 'What if he starts asking awkward questions

6

about Mum and Tommy . . . and us?'

'Well, you'd better go and say hello. He was Sybil's husband, after all. He must've found out about her funeral and come to pay his respects.'

'They never got divorced neither. Mum told me that. But we don't know him any more . . . '

'Reckon it's time to put that right,' Ed said gruffly. He'd come up unobserved behind Ruby, making her jump. 'It's been a long time, love. Too long. Wish now I'd mended bridges sooner instead of waiting until this sad day.'

'Too much water gone under this particular bridge.' Ruby wriggled her fingers free from his clasp. 'Mum could've done with some help while she was still alive. She might not have ended up in such a bleedin' state if we hadn't had to doss down in a slum.'

Ed flushed at the rebuff. 'You're still a lovely-lookin' lass,' he gamely persevered. 'How's little Mickey? Not so little now, I'll bet.'

'You've probably just walked straight past him in the street. So that says it all really, don't it?' Ruby snapped. 'You don't know us and we've nothing to say to you. So go away and leave us alone.'

'Aw . . . don't be like that, love. When I heard about Sybil's accident I wept me heart out.' Ed shook his head. 'Not saying I didn't hate her at one time fer what she did to me, but I kept me distance and let her live her life as she wanted. Didn't interfere even though I've not been that far away.' He glanced at his eldest niece who'd been quietly listening to the exchange. 'How's your lot, Olivia? I heard that Tommy had passed

7

on. Not going to be a hypocrite and say I was sorry. He and me wife between 'em ruined my life. Nobody deserves to go the way he did, though.' He paused. 'Ever find his murderer, did they?'

Olivia shook her head, giving her uncle a small smile. She respected his honesty and couldn't blame him for the way he felt. Only a saint would easily forgive and forget being made to look a fool by the people closest to him. In a way Olivia was glad her mother was no longer around and had been saved the humiliation this man had suffered.

'So where've you been then?' Ruby was incensed that they'd been struggling to keep a roof over their heads in the worst street in North London when this man could've pitched in and helped.

'I found a place over Edmonton way. I picked up with a widow and we're happy enough.'

'Oh, good fer you,' Ruby said sarcastically. 'So what's brought you back here then? Me mum didn't have two ha'pennies. If you've turned up hoping fer a pay-out as her next-of-kin, you can forget it.'

Olivia cautioned her cousin with a frown. Ruby was so het up that she'd let her voice rise and hadn't noticed that her neighbours were taking an interest.

'Shut up now till we're on our own.' Ruby gave Ed a fierce glare. 'I'll get rid of this lot.' She made a pecking movement with fingers and thumb, mimicking gossips at work, then began grabbing cups and plates out of her neighbours' hands, receiving some indignant tuts. 'Thanks for coming, but I'm clearing up now.'

'We'll be off too and let you have a private talk,' Olivia said. Her sisters had returned from the backyard where they'd shared a crafty cigarette. They remained loitering by the door, uncertain what was going on but sensing a bad atmosphere. Olivia could remember her uncle but he was a stranger to Maggie and Nancy. They'd been toddlers when he disappeared, and her brother had been a new-born baby.

Once the parlour had emptied, but for family, Ruby blurted, 'I want you lot to stay.' She grabbed Olivia's arm. 'After all, I ain't *really* any more his daughter than you are. We both know Tommy Bone fathered the lot of us. And if Ed don't already know that, then it's time he did.'

For a long, embarrassing moment there was a leaden silence in the room. Then Ed laughed . . . a shrill sound of disbelief. 'Who told you that nonsense?' He shook his head. 'Sounds like the sort of claptrap Sybil would come out with when she'd had a few. She liked to be the centre of attention. *I'm* yer dad, dear.'

'You're not. And neither is Mickey yours.'

''Course he is!' Ed looked to be getting narked now. 'The boy's got a bad foot. Wish he didn't, of course, but . . . ' He shrugged. 'Me father's to blame fer that. He was afflicted 'n' all. He died quite young . . . in the Boer War. He might've been a cripple but he didn't let it hold him back, God rest 'im.'

'You'd say anything, wouldn't yer, to get round me? Well, it won't work.' At first Ruby had

9

been shocked, as they all had, when her mother had announced that Tommy Bone had fathered the lot of them. The girl had got used to the idea now, though, and liked being half-sisters with Tommy's daughters. She didn't want this man coming back into her life, stirring things up. Yet what he'd said about his father having a crippled foot was making her wonder. He'd not had time to make it up; it had come straight off the cuff.

Maggie and Nancy were rudely elbowed aside on the threshold as a broad-set, dark-haired fellow barged into the room. 'Who's dis now?' he slurred while swaying on his feet and glowering at Ed Wright. Riley McGoogan was Ruby's boyfriend. She'd banned him from her mother's funeral on two counts. Sybil couldn't abide him, and he used a wake . . . or any gathering . . . as an excuse for a booze-up. And when drunk, he was keen to pick a fight.

'Clear off and sober up. I told you to stay away.' Ruby turned her back on him.

'I stayed away, so I did, until I saw de old gels leavin' . . . '

'Well, you're still too bleedin' early showin' yer face,' Ruby replied through gritted teeth. 'So piss off fer a bit longer.'

'If this fellow is upsetting you, dear, I'll get rid of him.' Ed was keen to show his protective, paternal side to win her over.

Riley was nice-looking, and when sober a fairly pleasant individual. But today he was neither of those things. His hair and clothes looked dirty and dishevelled as though he'd already been in a scrap. He looked to be spoiling for another as he turned a sneering look on Ed. 'No, I'll get rid of *you*.' He pointed a finger. 'Through that fookin' window!'

Olivia hastily steered her uncle towards the door. 'He's Ruby's boyfriend,' she informed Ed in a murmur, escorting him into the corridor.

'We're off. We'll wait for you by the bus stop.' Maggie glanced nervously past them at the wild-eyed Irish fellow in the room beyond, swinging his arms about while arguing with Ruby.

'You'd best get going too, Uncle Ed. There's no reasoning with Riley when he's under the influence. Perhaps come back and see Ruby another time when things aren't so . . . sensitive.' She gave him a sympathetic look.

'I didn't want nuthin' of Sybil's,' he protested. 'That ain't why I come. Tell Ruby that, will you? Just thought . . . oh, it don't matter.' He sighed. 'Made a mistake coming today of all days. But I do want to make it up with me kids if I can. Sybil turned 'em against me. But now she's gone, there's a chance for us to muddle along.' He shook his head. 'They *are* my kids. Why me wife would tell such a wicked lie about it is beyond me.'

Olivia reckoned she knew why. It had been Sybil's greatest wish to get Tommy Bone to marry her. Perhaps she thought she'd hit upon a way to do it by telling him he'd fathered her kids. Tommy probably hadn't got a clue if he was responsible or not. All of them were blonde and had similar looks. Whatever the truth of it, Ruby had told her something earlier that she hadn't known. Ed Wright and Sybil had never divorced, so there could have been no legal union between her father and aunt. If Sybil had lied to Tommy about being divorced, perhaps she'd lied to him about other things too.

'What did Tommy say about it all?' Ed was like a dog with a bone, worrying at it. 'Did he claim he'd fathered 'em?'

'Dad would never talk about it,' she answered truthfully.

'They set up home together, so I heard. Tommy passed on not long after, didn't he?' Still Ed chipped away.

'They lived here, in our old house.' Olivia glanced back at her childhood home. Once upon a time the place had held happy recollections of when her mum had been alive, and the rooms had been bright and clean and full of love and hope. Those memories had withered now and for Olivia it was just like any other building in the street. Nothing special. Her home now . . . the place where she felt content . . . was in Islington. The property her soldier fiancé had left to her in his will.

'If I'd found out she'd been spreading such lies, I'd've been back sooner.' Ed sounded quite emotional. 'Made a laughing stock of me twice over. Cheating on me then telling everybody I couldn't father me own kids!'

'It wasn't like that.' Olivia patted his arm. 'None of us knew until quite recently. There was a big upheaval in the family when I met my fiancé and left home. It just came tumbling out then. Only us kids were told, though.' The scandal *had* leaked out more generally, in fact, but Olivia thought it best to play that down to save her uncle's feelings.

'So you're getting married, are you?' Ed managed a smile. 'He's a lucky man. You always was a lovely kid. Pretty as a pitcher. Just like yer mum.' He gave a rueful chuckle. 'I liked Aggie, y'know. Bet Tommy never knew that. But Sybil did. I told her it'd be a good thing if she could act a bit more like her sister. Your mum was a proper lady.'

'I still miss her something terrible,' Olivia said wistfully. 'But I'm not getting married. My fiancé died at Ypres.'

Ed gave her a clumsy hug. 'Dreadful the way the war's dragging on. I've volunteered part-time for the Home Front. We've all got to show willing and I can fit it in between me work shifts.'

'I'm a VAD, serving in a French hospital . . .' The rest of what Olivia had been about to say was drowned out. The argument that had been rumbling inside the house broke out in earnest. The sound of missiles being thrown could be heard. Riley burst out of the door and stomped off, swearing, having given Ed an evil-eyed stare on passing.

'He don't seem the sort any man would want his daughter involved with.' Ed grimaced. 'I know I've got no right to tell Ruby how to live her life though. She's a grown woman.' He glanced along the street to where his son was playing football. 'Glad to see the boy's not too down about losing his mother. Life goes on, don't it?' Ed sighed. 'I'd best be off. You take care of yerself, Olivia.'

'You too.' Olivia looked at Mickey. He might seem as though he'd bucked up quickly but Ruby had told her he'd howled like a banshee for days after finding his mother dead. It must have been a dreadful scene for the poor lad to come home to. Yet when Sybil had been alive he'd had to be quite independent. His mother had been flaked out on her bed a good deal of the time, nursing her 'nerves' and her gin bottle. Olivia turned back to the house, knowing she should say goodbye to Ruby before escaping home to some peace and quiet.

Ed kept a careful distance behind Riley's lumbering figure. He came abreast of the boys playing football and stopped for a moment to watch them. He stepped off the kerb as though to talk to Mickey but then seemed to change his mind. He continued up the road and his son hobbled after the football his cousin had just booted past him. The crippled lad was oblivious to the fact that his father was close by, peering over his shoulder at him.

Ed was unaware that he, in turn, was being observed. The watchful man rolled himself a smoke while keeping a crafty eye out. But as the football bounced close to the hedge behind which he'd stationed himself, he pulled the brim of his cap low over his long, lank hair and quickly disappeared along the alley.

# 2

'I had a feeling Ruby'd go mad if her dad turned up out of the blue.' Connie Whitton crossed her arms over her chest, looking sulky. 'Weren't my fault though. Mrs Keiver come across him wandering about like a lost soul outside her house.' Connie prodded Olivia on the arm to gain her attention. 'Mrs K told him I was on me way to the wake and he could tag along. What could I do then 'cept say alright?' Connie's grumbling tailed off as the bus pulled up at the stop in Wood Green High Street.

They all trooped on. Maggie and Nancy took a seat together. Connie immediately plonked herself down next to Olivia so Alfie had to sit behind on his own.

'I reckon Ruby's gonna have to get used to him being around.' Connie continued where she'd left off.

'I always quite liked Uncle Ed,' Olivia finally got a word in edgeways.

'I thought he seemed nice enough,' Connie agreed. 'Paid me bus fare over from Islington, he did, by way of thanks.'

'I wish Riley'd stayed out of the pub today of all days.' When Olivia had said goodbye she'd found Ruby in tears. Dealing with her prodigal father and her belligerent boyfriend on the same day as her mother was buried had been too much for her. Olivia had left Mickey making his sister a cup of tea. The boy was used to the couple rowing. He thought a lovers' tiff with Riley had set her off. He'd not been told that his supposed father had turned up out of the blue.

'Riley's been on the turps since he got his call-up papers.' Connie stuck a cigarette between her scarlet lips and struck a match. 'He probably thinks if he drinks hisself to death he'll be given an exemption, the thick Mick.' She started to chuckle.

At the start of the conflict men had willingly done their patriotic duty. But reports of the carnage on foreign battlefields and the grave-yards filling up had changed all that. The likes of Riley McGoogan didn't want to enlist but didn't like the idea of being beaten by the Hun either. Riley and his pals would often be seen spouting off about military tactics outside the pubs, like kerbside generals.

'There she is!' Connie had spotted a rough-looking, fiery-haired woman and jumped up as the bus started to pull in at the stop in Islington. 'I'll have her, getting me in trouble with me best friend like that! She should've kept her gob shut.'

'Good luck,' Olivia said. The idea of petite Connie 'having' Matilda Keiver — a bruiser of a woman who'd been known to bend a poker over the head of a burly man — was rather comical.

As expected, Connie did no more than glower in Matilda's direction before tossing her blonde head and hurrying off towards the bottom end of Campbell Road — or the Bunk as it was nicknamed due to the doss houses and tenements that lined both sides of the street.

The older woman raised a hand and waved as she spotted the Bone family alighting from the bus. Maggie and Nancy said their hellos and carried on towards their home in Playford Road. Olivia always stopped for a chat. The Keivers might be slum dwellers but they were good friends who'd helped her in the past.

'Went off alright for your aunt, did it?' Matilda enquired about the funeral in her rough tone.

Olivia rolled her eyes. 'Apart from Riley turning up drunk and threatening to chuck me uncle through a window, you mean.'

'Pretty normal sort of funeral then,' Matilda remarked, grinning. 'Don't think I've ever been to a wedding or a funeral that didn't finish in a punch-up.'

'Ruby wasn't happy to see her dad. She told him she and Mickey are Tommy's kids. That really upset him.'

'Didn't he already know?' Matilda sounded surprised.

'He didn't. Said it was all rubbish in any case. I'm wondering if he was right.'

'Well, there's only one person who'd know, and she ain't telling.'

'Perhaps Sybil didn't know either . . . not for sure.' Olivia shrugged.

'You could be right. Maybe she couldn't keep track with two men on the go.' Matilda settled her chapped hands on her sturdy hips. 'Anyway, I never had nothing against Ed Wright. He was always a decent enough chap when I knew him

17

way back. I was just a kid then, though.'

'Didn't know you were acquainted with him, Matilda.' Olivia sounded surprised.

'When he was a lot younger he'd visit his nan who lived in the street. She's long gone now. That's how Sybil knew about this place and came here for a cheap room after things turned sour for her. Ed thought she still lived this way so I put him right on that and told Connie to take him along to Wood Green so he could pay his respects.'

'So Connie said.' Olivia pulled a face.

'That tart needs to learn some manners. Only time she's got a smile fer a man is when he opens his wallet then his trouser buttons.'

Olivia blushed. Although she'd known Matilda for several years she still found the woman's coarse comments a bit much. Matilda wasn't casting aspersions groundlessly though. Connie *was* a part-time tart. The reason she got on with Ruby was that they dabbled in the same game to boost their regular wages.

'Have you heard from Jack?' Olivia hastily changed the subject. Matilda's husband had volunteered just after Christmas and the woman and her daughters had naturally been upset to see him go to war.

'We got a letter a few weeks back. He's well . . . or so he tells us. Alice writes to him regular. Been waiting a while now for a letter back from him.' Matilda's expression had hardened due to her having clapped eyes on her brother-in-law sauntering along on the opposite pavement. 'That one'd suit khaki 'n' all.' She snorted with contempt. 'Me sister reckons he's too poorly to go though.'

'Looks alright to me.' Olivia glanced over her shoulder at Jimmy Wild. He was a fellow with a high opinion of himself yet few people liked him.

'Nothing wrong with him. Apart from his yeller belly. Doctor ain't got a cure fer that.' Matilda patted Olivia's arm in farewell then disappeared indoors.

Olivia continued up the street. In the distance she could see her sisters strolling arm-in-arm. Alfie was trailing in their wake bouncing his football on his knees as he went. Olivia smiled. It was nice to be home with them. She had a few days left before she had to be at Charing Cross railway station at the crack of dawn to start her journey back to northern France. Her mind turned to the patients she'd left behind at St Omer camp hospital. She wondered which of them would still be there when she got back. Some would have been passed as fit for active service, some . . . the lucky ones . . . would have travelled home to convalesce. Others would have made their final journey to the cemetery at Wimereux.

And then Olivia thought of Lieutenant Lucas Black. She'd last seen him in Wimereux Cemetery on a bitter cold January day. They'd turned up separately to visit the graves of men they'd known and had recently lost to the war. It had been a strange chance meeting yet wonderful too because he'd told her she was precious to him, and she had returned the sentiment. He had given her a lift back to the

19

hospital where they'd parted in the way of people who had much more to say to one another yet were cautious of uttering it too soon and tempting fate. They had settled on 'take care' and 'good luck'. Yet later on, in her dormitory, Olivia had changed into her nurse's uniform berating herself for not having made more of those last moments spent gazing into his deep blue eyes while their breath mingled and turned misty in the bitter air.

Olivia prayed he was safe, wherever he was. She wished she could write to him. It wasn't just the war keeping them apart. Lingering jealousies and family problems had conspired against them. Even so she knew she'd fallen in love with Lucas. And she believed he felt the same way about her.

★ ★ ★

'Oh, he's such a sweetheart. I think I might take him home with me.' Olivia bounced her friend's son on her knee, making the little chap gurgle and dribble down his chin. It was the first opportunity she'd had to see the infant, now almost three months old. Olivia had been determined to set aside an afternoon before she returned overseas to visit and bring him a present. The teddy with a blue satin bow tied around its neck had been propped up in a corner of the sofa. It looked almost as big as Master Robert.

Cath Williams wiped her son's face with a hanky. 'I wish you could come over on leave more often, Livvie. I miss you something rotten, y'know.'

'Miss you too,' Olivia replied. Less than a year ago they'd worked together at Barratt's sweet factory in Wood Green. Then they'd both headed in different directions in life: Olivia to the Western Front as a trainee nurse and Cath to her new role as a wife and mother. In the few years they'd known one another they'd shared confidences that had drawn them very close indeed.

'Sometimes I wish . . . ' Cath's voice tailed off and she gazed wistfully into space.

'What d'you wish?'

'That I'd gone with you to France as a VAD like we first planned.'

'Daft ha'porth!' Olivia tutted mockingly. 'You were already pregnant when I left. You'd've been sailing back to Blighty pretty sharpish if you had gone.'

'I wouldn't . . . not if I'd've taken another trip to Lorenco Road first.'

Olivia stopped jigging the child on her lap and locked eyes with her friend. She couldn't believe she'd heard aright. 'You don't mean that, Cath. You wouldn't be without this little one.'

The hint that Cath wished she'd had another abortion had stunned Olivia. She was tempted to tell her friend she'd sounded horribly callous. But she held her tongue, aware Cath must be very unhappy to say such a thing. She wondered if her friend was suffering from a bout of new mum's blues. She'd heard one of the nurses at St Omer talk about having come across the condition when working as a community midwife.

The first time Cath fell pregnant, she and her fiancé hadn't enough saved to set themselves up in a home of their own. Unable to contemplate starting married life cooped up with her in-laws, Cath had asked Olivia to accompany her to an abortionist. Olivia would never forget helping her out of the seedy house in Lorenco Road on that dank autumn night.

'Trevor's still feeling chipper, is he?' Olivia tried to lighten the mood. Cath had written in her last letter that her husband was showing a slight improvement after being invalided home from France.

'He's taken a job in the ticket office down the railway station,' Cath replied. 'He knows he'll never be fit enough to labour out in the yard again. Sometimes a loud noise sets him back and he acts bonkers for a few days . . . ' Her eyes were shimmering with tears. 'Anyway, it's a wage and it gets him out of the house.' She wiped her face and stuffed her damp hanky in her pocket. 'It gives us both a break, and something to talk about when he comes home.'

Olivia felt such sympathy for Cath, and for Trevor tormented by shell shock. Olivia hoped that their darling son would restore some of the happiness they'd once shared.

'He still don't know,' Cath blurted. 'I never told him about Robert not being his.'

'I don't blame you. Bet he dotes on him.' Olivia stroked the baby's warm pink cheek with a forefinger.

22

'Idolises him,' Cath said gruffly. 'The moment Trev gets in he takes Robert out of his pram and fusses over him. Pays him more attention than he does me.'

'Well . . . there you are then. Nothing to worry about.'

'It makes it worse, though, Livvie. What if he finds out?' Cath whispered in anguish. 'It'll finish him.' She took her son from Olivia, holding him up and examining his small features. 'What if one day Trevor looks at Robert and sees his best friend in him?'

'They won't *be* friends if the truth gets out,' Olivia said bluntly. She stood up and gave Cath a searching look. 'At the moment only you 'n' me know. I can't ease your conscience for you.' Olivia bit her lip, trying to find the right words. It was a tricky situation. 'Look . . . why not let sleeping dogs lie?' She glanced at Robert, drowsing contentedly on his mother's shoulder. 'I wish my dad had taken his secret to his grave. He'd been carrying on for decades with my aunt yet it only came to light a few years ago. They've all gone now . . . but I can't forget what I know.' She paused then added, 'How will you feel if Robert finds out about it when he's older?'

Cath vigorously shook her head. 'I don't want him ever to know.' She put the boy back in his pram. 'I've been so looking forward to seeing you and now I've spoiled it, acting like a bloody misery.'

''Course you haven't,' Olivia reassured her. She glanced at the clock on the mantel and groaned. 'Oh, blast. Look at the time. I've got to finish packing. My train's leaving Charing Cross first thing in the morning.'

'Just stay for one more cup of tea,' Cath coaxed.

'I'd love to, but I can't. I shouldn't have left everything until the last minute.'

'Don't forget to write, will you?' Cath pleaded. 'I love hearing what you're up to. And keep safe.'

The friends embraced then Olivia peered into the pram. 'Robert looks like you,' she said honestly. 'That's what Trevor'll see when he looks at his son. His wife.'

'You always cheer me up.' Cath fondly rested her head on Olivia's shoulder.

'Likewise,' Olivia said stoutly, if not totally truthfully. 'Heard any scandals from the factory?' She was prepared to dawdle for a few more minutes so they could have a gossip and part company in fits of giggles, as they usually did.

'I have actually. D'you remember Deborah Wallis, the snooty secretary?'

''Course I do! She was always on at me about something.'

'She was always on at you 'cos she was jealous you had the managing director wrapped around your little finger.' Cath chuckled. 'Bleedin' hell, Livvie! We was all jealous of you about that.' She arched an eyebrow. 'And how is our dashing Lieutenant Black? Seen him recently, have you?'

'Not since I bumped into him at Wimereux Cemetery, months ago. I already wrote and told you about that.'

'I know there's more between you two than you're letting on.'

24

Olivia smiled, hoping to leave it at that. She couldn't tell anybody what was between them when she wasn't sure herself of what that was.

'Has our handsome ex-boss finally managed to make a dishonest woman of you?' Cath suggested.

'Not me.' Olivia hoped she'd pulled off sounding breezy.

'Sounds intriguing.' Cath cocked her head. 'Who then?'

Olivia knew she'd get no peace until she told her friend a little bit of gossip. 'A girl followed him out to France. She worked as a VAD in a hospital. Not my hospital, but I think I might have liked to meet her.'

'To scratch her eyes out?'

'No! She's a fellow nurse, it's always nice swapping notes. Anyway, I've heard she's quite refined so maybe she wouldn't have liked talking to me.'

Cath hooted a laugh at Olivia's denial. 'This is me you're trying to kid, Livvie,' she scoffed, making her friend blush and shrug. 'Anyway, don't reckon Lucas would have been keen on you two having a natter, the two-timing swine.'

'He's not cheating on her with me,' Olivia stuck up for Lucas. They'd never been a proper couple although they'd been out together on a couple of occasions. And they'd shared one passionate kiss. It seemed a long time ago now. Yet not a year had passed since that late-summer evening when he'd kissed her as if he meant it . . . after she'd instigated it. Not long after that she'd heard that Caroline Venner had pursued him to France and was claiming to be his pregnant girlfriend. And Olivia *was* jealous. There was no fooling Cath or herself on that.

'The cow must *really* want to get her hooks into him, chasing him abroad.' Cath snorted disapproval.

'It's fizzled out since. She's engaged to his brother. Could be they're married by now.'

'Crikey! That's a bit of a tangle then for the Black family. Is Lucas upset?'

'He said he'd no intention of proposing to her himself and was looking forward to being an uncle.'

Cath raised an eyebrow.

'He denies the baby's his.'

'But you're not convinced, are you, Livvie?' Cath said softly.

Olivia shrugged. 'He didn't deny sleeping with Caroline in France. But I've no right to pry. I chose Joe over him. Joe wanted a wife and Lucas wanted something else. He seems happy with a girlfriend, or mistress as I believe posh people call them.' She smiled wryly. 'And that brings us back to Deborah Wallis. You were going to tell me something scandalous about her. Has she cooked the books?'

'Sort of . . . how did you guess? The official version is that she quit of her own accord but apparently Mr Barratt sacked her for financial misconduct. Or, in other words, she nicked the petty cash.'

Olivia was shocked. She'd been joking about cooking the books. Miss Wallis had been at Barratt's for years and had never seemed the sort to get involved in something as distasteful as pilfering. She'd kept up a good show of being morally superior to the factory girls.

'What a fool to risk her job like that. I bet she was on a good wage,' Olivia said, ever practical.

Deborah had envied Olivia's close relationship with Lucas when they'd worked at Barratt's. In her turn Olivia had envied the secretary her job. Deborah had always looked clean and well groomed, lording it over the female shift-workers from her own pristine office. The likes of Olivia and Cath had toiled in sugar-stained sacking aprons, and spent long hours breathing in sickly air on the factory floor while rolling out sweets.

There was a person who was never usually mentioned between the friends but as Cath showed Olivia to the door she blurted out, 'How's Ruby? I was sorry to hear her mum died in an accident.'

'She's as well as can be expected. You know Ruby.'

'Oh, yeah,' Cath said sourly. 'I do 'n' all.'

Ruby flirted with any man who crossed her path. It never bothered her if he was spoken for. Cath's Trevor had succumbed to Ruby's flattery. They'd had a fling and it had almost broken up Cath and Trevor. That was in the past now, although Olivia knew her friend would never forgive Ruby for humiliating her. Cath's tit for tat affair had resulted in her son's birth.

Olivia turned and waved double-handed before disappearing around the corner. When the talk had turned to Ruby it had reminded Olivia that she was only a couple of streets away from

27

her cousins. She felt she ought to pop in and see them as she wouldn't be back on leave for months. She was very fond of Mickey and although she couldn't say the same about Ruby, they were all family.

Possibly even half-siblings, depending upon whose version of events was to be believed.

# 3

The short visit Olivia had planned had ended up as a stay of almost two hours. Mickey had been out but Ruby had been glad to have some company. She'd told Olivia that she'd not seen hide nor hair of her father or of Riley since her mother's funeral. Her boyfriend's absence was all that bothered her.

It would've been rude to leave the moment she'd finished the tea and stale biscuit her cousin had pressed on her, but Olivia knew that if she didn't get cracking soon she'd still be packing her trunk in the early hours. She needed a good sleep in order to face the lengthy rail and sea voyage in front of her. She was getting to her feet, doing up her coat buttons, when Ruby came out with something that made her stop and sink back down into the battered old armchair.

'Are you sure about that?' Olivia sounded dismayed.

Ruby nodded. 'I saw 'em out of the window. They were by the alley. Maggie didn't come further down the road. Perhaps she was worried I'd spot her and grass her up. And I have.' She pulled a face. 'Truth is, Livvie, I didn't know whether to say anything to you about it or not. If your sister *is* knocking about with Harry Wicks again, there's nothing much you can do about it when you're in France.'

Olivia sprang to her feet. 'Well, there's still

time to have it out with her before I leave.'

'Might be nothing, though.' Ruby looked as though she wished she'd kept her mouth shut. She'd nab any woman's man but she had her own code about snitching on the sisterhood. 'They was only talking. Then Maggie went off up the road and he crossed over to his house and let himself in.'

Olivia's teeth nipped at her lower lip as she thought it through. Perhaps she *was* reading too much into it. But Harry Wicks had caused such trouble in the past for Maggie that it was difficult not to be anxious if their names cropped up in the same breath.

The Wicks family had lived over the road from the Bones for as long as Olivia could remember. Maggie and Ricky had walked to school together but hadn't been sweethearts until years later when Ricky went to war. At first the older of the two brothers had caught Maggie's eye. The daft girl had started encouraging Harry's attentions, thinking him more sophisticated than boys her own age. Maggie hadn't understood that his offers of booze and cigarettes came at a price. He'd callously taken advantage of her infatuation with him, getting her pregnant at fifteen. A self-induced abortion had followed. When Maggie told her sister she'd finally seen through the dirty swine, Olivia had breathed a sigh of relief. Ricky had been kind to Maggie, helping her get over his older brother's mistreatment.

Six months ago the young couple had been on the point of getting engaged . . . Maggie had even chosen her ring. But as for so many lovers, the war had turned their dreams of a future together to ashes when Ricky had been killed.

'Where've you been?' Ruby asked her brother, who had just sloped in looking red-cheeked and dishevelled. 'You've got school in the morning and should've been home ages ago. Get yourself some supper and turn in.'

Mickey set about sawing off a hunk of bread then spread it with bacon dripping. 'Alfie's gone to catch the bus. I expect he'd've waited for you if he'd known you was here, Livvie. We was playing hopscotch in the alley but it got too dark to see the lines.'

'Alfie ought to be indoors as well,' Olivia said. 'I'll have something to say to the little tyke.'

Mickey pulled open the sideboard drawer. 'Here . . . you can have these, Livvie.' He handed over a large bag of toffees. 'I've already let Alfie have some. Bet you nurses over there like a few sweets, don't you?'

'That's kind of you, Mickey,' Olivia said before suspicion set in. She glanced at Ruby and her cousin tapped her nose. 'Don't ask . . . won't tell yer no lies.'

'Right.' Olivia took the bag and pocketed it. It seemed churlish not to even though she realised Ruby had filched them from Barratt's sweet factory.

'Look after yourself over there, Livvie,' Ruby said, as they parted on the step. She began scouring the heavens, pulling the door to behind her to block out the light. 'Never know when they might come over, the baby-murderin' bastards.' She pulled her cardigan about herself

31

and gave a shudder.

Olivia peered at the night sky as well. The Zeppelin raids on London had resulted in scores of fatalities so far, many of them children. People were jittery and careful about observing the blackout, keeping curtains pulled after dusk.

'I hope Riley don't go off fighting without saying goodbye.' Ruby pouted. 'He's supposed to be bringing me in his share of the rent. You know what the landlord's like. The old miser don't take prisoners.'

Olivia did know what the landlord was like because she'd dealt with settling up on rent day when the Bones had lived in this house.

'Riley won't like me taking in a lodger to make ends meet after he's gone. He gets jealous.'

'Plenty of women are after a room, y'know.' With that parting shot, and a wave, Olivia set off. She broke into a jog as she turned the corner, hoping that Alfie would still be at the bus stop so they could travel home together.

Her brother had been in the queue and because he'd spontaneously rushed over, whooping happily at the sight of her, Olivia had toned down her telling off of him. They'd always had an especially close relationship.

The moment they got indoors Alfie headed off obediently to his bedroom to don pyjamas and Olivia called out to Maggie. And got no response. She headed up the stairs to find Nancy alone in the room the girls shared. Her youngest sister was lying on her bed flicking through a copy of Woman's Own.

'Where's Maggie?'

'Gone out with friends.'

Olivia felt a niggle of anxiety, wondering if she was with Harry Wicks. 'Workmates?' she suggested optimistically.

''Spect so,' Nancy said, studying a picture of some fancy buttoned boots.

It was unusual for Nancy to take an interest in fashion; in the past she'd pored over books of ballet dancers. But she'd outgrown that, Olivia supposed.

'Nance . . . ' As her sister looked up, Olivia blurted out, 'Tell me the truth now: has Maggie been going out with Harry again?' She didn't need to wait for a reply. Nancy's startled expression was answer enough. 'Is she with him now?'

Nancy sprang off the bed. 'She don't tell me nuthin' since I let her know what I think of her giving *him* the time of day after what went on . . . ' She broke off as the front door was slammed shut and footsteps sounded on the stairs. 'You can ask her about it yourself. I'm getting me supper.' She squeezed past as Maggie appeared in the doorway.

'What's up with her?' Maggie frowned.

'Where've you been?'

'You two been talking about me behind me back?' Maggie sounded defensive.

'Nancy hasn't told me anything. I have heard that you've been spotted with Harry Wicks again though.'

'That's not surprising, is it, seeing as he lost his brother and I lost me fiancé when Ricky died?' Maggie retorted. 'We're both grieving,

33

Harry said, and can help one another get over it.'

'I know you're terribly upset about Ricky . . . '
Olivia started quietly.

'Do you?' Maggie interrupted with a snort.
'Well, you never bloody showed it at the time! If
you'd come back to help me through it, I might
not have needed Harry to lean on. You're never
here to lend a hand with anything. We all have to
cope on our own, don't we?'

'And you're doing well at it,' Olivia soothed
her. 'Times are tough for everyone and we've all
had to make sacrifices. You're not a kid anymore,
Maggie.'

'I know and that's why I can make up me own
mind about Harry. If I want to see him, I will.'
She sniffed, looking more conciliatory. 'There's
nothing to it, anyhow. He reckons he needs me
to talk to, as much as I need him, 'cos losing
Ricky has sent his mum off her rocker. He said
it's hell living at home. I remember how it was
when we was all under one roof with Dad and he
made our lives a misery. So I understand how
Harry feels.'

'If he hates it at home, why doesn't he get
himself back to Flanders and help win this war?'
Olivia asked, a touch sourly.

'He can't. The wound on his leg's still not
healed.'

Olivia knew why that was. Harry Wicks had
tampered with his injury so as to stay signed off
active duty. He'd never wanted to enlist in the
first place. Olivia had manoeuvred him into it, to
get him away from Maggie who had been just
fourteen when the lecher started touching her

34

up. Olivia suspected he'd raped a nun and that had given her the ammunition she needed to force him to join the army. If he hadn't been guilty he wouldn't have gone along with it, in her opinion.

But she didn't want her last precious day at home to end in an argument so blocked thoughts of Harry Wicks from her mind. She sank down to sit on Maggie's mattress. 'You know I tried my hardest to be with you when I heard about Ricky's death. I couldn't get leave. I'd just got back after the Christmas holiday and we were short-staffed because so many of us had the runs . . .'

'Oh, you don't need to bother with excuses,' Maggie muttered. 'It don't matter now, anyhow. It's all in the past.'

'You make it sound as though you're over Ricky already, yet you wanted to marry him just months ago.' Olivia was surprised by her sister's indifference.

'You got over Joe pretty quick with Lieutenant Black,' Maggie returned.

'That's not true. Joe's been gone almost eighteen months and yet I think of him every day. And Lieutenant Black's a friend from my factory days.'

'Yeah . . . you've been saying that for a good long while. I still don't believe it, and I don't reckon anybody else does either,' Maggie sniped. 'You'd run to him if he crooked his little finger.'

That blunt remark hit home, making Olivia blush. She'd hoped she'd not made her growing feelings for him too obvious. Sometimes, when she couldn't get it out of her head that Lucas was rich and well connected and she was just a poorly educated factory girl, she wondered if they'd drift apart. And perhaps that would be for the best if she were to safeguard her heart.

'Didn't mean to upset you, Livvie.' Maggie had been observing the contradictory emotions darkening her sister's green eyes. 'I know you really like Lucas, and he feels the same about you. He makes that obvious,' she said softly.

'I do like him a lot. But I've not heard from him in months, and I'm getting a bit worried.'

'He'll be alright. He always is.' Maggie rushed to give her a hug. 'Ricky told me he was the best commanding officer any soldier could have.'

Although it was nice to have Maggie's comforting arms about her, Olivia made herself buck up. 'Yes . . . he'll be alright,' she echoed. 'Now how about we get some fish and chips for our last supper together, as a treat?'

Maggie smiled agreement. 'You don't need to worry about me, Livvie. I saw Harry at the flicks with a girl a couple of weeks ago, and I didn't even care.' She reinforced the fib with an idle flick of her finger. For more than an hour she'd watched the couple canoodling rather than swoon over Rudolph Valentino.

'Well, I don't envy the girl, and I'm bloody relieved you don't either.' Olivia spread her arms, getting up off the bed. 'Give us a hug.' Maggie bounded forward and Olivia enclosed her in a fierce embrace. 'You're doing a grand job running this place and keeping the others on their toes. Mum 'n' Dad would be so proud of you, Mags.' Olivia held her sister at arms' length, studying her. 'When I get back to France, I'll visit Ricky's resting place and lay some flowers for you. It's been cool and the woods behind the camp might still have bluebells.'

'Thanks.' Maggie sighed. 'I do miss him, but I wasn't ever head over heels with Ricky. We just sort of got together after I had the miscarriage. He didn't want to die never having had a wife and kids, so I said I'd marry him. In the end he did, though, didn't he? I wish now we'd got married straight away, for his sake.'

'I know,' Olivia said gently. 'I think you did the right thing waiting though.' She made a determined effort to cheer them both up. 'Right. I'll get off to the fish shop or he'll've sold out of haddock.'

'I wasn't with Harry tonight, honest,' Maggie said, stopping her sister by the door. 'I've just been round to Mrs Keiver's. Alice was upset at work 'cos they'd not heard from her dad in a while. He normally writes regular as clockwork. You can ask Matilda if you don't believe me.'

''Course I believe you!' Olivia felt a twinge of guilt. She felt anxious too. She liked Jack Keiver and hoped he was alright. Whatever was brewing around Ypres might have stopped thousands of soldiers' letters from getting through to loved ones. Including Lucas's.

By the time she reached Seven Sisters Road Olivia's frown was back in place. She tried to dislodge from her mind the worry that Harry might talk Maggie round. Her sister was older, more knowing about men's ways now than she had been when she'd fallen pregnant at fifteen. But not getting knocked up again, and not falling back under Harry Wicks's spell, weren't the same thing.

★ ★ ★

'Fer a dead man you look pretty good, mate.'

The sour comment had the dead man spinning about, startled. He saw behind him a wiry, grey-haired fellow leaning against the wall.

Inaudibly, Herbert Hunter cursed the fact that he'd been rumbled. He'd hoped to pick his time for the big reveal that he was still very much alive. He stepped closer to the stranger, trying to get a better look at him through the fading light. There was something familiar about him but he couldn't quite put his finger on what it was. While pondering he tried some diversionary chit-chat. 'Be bleedin' glad when this war's done with, eh?' He busied himself prising the lid off a tobacco tin.

'Amen to that.' Ed Wright glanced up. It was on this sort of moonless night that Zeppelins would come gliding over the horizon like a shoal of silver fish. But he had something more important on his mind now than an air raid. 'Don't recognise me, do you? Bet you wish I hadn't recognised you, don't yer, Herbie, now you've gone to the expense of buying yerself a new barnet?'

'How about you introdooce yerself then?' Herbie retorted. He'd heard the mockery in the other man's voice when he'd mentioned the wig.

38

With a show of insouciance Herbie fumbled with tobacco strands and a Rizla.

'You knew me late wife better'n you did me. You shacked up with Sybil for a while in Wood Green. Didn't treat her so well, so I heard.'

★   ★   ★

The penny finally dropped and Herbie recalled where he'd seen this fellow before. At Sybil's wake. Herbie, concealing himself in the shadows, had wondered at the time who was chatting to that little cow Livvie Bone. 'According to Sybil, *you* never treated her well, Ed Wright. She never had a good word for you.' Herbie stuck the finished roll up in his mouth and it wagged about as he added, 'Ran out on her, didn't yer, when the boy was still a babe-in-arms?'

'Had me reasons . . . good ones at that,' Ed snapped. 'What were yours for laying into her?' He could tell he wasn't going to get an answer to that. Herbie had pulled his hat brim down, shielding his expression as he puffed out smoke.

Ed didn't need an answer in any case. He'd made it his business to talk to the busybody living next door to Ruby. He'd not wanted his daughter knowing that he was spying on her, so had waited until she went to work before knocking up Mrs Cook. The woman had been suspicious of him at first, although she'd remembered him from Sybil's funeral. When he'd told her he was her deceased neighbour's husband, Ethel had opened up. He'd found out that Herbie and Sybil had lived there alone for a period and that a fight would erupt every rent day, ending with Sybil screaming because she'd taken a right-hander.

Ed had felt like knocking the living daylights out of his wife when he found out she'd been cheating on him with her brother-in-law. But he never had. He'd gone after Tommy Bone instead. He didn't hold with beating women. And he despised men who did.

Herbie had racked his brains but couldn't come up with an answer as to how this fellow knew him . . . unless he'd seen him coming and going at Sybil's place.

'I never lived in Campbell Road meself but I had family who did, so I know all about you.' Ed put him out of his misery. 'Years back you thought you was Jack the Lad, didn't yer? Didn't need a syrup then with yer wavy brown hair. Yeah, I remember you. You was run out of the Bunk for ill-treating yer wife 'n' kids.'

Herbie sniffed, mouth turned down in a mean smile. 'Yeah, well, all water under the bridge now, ain't it?'

'Shame you didn't stay in water under the bridge . . . ' Ed jibed. Mrs Cook had told him that Herbie Hunter had gone missing then his body had been found, drowned. So the puzzle was, if Herbie was alive, who was the fellow they'd pulled out of Carbuncle Ditch?

'What is it you want, old man?' Herbie snarled through his teeth. 'If you've got a beef with me 'cos you think I was poking your old woman, you're wrong about that.' He snorted in disgust. 'You must be joking! All I wanted off her was a place to kip. Sybil weren't my type. She weren't any self-respectin' bloke's type. She was a drunken old slut. You'd know that if you'd seen her lately.'

'Have *you* seen her lately?' Ed pounced at once. 'She had an accident, y'know. Me son found her dead on the floor, poor lad.'

'So I heard,' Herbie said carefully, crossing himself for good measure.

In a rare civil conversation between them, Sybil had once told him that her husband was just a couple of years older than she was. So Ed wasn't a pensioner, although he looked like it. Sybil had also said she'd not clapped eyes on her husband in years and nor did she want to. Herbie was wondering what had rattled Ed's cage. Herbie hadn't lied about not sleeping with her. Although he would've. Any woman was better than none when the lights were out. But she'd no interest in that sort of thing and the ragbag hadn't been worth pushing into it.

'Did me wife know you was still alive, Herbie? Call on her, did you, to give her the glad tidings?'

Herbie dismissed the taunt with a lazy smile. Beneath the brim of his cap he darted furtive glances to and fro. He'd been about to go and get himself a ha'porth of chips but had retreated back into shadows when he'd spotted Olivia Bone entering the fish shop. He didn't look the same now he was wearing a wig and would've liked to think that she'd not recognise him. But he'd chickened out of putting that to the test. The girl had been his dead son's fiancée. In the past when they'd crossed paths she'd made it clear she'd no time for him. And he hated her. It was because of Livvie Bone and her friends in high places that he'd ended up dumped semi-conscious in a ditch and left to drown. Those responsible should pay. His dead son's house should belong to him, as next-of-kin, not Olivia Bone. Joe had never married her after all.

'How about you then, Ed? Strange you showing yer face here again after all them years in the wilderness. Wanted to make it up and get your boots back under the bed, did yer?' Herbie sucked his teeth. 'I bet Sybil weren't having none o' that. And now she's snuffed it,' he added craftily. 'Very strange . . . '

'I ain't spoken to her in years. I turned up for her funeral, to pay me respects. *I* never laid a finger on her in me life. I've heard that you and her went at it hammer and tongs every rent day.'

'Who told you that? Nosy cow next door?' Herbie straightened up. It was time to go before he said something he shouldn't. 'Well, nice talking to you, but I've got somewhere to be.' He shuffled away, brooding on things.

Ed Wright had taken a lucky guess and hit the nail on the head. Herbie *had* seen Sybil and he *had* been responsible for her falling off a chair on the day she died. But it had been an accident, and her own stupid fault. Herbie still had a key to the property in Ranelagh Road and had let himself in, hoping to sweet talk her into giving him lodgings again. He'd known he couldn't lie low for ever. He'd been staying with his sister in Southend for months but she'd finally thrown

42

him out. He'd ended up dossing under the pier. Then the weather had turned chilly and he'd known it was time to show his face again with a pitiful tale to tell.

On the evening he'd disappeared he and Sybil had had a fight. He'd planned on saying to her that he'd put distance between them so they could both calm down, but had missed her so much he'd come back a changed man, for her sake. He'd hoped that he'd not choke when he came out with such garbage, or that she'd laugh in his face and make him clump her. He'd truthfully not known that a body had been found that was thought to be his. He'd lost his hip flask in the water so could see how conclusions had been jumped to when it was recovered with a decomposed body. Herbie felt sorry for whichever poor sod had taken a tumble in the ditch . . . or been thrown in, as he had.

On the morning he'd called he'd found Sybil wobbling on a chair, reaching for a bottle of gin on top of the wardrobe. Eager to start off on the right foot, he'd offered to get it for her. She'd peered over her shoulder, looking like she'd seen a ghost . . . which was only to be expected, all things considered. She'd recognised him, wig 'n' all, and upset the chair. She'd gone down with a terrible crash, bashing her head. With hindsight Herbie knew he should have shown more sense than to risk startling the life out of her. He felt lucky that she'd not drawn breath to scream and brought the neighbours running. As it was he'd chosen to turn up on a Monday morning when he knew all the women would be in the washhouses out the back. Apart from Sybil. She'd long been a stranger to clean clothes. So he'd got nothing out of that visit other than the silver and copper from the kitty jar on the shelf.

Ed followed Herbie along the alley. He'd not finished with him yet. 'Where you off to then?' he called. But he got no reply and Hunter speeded up.

'See yer then, mate. I'll put it about that yer alright after all, shall I?' The subtle threat had the desired effect. Herbie scuttled back towards Ed.

'I've got a tongue in me head and can pass on me own messages. No need for you to interfere in me business.' He calmed himself down with difficulty. 'Don't want any bad feeling between us. How about a drink, Ed? Raise a glass to Sybil, God rest her.' He jerked a nod down the road. 'Ain't keen on the boozers round here. Fancy a walk back down the hill? Could wet our whistles in the Red Lion.' Herbie would rather be somewhere he wasn't known while he brooded on his next move.

'Thought you had somewhere to be?' Ed reminded him.

Herbie shrugged. 'Just a gel . . . she'll wait.' He had intended to head for Chapel Street after he'd bought his chips, to find a tart. There was one who was a friendlier sort than some of the younger, better-looking brasses hanging about the market. Sometimes she'd let him at her for a tanner if she'd had a quiet night and was glad of any punter. Herbie'd had an itch in his trousers but it was flagging now he'd worries on his mind. He didn't want it getting out that he was

44

alive until he was good and ready.

Ed was amenable to staying in this man's company a while longer and finding out what he could. He regretted having left it too late to bury the hatchet with his estranged wife. But Sybil had always been a funny woman. He'd not wanted to turn up and be humiliated by her in front of his kids. In the end when he'd turned up he *had* been humiliated, not by Sybil but by his daughter. He reckoned he'd deserved it too.

He'd come to the Bunk this evening to see Matilda Keiver. He knew she drank in the Duke and had planned to buy her a whiskey. He'd always liked the woman and without her help wouldn't have made it to Sybil's wake in time. A chinwag with Matilda could wait though. Grilling Hunter couldn't. Ed had a feeling that the weasel could easily disappear into thin air again.

Half an hour later, Ed was heading in one direction and Herbie in the other. Ed reckoned it had been a waste of time buying the man a drink. Hunter hadn't bought him one back and had let nothing slip about seeing Sybil recently. Ed only had a hunch to go on that his wife would still be around if Herbie Hunter hadn't turned up again.

# 4

St Omer Camp Hospital,
Western Front, Late-June 1916

'Oh, no! Did he leave me a letter?' Olivia cried in consternation.

'He didn't, I'm afraid . . . just a message that he was sorry he'd missed you. Lieutenant Black came with a few of his wounded men, saw them settled and then was gone.' Matron added dryly, 'I use the term 'men' loosely. All of them were very young. Two were well enough to be moved on after a week. The youngest one of all is still with us. Private Carter doesn't look a day older than his fifteen years either. Those recruiting sergeants want shooting . . . ' She clucked her tongue. 'Hardly an apt remark for a ministering angel! Nevertheless you get my drift, I'm sure.'

Olivia wholeheartedly agreed with her superior that boy soldiers shouldn't be here even if in their innocence they'd been enthusiastic recruits. Lucas had told her that Ricky Wicks had just been acting his age when he got into a snowball fight with a pal. He'd dodged an icy missile by leaping onto a firestep in his trench. For a second he'd forgotten where he was, giving a German sniper the perfect opportunity to find a target. Maggie's fiancé had died laughing because the snowball his pal had lobbed had missed him. He'd not known what had hit him.

46

Olivia had comforted men battling for a final breath and realised that, in a way, his clean death had been a blessing and Ricky had been one of the lucky ones.

Her eyes were filling with tears at the awful disappointment of having missed seeing Lucas. It was as though fate was conspiring to keep them apart. Knowing he was alive and well gradually overtook her frustration, though, and she felt a glow of relief.

Matron pushed back her chair from her desk, getting to her feet. Her office was housed in a hut that felt damp despite the approach of July. The persistent rain had seeped into its wooden boards and a constant chill permeated the air. She held her thin fingers out to the heater clogging the atmosphere with its pungent fumes.

'Well, how was your voyage? No scares en route, I trust?' Gladys Bennett rubbed her palms together. 'Fritz seems determined to make colanders of our ships with those blasted U-boats skulking in the deep.'

'It was a good crossing. I kept my breakfast down. I'm always glad to be back on dry land, though,' Olivia said simply.

'I'm certainly glad to have you back, Sister Bone. Our lot are gearing themselves up to make a big push around the Somme and unfortunately we're already counting the cost of it. Not many walking wounded came in the last convoy.' She sighed. 'We're short-staffed again, so off-duty time has been cut. The orderlies and the padre, bless him, have been helping out, making tea and buttering bread. Everybody's pitching in too with washing and delousing the new arrivals.'

'Haven't any more VADs been allocated to us?' Olivia asked, frowning.

'A few, but as fast as we take on we lose sisters to the barges ferrying the worst cases away from the front. The clearing stations and hospital trains are stealing our people too. We mustn't begrudge them; I know that at times their need is greater than ours.'

Gladys Bennett had been one of the first nurses to arrive in France in the early days of the war. She'd done a stint at one of the casualty clearing stations and her own younger brother had been one of her first patients. The primitive amputation he'd undergone hadn't saved him and she'd vowed never to return to one of those grim outposts close to the line. She'd since served in various base hospitals but could rarely be drawn into speaking of her loss or her private life.

'The VAD who arrived just as you went home has a raging toothache. She needs it pulled but refuses — from vanity, I think.' Matron tutted. 'Nurse Booth's a conscientious worker but if it worsens, she'll regret being stubborn.' Settling back down at her desk, she studied the staff rota. 'Then yesterday Flora Thistle twisted her ankle on the road to the village. She should have remained on site as the rain's churned the lanes into a bog. Luckily she managed to get help and arrived back on a farmer's cart, smothered in silt up to her waist. He wouldn't take a bean for his assistance and kindly donated three dozen eggs, too. We made egg flip and it was much appreciated by the boys.'

Olivia hadn't warmed to Flora Thistle and she knew the feeling was mutual. Flora thought her an upstart who had no business calling herself a nurse — and perhaps she was right. But Olivia resented its being rubbed in. For her part, she thought Flora a snob although she readily accepted the older woman was good at her job. Olivia might be far behind the others in skill and experience, but she was keen to learn. She dispensed medicines, bathed and fed patients, and knew how to take temperatures and apply ointments and dressings. She also made no bones about scrubbing and disinfecting equipment, or about giving the laundry maids a hand when the washing piled up and bandages and sheets were in short supply. She believed her hard work and generosity of spirit worthy of appreciation, if nothing else.

Despite some differences with colleagues, Olivia strove to be friendly, and to fit in. They all wanted the same thing after all: to ease the suffering of the soldiers brought into the hospital. She didn't blame Flora for wanting to escape into the outdoors, even in bad weather when it might have been more sensible to stay in. Every nurse used her precious off-time to breathe air that wasn't fouled with the smell of disease or disinfectant.

Olivia loved to walk up on the banks alongside the narrow roads or to trek through the dappled woods behind the hospital. The musky scent of peat and forest flowers, a breeze bringing the tang of hay ... those were pleasures to be

49

cherished. The grizzled men who came into the hospital would talk . . . often deliriously . . . of where they'd been and what they'd seen and smelled. She knew that just seventy kilometres away to the west was countryside where no trees remained standing. A landscape of charred stumps and churned earth embedded with metal was all that survived. Over that way the only brambles were man-made and instead of fruit bore scraps of ragged humanity on their deadly barbs. And whenever she allowed the desolate scene into her mind, she prayed again for Lucas's safety.

'Lieutenant Black might have posted you a letter. Mail arrived for you yesterday. It's been put on your nightstand.' Matron's tone turned brisk as she got to her feet once again. 'I've no choice but to throw you straight back in at the deep end, I'm afraid. We're all on double-shift this week. You've just two seniors in your section, so pay close attention as you might be unsupervised at times.'

Olivia went off like a homing pigeon towards her dormitory. Moments later she blasphemed beneath her breath, swung about and proceeded in the opposite direction. She'd forgotten that she was one of the nurses who'd been evicted to a different dormitory. Staff quarters were regularly turned over to ward space when more hospital capacity was needed. As she hurried along her thoughts were again with Lucas, and the rotten luck that had brought him to St Omer while she'd been in England attending her aunt's funeral.

The following morning the rain had stopped, the air was humid and the orderlies had rolled back the canvas walls of the tents. All that remained of the ward's structure was a canvas roof and a board floor. Those patients confined to bed could now appreciate the dull and misty outside world. Olivia, feeling ready to pitch back in after her break in England, made a point of searching out the casualty from Lucas's platoon. She reasoned that as she'd been denied a chance to speak to Lucas himself then a conversation with his young private was the next best thing. She found the lad on C4, her usual stamping ground. Matron hadn't exaggerated how youthful he looked. With his snub freckled nose and fair colouring, he reminded Olivia of her brother Alfie.

'So you're Private Carter, are you?' she greeted him, taking up his record chart.

'That's me right 'nuff, Sister.' The lad grinned. 'But you can call me Albert if yer likes.'

'Righto then, Albert, what's brought you here malingering, might I ask? You seem right as rain to me,' Olivia teased, noticing that he had the beginnings of a moustache feathering his top lip. His shoulders beneath his pyjama jacket were narrow but a bump of muscle contoured the cotton, developed no doubt from wielding a rifle and trench tool, and marching with the full humpy. His voice hadn't properly broken, though, and was uneven in pitch.

'Copped shrapnel in me calf, Sister.' Eager to

display his wound, he yanked up his baggy pyjama leg to let her see a large patch of puffy, inflamed skin.

'That's a fine bit of needlework. Once the infection clears up you'll be back on your feet in no time.'

'Lieutenant Black said it's a Blighty One.' The youth beamed. Every patient wore the same beatific expression when anticipating being allowed home to convalesce.

'Let's hope Doctor agrees with your commanding officer.' Olivia certainly expected him to. The boy shouldn't have been in France in the first place and the only right thing to do was to send him back to his mother.

'The lieutenant brought us here himself, y'know.' Carter sounded proud.

'That was good of him.' Olivia felt a fluttering inside her at this mention of the man constantly in her thoughts.

'Weren't just fer us he did it. He wanted to see a nurse. He said so.'

'Oh? What was her name?' Though her heart was drumming, Olivia looked a picture of ease as she sorted through the thermometers, standing in a jar of carbolic solution.

'He wouldn't tell. But I know it's you.'

'Do you now? How d'you know that?' Olivia selected a thermometer and shook it, avoiding the boy's twinkling eyes.

''Cos you're Nurse Bone. Me best pal told me the lieutenant was acquainted with you and your family. Wicksy said the lieutenant used to be the guv'nor in the sweet factory where you worked.'

He grinned cheekily. 'Brought any samples with you, Sister? I love liquorice.'

'I did bring some sweets back with me but the gannets in my dormitory devoured the lot.' Olivia had shared out the bag of goodies her cousin Mickey had given her. Her roommates had fallen on them, exclaiming they missed a good English stick-jaw toffee. Even Flora Thistle had cracked a smile and helped herself to one.

Private Carter suddenly sank down in the bed and turned his face away, as though he no longer wanted to talk.

'What's the matter?' Olivia frowned at Albert's sudden withdrawal. She didn't think he could be that upset about missing out on a few sweets. She'd hoped to find out Lucas's whereabouts from him.

There had been two letters on her nightstand, neither of them from Lucas. Hilda Weedon had written to tell her she was on her way to a hospital in Malta as a staff nurse now the Turkish campaign had foundered. Olivia's friend Rose Drew had also written. Rose was an ambulance driver and her letter had contained a promise to stop by when she was next picking up supplies from Wimereux and give Olivia another driving lesson.

'Are you feeling tired, young man?' Olivia put a gentle hand on Albert's hunched shoulder.

He shook his head. 'I miss me pal,' he croaked. 'He copped it. Wish it had been me 'stead of him.'

The identity of the snowball thrower suddenly became clear to Olivia. Private Carter was feeling guilty for skylarking with Ricky, with such tragic consequences.

'I think I know who you're talking about,' she said quietly.

The lad made a snuffling sound and pulled the sheets up to his chin.

She perched on the edge of Albert's bed and leaned over to comfort him. 'It's not your fault. You didn't know Ricky would jump up onto the firestep.'

Albert glanced over his shoulder with glistening eyes. 'Wicksy looked after me. Wasn't that much older but he treated me like he was me big brother. He stopped the others pickin' on me.'

'He was a nice lad,' Olivia said quietly. 'I liked him very much.'

'I've been lonely without him. Just wanted me mum after he'd gone.' Albert let out a sob. 'Felt ashamed too, 'cos when it happened . . . ' He paused as though he didn't want to finish what he'd been about to say.

'What about when it happened?' Olivia asked gently. Her heart went out to the lad; he obviously had a lot bottled up.

'When it happened I was relieved it was him an' not me,' he gasped, then pulled the covers over his head as though to hide himself.

Olivia squeezed his shoulder to let him know she understood. Of course she did. She imagined there wasn't one patient at St Omer who hadn't thanked his lucky stars to be the fellow going to the hospital instead of the cemetery.

'There's no need to feel ashamed, Albert.'

'But I do.' He lowered the sheet, revealing a pair of bloodshot blue eyes. 'You won't tell me lieutenant what I said, will you? He reckons I'm brave.'

'You are very brave . . . and, no, I won't tell him.'

Albert emerged further from the covers. 'We was happy when we went off duty that night. Our sergeant had told us the post had turned up. Me mum had written to me, telling me to come home. She does it every letter. She don't understand that I can't, though.' He sniffed. 'Wicksy had a letter too. He never got to read his.'

'It was from my sister. She had it returned to her.'

'He told me he was engaged to Maggie Bone.' Albert squirmed up on his elbows, chin sunk onto his chest. 'He was real proud of her, said she was a smasher.' From beneath his brows he gazed at Olivia's lovely face and wide green eyes. Her rosy cheeks were curtained by sweeps of golden hair that were neatly pinned at her nape. 'If she's like you, Sister, I can see why Ricky was head over heels. You're a looker.' Feeling shy after his outburst he wriggled back down the bed. 'Wicksy couldn't wait to get married. He said all he wanted was a wife and some kids and his job back when he got home.' Albert miserably shook his head. 'I want to go home. Don't care if I sound like a coward. They don't tell you what it's *really* like.'

'You're *not* a coward.' Olivia's voice was rough with emotion. The boy was discreetly using the sheet to wipe his eyes. 'Your mother will tell you that too. After she's done with boxing your ears for coming out here in the first place!' She curled into her palm the fingers that itched to reach out and smooth his hair. He looked so young and innocent. He wasn't . . . not any more. He'd seen and done things that were usually only for men to know and do. Private Carter had come of age no matter how few years he'd lived. And, please God, would see many more. She approached with the thermometer and he obligingly opened his mouth.

As soon as she'd removed it he rattled out, 'Me mum will tear me off a strip 'n' all. She's always telling me I ain't too big fer a slap, and not to forget it.'

'That seems to be a favourite expression with all mothers.' Olivia gave him a wink while writing on the obs chart.

'Did your mum give you a clip when you was a kid?'

'Yes, she did.' Olivia chuckled at the memory of her mother's wagging finger. She'd command her daughter to behave or else she'd be for it. And sometimes Olivia had been stung on the backside for overstepping the mark.

'Bet your sister's cut up bad over Ricky.' Albert's smile had vanished. 'Tell her I'm sorry, and it were my fault.'

'You mustn't say that! It's nobody's fault, Albert. Just this wicked war to blame.' Before he could sink again into melancholy Olivia said briskly, 'Your temperature is almost back to normal. No fever means you're well enough to

56

travel. I reckon Doctor might find you a Blighty pass.' She gave him a smile then briskly moved on to the next bed.

A fellow in his mid-thirties was fidgeting on top of his bedcover. He'd been brought in a short while before Olivia went on leave and was now well enough to be up and about with the aid of a crutch. But he chose to stay where he was, away from the others. He was recovering from a gunshot wound in the foot. As it was believed to be self-inflicted, he was being detained on suspicion rather than evacuated. It wasn't just his comrades who cold-shouldered him. Some of the nurses treated him frostily because of what he was alleged to have done. Olivia felt sad for him, and for his family. Foolishly, he'd told differing versions of how the wound had occurred, the last being that a chunk of shrapnel had landed on his foot just as he was about to pull on his boots. Not a bright idea as it was clearly a bullet hole. Olivia guessed he'd be moved from hospital to gaol when he was fit enough. After that, who knew where Private Jones would end up?

'See them up that end?' Jones hissed as she came to a halt, bearing the jar of thermometers. 'Turned up when you was off, they did. You stay clear of 'em, luv.' He made a noise of disgust. 'You let the old dragons see to 'em. Those dirty gits'll go for a pretty young gel like you.'

Olivia didn't follow the direction of his rolling eyes. She knew very well that he was referring to the prisoners-of-war. That morning at the staff meeting she'd been told about two Germans having been admitted.

'Ain't right expectin' us to lie shoulder to shoulder with the likes of them,' Jones spat. 'Me pal got blown to bits at Loos. And the new arrivals are saying there's so many dead on the ground at Beaumont Hamel, you gotta climb over 'em to get shot.' He gave a guttural noise of disgust. 'We should be outta here by now and back home. They promised us it'd be done by last Christmas.' He hoisted up his bandaged limb with both hands. 'I've got an infection in it so I've got the gripes in me belly 'n' all.' As though to prove his point, he broke wind.

'If you were captured you'd want your wounds looked at by a German nurse, wouldn't you?' Olivia ignored his blushes and the bad smell. But his attitude to the Germans wasn't unusual; she'd heard similar complaints from men when other prisoners had been brought in for treatment. Being nursed back to health next to an enemy you'd be expected to kill when back on your feet, seemed a queer thing.

'You make sure you keep yer scissors out of reach.' Private Jones snatched at her sleeve and gave it a shake. 'They'll have 'em off you and stab us lot while we're akip. Gawd awmighty! Would've been safer stayin' in the trenches.'

Having noted down his temperature, Olivia was about to move on when he caught her arm again.

''S'cuse my language, Sister.' He looked bashful for having blasphemed. 'Was gonna ask you if you'd write me a letter to the missus. Won't ask the other sisters 'cos I know some of 'em's snooty. But you're a nice gel . . . East Ender like me, ain't yer?'

'Of course I'll write a letter for you,' Olivia replied, removing his plucking fingers from her blue sleeve.

'Just . . . me wife's still sending me stuff over, custard creams and jars of Pan Yan pickle and so on. Love a bit of Pan Yan, I do, normally, but I can't eat it till me belly settles. She should keep the treats fer herself and the nippers till I'm well enough to get back to the trenches.' He slid a glance at Olivia from beneath bushy eyebrows. 'That's me aim, y'see . . . to get back to me muckers and give Fritz what for. If you'd tell the wife all o' that, in a letter, I'd be real grateful.'

'I'll come back teatime when I finish shift.' Olivia knew if a convoy came in there would be no usual finishing time.

It was obvious Private Jones regretted what he'd done now he understood how much trouble he was in. She didn't mind at all writing letters for him or any patient who was illiterate or incapacitated. Such little kindnesses were vital to their recovery, in her opinion. She gladly listened to them talk of their families, oohing and aahing over precious photographs of bonny infants seated on their mothers' laps. The majority of the casualties she saw were infantrymen from working-class stock. Men, like her beloved Joe, who might have been her neighbours in Islington. She knew they opened up to her because she sounded common . . . as did they.

'Shame they ain't all like you. You're a good 'un, you are . . . ' Private Jones's praise followed

59

Olivia as she moved on.

She was aware of receiving the two Germans' scrutiny as she drew closer to their beds. The younger, auburn-haired fellow might have been in his mid-twenties and appeared to have suffered the worst physical injuries. He was propped up on pillows with his pyjama jacket unbuttoned over bulky chest bandages. The other man was perhaps five years older, fair-haired and thin-faced. He was sitting in a chair with a beaker held on his lap. One of his legs was held stiffly in front of him as though he was unable to flex his knee.

'Fräulein,' the older of the two called querulously as she drew level. '*Wasser, bitte.*' The bandage covering his forehead didn't disguise the fact that he was a good-looking man.

'He'd like some water, please,' the younger man translated in good English.

Olivia poured him a beakerful and received a '*danke*' in return which she'd heard before and so understood she was being thanked. She was aware of the men in the other beds taking an interest in what was going on between Sister Bone and the despised Boche.

'I am Unteroffizier Ernst Fischer,' the younger man introduced himself politely. 'He is Hauptmann Karl Schmidt.' The older fellow, clutching his water, seemed to have slipped into a fantasy world. His lips were writhing over his teeth as though he were talking to himself, but no sound emerged.

The Unteroffizier tapped at his head. 'He is

hurt badly . . . up here.' He gazed forlornly at his superior.

Olivia nodded and removed the empty beaker from the Hauptmann's tense fingers. She refilled it and gave it back for he had looked startled to lose it.

Flora Thistle was watching her from a few yards away, a pleat between her brows as though she disapproved of what she saw. She was Olivia's supervisor today. It was unusual for them to be on ward duty together but since the battles around the Somme had worsened every nurse simply went where Matron directed them. Sometimes there was no time for a break and they all ended their shifts hungry and exhausted.

Olivia wielded two thermometers and the Germans dutifully cooperated. She wrote down their readings then, with a neutral smile, moved on to the next bed. It always seemed inappropriate to chat with prisoners in the way she did with the Allied patients. But she guessed German soldiers were no different in simply wanting to go home and convalesce. The officer with the head injury would probably take longer to recover than his comrade. One thing she had learned was that flesh often healed quicker than the mind.

Ernst Fischer and Karl Schmidt might get a Blighty pass but it would take them straight to a hospital ward in a prisoner-of-war camp. Or when fit they might be put to hard labour in France, though they'd not willingly build roads and tunnels that could bring about their enemy's victory, even if that enemy had saved their lives.

# 5

'Are you going to admit defeat now and have that rotten gnasher pulled?' Olivia asked.

With a weary sigh, she flopped down on her hard camp bed and gave her roommate a sympathetic glance. The girl was the unlucky VAD with a gumboil, and overnight it seemed to have ballooned. Valerie Booth was a tall, plain young woman with short brown hair cut in a neat boyish style. At present she was staring morosely at her distorted profile reflected in the spotted mirror hanging on the hut wall. She'd been swilling her mouth diligently with diluted hydrogen peroxide in the hope it would kill off the infection, to no avail.

'I'll come with you to the dentist and lend you an arm to lean on if you feel groggy after the gas.' Olivia had just come off shift. She had trudged back to the dormitory in the early-morning light. But she no longer felt like going to bed. She was always glad to finish night duty, having listened to tormented souls whimpering or whispering gibberish into the darkness. Their pain, their fear . . . all seemed worse in those interminable hours. It was extraordinary that the first streaks of dawn could soothe traumatised men more quickly than a sedative. They slumbered best when the day was breaking. For her, though, it felt odd to be drawing the curtains against the light.

'You just want to make sure I don't miss my shift.' Valerie's wry comment was muffled by the hand cupping the side of her throbbing jaw.

'True. Oh, don't be a baby.' Olivia rolled onto her stomach on her bed and assessed Valerie's reflected physog. 'I'm not going to spare your feelings. That's got a lot worse. And a fat chin is uglier than a gap between your teeth in any case.'

'Can you keep a secret?' Valerie asked.

''Course . . . '

'I can't stand the sight of blood. I'm alright with the patients, but when it's my own . . . ' She shuddered. 'Don't tell Matron, will you? She's already taken against me. I'll be sent home in disgrace if she ever finds out. Don't want that now I've made my mother proud at last.'

It wasn't the first time Olivia had got the impression her roommate had a difficult home life. She sympathised; she'd had a hard time of it herself with her own father and knew how unpleasant such a parent could be. Valerie was quite clearly upper-crust and the cut of her clothes and quality of her luggage proclaimed her to be from money as well as breeding. 'Your mum should be proud of you for volunteering.' Olivia said in stout support.

'I didn't volunteer. *She* put my name forward to the Red Cross. Said it was time I did something useful and got out from under her feet. I wanted to go to art school as a mature student, then travel the world painting cathedrals and things. But she wouldn't let me. Find a husband or find a career. That's her way.'

Olivia was surprised to hear that the girl was

still so firmly under her mother's thumb. Valerie looked to be at least five years her roommate's senior, so was about twenty-six. And she was a talented artist. She'd shown Olivia some drawings of the French coastline, sketched from the rail of the ship on the way over. Most of the VADs had a photograph of family, or else a sweetheart, displayed on their dormitory nightstand. Olivia had one of her brother and sisters that she pressed to her lips every night before turning in. Valerie Booth had just a charcoal outline of the Opal coast propped against the wall.

'How about your father? Did he want you to join the VAD?' Olivia began loosening the length of starched linen that served as her nurse's cap.

'Don't think he's aware I exist.' Valerie snorted a giggle. 'He's a bigwig in the City and wanted a son and heir. All he got was me. No brothers or sisters to take the spotlight off how much of a disappointment I am, either.'

'I'm sure you're not!' Olivia exclaimed. She felt for her friend although Valerie had sounded quite offhand about her parents' neglect. Olivia's own father had been self-centred and prone to drunken rages but, oddly, that seemed better in a way than having people too cold and remote to bother noticing you. She injected some lightness into her voice. 'As for Matron, she's alright, y'know. I think she's just worried you'll keel over with blood poisoning and take up a bed. The dentist will knock you out before pulling that bad tooth and I'll clean you up if you dribble claret down yourself.'

'I should have had one of your toffees, after all. That would've pulled it.' Valerie had refused a sweet, fearing the painful consequences.

Though she had been suffering she'd conscientiously never missed a shift. But Matron *was* out of patience. If things hadn't been so frantic, Olivia guessed her roommate would already have been sent packing. 'The anaesthetic will be in short supply if another convoy comes in. Are you brave enough to do without?'

It was a valid point and had the desired effect. With a pathetic groan, Valerie put up her hands in surrender then allowed herself to be steered outside into the sunshine. It was an early morning on the Sabbath, and the guns were already chuntering in the distance. Yet on the breeze wafted a scent of mimosa and rose from the small flower garden by the vegetable patch. With such a treat for the senses came the weird notion that the rumbling sound might be celebratory. Fireworks or a gun salute . . . but it was a short-lived dream. In front of them Olivia could see a group of maimed men enjoying the summer morning. They were dressed in hospital pyjamas, their baggy trouser legs and sleeves pinned up, air where limbs should have been.

'Wonder if that's our lot letting loose.' Olivia frowned as another salvo desecrated the glorious day. If the Allies were under bombardment there was sure to be another rush of casualties before nightfall.

They proceeded along a cinder path in the direction of the hut that had a wooden plaque nailed outside with the word 'Dental Surgery' stencilled on it in black paint. Suddenly Olivia heard her friend's little gasp of dismay. Nothing other than the sight of the two German patients could have caused it. The Hauptmann and Unteroffizier were in wheelchairs that had been pushed under the shade of a tree. The officer remained seated but seemed to recognise Olivia as the nurse who'd fetched him a drink. He raised his face then a hand in greeting before his chin dropped back to his chest. The younger man got gingerly to his feet, gave a polite nod and said, 'Good morning.'

Olivia was surprised when her colleague squirmed in discomfiture as they drew alongside because Valerie hadn't displayed any hostility before towards the prisoners.

'Oh, damn! Didn't want to bump into *him* now I look like a bloody dormouse.' Valerie averted her swollen profile and marched on.

'Your friend is not well?' The young Unteroffizier was gazing after Valerie's tall striding figure.

'Good morning. She's just got toothache,' Olivia briskly rattled off while passing by. 'What was that all about?' she demanded, having caught up with Valerie. 'Has he been difficult?'

'Far from it,' her roommate mumbled. 'I think he's really rather charming.' After a moment she added defensively, 'Some of our boys could learn better manners from those two. Even the barmy one. It's not their fault they're here. They don't want to be. I feel sorry for them. Nobody likes them.'

'I feel sorry for them too. But it's hardly

66

surprising they're not welcomed with open arms,' Olivia reasoned. 'They're being fed and nursed. What more can they expect when they're our enemy?'

'I'm going to bring them along to the concert in a few weeks, if they want to come and are still here.' Valerie sounded defiant.

'Well, I doubt anybody *would* object.' Olivia's tone was doubtful though. 'If they sat a little apart from our lot . . . in case things get heated.' Valerie's heightened colour confirmed Olivia's suspicions. Her roommate was soft on Ernst Fischer and if that became common knowledge it was sure to stir up trouble. 'Perhaps you should have a word with Matron first, though, about the concert. Be on the safe side,' Olivia cautioned.

Valerie answered with the briefest of nods. 'Come inside with me, Livvie?' she appealed as they reached their destination.

'If you want me to.' Before following her into the dental surgery Olivia glanced back. Fischer was still on his feet, smoking a cigarette and watching them.

★  ★  ★

At the sound of the church bell Olivia propped herself up on her pillow, cupping her chin in her hand. 'Are you fit to come along to the evening service, to help out?' she asked Valerie.

After they'd got back from the dentist they'd both taken to their beds: Olivia to catch up on some sleep before she went back on duty and

67

Valerie to quell a feeling of nausea as the anaesthetic wore off.

She removed the wedge of cotton wool stopping the hole in her gum. ''Course I'm coming, I feel quite chipper now.'

Olivia got up and stretched, undulating her shoulders. Lifting the china jug, she splashed water into the bowl then gave her face and hands a wash with some lovely scented soap she'd found in her luggage. When she'd unpacked, some toiletries had emerged from the folds of her chemise. She imagined her sisters had put the Yardley's lavender there as a treat for her. It was sweet of them to do it, but Olivia wished she could stop herself wondering how they'd come by the luxuries.

Maggie had told her months ago that she'd caught their sister Nancy shoplifting lipsticks from Gamages. There had been another occasion too when Olivia had been suspicious about a fancy hat Nancy had come home wearing. She'd asked her youngest sister about it and it had been explained away as a bargain buy off a friend who'd decided it didn't suit her. Olivia didn't want to fret about what her sisters got up to in her absence . . . but the truth was, she couldn't blot out of her mind the past scrapes they'd been in. She put the soap carefully away in its box in the drawer. There was little she could do anyway even if her suspicions were well founded and she was in possession of stolen goods. So she supposed she might as well enjoy it. She splashed lavender water onto her skin and rubbed it in. The afternoon sun had warmed the hut and it felt quite humid inside.

Her uniform was hanging on a hook embedded in the hut wall. She started pulling it on. There was a lot of it, but with practice she'd now speeded up considerably at getting herself dressed for work. The black stockings went on first then the plain blue lustre dress, buttoned at the front. A full-length bib apron was cinched at the waist with a starched linen belt. Then the over-sleeves were put on and a soft, turn-down collar of white linen fastened at the front with a safety pin brooch bearing the Maltese Cross emblem of St John Ambulance Brigade. Finally she wriggled her feet into her regulation black boots and stooped to lace them before attending to her headgear. It had taken her a while to master the Sister Dora cap but now she could fold and fasten the starched cloth with a safety pin in seconds.

'Only shows when you laugh,' she teased Valerie, having noticed her friend once again examining her changed appearance in the mirror. On their way back from the dentist they'd bumped into Matron. Valerie had blossomed beneath Gladys Bennett's praise for having finally grasped the nettle.

'It's alright for you, Livvie. You're so pretty you could afford to have an imperfect smile. You'd still have fellows running after you. When you're mousy like me, it's not easy hooking a man.' Valerie sighed. 'I'm twenty-seven next year and, as I can't afford to travel the world painting once this blasted war's over, I would sooo like to get married.'

Olivia screwed the cap back on the lavender water. 'So you can escape from home, you mean?'

'Too true!' Valerie replied with feeling. 'I'm glad Mummy made me volunteer. We're surrounded by young fellows all the time here. And most of 'em can't run away.' Her cheeky grin was accompanied by a wink. 'Can I have a bit of your lavender water?' she asked, primping her fringe with a hair brush.

'Have you got your eye on somebody already?' Olivia handed over the bottle then perched on the edge of her bed.

Valerie looked bashful while dabbing the scent behind her ears.

'Ernst Fischer?' Olivia cut to the chase.

'He is very sweet,' Valerie admitted, rather defensively. She glanced at the door as though worried somebody might turn up and overhear their conversation. 'When I was on night duty earlier in the week, he couldn't sleep so I kept him company . . . just chatting,' she qualified in a whisper. 'Ernst speaks such good English because his grandmother was English and he used to visit her in Norfolk when he was a boy. He said his lot want this bloody war over with as much as our lot does.' She rattled on, 'He's taught me a few German words. *Schon* means pretty. *Liebling* means darling. And he gave me some *Schokolade*.' She pulled open a drawer, broke a piece off a bar then quickly lobbed it onto Olivia's lap. 'He said he thinks I'm an angel . . . Don't you breathe a word about any of this to the others, will you?'

Olivia gestured that she wouldn't. She glanced at the chocolate, knowing it would be rude to refuse it just because of where it had come from. She popped it into her mouth, enjoying its silky sweetness. She circled her tongue round her lips to catch all the crumbs. 'I agree it doesn't hurt to treat the Germans nicely but . . . '

'But you think they're not really as nice as us? *We're* all good and *they're* all barbarians, I suppose.' Valerie sounded peeved.

'I don't think that at all! It's about loyalty to our men, and our country.'

Valerie crossed her arms over her flat chest. She was still in her petticoat, and though it was a pretty style it couldn't conceal her lack of curves. 'I want us to win but I don't want people like Ernst to die so that we can.'

'Neither do I,' Olivia said immediately. 'I agree it's all madness.' She gave a hopeless shrug. 'I'm not even sure any more why it started. Whatever the reason, it wasn't worth all this. But we're too deep in to walk away now. I couldn't bear it if my fiancé, or any of the others, had perished for nothing.'

'Oh, sorry . . . didn't know about your chap.' Valerie sounded contrite and sank down next to Olivia on her mattress, putting an arm clumsily around her.

'It seems as if everybody's lost somebody now.' Olivia used her knuckles on the tears prickling in her eyes. Any mention of her dear Joe always made her choke up. She gave her friend a wan smile. 'Ernst seems nice. Can't deny the Germans are both always polite and grateful for what's done for them.'

'Mmm, and that can't always be said for our lot,' Valerie remarked pithily. 'That self-inflicted was grumbling again yesterday about the doctor refusing him a Blighty pass. Then in the next breath he says he's going back to the trenches.'

'I expect he'd sooner take his chances there than embarrass his family by ending up in gaol.' Olivia's voice held a note of sympathy. 'Ernst Fischer seems to be on the mend. He'll be leaving here soon, y'know.'

'He's resigned to being sent to a prisoner-of-war camp.' Valerie sighed, getting to her feet. 'He's begged me to write to him when he gets to England. I've said I will.'

The bell pealed again, hurrying the congregation to the evening service.

'Are you going to church dressed like that?' Olivia teased, jerking a nod at her friend's petticoat.

'Give the poor vicar a fright if I did!'

'Might cheer the other fellows up though,' Olivia said saucily, making her friend snort a laugh and peer down at her slight bosom.

'Not exactly Lili Marlene, am I?' Valerie sighed.

A few minutes later they made their way outside, walking purposefully but in silence, deep in their own thoughts. They headed for the ward where a group of patients were waiting in wheelchairs. Those able to make it under their own steam or with the aid of crutches, had already gone ahead. Olivia and Valerie, and about half a dozen other nurses, took a

72

wheelchair each and set off, chatting about this and that, but mainly about the guns having fallen silent for a while. But their relief was muted; nobody believed it would last.

The church was just another tent, with an improvised chancel and a few planked benches serving as pews. The bell that had summoned the worshippers was an empty shell casing strung through the middle with a lump of metal that served as a clapper. Most of the patients liked to attend the service, no matter what their denomination. It gave everybody a change of scene and the men a chance to mingle with fellows from different wards. Even dour Private Jones had come along on his crutch although he appeared to be as isolated from the other patients as the Germans were. He stopped glowering long enough to smile and nod at Olivia in thanks for her having posted his letter yesterday.

The church was set at the back of the field so a visit to it exercised legs as well as lungs. And sing the men certainly did. Hymn after hymn rang out, their lusty voices drowning the nurses' softer tones. They all prayed too, with the quiet fervour of people who have much to ask for.

At the end of the simple service the church started to empty and in the candlelight Olivia spied young Albert Carter seated on a bench. He struggled up with the aid of a walking stick then waved it at her to make sure she'd seen him.

Olivia asked another nurse if she'd mind pushing her charge's wheelchair back to the

73

ward. Then she went to speak to the young private.

'Have you seen him?' His excited question greeted her as soon as she was within earshot.

Olivia frowned. 'Seen who, Albert?'

'Me officer's turned up,' he gabbled. 'Lieutenant's got furlough and come over to see how I'm doing. I reckon he's here for you really, though, 'cos he missed you last time.'

Albert gave her a cheeky grin. 'I told him you'd been on night duty but you'd be sure to turn up in church later, after you'd had a kip.'

Olivia's sheer joy must have shown on her face because his smile grew wider.

'He's really here?' Already she was pivoting on the spot, going on and off tiptoes to peer over the remaining heads.

'Don't reckon he come in the church. 'Spect he's waiting outside for you,' Albert suggested helpfully. 'Want me to go and find 'im, Sister Bone?'

'No . . . stay with your friend.' Olivia nodded at a young fellow seated on the bench, one trench-slippered foot propped on the pew in front. Her heart was beating so frantically that she felt quite faint. She managed to say goodbye before zigzagging between the pews to emerge into the fresh evening air.

The majority of the congregation had dispersed. Just a few stragglers were making their laboured way over the grass. It was suppertime and all were keen to get to the toast and jam and Madeira cake and hot strong tea, before settling down for lights out.

She shielded her eyes against blinding light as the sun settled on the horizon in a blaze of coral. She glimpsed him at the same moment that he spotted her. 'Oh, Lucas,' she murmured, an agony of emotion tearing at her throat at the sight of him. His ebony hair looked too long and was flopping into his eyes as the evening breeze lifted it. With a gasp, Olivia grabbed her skirt, hoisting its material off her boots, then sprinted over the springy turf towards him. Two strong arms immediately crushed her to him in an eager embrace then spun her off her feet.

# 6

'I've been so worried about you!' Olivia pressed herself against his solid body, rubbing her cheek against the musky khaki tunic. 'What's happened? Why haven't you written? Oh, thank the Lord you're safe!'

While she'd been speaking he'd lifted her in his arms. With her toes skimming the turf, he carried her out of sight of any onlookers back into the empty church.

'Where have you *been*, Lucas?' His jaw felt rough with stubble as she eagerly cupped it between her hands. 'I asked young Albert this morning but again he just tapped his nose and said he wasn't sure he could say.'

'It's not a secret now we're back on our side of the barbed wire. Half the platoon got trapped behind enemy lines for a while.' Lucas's voice was husky, his ravening gaze fixed only on her. 'Young Carter wasn't one of them, thankfully. A couple of my men got hit as we made a dash for it but we managed to bring them back. Neither of them survived . . . ' He closed his mind against the memory of scrambling over cratered ground with a groaning man over his shoulder, praying in vain that they'd reach an aid post in time. And though he'd had years of doing the same thing . . . ever since he'd carried Joe Hunter to his final resting place on a bitter winter's day in 1914 . . . it hadn't got any easier for Lucas. The sense of guilt and failure he felt was as strong every time he fumbled at a dead man's neck for his dog tags.

'Thank God you escaped capture.' Olivia's eyes widened in alarm as she imagined the dangers he must've faced.

'Came close to being caught on two occasions. But we kept our heads down and survived on rations and the kindness of some locals. They sheltered us and gave what help they could until relief turned up. We had enough cover then to chance making a run for it.'

She gazed up at him. Lucas was thinner in the face these days and his vivid blue eyes appeared haunted, evasive, as though they had seen things he must conceal from her. 'Were you injured?' Again she looked him over for signs of harm.

'I took a few knocks but nothing major. Bad guts was the worst of it. Not very pleasant. Drinking foul water gave us all dysentery. When we got back we spent some time recuperating in hospital. Better that than catching a bellyful of shrapnel.'

She felt jealous of the nurses who'd had him in their care. She wished she could have tended him herself. Olivia closed her arms about him again, hugging him in sheer relief that he'd survived. She knew he hadn't suffered a worse ordeal than thousands of other soldiers, but he was the one she prayed for every night. Lucas and her family were always in her thoughts just before she slept and first thing on waking in the morning. 'We've a couple of German prisoners on the ward,' she told him. 'By all accounts they're just as sick of this bloody war as we are,' she announced with feeling.

'Trouble is, Fritz wants it finished on his terms. We on ours. That's why we're fighting it out.' Lucas gave an ironic smile. 'So, you're nursing Germans, are you?'

Olivia nodded. 'My roommate's taken a shine to one of them. They seem ordinary folk . . . nice enough.'

'I'd seem nice enough in a German hospital,' Lucas said dryly. 'It wouldn't stop me wanting to be out of there and back with my own kind. Unless one of the nurses looked like you, of course.' He dipped his head, brushing his lips over her warm cheek and drinking in the scent of her skin.

'You smell heavenly. Like an English garden.'

'My sisters hid a surprise bottle of lavender water in my trunk. It was lovely finding it when I got back.'

'Your matron said you'd gone home for a funeral when I brought Private Carter in.' His fingertips with their ragged nails touched her face so delicately.

'My aunt passed away. You know we didn't get on but it was still a shock to hear about her accident. She fell and hit her head. I couldn't believe it when I got back here and Matron told me I'd missed you. I thought it might be months before you'd manage to come this way and see me.' Despite the glitter in her eyes, she gave him a sunny smile. 'You're here now though. That's all that matters, Lucas.'

Her sweet attempt to be light-hearted for his

sake melted his self-control. With a soft murmur, he pressed a hungry kiss onto her mouth.

'God knows I've missed you, Olivia Bone,' he breathed after a while. 'Can you come out somewhere with me . . . now? There's so much I want to say to you. I need you so much . . . '

'I'd love to, Lucas, but I'm on duty. I can't just swan off,' she sighed. 'I've been on nights all this week. Come and have some supper with us? Matron won't mind.' She hugged him then took his hand to lead him out into the open.

'I know you've work to do but let me have a few minutes more alone with you . . . please.' Lucas resisted her attempt to tug him outside; he didn't want others to spoil this longed for reunion. 'I've been dreaming about this moment. Yearning to touch you . . . talk to you. All I've had is the phantom inside my head and she's a poor substitute for the real thing.' He slid back Olivia's starched cap to slide his fingers into her golden hair, luxuriating in the silky feel of it on his blistered skin.

'I've been counting the seconds too. Wondering if you'd come back this time. I've been scared, Lucas. So many are dying. It's hard to comprehend that what the men tell us can really be true. They speak of seas of bodies around the Somme. Too many mown down to count, or to get past. And sometimes no advantage gained for it . . . ' Her words faded on a sob at the obscenity of it.

When she'd lost Joe, she'd not had much idea about what was going on in France. Oh, she'd read newspaper reports, discussed the war with colleagues over the work benches at Barratt's. In those early days people had still been optimistic about a quick victory. Things were different now. She was in the fray with eyes wide open, and the likely outcome for Lucas, for Jack Keiver, was all too clear. They might yet fall and be trampled into the yellow earth, then get just a bit of tin and a blanket of poppies for what they'd sacrificed. For their grieving families, though, life's battles would go on.

'Hush.' Lucas brushed his lips over her cheekbone, tasting salty tears. 'I'll always come back to you, I swear. Look . . . lucky charm.' He slid a hand into his jacket pocket and produced a pewter cigarette case. It had belonged to her father. Lucas had asked her for it, saying it was his talisman even if it hadn't done the late Tommy Bone any good. Countless indentations covered its dull grey surface.

'You've still got it then,' Olivia said softly, cradling the battered metal in one palm.

'I won't part with it, Livvie. I told you, it's my amulet.' He lightly thumped the pocket over his heart where he always kept the case.

She wrapped her arms about his neck. 'You and your fancy words . . . say 'lucky charm'.'

'You know what I mean. Anyway, I thought you wanted to be educated? You wished you'd stayed at school so you'd be clever like me, you once told me,' he teased.

She remembered that day before the war when they'd strolled on the lawns at Alexandra Palace and learned a little bit about one another. She'd envied him his fine education, having been

80

allowed so little of it herself. At fourteen she'd been expected to leave school and earn . . . as well as to keep house for her father in her spare time. 'It all seems a long, long time ago now.'

'Schooldays or Barratt's days?'

'Both . . . and I'd go back in a tick to either time if I could,' Olivia said whimsically. 'Compared to this, things were just so easy, back then before the war.' She shrugged off a tinge of melancholy. This was the happiest she'd felt in ages and she'd not spoil it by being maudlin. 'Right, come on, suppertime. You'll get me shot, Lieutenant Black, if I don't show my face soon. They'll think I've deserted.'

Again he reached for her but she backed away, eyes locked with his. He wanted to kiss her. Much as she longed to linger here and love him while their bodies were romantically bathed in the light of a rose-coloured sunset, she knew she couldn't delay any longer. One of the sisters would be waiting to be relieved. She pulled him out of the tent.

A faint noise to one side of them made Lucas turn, frowning, hand instantly at his hip where his pistol was kept. All soldiers were alert to unseen danger even when it was unlikely to be present, as now.

The padre suddenly appeared from the tent, pulling the flap closed behind him. 'I do weddings as well, you know.' He doffed his cap to them with a twinkling grin before heading towards the refectory.

'Do you think he was in there all the time and heard us?' Olivia squeaked, caught between embarrassment and amusement.

Lucas relaxed and resumed stalking her with a wolfish glint in his eyes. 'So what if he did? He made a good point. I've got a ring.' He slid a hand inside his shirt collar and pulled out his dog tags. On the string next to the green and red discs was a thin gold hoop.

'It's Romany gold. Belonged to my mother.' He slid it onto his little finger. 'It'll do as a standby.'

'Is that a proposal?' Olivia's whispered question was followed by an uncertain smile, and she barely breathed while awaiting his reply.

'It's a pretty paltry one, I know. And not the way I wanted it to be. But champagne and a diamond aren't easy to get hold of out here. If I wait for the perfect time, it might never happen.' Lucas took her fingers in his, bringing them to his lips. 'Truth is, Livvie, I've never found the courage before to tell you how much I love you . . . desire you . . . ' That last bit caused him to smile crookedly. 'I want to make love to you, but you already know about my wicked side. It's not just that any more though. I'm not sure it ever was just that. I think you had my heart from the first moment I saw you at the factory gate. But Joe Hunter was worthier than me. It was right he won you then. He was younger but more mature and didn't shy away from the responsibility of having a wife and children whereas I wanted to have my cake and eat it. In my conceit, I thought I could, too. Up to then, I'd always had what I wanted.'

He gazed at her with wry admiration. 'But you

had different ideas. And a choice. You saw through me and my cheap offers of the good life. You're honest and principled and I've not known many women like that.' His head bowed lower as he poured out his heart to her. 'I've never before asked a woman to marry me. I never thought about having a wife or a family until I met you. I know it's not the right time for all of this.' He rubbed a hand across his nape in an endearingly diffident gesture. 'There's a lot I need to explain about myself and I hope you'll be merciful when I do. There are things in my past that I'm ashamed of . . . mainly to do with me being an arrogant bastard. But you know that about me already. So perhaps it won't all come as too much of a surprise when I tell you. Now's not the time though. I won't leave you a pregnant widow. I will come back to you . . . one way or another. I'd crawl over barbed wire if I had to . . . '

Olivia nestled her head on his shoulder. She knew why he'd waited, just as she knew why she hesitated before answering him. There was more troubling her than the prospect of ending up alone with a child. 'I will marry you, Lucas, because I do love you with all my heart,' she said, in a voice that throbbed with emotion. 'But we can't get married today, or even tomorrow.' She had a duty that went beyond that owed to her patients and work colleagues. Her siblings might be more independent since she'd joined the VAD but they still relied on her, financially and emotionally. She'd never abandon them. They deserved to know if she was about to make great changes to all their lives. They'd be anxious about their own futures.

Then there was Lucas's family background ... things that were complicated ... as yet unexplained. He wore gypsy gold on a string about his neck yet he'd once said he knew little about the woman who'd given birth to him. Now it seemed he had found something of hers. Olivia had a host of questions. She wanted to talk to him, *really* talk to him, about his background. The muddle of his natural and adoptive parentage, and the affair he'd had with his brother's wife, all remained a near mystery to her. Excusing it as his arrogance, saying he hoped she'd understand, wasn't nearly enough on which to build trust and understanding between them.

She searched his deep blue eyes and told him, 'It would be wrong to act on the spur of the moment. At the very least, I owe it to the kids to tell them I'm getting married. There are living arrangements to work out ... it's only fair to warn them.'

'I know you come with your family or not at all. That's never bothered me,' he told her with a shrug of his shoulders.

'I love you, Lucas, and I trust that you love me ... and that's the best thing of all. We don't need a hasty wedding ceremony. I've got an afternoon off next week so if you're still on leave then we could go out somewhere and talk properly ... '

'Livvie!'

Olivia screwed up her face in frustration at the sound of her name being called. 'That's my roommate,' she whispered. 'Bet Matron's sent her to find me. I'm in hot water then.'

'Blame it on me.'

'I will, don't worry,' she returned ruefully. She pulled him behind her by the hand. 'Come on, I'll introduce you . . . she's a nice girl.'

'Oh, sorry.' Valerie had just glimpsed her friend stepping over some tent ropes, leading a fellow into view. 'Didn't mean to butt in.' She sounded awkward. 'Just . . . the dragon's on the warpath, wondering where you've got to . . . ' She abruptly stopped talking and stared at Lucas. Then she looked at Olivia with an expression of mingled amazement and admiration.

Olivia was used to seeing women staring at him like that. Lucas was a distinguished-looking man. 'A dreamboat' her friend Hilda Weedon had called him. Apart from his good looks, he had a casual yet confident manner that most people responded to. When she'd worked at Barratt's, Olivia had noticed that her then boss commanded respect without doing or saying much at all. Even her father — a surly, defiant character if ever there was one — would watch his Ps and Qs if Lucas Black was about.

But as Valerie continued to stare and shuffle her feet, Olivia sensed there was more to this.

'Oh . . . well . . . what a surprise,' Valerie gabbled. 'I'd no idea you two knew one another.' She smiled uncertainly at Lucas. 'Didn't know you were here, Lieutenant Black . . . well, of course I knew you were serving in France, Mummy told me. I expect she got it from

Caroline because . . . ' Valerie bit her lip, darting glances between the couple. 'I expect it's best if I shut up now,' she mumbled.

'You two are friends?' Olivia turned to Lucas, her contentment ebbing away. He'd worn that cynical expression before, on the day she'd confronted him over his relationship with Caroline Venner and demanded to know whether he'd fathered the baby she was said to be carrying. He'd said he hadn't, though he'd admitted they'd been lovers while Caroline had been a nurse in France. She had then returned home and got engaged to Lucas's brother at Christmas. Olivia imagined the couple might be married by now, for the child's sake if no other.

'We've mutual acquaintances.' Lucas's voice was toneless.

'I must get back.' Olivia evaded his hand as it reached for hers. 'Come and have some supper, if you want. I'll have to go straight to the ward though. I'm long overdue.'

'I'll run ahead and tell Matron you're on your way.' Valerie seemed keen to escape. 'Give you two a chance to say toodle-oo.' She began backing away. A moment later she'd turned and dashed off.

Lucas barked a short sardonic laugh. 'Well, that was unfortunate. When I came to see you last time we were interrupted midway through another heart to heart.'

'We could talk for hours and I think there'd still be things left to say.' Olivia couldn't keep an acid note from creeping into her voice. 'The thing is, would you say it?'

'Meaning?'

'It doesn't matter. I'm late. I have to go.'

He caught her wrist, preventing her from marching off. 'You think I'm not being completely honest?'

'I think if I said I wasn't bothered about knowing everything about you, it would come as a relief, wouldn't it?'

'Right now I'd take the easy way out . . . yes. The whole truth doesn't seem important. I love you and you love me. What else is there of any real consequence? Who I was . . . what does it matter when I don't know who, or if, I'll be tomorrow?'

'What d'you mean by that?' Olivia felt alarmed by his tone. 'You promised you'd always come back to me.'

'There are ever-present perils, but I'll do my damnedest to outrun them and keep that promise to you.'

The ever-present perils chose that moment to make their presence felt: the guns that had been silent for most of the evening started to grumble in the distance.

'Promise me something in return.' Lucas took a step towards her. 'Give me something.'

'I swear that whatever you tell me about yourself, Lucas, I'll believe.' Olivia watched the glimmer of a smile touch his mouth.

'Give me something else to seal those vows.'

She kissed him, sweetly and tenderly, and though she'd been expecting him to imprison her in his arms, he didn't. He let her go when she took her mouth from his.

'Valerie Booth's Caroline's cousin,' he said. 'Their mothers are sisters.'

Olivia contained her surprise. 'I know Valerie's from well-to-do parents. They sound a bit odd though. Cold and unfeeling.'

'They don't sound odd to me,' he said sarcastically.

'You're not cold and unfeeling — far from it,' she said gently.

'I'm different since I met you.' He made to reach for her but seemed to change his mind and plunged his hands into his pockets instead.

'Your brother got married then?' There was something she very much wanted to know before they parted. 'Has the child been born?'

'No . . . Caroline miscarried.'

'I'm sorry,' Olivia murmured, for want of anything else to say.

'Yeah, I'm sorry too.' He caught at her hand and started off at quite a pace towards the lights of the mess tents.

Marching silently at his side, Olivia guessed his regrets were not so much for the loss of his unborn niece or nephew as about the likelihood of Valerie revealing something he'd intended to disclose himself . . . when he thought the time was right.

'Are you stopping for a bite to eat?' she asked him.

He shook his head and skimmed his lips over her cheek in farewell, in the way he used to before they'd permitted their true feelings for one another to show and kissed like lovers.

'Please take care of yourself, Lucas. Remember your promise to me.' She gazed up at him through the deepening dusk.

'You too,' he said hoarsely. 'I meant what I said. Every word. Remember that.' He walked away towards the driveway where he'd parked his car.

# 7

'You've got a cheek, making me wait like this! I've been run off my feet and not yet had a bite of supper.'

Noticing Flora Thistle's hard eyes fixed on her cap, Olivia quickly straightened it. The memory of Lucas's caresses was making her blush in retrospect but she knew her colleague had a right to feel annoyed. 'I'm really sorry to be so late.' She spoke quietly, conscious of the hour and the men settling down for the night. 'I was just saying goodbye to somebody,' she explained in a whisper. 'Not seen him in a while and I've been worried about him . . . '

'A professional would put their duty before any personal concern,' Flora primly interrupted.

'I might not be a professional, as you term it, but I am human and I care about this man.' Olivia's guilt was being replaced by indignation. She was doing her best to be conciliatory and wasn't going to apologise again. 'He deserved a proper goodbye. I couldn't just brush him off, for you or anybody.'

'Can't blame her for staying out with him,' another sister interjected, giving Olivia a conspiratorial wink. 'Lieutenant Black's gorgeous. Val Booth told me he's a family friend of hers. I'm angling for an invite to her house when we get home!' The older woman had just nipped in to cadge some laudanum as they were running low in B section. She was a Queen Alexandra nurse but an easy-going colleague, unlike Flora who believed herself superior to the St John Ambulance and Red Cross recruits.

'Sister Barr is your supervisor this evening,' she informed Olivia stiffly. 'She's been called to the post-op ward to help out as the surgeons are still at it.' A studied lift of one eyebrow preceded the announcement: 'Things are ticking over nicely in here now so you *should* manage to hold the fort until she puts in an appearance.'

Once her two colleagues had gone Olivia settled down at the nurses' station, which consisted of a pair of hard chairs set behind a desk close to the ward's entrance. From this vantage point a duty nurse had an uninterrupted view of a row of grey-blanketed bedsteads receding into the gloom to either side of a long functional refectory table where the ambulant patients congregated to eat. Olivia had scrubbed the pine top of that with Cresolis many a time when she'd started work at St Omer as a ward maid. She still did roll up her sleeves and pitch in when they were understaffed and made no bones about it. She'd acted as her father's char and washerwoman from the age of ten so was no stranger to hard graft.

Upon the table stood hospital paraphernalia: jugs and lotions and bowls of dressings. Along the perimeters of the marquee hung lights, dimmed in the evenings by draped squares of red cloth. The warm glow seemed to assist the men to drowse but few of them slept properly. Even those who might have liked to drop off, found they couldn't with a fellow tossing and turning close by in the next bed.

Olivia was at her least confident while on night duty. She had her supervisor to call on but a night sister often had three wards to cover until dawn, whereas the VADs assisting her patrolled just one each. Olivia did her best to cope alone because she knew there were more urgent cases requiring her senior's skill. For the most part C4 was home to patients who were making good progress, or were pending transfer home to convalesce. The unlucky ones were biding time until they were sent back on active duty.

But when they'd been short-staffed she'd served on other wards with more gravely ill patients. Those suffering nightmares were hardest to cope with. When still new to nights, she'd felt terrified of being drawn into one shell-shocked fellow's delirium. As though he could divine exactly when midnight was, he'd jack-knife upright in his bed and jab wildly at the unseen imps tormenting him, circling overhead. Another patient, long since gone to the cemetery at Wimereux, had regularly struggled out of bed on his bandaged stumps, to put out the fire he imagined burning beneath it. Olivia had learned not to explain away the patients' grisly fantasies but to find solutions to them instead. She'd thrown imaginary jugs of water onto flames and had shooed unwanted visitations away by yanking off her cap to flap it at them. She'd comfort the men until their minds and bodies relaxed, breathless sometimes from the exertion of restraining them and urging them back to bed.

In those critical wards it was rare for her to sit for more than a few minutes at a time. On a particularly bad night, she would stand with her back to the canvas wall, trapped in a state of tension and vigilance, primed to dart left or right. Presently, the atmosphere in C4 was peaceful. No murmurings could have penetrated her mind in any case, crammed as it was with memories of Lucas and confusion about what remained unsaid between them. But it was too late now to tell him that he'd been right. They loved one another, and that was enough with ever-present perils threatening.

A call alerted her to a problem on the ward. Olivia got up, padding quietly towards a bed. The patient was too hot, he said, so she rearranged his tangled covers, adjusting the cradle protecting his fractured leg that had been knocked over when he'd kicked off the blankets. She was halfway back to her seat when another plaintive call of 'Sister!' reached her ears.

'Got a clean handkerchief for me, ducks?'

'I'll find one, lie down now,' she soothed. He seemed quite an elderly fellow to be serving in the infantry. He said he was forty but looked as much as a decade older. He was often awake the night through, pulling letters and photographs out from underneath his pillows then holding them to the shaded lamp to gaze at while tears dribbled down his rose-tinted cheeks. When she came back with the clean hanky, he caught her hand and patted it. 'My Maria's written me. Would you read it aloud,

Sister? Me light's on the blink.'

'I'll fetch a candle,' she whispered, noticing that the bulb by his bed was out. She pretended not to notice him dabbing at his eyes with his clean hanky while she read slowly from his wife's letter, telling him about his grandchildren. The paper was frayed with handling and she folded it carefully to slide back inside its envelope. What he really wanted wasn't the news from home — he already knew that off by heart — but some company to while away the lonely hours.

'Ta, luv.' He took back his precious letter and folded his hands over it on the bandages protecting his burned chest. He closed his eyes, serenity softening the lines of his tired face.

On the way back to her chair she stopped by Albert's bed as she often did. He was gazing up at the pitched canvas ceiling. His blank expression grew more animated when he saw her. He rolled in her direction, propping his chin on one fist. 'See the lieutenant, did yer?' he whispered.

Olivia nodded, a smile twitching her lips.

'Good . . . can see you had a nice chat. You look proper chirpy.' He grinned and hiked a fair eyebrow at her.

'Coming back soon, is he?'

'Hope so,' Olivia replied fervently. 'I really do.'

'He will,' Albert reassured. 'And reckon he'll be asking you something special . . . if he ain't already?' He chuckled, having read her bashful expression. 'Good on 'im!' Albert settled on his back again, pillowing his head on his hands. The lad looked the picture of contentment now.

Olivia had just sat down again behind the desk and opened the night ledger when approaching footsteps made her glance over her shoulder. She closed the book and welcomed the newcomer with a smile although anticipating she might be about to hear something that was not to her liking.

'Bloody hell! Sorry to have barged in on you like that, Livvie,' Valerie hissed beneath her breath, perching on the vacant chair by the desk. 'I got quite a shock, seeing Lieutenant Black, I can tell you. I'd better tell you how I know him . . . '

'You're Caroline Venner's cousin. He did explain to me.'

'Phew . . . glad *she's* out in the open. Thought I might have put my foot in it, letting on I knew Lucas. But then I couldn't really not, could I?' Valerie's eyes widened. 'How do *you* know him? He's not your boyfriend, is he?'

Olivia detected a note of incredulity. Valerie might just as well have said she didn't believe a cockney girl could hook a sophisticated man like him. Olivia took no offence though. It was an understandable reaction. Her own kith and kin would be surprised to learn her old boss had proposed marriage to her. Besides, she liked her roommate's blunt ways. Valerie Booth was of good stock yet she reminded Olivia of her Barratt's pals, so plain and unaffected was her manner. But Olivia guessed that Valerie, unlike herself, didn't always mean to be that way.

'Sorry, didn't mean you aren't good enough for him 'cos you bloody well are!' Valerie said stoutly. 'It's just he's always being chased by Mayfair totty. Anyway I remember you said you'd had a fiancé who'd died, but that won't stop you finding somebody else.' She stopped and pulled a face. 'I could be more tactful sometimes, I know.'

Olivia shrugged and smiled, and almost blurted out that actually Lucas might like Mayfair totty but he loved a Wood Green factory girl. But she didn't. It wasn't in her nature to be boastful. Also it was far too soon to tell anybody about future plans that were so exciting and precious she'd rather keep them to herself for the time being. Young Albert had guessed she'd received a marriage proposal. Valerie was not so acute.

'I know Lieutenant Black for a couple of reasons,' Olivia began. 'He was a director at Barratt's sweet factory where I once worked. Then he was my fiancé's commanding officer. After Joe was killed, Lucas Black came personally to tell me what had happened. I was so pleased he did that.'

'Gosh, sorry.' Valerie grabbed Olivia's slender fingers in her own square, mannish hand, patting them. 'It must have been a terrible time for you. Stupid me! I imagined that you two were canoodling when I interrupted.' Valerie nudged her and whispered wickedly, 'Fancy a gossip about him then? I know Caroline's my cousin but I can't stand her! She's the standoffish sort. Put her near a rich man, though, and it's the complete opposite.' Valerie rolled her eyes. 'Fur coat . . . no knickers, that's her! It's absolutely true. I eavesdropped on Mummy talking to a friend. She said that Caroline might be her niece but she'd acted like a cheap tart, turning up at a man's apartment wearing nothing but a mink coat.' Valerie snorted in amusement.

Olivia could tell her friend expected her to laugh at that. So she did and spluttered, 'Really . . . who was the man?'

'Didn't find that out but I can guess.' Valerie gave a significant, slow nod. 'Caroline followed Lucas to France, y'know. That didn't go down well in the family. She was being courted by his brother at the time. Just upped and left poor old Henry, she did. Silly girl was wasting her time bothering with Lucas though.'

'Was she?' Olivia asked, opening the night-duty ledger. But her writing was clumsy as she filled in the charts.

'Lucas had somebody else. He never has just one woman on the go,' Valerie continued. 'Caroline thought nothing could come of that, being as her rival was already married to an aristo. But the old boy popped his clogs and everybody thought, aha!' Valerie softly tapped the table top for emphasis. 'Lucas Black'll make an honest woman of her after a decent interval. She was left *filthy* rich, the lucky thing. But he didn't. It all fizzled out with the viscountess. It always does with him.' Valerie gave an exaggerated shrug. 'Caroline saw her chance then. Even though she was expected to marry Henry, she *really* went after Lucas. But to no avail. So she came back to England and now she's cosy with Henry again. They got married even though he's not the full ticket. He was always an odd one, even as a boy. So my cousin's not to blame for driving him bonkers, even though Mummy always says Caroline's enough to try the patience of a saint.'

'What's wrong with her husband?' Olivia enquired. She knew that Lucas was the person she should be asking about this. But she'd no idea when she'd see him again and she was desperate for some answers. She was tempted to ask about his rich widow, too, but didn't. Their affair had taken place before she'd even met Lucas. And it had come to nothing. As they all did, according to Valerie. Olivia knew he wouldn't want her prying into his past. She wouldn't like it if he gossiped about her. Not that she had anything to hide. Joe had been her one and only proper love, and Lucas had known all the ins and outs of that.

'The poor chap was born with problems up here.' Valerie tapped her head. 'He's not bad-looking, but nowhere near as handsome as Lucas. His mother dotes on him even though he flies off the handle easily and acts very oddly. Caroline used to say that the old man had no time for his idiot son. I think that's one of the reasons she set her sights on Lucas. She knew that although he was younger, he'd inherit everything when his father shuffled off.' Valerie suddenly fell silent. 'Rather bad of me to discuss their business like that.' She grimaced. 'Good job I know I can trust you.'

'Sounds a bit of a tangle for them,' Olivia said. Oddly, she felt a twinge of pity for Caroline, acting like a fool over Lucas then returning with her tail between her legs to her future husband.

'It's that alright! Caroline's a gold digger. Takes after her mother, so my own dear mama informs me. Lucas is a Romeo. None of us believe he'll ever settle down . . . '

This time when Olivia heard a patient call out it came as a welcome distraction. She was starting to feel guilty about discussing Lucas behind his back, and pretending she was an impartial bystander in his life. She jumped to her feet with a faint, 'Better get on now. Private Jones is waving his handkerchief at me.'

'I'm going to say goodnight to Ernst.' Valerie glanced towards the Germans' beds with a secretive smile. Her favourite patient was propped up on his pillow and appeared to be reading a book in the dim light. 'He can teach me some more German if he likes. Then I'd better turn in. I'm on earlies all week.'

Olivia set off. On drawing closer, she noticed Private Jones was looking agitated.

'I'm keeping me peepers peeled tonight, alright,' Jones hissed as soon as Olivia reached his side. His chin jabbed repeatedly towards Ernst Fischer's bed.

'You should try and get some shut eye,' Olivia said. She was growing fed up with Jones's constant complaints about the Germans. They were the least troublesome people on the ward. 'Nearly everybody else is asleep, y'know.' It was a good trick to tell a restless fellow that he was the only one still awake. Invariably he'd then slide down in bed, looking sheepish. But not this time.

'*He* ain't akip,' Jones growled. 'And I don't reckon his mate is either, though he's makin' out different. I got a nose fer trouble.' Jones reckoned he did too. He'd felt the same intuitive disquiet on the day he'd taken aim at his own big toe. He'd survived to see another sunrise whereas eight men he'd been due to go over the top with had dropped as rat fodder on no-man's-land. The same sixth sense told him now that something was up.

He suddenly threw back the blanket and shuffled to the edge of his bed. Wondering if he was delirious, Olivia tried to press him back by the shoulders, murmuring soothingly. The thud that followed made her think for a moment he must have knocked something over with his thrashing about, although she'd seen nothing fall.

She spun about then groaned at the sight of a crumpled form on the floor. Olivia was too far away to be able to identify which of the Germans had taken a tumble out of bed. It then dawned on her that Valerie must have changed her mind about talking to Ernst and gone straight to the dormitory because she was nowhere in sight.

Leaving Jones to his own devices, Olivia quickly skirted around the table to the opposite side of the room. It was a shame Valerie hadn't hung around. She could have helped get the fellow upright and save the need to call an orderly. Olivia's pace slowed as she drew closer and a prickle of unease stole over her. The body on the floor was now more distinctly visible, the head plainly poking out beyond the legs of a bed.

It had short mousy hair . . . as the shoulders came into view, Olivia saw they weren't clothed in regulation blue pyjamas but instead a blue bodice with white pinafore straps over the shoulders. A white flag of cotton lay close by that Olivia recognised as a nurse's cap.

She sprinted the last few yards and dropped to her knees next to Valerie, noticing a bloody contusion on her cheek. She felt for her friend's pulse while glancing up at Ernst, who was peering down at her. 'What's happened here?' Olivia panted.

He shook his head, all innocence. 'I think she tripped over.'

Olivia shot to her feet, staring at the German patient. He'd spoken with his customary politeness. But he looked different somehow . . . shifty.

'What have you done to her?' She glanced over at his comrade's bed. The dim lamps outlined a form under the covers but there was something odd about it. Olivia pounced on the blanket edge and whipped it back to reveal just a bundled up sheet and a pillow. Karl Schmidt — the deranged German with a limp — had gone.

Ernst gave a laugh. It was barely audible, but a nasty triumphant sound nonetheless. 'Don't waste your time fetching help, *gnädige Schwester*,' he sneered. 'The Hauptmann has had a good start. With better lungs, I would have gone also.' He made a noise of disdain. 'You English are so stupid. You have no chance of winning this war.'

It took her a moment to grasp his meaning. It seemed they had all been duped about the

101

Hauptmann's mental state, even the doctors. Olivia staggered in shock, curling her fingers about the iron rail of Fischer's bedstead to steady herself. A prisoner had escaped and she had to raise the alarm! Out of the corner of her eye she glimpsed Private Jones speedily tapping his way towards her, balancing on his crutch. She pivoted on the spot to see other men sitting up in bed to discover what the mounting commotion was about. For a second longer Olivia dithered as her eyes were drawn to a circle of blood slowly widening over the floor by Valerie's head. Olivia instinctively fell to her knees, dragging up her pinafore to use to staunch the flow.

'I told yer they was up to no good.' Jones had puffed to a halt beside her. 'Bleedin' Hun bastards! Come on, you lot,' he yelled, rallying the other men by shaking his crutch in the air. 'Look what they done to one of the sisters. Come on . . . let's get 'em!' Hanging onto the bed for balance, he used his crutch as a lance, jabbing it at Fischer's face.

The German sprang forward with a pair of scissors he'd had secreted in the blanket, stabbing his opponent and drawing a surprised grunt from him. As Jones tottered back, holding his side, Ernst swung the weapon again, to finish him off, but Olivia intercepted, making a grab for the scissors. Her outstretched arm was slashed by the open blades.

'Stay back and keep them all quiet or you'll get the same as that cowardly fool.' Fischer curled his lip in contempt. 'You should have let me finish him off. It would have been better for him that way.' He smirked callously. 'Such heroes, your English Tommies.'

Despite her wounded arm Olivia caught Jones, who'd started sagging to the floor, but his weight took her down too. Frantically, she scrambled back to her feet, sobbing in panic. She knew if she didn't raise the alarm a riot would ensue and more blood would be shed. Several patients were already stumbling to their feet and shaking the shoulders of men in adjacent beds, to alert them to danger. The rumble of threats and curses was mounting in volume. The guards would be outside, patrolling the perimeters of the compound. Olivia knew she must flee to fetch them. But Fischer was out of bed too and, though wheezing with the effort, dodging to and fro to block her path.

She jerked backwards to evade the fingers he'd tried to clamp around her throat. Still she felt unable to strike the injured chest of the man she'd recently put clean bandages on. He had no such qualms about hurting her and swung his fist, sending her flying into the nightstand.

Olivia tried to steady herself and keep upright. But things were eddying around her, turning black. And then she saw a flitting shadow, fair-haired and fair-faced . . . just like her brother Alfie. She tried to scream at him to stay back but couldn't even whimper. A second before she lost consciousness she glimpsed Private Albert Carter launch himself into mid-air, roaring a battle cry, and land on top of the German.

# 8

'You really should eat something, my dear, try and regain your strength.' Matron sounded mildly cross, frowning at the untouched food on the tray.

Olivia had been reading a letter she'd received from Cath but dropped it on her lap to cast a jaundiced eye over the chicken soup. She'd swallowed more of the insipid stuff over the past few days than any person should be expected to down in a lifetime. The offer of a nice plate of mutton stew with dumplings might have helped her appetite to pick up. She knew that was what the patients had eaten at dinnertime as she'd opened her window and the savoury aroma had wafted in.

The doctor who'd been attending her had instructed her to stay on a light diet. He'd diagnosed concussion after she'd vomited for twenty-four hours. Her face had been bruised and swollen in the skirmish following Karl Schmidt's escape. As she'd fallen to the floor after being punched, she'd bashed her head on a nightstand. Apart from a thumping headache she'd also suffered a nasty gash on her lower arm from the scissors. The wound had required a few stitches; she'd removed the dressing herself, allowing the air to it once the scab had formed.

Olivia wanted to believe her nausea was due to anxiety, rather than the shock of being punched by Ernst Fischer. She didn't want to allow him that sort of power over her. She'd not clapped eyes on him since but had been told he'd been taken away in handcuffs by the Red Caps, still smirking.

One of the orderlies had carried her back to her dormitory, unconscious. From the moment she'd come to in her bunk she'd fretted over the fate of the others who'd been caught up in the fracas. At first nobody would tell her the details, fearing it would set her back. But she knew all of it now. The good and the bad. She'd also learned she wasn't as mentally or physically robust as she'd believed herself to be. She still felt jumpy, days later, as though her guts were tied in knots. Most upsetting of all, though, was the guilt she felt for not having reacted more quickly. She should have raised the alarm the moment she spotted that evil glint in Fischer's eyes. The patients had been in her care and she'd failed to protect them.

Private Jones had perished on her watch. The soldier who'd been shunned as a coward had been fatally stabbed by the German prisoner-of-war and was now being hailed as a hero. As was young Albert Carter, who'd needed to be pulled off Ernst Fischer. By all accounts, he'd pummelled the German mercilessly, mad as hell to see the filthy Kraut knock Sister Bone down.

'You look thinner.' Matron sat down on the chair by the side of Olivia's bed. 'How about some tapioca pudding instead of soup?'

Olivia grimaced her aversion to that idea and brightly suggested, 'Toast and jam?' She enjoyed

105

nothing better than a bit of toast and jam. Now she was sitting up in bed — and itching to get out of it — she was sure the doctor wouldn't object to that modest treat.

'I think it could be arranged.' Matron stirred the greyish chicken soup and frowned.

'I'll never again shove a spoonful of gruel down one of our boys' throats now I've tasted it myself,' Olivia declared.

'I bet you will,' Matron ruefully contradicted. 'You'll do what's good for them, as I will for you.' She allowed the spoon to rest and turned to Olivia. 'You're one of the best VADs I've encountered since this cursed war began. But you need to go home to recuperate. That's what I've come to tell you. And I won't take no for an answer.' Matron held up a silencing hand as Olivia started to protest. 'I don't want to lose you, my dear. Heaven only knows, we need every pair of capable hands we can muster. But you need time to get over this, don't you?' Her kindly eyes locked with Olivia's, demanding an honest answer.

Olivia gave a slow nod. Her eyes began prickling with tears but she blinked them back. She wouldn't allow self-pity to creep in. For her the confrontation on the ward had been just an isolated incident, something she was unlikely ever to face again. The men taking sanctuary in hospital knew that if they were sent back to the front line, every second would hold the prospect of grappling with the enemy . . . and maybe losing the fight. 'I do have nightmares,' she began. 'But there's no let up in the fighting

106

around Passchendaele. We're already struggling to cope with the convoys coming in one after the other.'

'I know all of that, and appreciate your conscientiousness,' Matron gently interrupted her. 'Nevertheless I still insist you go home, my dear.' She approached Olivia's bedside to place a comforting hand on her crown of fair hair.

'You've been brave, coping with a situation no nurse should encounter. But I can tell you've had the stuffing knocked out of you. I've made arrangements for you to sail from Boulogne at the end of the week.' She ran a professional eye over Olivia. 'You'll be fit enough to travel.'

'Is Valerie fit too?' Olivia asked. She had been thinking a lot about her unfortunate roommate, wondering how she was doing and what the future now held for her.

'Yes, she is. She will be going home on the same voyage.' Matron frowned. 'She's upset, of course. After what happened, though, there's no option but for her to leave with as little fuss as possible.' Matron smiled at Olivia. 'When you're feeling ready, I'll welcome you back with open arms. But there's no rush. Remember that. And if you do decide to rejoin us then I'll ensure you get paid the going rate. You're worth every penny of a nurse's salary. I insist you have it.'

Olivia smiled gratefully. The money she'd borrowed against her house to meet her expenses as a volunteer was dwindling and she didn't want to go back to the bank and ask to borrow more.

Since the night of the German's escape Olivia had had the dormitory to herself. Her roommate was now in disgrace and had been moved in temporarily with Flora Thistle so the camp stickler could keep an eye on her. Ernst Fischer's intention had been to give the Hauptmann a good head start and prevent anybody from reporting his comrade's absence until the following morning. Valerie had been the first to put paid to his scheme by approaching their beds unexpectedly to wish them good night. Fischer had knocked her unconscious before she could fully grasp the situation and raise the alarm.

Everybody who'd been on the ward had been interrogated by the Military Police. Valerie had admitted that she'd befriended Fischer and accepted gifts of chocolate from him. A few of the patients had noticed how she favoured him. But worst of all was the fact that the Unteroffizier had got the scissors he'd wielded from her. Valerie had lent him them to cut off his pyjama buttons because he'd complained they dug into his sore chest when he rolled over at night. Although it was against the rules it had seemed an innocent enough request to her, considering that he'd always been such a docile and charming fellow. And he'd called her an angel . . .

Had Fischer not attacked her, Valerie might now have been facing a far worse punishment than a severe dressing down and dismissal from the Voluntary Aid Detachment. Olivia was certain her roommate had just been foolish and gullible. But rumblings of collaboration and aiding and abetting had started and needed to be quashed. Overall, the gravest injury Valerie had suffered had been to her reputation. Although her scalp had bled profusely, and her eye had turned black, she'd not been concussed as Olivia had.

'Valerie must be very upset to be sent home,' Olivia said.

'Indeed she is,' Matron replied. 'She's been tearful and most apologetic. But it's hard to feel proper sympathy for her. The silly girl has invited trouble on herself. I expect her parents will be very disappointed.' She added briskly, 'How about your family? Have you written to tell them what's happened to you?'

'No!' Olivia burst out. 'And I don't want them worried now I'm on the mend. I'll soon be home and will explain in my own way when I'm back with them.' She smiled wistfully. 'I can't wait to see them.'

Flora Thistle suddenly poked her head around the door and addressed Matron. 'An ambulance driver has turned up and says she won't leave until she's seen Sister Bone. She's waiting outside in the corridor.'

'Oh, is it Rose Drew?' Olivia spontaneously threw back the bedclothes. The prospect of seeing her good friend had joyously transformed her expression.

The two girls had first met when journeying out to France together. That rolling ship's voyage had made Olivia dreadfully seasick. During those long, turbulent hours she'd bitterly regretted having been mad enough to volunteer. Now that blustery day seemed half a lifetime ago, and the shipboard malaise a minor inconvenience. Yet barely a year had passed since she and Rose had disembarked onto French soil as firm friends and made a solemn promise to keep in touch, wherever they were posted. Rose Drew had gone into the ambulance service as she was an experienced driver. On their days off they'd meet up and Rose would teach Olivia how to drive. Although she knew she'd never have Rose's skill, Olivia was pleased that she'd mastered the rudiments of engaging the gears and using the accelerator and brake pedals.

'I believe Rose *was* the name she gave.' Flora treated Olivia to a rare smile.

'Very well, send her in.' Matron was pleased to see her patient's excitement. Livvie Bone had always been a cheery sort but this bad episode had affected her morale and she needed perking up.

When she was left alone Olivia proceeded to make herself presentable for her visitor. Rose was the same age as Olivia, but whereas she was slender and had a fair complexion, her friend Rose was buxom, dark-haired and dark-eyed. When they got together, they always made it an occasion and took extra care with their appearance. Olivia didn't want to let the side down so dragged a brush through her untidy blonde locks and tipped some lavender water into one palm, rubbing it over her temples and neck. She unhooked her dressing gown from the peg on the door and belted it over her nightdress. She was approaching the chair to sit down when her visitor bounded in.

'You'll do anything to get a few days off in

bed, won't you?' Rose chided her.

The two young women flew into a tight embrace. 'How did you find out I've been swinging the lead?' For all Rose's drollery, Olivia guessed her friend had been frantic with worry. Rose seemed reluctant to let her go. 'Come and sit down and I'll tell you all about it.' Olivia linked arms with the other girl, drawing her towards the visitor's chair. ''Course I'll have to swear you to secrecy.'

'Bit late for that.' Rose snorted a giggle. 'It's all over Wimereux that two nurses were attacked when a German escaped from St Omer camp hospital, leaving his mate behind to cause havoc.'

'That's about the gist of it,' Olivia said with studied disappointment. 'Not much else to tell now.'

'Come off it! I heard the younger nurse was a heroine and got slashed trying to save a Tommy. Take it that was you, showing off as usual?'

''Fraid it was.' Olivia grinned. 'It's just a scratch though.' She held out her arm to display the neat, healing wound.

'I've just been to pick up supplies from headquarters. I was planning on stopping by to see you anyway. But as soon as I heard the gossip I just knew you'd be involved. I dropped everything and started up the motor. I've had lead in my boot all the way here. Hope the tyres'll hold up or I won't get back. I bounced straight over a few potholes.'

'Reckon you could get yourself home on bare metal.' Rose was a marvel and had already received several commendations, picking up

111

patients while under fire from enemy aircraft. Olivia was in awe of her courage and driving skill. But her friend never bragged and spoke as though it was nothing much to race from aid post to base hospital with a vanload of groaning casualties while Fokkers screamed overhead.

'Does it smell of sick in here?' Olivia had noticed Rose looking around, wrinkling her nose. 'I have been throwing up . . . ' She took out her lavender water and liberally shook it into her friend's palm.

'No, it's that . . . Gawd! What is it?' Rose rubbed in the scent while grimacing at the soup. 'Couldn't you find a bucket?'

'It's not vomit!' Olivia guffawed, the first time she'd really laughed in a long while. 'It's gruel and it's good for you, is what it is.' But she opened the hut window and tipped it out. She felt so glad to have Rose's company as she wiped tears of mirth from her eyes. They'd settled straight back into their easy camaraderie. It could have been only yesterday they'd had coffee and eclairs in a café in Boulogne instead of long months having passed since their last excursion.

'Come on then, spill.' Rose settled herself in the visitor's chair. 'From the top — and don't leave anything out.'

By the time Olivia had finished, Rose's jaw was sagging. 'Bloody hell, Livvie,' she murmured. 'Why on earth did your roommate act so idiotically?'

'She had a soft spot for Fischer. Valerie was daft in handing over the scissors, but she wasn't alone in being taken in by those two. Only

Private Jones had their number. I saw Lucas recently and told him that the two Germans seemed nice, ordinary folk. They'd put on a great act. I fell for it too.'

'So you've seen Lucas, have you?' Rose asked archly. 'And how is the on-off romance with our dashing lieutenant?'

'That's another story and far too long to go into now.' Olivia rolled her eyes to put Rose off the scent. She and Cath were Olivia's closest friends. Even so, intuition was telling her to hang back on breaking that news.

'He doesn't know about your heroics, does he?'

Olivia shook her head. 'I must tell him when I've worked out how to.' And she knew she must do it soon. She didn't want Lucas finding out from somebody else. He'd risk his liberty going AWOL to see her or, worse, his life by going into battle while distracted by thoughts of what she'd suffered. So she must write to him, saying she was fine. But she wasn't completely fine, even if her body was healing. She felt she didn't deserve to be praised for what she'd done when poor Valerie's behaviour was considered beyond the pale.

'Got a ciggie, Rose?' she asked. 'I've not been out in days and I've none left. I'm gasping.'

Rose delved into a pocket, producing a packet of Woodbines. Once they'd taken one each and lit up, Olivia padded to the window and opened it again, explaining, 'So Matron won't know. She's not a smoker . . . doesn't like it . . . and refused to bring me a pack back from her

113

shopping trip. Said my lungs needed a rest.'

'She cares about you. Anybody can tell that. She's an alright sort. Better than our commandant. She really *is* a bitch. Some of the girls call her the Gorgon.'

'Ugly, is she?' Olivia took a deep savouring drag of tobacco smoke, propping her elbow on the windowsill and gazing out into a twilight studded with emerging stars.

'Nah . . . she stinks. Cheesy feet . . . phew!'

'Short for Gorgonzola?' Olivia guessed, and Rose gestured with her cigarette that she was quite right. Olivia wafted her hand to and fro to disperse the fumes after she'd pitched the dog end out of the window. She felt quite mellow now: the combination of nicotine and Rose's company seemed to have settled her down.

'It wasn't just Val's doing. I was at fault, too,' she confided, wanting to get it off her chest. 'I just froze. Things might have been different if I'd reacted faster. But I felt paralysed, as though I was watching everything instead of being stuck in the middle of it.'

'Anybody would've been in shock.' Rose gently reassured her, coming over to dispose of her own stub out of the window. She put a comforting arm round Olivia's shoulders. 'You'd just found a colleague out cold on the floor.'

'At first I thought Val had had an accident. It didn't occur to me that Fischer was to blame until I asked him what had gone on and saw the hatred in his eyes. The previous day I'd chatted to him — oh, he speaks excellent English — while I renewed his dressings. It was as

114

though a different person was snarling back at me and trying to slash me with the scissors. I do understand how he won Val's confidence, though.'

'Falling for his spiel's one thing. Giving a German a potential weapon's another. No excuse for that, is there? Bet the poor cow's in hot water.'

' 'Fraid she is,' Olivia sighed, leaning her head on her friend's shoulder. 'She's nice too. I do feel sorry for her.' She slid her arms about Rose's waist and they clung together. 'Karl Schmidt might've faked having a screw loose but he didn't make up that leg injury or the bash on the head. It was all healing well but he'll have a limp and that'll slow him down, wherever he's scarpered to.'

'The Red Caps will be after him. He won't get far in hospital pyjamas.'

'He's already dumped those. A woman in the village reported a man's shirt and a pair of trousers had been stolen from her washing line.'

Olivia remembered what Lucas had said about how he'd feel if he was being treated in a German hospital. He'd want to be back with his own kind, he'd said. Schmidt would be heading for the front line, hoping to reach the German trenches.

The girls broke apart then, returning to sit down, Olivia on the edge of the bed and Rose in the visitor's seat.

'What's happened to the bloke who attacked you all?' Rose asked. She offered her cigarettes but pocketed them when Olivia shook her head.

'He was driven away the next morning by the Military Police.'

'Didn't anybody spot the Hauptmann skulking about?' Rose settled her chin on her fist, absorbed in the mystery.

'Oh, they'd timed it just right,' Olivia explained. 'On Sunday evenings, if there's no mad rush with a convoy, there's a church service at the far end of the compound. Most of the patients go along and a good number of the staff are tied up pushing wheelchairs. Those left on duty concentrate on the critical wards. Schmidt crawled under his bed and out through a rip he'd made in the tarpaulin. He must've memorised the sentries' patrols and knew when to make a dash for it.' Olivia's expression displayed her grudging admiration. 'He knew none of us thought him capable of any such thing. Those two Germans played on our sympathies and turned us into pathetic stooges.'

Flora Thistle had been on duty when the escape had taken place. Nobody blamed her though. In the low nighttime lighting in C4 everything had seemed familiar and in its place. Only Private Jones's prejudice had kept him vigilant. He'd cottoned on to something and, unfortunately for himself, drawn Olivia's attention to it.

A tap on the door brought her to her feet. Matron entered, bearing a tray of tea and jammy toast. 'This is positively the last time I wait on you, Sister Bone. I can see you're feeling much better.' She deposited the tray on the nightstand, sniffing the smoky air and giving Olivia an

116

old-fashioned look. 'Now have your supper, then get started on your packing. Any large trunks need to be delivered to the port in advance of sailing.'

'Crikey! You've been getting spoiled!' Rose accepted the cup of tea and plate of toast Olivia held out to her.

'Indeed she has.' Matron made a point of closing the window with a snap. 'That's why I've allowed her a visitor. But you are now outstaying your welcome, Rose Drew, and getting my nurse into bad habits to boot,' she scolded with a twinkle in her eye. 'So drink that up and get going or I'll have to throw you out. I run a tight ship here at St Omer.'

'So I've heard,' Rose muttered darkly as Olivia's superior left them alone. But she emptied her cup and stood up. 'She said you've packing to do. You're going home then?'

'At the weekend,' Olivia informed her, and added firmly, 'I'll be back though.'

'Wish I had leave,' Rose said simply. 'Not seen Mum since Easter.'

'And your dad?'

'Still missing in Turkey,' she said huskily. 'Me brother's been back home though. We were on leave together for a few days. Mum was over the moon. Then she nearly cried her eyes out when *he* had to go back. Didn't shed a tear for me. Helped me pack, she did.' Rose chuckled. 'She knows I can look out fer meself, that's what it is.'

'You can, too,' Olivia said simply. She had a feeling if Rose had been on the ward when Fischer went on the rampage, her friend would have knocked the fiend sparko.

'Ever wish you'd not come out here, Livvie?' Rose asked quietly.

'All the time.' Olivia pulled a wry face. 'But if we don't do it . . . who will? Not enough of us volunteers as it is now everything's gone crazy round Passchendaele.'

'You really reckon you'll be coming back?' Rose cocked her head and considered her friend. 'You've done a good stint and taken a bad scare. Nobody'd blame you for calling a halt to it now.'

''Course I'm coming back! You take a bad scare every time a bloody Hun opens his bomb hatch over your ambulance. I'm not having you being braver than me, y'know. Anyhow, you've still got to teach me to get out of third gear.'

'Daft mare!' Rose clucked her tongue and chuckled.

The girls hugged, swinging each other to and fro in fierce affection, eyes squeezed shut. Then after Rose had left Olivia sat down, finished her toast and cleared the crockery onto the tray. She reseated herself in the chair by the bed, staring into space. Her eyes suddenly started to water, then huge sobs that she tried to stifle with her hands broke from her throat. She wasn't sure exactly why she cried. She didn't feel sad for herself . . . far from it. She had survived a fight with a German and felt privileged, as well as relieved, to have been spared. She quietened and wiped her eyes on her dressing-gown sleeve, saying a prayer for Lucas and Rose and all the people working on through their fears and the filthy carnage.

She needed to go home to ease her mind. If she stayed here she'd be little use. Matron had known that. But Olivia would come back. She found some writing paper and rested it on a book and started to write to Lucas, telling him she'd be in England for a while. But not to worry, because everything was fine.

# 9

'I'll understand if you don't want to . . . but please would you keep in touch with me, Livvie?'

'Of course I will. Try and stop me.' There'd been a pitiful note in Valerie's request that'd made Olivia rouse herself from her tiredness to sound cheerful.

They had just disembarked on Charing Cross station platform, their journey home to London finally at an end. The sea voyage had been the worst Olivia had faced so far, and she'd traversed the Channel on almost a dozen occasions. The ship had been raked fore to aft by a Fokker's Gatling guns before their battleship escort sent it spiralling away, trailing smoke. Then a submarine had been spotted and life rings had swiftly been distributed. Luckily the sub had turned out to be friendly. But by then alarm had spread. Even the crew had looked jittery. A group of white-faced wives and mothers who'd been hospital-visiting at Étaples had huddled together, crying and crossing themselves. For two VAD nurses, fresh from closer combat with the enemy, it hadn't seemed the end of the world. They had slipped into professional mode and comforted the hysterical women, telling them that their wounded boys would be well looked after by VAD colleagues back in France.

Discretion had kept the girls from discussing their own recent hair-raising drama on packed public transport. But it hadn't been forgotten. Now, with the journey complete, they were on the point of parting, but still had much to say to one another. This wasn't the right time or place though. They were both too exhausted after the long journey for much conversation.

'Are you getting a cab home to Islington?'

Olivia nodded. 'How about you, Val?'

Instead of replying she jammed her hat further down on her head as though to disguise herself. 'Oh, for Christ's sake!' she groaned. 'Mummy's over there. I could've done without her coming to fetch me as though I'm a naughty kid expelled from school.'

Olivia swayed to the left, taking a glance past her friend at a woman sporting a feathered hat and fur-trimmed coat. Her elegant attire did nothing to soften her stony expression. Olivia felt sorry for Valerie, returning to that reception. 'Buck up!' She gave her friend's arm an encouraging shake. 'We're home in one piece. How about we settle down for a couple of days then go out somewhere later in the week? We could meet up at the Angel, Islington if you'd like?'

Valerie's expression brightened immediately. 'You're not embarrassed to be seen out with me? That bitch Flora Thistle said she'd cut me dead if she ever saw me in civvies.'

'No need to worry about what *she* says,' Olivia replied flatly.

'You really want to stay friends after all that's gone on?'

''Course, I do.' Olivia dug in her pocket and

found a pack of strong French cigarettes. She'd bought them in Boulogne to see her through the homeward journey. There was only one left. She tore off a strip of carton and quickly pencilled her address on the back of it. 'There . . . If you feel like popping round some time that's where I live in Islington.'

Valerie pocketed the address and spontaneously grabbed Olivia in a bear hug, pressing a kiss to the side of her head. 'You're a good sort, Livvie. See you Friday at the Angel, Islington. Seven o'clock?' she suggested eagerly.

'Seven o'clock,' Olivia confirmed. She watched Valerie stride off and was pleased to see her friend straighten her shoulders as she drew closer to her mother. 'That's it. Chin up,' Olivia urged beneath her breath. About to put away her Gauloises, she instead emptied the pack and struck a match. She stood alone on the platform, smoking and watching mother and daughter heading off. Mrs Booth's mouth was already working nineteen to the dozen. 'Chin up, Val,' Olivia repeated, reaching down for her luggage.

In her mind she heard the echo of a rough female voice giving her that same advice. It was a memory that brought a smile to Olivia's face as she trudged on, a suitcase held in each hand and a cigarette clamped between her lips in a most unladylike fashion. 'Chin up, Livvie,' Matilda Keiver would bark at her when times had been tough. 'That's what us women do round here and you'll have to 'n' all, if you want to stop here a while.'

Olivia *had* stopped a while in the neighbourhood of Campbell Road. Now she'd no intention of ever going anywhere else. The dirty glamour of the Duke public house, with its smoky, yeasty atmosphere, seemed newly appealing to her on her return. She yearned to push through its doors and relax in the company of her family and friends. A contented sigh expanded her chest as she dropped her luggage to hand over her ticket at the barrier. After a final drag on her cigarette, she stepped on the stub. Then, suitcases again at the ready, she walked out into the street to find a cab to take her home.

*   *   *

Olivia gazed up at the front of her house on Playford Road, feeling both proud and critical. Although dusk was settling, she could see the nets needed a wash and the front path could do with a broom pushed over it. It was September and the leaves were fast coming down. The solid red brick, ornamented with four sash windows and a neat portico, seemed to radiate memories of good times. Joe had first taken her home to his house on an autumn evening. They'd sat in the cosy parlour in fireside chairs, and he'd asked her to be his wife. Three months later he had been dead. Nearly two years had passed since then but she still felt such affection for him and this precious gift that she would have hugged the house's gritty walls, if she could.

On opening the front door she heard the sound of raised voices. Nothing much had changed then, she thought wryly.

Having quietly closed the door, she shoved her cases against the wall. She'd not seen her family since their aunt's funeral back in the early summer. She hoped to surprise them, sure the pleasure of her unexpected arrival would light up their faces and stop them arguing. It dawned on her then that even had she crashed in they might not have heard above the racket they were making.

'Livvie!' Her brother had just come out of the kitchen, holding a plate of toast. For want of anywhere else to deposit it, he dumped the plate on the stairs then rushed up to clasp his arms about her waist.

Olivia caught him in a tight hug. A year or two ago she would have lifted him off his feet. But he was a solid lad now, almost as tall as she was and too heavy for her to carry. She dropped a kiss on his fair head, easing her bad arm away from him as his exuberance made her wince.

'Your sisters are having a ding-dong then?' She raised her eyes to the ceiling.

'They never stop.' His voice was muffled by her coat. 'You should've let us know you was coming home.'

'I thought I'd make it a nice surprise this time.' She put Alfie away from her, troubled when the noise upstairs increased in volume. She couldn't get the gist of the argument. 'What's up with them?'

'It's about the wedding,' Alfie said, wrinkling his nose in disgust.

'Who's getting married?' Olivia had reached

the foot of the stairs, about to go up and make her presence known, but turned back to Alfie with a frown.

'Maggie. Nancy reckons she's nuts. And so do I,' he said darkly. 'Can't stand *him*.'

'What?' Olivia barked in astonishment. She was torn between interrogating Alfie further and charging upstairs to get it straight from the horse's mouth.

'You heard right. I'm getting married.' Maggie was leaning over the banister, her expression a mixture of shock at seeing her big sister and defiancé that her news had leaked out too soon. 'How come you're back without warning us?' she demanded. 'You always write and let us know when you're due to turn up.'

'Something happened — there wasn't time to write and let you know this time.' Olivia felt disappointed by Maggie's tone of voice. There was no glad welcome from her. She bit back the reminder she wanted to give that this was her house so she'd turn up whenever she pleased.

'What's happened?' Alfie asked. 'Did you get the sack?'

'No, but I'll explain later. Sounds as though Maggie's got something more important to say.' Olivia glanced up at her sister. She sensed Maggie was agitated and not just because she'd been arguing with Nancy. The kettle whistled in the background, cutting into the silence. Olivia relaxed and suggested, 'Anybody like to make me a cup of tea then?' Walking straight back into the middle of family problems was the last thing she'd wanted so she decided to approach things

125

gently. She wasn't sure she felt up to more than that right now.

'I'll do it,' Alfie offered, and trotted back to the kitchen.

Maggie came down the stairs, stepping on her brother's unseen plate of toast on her way. She cursed as she upset it. 'I am glad you're back, Livvie.' She gave Olivia a quick hug.

'How long are you staying?'

'Not sure yet,' Olivia said, returning the embrace. She noticed one of Maggie's cheeks had a faint red weal on it. It had been a proper fight then. Her younger sisters would set about one another with their hairbrushes when really het up. 'Nancy won, did she?' Olivia teased, touching the mark.

Maggie jerked aside her face. 'How long d'you reckon you'll be staying?' She sounded impatient.

'I'm not sure. I've not been well. That's why I'm home.'

'Oh, I see. Are you better?'

Olivia nodded.

'That's good then.' Maggie quickly followed Alfie in the direction of the singing kettle without bothering to enquire further.

Olivia stared dispiritedly at the mess her sister had left behind on the stairs.

''Bout time you showed up here to sort things out,' Nancy said, stomping down from her bedroom. She stopped a few treads above Olivia, busy clearing up the debris. 'She's just about driving me crackers. Soon as I've got enough put by, I'm moving out. Ain't living here with *them*.'

She gave Olivia a perfunctory peck on the cheek before slipping past into the parlour and slamming the door behind her.

'Welcome home, Livvie,' Olivia murmured ruefully beneath her breath while carrying toast crumbs and cracked china into the kitchen.

* * *

'You're catching me up.' Mrs Keiver nodded at the empty port glass by Olivia's elbow, asking, 'One fer the road, gel?'

'Why not? Thanks, Matilda.'

Within a minute of Matilda beckoning him with a shout, the landlord had deposited their fresh drinks on the table. The restricted drinking laws that had been introduced in an attempt to promote sobriety during the war were regularly flouted in the Bunk. As were plenty of other rules and regulations. These people were a law unto themselves and the Duke's landlord knew if he wanted to keep their custom he'd turn a blind eye when the clock struck half past nine or if somebody bought a drink for a pal. He'd especially turn a blind eye for Matilda Keiver. She kept him in profit more than the rest of his punters put together. And as the coppers were too nervous to pound the beat around the neighbourhood of the worst street in North London the landlord reckoned that his licence was safe enough. Nevertheless he dimmed the lights and locked the doors . . . just in case.

The clamour that had started the moment

Livvie Bone stepped inside the pub had long since petered out. People always flocked around at first to find out how she'd fared and what was *really* happening over there. Everybody had kith or kin away fighting and wanted to know whether Sister Bone had any news of them. Having heard their fill, they'd all now drifted back to their regular spots propped against the bar, leaving Matilda and Olivia alone at a corner table. The older woman saw an opportunity for a private talk at last.

'It's cheered me up no end, you being back, but you don't look that happy about it, love.' Matilda could see behind Olivia's polite smiles and chat and knew something wasn't quite right. 'What's up?'

The answering shrug was non-committal but Matilda was no fool. 'Come on, Livvie, problem shared,' she coaxed. 'Ain't like you to be in the pub till this time o' night, downing booze like there's no tomorrer. That's my job,' she tacked on dryly. 'Thought you'd still be catching up with yer sisters and brother. Ah . . . ' Matilda paused, having glimpsed a certain expression flit over the girl's features. It was a look that she recognised, having ground many an axe with kin herself. 'So it's a family problem, is it? I'm guessing one of your lot's been up to mischief while you've been away. Young Alfie been fighting again, has he?'

'He seems the most sensible of the lot of 'em.' Olivia took a sip of port then another although she already felt quite tipsy. People had been kind, refilling her glass by way of welcome home.

Matilda was right, though: it wasn't like her to stay out so long, or drink so much. Or smoke so much either. Sometimes she barely recognised herself and wondered where the virtuous factory girl who'd worked at Barratt's had gone. But then nothing was the same as it had been before the war.

This evening she'd stayed out late because she didn't want to go home. Normally she never shirked an argument but she hoped they'd all be in bed when her key struck the lock later. She ached in body and mind and didn't feel up to another shouting match with Maggie. On her first night home she'd managed to curb her temper once she'd heard her middle sister out. Privately she'd thanked God that fate had been at work, bringing her back at this vital time. Maggie hadn't written to her in France for a while, and her own letters, loaded with questions about how they were all doing back home, had lately been briefly answered only by Nancy. Now Olivia knew why she'd been getting so little news from them. Maggie, in particular, hadn't wanted her to know what had been going on.

Aware that Matilda was still patiently awaiting an explanation, Olivia offered her pack of cigarettes to buy a bit more time. She knew once she started talking about her woes, it would all tumble out.

'This poison's enough fer me.' Matilda waggled her glass of Irish whiskey before gulping from it.

'Maggie's in the family way again.' It felt as

though a weight had been lifted off Olivia once she'd said it.

Matilda's expression barely altered. She put down her glass, licking whiskey from her lips. 'Want me to have a word with Lou about payin' a visit?'

'He's asked her to marry him this time.' Lou was a handywoman who'd helped Maggie before when she'd got pregnant. On that occasion the culprit had wanted nothing to do with babies or weddings. Now it was different, Maggie had said, looking pleased as punch. And unfortunately Olivia believed her.

'Same bloke, is it?' Matilda sounded surprised. 'I remember you said he was a nasty git.'

'He is.' Olivia's tone quivered with an undercurrent of disgust. 'That's why me face is on me boots. But Maggie won't hear a word against him, and this time I'm not sure I can do anything about it.' She downed what remained of her port and pushed the glass away over the slop-stained table. 'She's turned seventeen now. Maggie's told me I'm not her mother and can't order her what to do. She's said I'm to leave her alone because it's none of my business. Perhaps she's right.'

'It'll always be your business for as long as you care about her,' Matilda said gruffly, patting Olivia's wrist. 'I know what you're going through, being as I've got exactly the same problem. My own sister's married to a nasty git.' A raucous guffaw made her eyes swerve to her brother-in-law. He was with his pal in the taproom. As though aware of being observed

130

across the bar, Jimmy Wild raised his tankard and gave her a smirk. Matilda jutted her chin at him before turning away.

'Maggie's been letting Harry Wicks stay overnight at ours.' Olivia took a deep drag on her cigarette then jabbed the dog end into the ashtray. The couple had actually used her vacant bedroom. The very idea of that swine, sleeping in her bed, made her want to throw up. When Nancy had told her what they'd been doing, Olivia had tackled Maggie over it and been tempted to clout her for taking such a diabolical liberty.

'Didn't you know about any of it?' Matilda sounded shocked. 'Can understand Maggie keeping quiet about doing that behind yer back. But why ain't your Nancy warned you what's been going on?'

'Nancy can't stand Harry either. She wants to move out and I don't blame her. She said she didn't want to worry me as I couldn't do anything about it from France. She was right about that, but I think there's more to it. I think, if Nancy grasses Maggie up, *she'll* get a taste of her own medicine.'

'What's Nancy been up to then?' Matilda was agog and leaned in closer.

'Let's just say she's got some nice new stuff in her wardrobe.' After the girls had gone to work yesterday Olivia had quashed any pangs of conscience and started to snoop. It was still her house, she'd told herself, and she was entitled to know what went on in it. Hidden beneath an old blanket on Nancy's side of the room she'd found two blouses and some pretty underwear of a quality far too good for a factory girl's pocket. They'd still had the price tags attached and Olivia had guessed Nancy intended selling them. But when she'd delved into Maggie's chest of drawers and uncovered a man's shaving kit and a comb full of brown hair and scurf, her stomach had really lurched. She'd known at once who owned those.

'So Nancy's been out lifting, has she? If she wants to shift any of it, send her my way,' Matilda whispered, giving Olivia a slow nod. She'd been ducking and diving herself ever since her husband had enlisted and she'd lost his wages. She'd fenced top-quality bed sheets recently for a woman in Lennox Road, for a cut of the takings.

Olivia rolled her eyes. 'You're supposed to be giving me helpful advice, Mrs K.'

'I am, love,' Matilda returned succinctly. 'Better Nancy moves it on than keeps it in the house. Especially if a wrong 'un's getting his boots under yer table. You don't want him nosing around and clocking what he shouldn't. All of yers could end up getting your collars felt then.'

'Harry Wicks is never putting his boots under my table again. I've told Maggie that. And I'll keep telling her till it sinks right in.' Olivia bit her lip. The last person she'd ever want unearthing Bone family skeletons was Harry Wicks. She prayed Maggie hadn't divulged any sensitive family stuff to him but feared it to be a vain hope.

'I don't want to fall out with Maggie. She's

been keeping things going while I've been away and that can't have been easy. She's told me she has to prise housekeeping out of her sister, and Harry's been a godsend chipping in for his board and lodging.' Olivia tutted in disbelief. 'I doubt he's given her a brass farthing. He's always been mean. She's probably putting in his share herself.' Olivia paused. 'I know Nancy can be tight-fisted. She's squirrelling away every penny so she can have her own place.'

Matilda wagged a finger. 'One day those kids'll remember they've got a lot to thank you for.'

'They say you reap what you sow. I wanted them to be more independent, less of a burden on me so I could be a VAD. Now I'll have to live with the consequences and let them off my apron strings.'

'I'm surprised by your Maggie though.' Matilda shook her head.

'She's been different since she hooked up with Harry Wicks. It was a relief when she turned to Ricky instead. Harry's used his brother's death to worm his way back into her affections.' Olivia sighed glumly. She'd intended to have a few pleasant relaxing weeks at home before returning to the fray in France. But it wasn't going to be that simple. And brooding in the pub wasn't going to help matters. 'I'd better get going. It's late.' She glanced at the clock over the bar; it was high time to head home. She knew she'd have a sore head in the morning. 'Let me buy you a drink before I do, Matilda?'

'Thanks, love, but I'm off to get a bit of shut eye meself. If I ain't banging on doors at the crack of dawn, half of 'em will have scarpered to avoid paying their rent. Then me guv'nor'll cut up rough.' It was rare for Matilda to turn down a free whiskey, rents or no rents to collect. But Olivia was a novice drinker and Matilda didn't want to find out she'd come a cropper in the dark, walking home alone.

A blast of chilly autumn air whipped the door back as Olivia ventured out, almost making her lose balance. She did up her coat buttons then jammed the hat down on her fair hair before plunging her hands into her pockets for warmth.

'Shame you ain't been out celebrating being home rather than drowning yer sorrows, love.' Matilda linked arms with her and they started up the road, chins huddled into collars.

The slap of frosty air on Olivia's face soon helped to sweep away the boozy fog from her mind. 'Has Jack been back on leave?' She turned the conversation to Matilda's husband as they walked. Enough had been said about her lot.

Matilda gave a morose shake of the head. 'Hope he'll come home at Christmas. He writes regular to us. I hate it when it goes silent and we don't hear nuthin' fer weeks and weeks. Me mind goes crazy, imagining what's happening. Jack makes out it's not too bad out there but he don't fool me.'

Olivia knew that Jack Keiver was right in the thick of things. As was Lucas.

Lucas . . . he was always there at the back of her mind. He would surely have received her letter by now and would know she was home. She prayed he was still safe. Her mind was haunted by what he'd told her about being caught behind enemy lines. Like Matilda, she was crazy with worry, especially now she knew how terrifying it felt to come face to face with an enemy intent on killing you.

'Thanks for bringing me home, Matilda,' Olivia said on a tipsy sigh. The two women slowed down on approaching her gate.

'You're welcome,' Matilda replied. 'Now get yourself indoors and have a good night's kip. I'll come by later in the week and have a word. I've some news to give you, actually.'

'Oh, what's that?' Olivia hesitated with a hand on the latch.

'Nothing worth bothering with at this time of night, love. We'll talk about that another time.' She put her hands on Olivia's shoulders. 'Now don't forget, if you want me to help you sort out Maggie's little problem . . . ' she jerked her head at Olivia's abdomen ' . . . you just say the word and I'll have Lou round yours in no time at all.'

'Thanks, Matilda, I can always rely on you.'

'You can, love.' Matilda started to walk away. 'G'night, Livvie,' she sent over her shoulder

''Night, Matilda.'

Olivia opened the door then glanced back as she heard a rustling sound. The wind was swaying the privet hedge to and fro. With a shiver, she hurried over the threshold.

# 10

'What was wrong with you then? You look alright to me.'

Olivia was surprised when her sister unexpectedly fired this question at her. The atmosphere between them had been strained for days although they'd not argued again. Maggie had retreated into sullenness and Olivia had let her be rather than attempting to coax her out of it.

'You said you'd come home 'cos you'd not been well,' Maggie continued. 'You don't look ill.'

Olivia up-ended the iron onto the hot range then folded her pressed chemise. 'I had a bit of an accident. I had some stitches put in my arm,' she explained, rolling back her sleeve.

Maggie seemed taken aback by that. She'd been seated on a hard kitchen chair, sewing a button back on her blouse. She got up to come and have a better look at the neat scar Olivia displayed. 'What sort of an accident?'

'You wouldn't believe me if I told you,' she answered flatly. She knew that even a cautious account would sound far-fetched. The incident seemed a long while ago even though only a little over a fortnight had passed since Ernst Fischer had sent her crashing, unconscious, to the ground.

She had intended to tell her family a watered-down version of it; she didn't want them

136

worrying that the St Omer hospital was a dangerous place to work. In the end Maggie's bombshell had trumped her sister's calamity. Now the moment had passed and it seemed too late to bring it up. 'All said and done, wasn't anything to write home about really.' Olivia smoothed down her sleeve, rebuttoning her cuff. 'You off to work when you've done your sewing?' She was keen to keep the conversation flowing. She hated stony silences.

'Yeah . . . hope I don't throw up, though. The smell of the solder makes me feel sick.' Maggie nipped the thread with her teeth then tidied away her needle and cotton in the sewing box.

'Do any of them at the factory know you're in the family way?' Olivia could detect a tiny bump beneath her sister's skirt. Luckily, a person unaware of Maggie's condition wouldn't have suspected she was pregnant. Her hips were still narrow although her blooming bosom had tightened the buttons on her bodice.

Maggie shook her head. 'Not even told Alice yet. She's nice but some of 'em would grass on me to the supervisor, to try and get their mitts on my nightshifts. Ain't losing those wages just yet.'

'Have you worked out when the baby's due?'

Maggie stroked a hand over her belly. She seemed pleased to be pregnant. Last time she'd been desperate to get rid of Harry Wicks's bastard and had injured herself in the process. But this baby wouldn't be a bastard, if he stayed true to his word.

'I reckon early spring.' Maggie cocked her

head, listening for another heartbeat, her eyes glowing. 'I reckon it's a boy.'

Olivia smiled too . . . wistfully. It could be so easy to delight in this first niece or nephew. Maggie was young to be thinking of getting married and being a mother, but what did age matter? Boys younger than she was were perishing on the Somme before they'd had their first kiss. Nobody took next year for granted now; there was a sense of urgency, an impulse to do something . . . anything . . . before the chance was snatched away for good.

Olivia had decided not to interfere with Maggie's plans, but she wouldn't pretend she approved. She was a realist. She didn't want her sister to have to face up to the ordeal of another abortion. And the idea of the abuse she'd receive as an unmarried mother was equally abhorrent. It might make Olivia boil up to admit it but Maggie only had one option if she was determined to keep her baby, and that was to marry the father. A ruined woman's prospects were grim and a good-for-nothing was considered better than no husband at all. So Olivia would grit her teeth and wish her sister all the luck in the world on her wedding day. Apart from that she had nothing to say . . . no advice to give. The baby had to come first now. The poor little mite deserved to have two parents named on its birth certificate, even if one of them wasn't worth spit.

It was possible that being a husband and father might bring out a different side to Harry. It seemed a forlorn hope but Olivia decided to cling to it for want of anything else. Her brother and sisters were getting more confident and independent, just as she'd hoped they would. So she couldn't complain if they didn't always follow a path she would have chosen. They were their own people and must suffer the consequences of their actions. She loved them all dearly and didn't want rifts to drive them apart as they turned into adults. There'd been enough ill will in the family when her father had been alive, skulking about with his sister-in-law and keeping secrets from them.

Olivia thought of her own secret then: Lucas had asked her to be his wife and the thrill of it warmed her from top to toe, obliterating any thoughts of Harry Wicks. She regretted having rebuffed Lucas's suggestion just to go off and get married. She'd wanted time to consider his family . . . her family . . . the trust and love and lies between them. Then, just hours later, she'd stared into the eyes of a vicious enemy, in the way Lucas must have done a thousand times. She'd understood then why he'd not wanted a delay. She should have snatched her chance to have him for her husband. She feared she had tempted fate and the wheel might never turn for her again.

'Harry'll be a good dad, y'know.' Maggie broke into Olivia's thoughts. 'It's true he's treated me badly in the past but he's different since Ricky passed away. He said he feels humble, being the lucky one who's still alive. He's sorry for all the things he's done.'

'Glad to hear it,' Olivia said crisply.

'I just couldn't forget Harry, 'cos he was me first boyfriend.' Maggie hoped to win her big sister over with this frank explanation. 'I wanted to hurt him by marrying his brother. I liked Ricky a lot 'cos he was kind. But I never wanted him like I did Harry.' She hung her head, ashamed of herself. 'Harry regrets telling me to get rid of the first baby. The trenches sent him cuckoo, he reckons. But he's better now and wants to take care of me and make his brother proud.' She gave a bashful smile. 'If it's a boy we're naming him after Ricky.'

'That's a nice thought,' Olivia said. 'I hope you're right about Harry this time, Mags. I honestly do.' Her voice throbbed with sincerity. But she remembered things differently and took Harry Wicks's vow about being a reformed character with a pinch of salt.

The first time he'd knocked Maggie up he'd fled back to his regiment to escape the responsibility of a wife and child. He'd cheated on Maggie with another girl even though he knew she was pregnant. Olivia made a determined effort not to dwell on his past crimes but give him the benefit of the doubt . . . for now. 'The time up to Christmas will fly by. Have you already booked the register office?'

'Harry's doing it next week. We want a December wedding.' Maggie sounded excited. 'He's fitting in extra shifts at the butcher's, to save up. I'll still be able to wear a decent dress if I watch me weight.'

'So he got his job back in Scully's, did he?' Olivia pushed the iron over a pillowcase.

140

'Shouldn't he be shipping out as he's fit for work?'

'He's been invalided home. His leg got infected again and he's limping. The doctor said he can't go back.'

Olivia knew she'd sound sour if she made a comment about having seen infantrymen soldiering on with far worse injuries, so she kept quiet. She'd heard on the grapevine that Wicks had damaged his own leg so as to be sent home. With that damning thought came others that were hard to ignore. Remembering his perverted interest in Maggie when she was only an adolescent still made Olivia feel sick. As did the memory of his rough hands on her. Olivia knew she wasn't the only woman Harry had tried to force himself on. But it seemed Maggie had managed to put aside the humiliation of having once been rejected by such a useless item, to forgive if not forget his ill treatment of her.

Olivia abruptly stopped picking it over before a catalogue of reasons to hate her future brother-in-law rolled off her tongue. She had to let the matter rest now.

'I'm off out this evening with a friend from the VAD,' she brightly changed the subject. 'We came home together on the same ship. D'you know what picture's showing round here?'

Maggie ignored the question. 'You'll be travelling back to France soon with your friend, won't you?' she demanded.

'Val's not going back. She's finished over there.'

141

'You're not though, are you?' Maggie sounded alarmed.

'I'll be going back when I'm ready. I've not been home a whole week yet.' Olivia gave her sister a sharp look. 'If Harry's pestering you to find out when the coast'll be clear, tell him not to bother. He's not living here when I return to work.'

'Ain't bothered about that,' Maggie replied, blushing furiously. 'We'll get our own place now we're properly engaged.'

'Are you?' Olivia shook out another pillow-case. 'Has he bought you a ring?'

'He's saving for it. Anyhow a ring ain't important. We've got to get things for the baby.'

'First you've got to find somewhere to live, unless you're planning on moving in with your in-laws.' Olivia tested the heat of the iron with a licked finger.

'No fear of that! Harry can't wait to move out. His mother's driving him crazy.' Maggie regretted having let the cat out of the bag. 'We'll get our own place,' she insisted.

'That'd be for the best.'

'You're being bloody mean! You'd sooner leave this place half-empty than let your sister and her little baby have a roof over their heads?'

'It's not that and you know it. You're always welcome.' Olivia sighed. Harry had caused far too much trouble between them over the years. It wasn't right that he wielded that sort of power over the Bone family. 'I'm not arguing with you about it. I'll sign where I need to so you can get married. But you've made your bed and you

142

must lie on it in his house, not in mine.'

'I will then!' Maggie stormed.

Olivia picked up the pile of pressed linen and went upstairs with her sister's sullen muttering following her. She felt sad that their truce had been so brief. Maggie wanted to make her feel guilty. But she wouldn't succeed. Olivia would never allow Harry to taint Joe's legacy. Joe had hated him too. He'd fought Harry on more than one occasion, to protect Olivia from the brute who lived over the road. She had Nancy and Alfie to think of too. They disliked him and it was *their* home, not Harry Wicks's.

'What's for tea, Livvie?' Alfie called out from his bedroom as he heard her coming up the stairs.

'Whatever you can find in the pantry,' she answered. 'I'm getting ready to go out.'

'Where are you off to?' Nancy had appeared in the doorway of the bedroom she shared with Maggie. She had her hair in curls, and rouge on her lips and cheeks.

'I'm meeting a colleague from St Omer. How about you? Where are you off to?'

'Nowhere special.'

Olivia wasn't fooled by Nancy's mumbled reply and casual shrug. But before she could question her sister again about dolling herself up, Nancy had shot back into her bedroom, pulling rags from her hair.

She'd turned fifteen now and that was older than Maggie had been when she'd started hanging about with Harry. Olivia realised that Nancy had probably attracted a boy. Her

143

youngest sister was prettier than Maggie, who had mousy fair hair and a slim figure. Nancy was golden-blonde, like Olivia, and her figure was already well developed. When she was younger Nancy had always seemed sensible for her age, so Olivia had tended to let the girl just get on with things while she sorted out the other two. Now she wasn't convinced that Nancy was sensible. She was crafty, that was for sure, if she'd been shoplifting and hiding stolen goods in the house.

If Maggie hadn't been hogging the limelight, Olivia would have made a point of cornering Nancy for a serious talk, not only about the shoplifting, but about how life in general was treating her. She wanted to know what Nancy got up to in her spare time, and with whom. But right now wasn't a good time for a lengthy chat that was likely to end in an argument. Olivia had promised Val Booth that she'd meet her at seven o'clock and she wouldn't let her down. She closed her bedroom door, put away the pressed linen in a drawer then concentrated on enjoying the evening ahead.

She felt a thrill of anticipation as she opened the wardrobe to unhook her best serge skirt and broderie anglaise blouse. Then she found her favourite hat in a box on top of the wardrobe. It was years old but reminded her of Joe. The first time she'd met him he'd retrieved it from the gutter for her. Harry Wicks had knocked it there during a tussle in which he'd tried to kiss her. Then Joe had knocked *him* into the gutter. She smoothed a hand over the soft blue velvet then quickly started changing her clothes. It wasn't just the prospect of having a chinwag about the drama they'd got caught up in at St Omer that was spurring her on to leave the house. Val was Caroline Venner's cousin and Olivia, like any woman in love, was keen to find out more about her future husband's former lover.

★   ★   ★

'I thought you might've changed your mind about coming.' Valerie held onto her stylish French beret as she rushed towards Olivia with a welcoming grin.

'Sorry I'm late.' Olivia squeezed her friend's gloved fingers. She'd walked to the Angel, thinking it would be quicker than waiting for the bus. But it had taken a while because on the way she had bumped into Matilda's neighbour. Olivia liked Beattie Evans and had politely stopped for a chat. Normally she was a jolly woman but tonight she'd been drying her eyes while recounting that her nephew, who was serving as a sapper, had been missing for months on the Western Front. Olivia was used to relatives wanting reassurance from her that the wounded soldiers all got better, and the missing always turned up. To comfort them, she went along with it even though both sides knew it was fraudulent kindness.

'Fancy a bite to eat in a Corner House before we go to the Empire?' Olivia suggested.

'Oh, rather!' Valerie beamed.

They set off in the direction of Highbury

Corner, passing a group of Bantams in khaki. The soldiers' appreciative glances and whistles followed the girls down the road. Valerie turned about to give them a come-hither smile. 'The tallest might just about reach my chin,' she said optimistically.

'You're in enough trouble 'cos of men.' Olivia tutted in amusement and pulled her on, linking their arms. 'How're things at home, Val?'

Valerie gave a theatrical groan. 'Mummy's frightfully angry. I've not seen my father. He's been staying at his club. I expect they've had words about me being a bloody disgrace.'

'You weren't arrested or charged with any crime. *And* you took a thumping from Fischer.' Olivia pointed out.

'Mummy loves a drama.' Valerie rolled her eyes. 'I know I made a mess of it over there but making me join the Voluntary Aid Detachment was the best thing she could have done for me. I thanked her for that but she didn't take it well.'

Olivia was pleased that her friend could find a bright side to the situation. 'We'll all want to forget about what went on when the war's done. Nobody'll bother bringing it up then.'

'*She* will. She'll harp on about it for donkey's years. She's already threatened to pack me off to an aunt in Scotland.' Valerie giggled. 'Better that than being banished to a nunnery, I suppose.'

'What's your aunt like?' Olivia pushed open the door of the Corner House and they gratefully escaped the dank autumn dusk to settle down at a window table.

'No idea, I've never met her. And I'm not

146

going to.' Valerie whipped off her beret and ran her fingers through her short bob. 'I'm going to volunteer again. I don't mind what I do or where I'm posted. Somebody'll take me on. Anything's better than being stuck at home or in Scotland.'

'Good for you.' Olivia gave her an admiring nod.

The waitress stopped by their table and they gave an order for tea and currant buns then sat quietly gazing through the window into the twilight, thinking about the people they'd left behind in St Omer.

'Did you tell your mother *all* about it?' Olivia asked as the tea arrived.

'Everything. I had to. She wouldn't leave me alone until I did.'

'What did she say about Ernst?'

' 'Well . . . if he's still alive after this bloody war's over, you can go and find him and good riddance! No decent Englishman will marry a traitor.' '

Valerie's impersonation of her mother's posh tones made Olivia giggle. 'You're not a traitor. You're just kind and a bit too gullible.' Olivia shrugged as if to say that this mild criticism was, unfortunately, merited.

A silence developed between them. Valerie was the one to break it.

'I've just remembered, I've got an invitation for you to have tea next week. You don't have to accept . . . I'll make your excuses, if you like.'

'Your mother's asked me round for tea?' Olivia sounded astonished. She'd not glimpsed any friendliness when her eyes had briefly met Mrs

147

Booth's at Charing Cross station.

'No!' Valerie sounded amused. 'Caroline has. I called on her in Belgravia. I told her about the rumpus with the escaping German and how brave you were. She'd already heard about you and would like to meet you.' Valerie had noticed Olivia's startled reaction and dismissed the invitation with a flick of her fingers. 'Don't worry. I'll tell her you're tied up with your family.'

'No . . . I'd like to go,' Olivia interrupted. A second later she wondered if she'd done the right thing. Lucas wouldn't want her getting to know his relatives behind his back. Especially not his sister-in-law. But if he'd spoken about *her* to Caroline, then perhaps Olivia had a right to know why, and what had been said.

'Caroline was terribly upset. Henry's a strange one though. He didn't seem bothered that his brother has been reported missing around Thiepval.'

'What?' Olivia gasped.

Valerie clasped her hands. 'Sorry! Should've been more tactful about letting that news out. Of course you're upset, too, being as you're good friends with Lucas. I could tell you were fond of one another. He looked so handsome when we saw him last, didn't he?' She sighed dreamily. 'This bloody war will be the death of us all.' She gulped tea. 'Sorry . . . done it again, haven't I?'

Olivia stared through the window into the dusk, her heartbeat thundering in her ears. 'He'll turn up,' she whispered. 'He always does. Luck of the devil, that's what he says he's got.'

148

She put down her teacup with a rattle of crockery, having taken just a sip. Val was chatting to her about the Bantams they'd just passed, saying the tallest one had been rather handsome. She continued on and on about him while spreading jam on her bun. Olivia absorbed little of what she was saying. She tried frantically to calm her fears. Lucas had gone missing before . . . been cut off behind enemy lines, like many other soldiers. But he'd been relieved by comrades and come safely back. And he would again. He'd promised her that.

# 11

'What's a toff like 'im know abaht shovellin' shit, day in, day aht?'

'Nowt!' chorused a few fusiliers with soil-streaked faces. They were squatting in a semi-circle around some smouldering twigs, trying to keep warm while sending dirty looks at their surprise visitors. A short while ago they had been using entrenching tools and a solitary shovel to carve dugouts from clay. It'd been hard graft, providing themselves with shelters, and they'd built up a sweat, stripping down to vests. But a few blasts of the fresh night breeze had soon raised the hairs on their bare arms when they'd downed tools.

'What's any of 'em wearin' pips know about this fookin' war?' a gruff Irish voice had asked, and brought forth a rumble of agreement from the group holding out their muddy palms to the flames.

'They sit on their arses in their bunkers, givin' orders, while we cop it.' A casualty had piped up this time. He adjusted the field dressing that was covering a shrapnel hole in his skull, secured by a grimy bandage. 'Few inches in it, that's all. Could've lost both me eyes. I never signed up for this! Recruitin' sergeant told me I'd be back home with me wife 'n' kids come that first Christmas.'

'We was all told that back when it started,'

another voice scoffed.

'I never volunteered. I got told, so I did, to come to this fookin' place.' The Irish fusilier scowled at the officer, who was crouching down and studying the map he'd spread out on some duckboard nearby.

'Manicured nails, I'll bet,' jeered the man who'd started the grumbling. He knocked out the bowl of his pipe on his boot heel before stuffing it again with tobacco.

'Lieutenants be sergeants wiv their brains bashed aht.' A young private offered up his gem of wisdom. He licked the edge of his Rizla, grinning.

'He's right, so he is.' The big Irish fellow praised the boy by punching him on the shoulder.

'Give yer tongue a rest, McGoogan,' an older man growled. He'd been listening to his comrades' whingeing without comment so far. He had been excavating with them earlier, using his trench tool, but now had his soiled fingers in a tin of tobacco. He'd been frowning at the posh officer from beneath his brows, not from resentment but because he thought he recognised the man. The scant glow from the fire was barely adequate to allow him to find his own hand in front of his face, let alone examine a stranger's features. But light and noise had to be kept low with Fritz within spitting distance.

Lucas knew the men were being insolent. They'd been stumbling about, lost and in need of rescue, and had become defensive. Their officer had been killed during the retreat from

151

Thiepval and these stragglers had got separated from the rest. Confused by the maze of interlinking boggy trenches clogged with bloated bodies, they'd wandered further into trouble.

But he didn't give a toss about any of that. He was too busy concentrating on finding a way to slip through Hun troops a thousand strong and rejoin C Company, to the east at Thiepval, without every man jack of them being annihilated, either by the enemy's machine guns or by their own side's mortar fire. He could have done without surly Cockneys to contend with as well. A few more riflemen were of little benefit to him; a regiment of them, or else a miracle, would be needed if they were spotted skulking in the middle of a German encampment.

Five days ago Lucas's platoon had been at the forefront of the advance before being cut off during the scramble to take the ridge. To remain undetected, they'd been forced further into enemy territory. Meagre shelter had been found in a bomb-damaged church, with trenches buzzing with Hun just one hundred yards away. In growing dismay, he and his surviving men had watched more German infantry arrive, swamping the surrounding area. Once murderous friendly fire started making the building collapse around them, they'd become too exposed. With little other option, they'd crawled and slithered over mud under cover of darkness, one by one, to an abandoned section of German trench. By then the platoon had been down to four able-bodied, one walking wounded and a Lewis machine gun out of ammunition. They'd stealthily dropped down at the furthest end from Fritz. Conscious of human voices and the soft thunk of shovels hitting clay, Lucas and his men had crept forward, stepping over rotting bodies. Then they'd rounded a bend and, instead of seeing German infantry, had come upon friends.

The most senior of them had narrowly avoided getting a bayonet in the guts; in a blind panic the corporal had rushed at Sergeant Dawson, swinging a shovel. That near miss had soured things between them from the start. But Corporal Swann had since participated in a civil conversation. Lucas didn't need to hear the fellow's excuses about why his lot had got left behind. Lucas knew how easy it was to become disorientated in the cratered landscape when trying to get back to what passed for home in this pitch black, Godforsaken hellhole.

The corporal had a chip on his shoulder but so far had resisted bellyaching about Lucas to his men. And so had one other fellow who seemed determined simply to stare at him. Lucas glanced up from the map on the ground.

The candle he lifted up illuminated his features. A grin spread across Jack Keiver's grizzled chops before he strode forward, holding out his hand.

'Believe I know you, sir, from back home. I bought you a drink in the Duke pub in Islington . . . quite a while ago now that was. We've got a mutual friend in me neighbour, Olivia Bone. Remember me, do you? Me name's . . . '

'Jack Keiver,' Lucas said, slowly straightening up from his crouching position. He tipped back

153

his cap and barked an astonished laugh. He gave Jack's face, beneath its smudges of mud, a thorough inspection. Private Keiver looked exhausted and gaunt, as Lucas imagined he did himself. He dropped the candle and they shook hands.

Lucas's smile soon faded away when he understood what this meeting would do to his sanity. So far he'd managed to block Livvie from his thoughts. He didn't want a jolting reminder of her stealing his attention at a time like this. But it was too late now. She was there again in his head, beautiful green eyes searching his soul, her soft, soft lips yielding beneath his . . . he could still taste her. He dropped his head, shielding the bright torment in his eyes from Keiver's notice as he picked up the candle stub and relit it. Lucas's throat felt dry when he asked hoarsely, 'How's your family doing, Private Keiver? Have you heard from them recently?'

'If you're really asking after Livvie Bone, I do know that she's back in Blighty.' Jack offered. He'd seen this man and Olivia together and knew the fellow was smitten by her. 'I got a letter just a few days ago. Me daughter Alice wrote and told me that Livvie's had an accident. She's fine, though.' Jack quickly added, noticing a ferocious glint appear in the lieutenant's eyes. 'As fer me own . . . they're all doing well enough, thank you, sir. Matilda's had a bit of a cold so Alice tells me.'

'Hope she's feeling better soon.' Lucas said gruffly.

'Yeah, me 'n' all,' Jack agreed.

Quiet ensued, as though they'd realised how incongruous it was to commiserate over Matilda's sniffles when all around them lay stinking carcasses.

'What sort of injury?' Lucas's thoughts were soon back with Olivia.

'A cut on her arm, I believe. Healing well, by all accounts.' Jack had instinctively understood to whom the lieutenant had referred. 'She's a brave lass, is our Livvie.'

'Yes, she is.' Lucas murmured huskily. 'How did it happen?'

'That I don't know, sir.'

'But she's alright?' Lucas persisted. And even Jack's firm nod wasn't enough to quieten his fears. He'd been berating himself for not having been honest with her before. They might have been man and wife by now if he'd had the courage to bare his soul and tell her all about himself. But he'd been ashamed of admitting to his former debauchery and his Romany mother. Now he felt shame for feeling ashamed. He couldn't change anything, but he was different these days. His mixed blood had brought him strengths as well as weaknesses. Had he not been his father's bastard, he might have suffered the same mental frailty as his brother Henry had inherited through the distaff side.

Lucas's reflections were interrupted by the sound of men hurrying over duckboard.

'We've recovered some water flasks and a couple of loaded pistols, sir. No ammo for the Lewis though.' Sergeant Dawson had come back along the trench with the other men from their platoon. They'd been scavenging dead bodies for whatever they could find that might be of use. The platoon's rations were running low and the Cockneys had next to nothing left either.

'We'll have to leave it then. No point carrying it empty.' It was a blow to have to abandon the gun. It had served them well and the men viewed it as their mascot.

'I'll carry it on me back, sir. Strap it there. Never know what we might stumble across once we get going.' Dawson handed over some dog tags to his lieutenant. 'Few of ours made it this far, sir.'

'They got a long way, poor sods,' was all Lucas said as he pocketed the discs. Most of the advancing Allied troops had been mown down on the march across no-man's-land, just minutes after quitting their own trenches.

As Dawson and the two others retired to try and nap in a dugout, Lucas turned again to Jack Keiver. 'We'll leave soon. I'll get you back.'

'Know you will, sir,' Jack said simply. 'Another one of our lot from Campbell Road's over there.' He jerked his head. 'The gobby Irishman is Riley McGoogan. Livvie knows him. He used to live in the Bunk with her cousin Ruby before they moved over to Wood Green.'

'I think I remember him,' Lucas said in surprise as he squinted at a bristly face tinted red by the firelight. On the occasion that Lucas had been at the Duke pub, McGoogan had been there too, watching his girlfriend and Livvie arguing. 'I could do with a pint right now,' Lucas said, his tongue circling his parched lips.

'Yeah . . . whiskey chaser to go with it, and a sing-song round the joanna. Then back home to some toast and drippin' fer supper before turning in.' Jack smacked his lips and started chuckling. He was aware his comrades had gone quiet and were watching this odd conversation. He knew he'd get some sneering remarks later. But he didn't care. He liked this man; had from the very first time they'd shaken hands in the pub and then had a good-natured disagreement about who was going to win the match at the Arsenal that Saturday. Lucas Black had stood his round of drinks and more besides, as Jack recalled.

'Reckon you'd like to be back in Wood Green, wouldn't yer, sir? Back in yer office in Barratt's, surrounded by sweets.'

'Amen to that,' Lucas said quietly, thinking of a blonde girl in a sacking apron, with sugar-stained hands. She'd come to his office to wish him luck when she found out he was leaving to enlist. But he'd fallen for her before then. Probably from the first day he saw her waiting at the factory gate with her father's packed lunch. Even Tommy Bone's belligerence didn't seem so bad in hindsight. At the time Lucas had been bored by Barratt's. He'd felt restless, angry with his father for having got him a directorship in a sweet factory, to try and discipline him and put an end to his playboy ways. The ploy had worked but not for any reason that his father would have understood. The yoke of routine work and responsibility had little to do with the change in Lucas that had kept him obeying his father's wishes. He'd fallen in love and had wanted to be worthy of the factory girl who'd tamed him.

What he wouldn't give now to be back with Livvie and their early skirmishes in Wood Green . . .

'I don't mind a few barley sugars,' Jack said. 'So if your factory pals send you out a few, remember me, won't yer?' He grinned, then after a salute to Lucas he returned to his pals.

'Arse lickin' was yer, Keiver?' McGoogan taunted.

'We surrenderin'?' the wounded man demanded.

'No, we ain't!' Jack said. 'We're takin' a run, when he says. I know him from back home and you lot can think yerself fuckin' lucky he come across us. One o' the best, is Lieutenant Black.'

'We're fuckin' surrounded with no grub and hardly no ammo neither,' the wounded man blasted out. 'We'd be better off surrenderin'. See it out in a camp.'

'Yeah?' Jack said and looked at them all fiercely. 'Well, I'm going home, and he's said he'll take me. Any of yers that fancy Fritz's hospitality as yer best bet . . . ' Jack pointed along the trench. 'You'll find 'im that way.' He walked off and picked up his jacket. He buttoned it through, dusted it down then sat and waited. He knew it wouldn't be long before they moved off.

He closed his eyes and prayed.

# 12

'Maggie told me you was back.'

'She told me about you, too,' Olivia said. 'And I pray that at least some of what she said's true as you're getting married.'

'Weren't expecting you to accept it. You've always been sour before where me and Mags was concerned.' Harry Wicks looked her up and down. 'Anybody'd think you was jealous.'

At one time Olivia might have laughed in derision at that. But there was nothing funny about her sister marrying this man.

'Got a welcoming kiss for yer future brother-in-law then, have yer, Livvie, now you've come round to the idea of me being part of the family?' He puckered his lips and tipped her a wink.

Olivia knew she was being goaded so refused to rise to it. Just a few sentences exchanged with Harry Wicks was enough to depress her. He hadn't changed one bit. She'd really wanted to believe, for Maggie's sake, that he was a better person now. But he was just as she remembered him: still leering at her, taunting her, his eyes fixed on her bosom.

Moments ago Harry had emerged from his mother's house and swaggered into her path, making a mockery of his claim to have a permanent limp. It was almost as though he'd been waiting for her to turn up and visit her cousins across the road.

'Nice place you've got in Islington. Very comfortable,' Harry said slyly. A couple of slow nods emphasised his point.

'I know you've been staying there so no need to rub it in,' Olivia snapped. For two pins she would have slapped his smirking face. 'And just in case it doesn't sink in when Maggie tells you, I'll spell it out for you myself. You're not welcome at Playford Road.'

'That ain't very nice.' He grinned, wiping down his bushy brown moustache with thumb and forefinger. 'Who's been sleeping in my bed?' he purred. 'Is that what yer thought, Goldilocks?' He tested a silky blonde tress of her hair between his thumb and forefinger. 'It was me . . . that's who . . . and I loved every minute.' He'd put his lips close to her ear and the stench of raw butcher's meat coming off him made her jerk away, tearing her hair painfully from his grip.

'Could smell you on the bed sheets.' Harry inhaled, groaning in ecstasy. 'Ooh, lovely that were, gel, almost like you was in bed with us.'

Olivia pushed past him, fists clenched at her sides. She knew it would be pointless recounting this episode to Maggie. Her sister was too wrapped up in wedding plans and dreams of babies to want to listen to anybody who would tell her how vile this man was.

Harry stepped in front of Olivia. 'Ain't finished talking to you yet.' He propped his hand against the alley wall, barring her way. 'Nipper'll be born in the spring. Ain't much time to sort out living arrangements.'

160

'I agree, so better get on with house-hunting, hadn't you?'

'No need to. I know where I'm living,' he said. 'Playford Road, with Maggie.'

'No, you're not,' Olivia told him, through her teeth. 'If you can't afford a place of your own, you'll have to stop with your mother.'

'Nah . . . Maggie won't have that. She wants somewhere nice 'n' cosy where she feels at home.'

'So do Nancy and Alfie. There's no room for you there, and even if there was, you'd not be welcome.'

'Nancy's moving out. Maggie told me. So there'll be a spare room. Won't use your bed no more while you're in France . . . promise.' He adopted a mock-solemn expression.

'Get your own place. I've nothing more to say.' Olivia was seething but had her temper under control. She knew he wanted her to shove him but she wasn't going to touch him. She stepped off the kerb to get past.

'You know what Nancy's been up to, do you, while you've been away?' he called after her.

Olivia hesitated then marched back. There'd been a triumphant note in his voice that had chilled her. She feared he knew too much about the shoplifting sprees.

'If you've got something to say, spit it out. Not like you to be shy, Harry.'

'Come up the alley.' He jerked his head at the pathway.

She hooted a laugh. 'What d'you think I am? A kid? That might have worked years ago when I was still stupid enough to think you'd stick to your word and act decently.'

'Ain't gonna lay a finger on yer.' He put up his hands in surrender. 'Just thought you might want this kept private,' he continued innocently. 'Your kid sister's behaviour don't bear repeating out in the open.'

'You've got no proof of anything,' Olivia said quietly. Inwardly she was berating herself for not having questioned Nancy sooner. But it'd be the first thing she'd do when her youngest sister got in from work.

'You don't know what I'm going to say,' he crowed.

'Oh, I do, I know all about it. So you can't shock me. And if you're about to threaten that you'll grass Nancy up . . . you've no proof.'

He smiled like a cat who'd got the cream. 'They sent you some of the Yardley stuff, didn't they? Nice, was it?' He leaned in to sniff her neck. 'Lavender water . . . love it.'

Olivia could feel herself blushing as she stepped back. She wished now she'd not used the bloody stuff.

'Nah, the shoplifting's only half of it. I was referring to the company she's been keeping. If you think I'm no good, you should meet the bloke Nancy's running around with. Makes your dead pimp seem like a choirboy.'

Olivia was determined not to show her shock even though she felt as though she'd been doused in icy water. 'You're a liar . . . you've always been a liar.' She gave a passable impression of being unconcerned by shaking her head and smiling as she walked on. But her insides were in knots.

Harry watched her go, narrowed eyes running hungrily over her slender figure. He'd always wanted her and not Maggie. Ever since Olivia Bone had been a girl, keeping house for her father, Harry had had a yen for her. But she'd rejected him and settled for Joe Hunter. When her father had found out she'd been seeing a pimp, he'd knocked her sideways then thrown her out. Livvie Bone had known what she was doing though. Pimping paid well. Joe Hunter had been a wealthy man. He'd owned his own house and had left it to her. Harry had always fancied having his own property, and now he could see a way of getting his foot in the door of one he liked very much.

Olivia Bone was a strong and independent woman . . . one of a new breed coming through with too much to say for themselves, in Harry's opinion. Suffragettes, union conveners in factories . . . he had no time for any of them. All women should be like his mother: under a man's thumb and doing what they were told, in bed and out of it.

But Olivia had a weakness: her family. She'd always mothered them and old habits were hard to break. Harry was banking on her not letting Maggie suffer, and Maggie wouldn't go against him. He'd already laid down the law that they either lived together in Playford Road or the wedding was off. And she was mad keen to have this baby. He'd been able to coax Maggie into doing whatever he wanted since she was fourteen. When she was engaged to his brother even, Harry had proved to her he still had power over her. He'd got her alone and she hadn't protested when he'd kissed her. She'd loved it, opening her blouse for him unasked. Harry had always known he was the brother she really wanted.

Just as Olivia was the sister he really wanted. And he hadn't given up on having her. Or her house.

Olivia refused to look back although she knew he was still staring after her. She banged on her cousin's door, praying that Ruby was in. She didn't want to have to turn around and walk back past Harry Wicks.

'I heard on the grapevine you was back 'cos you weren't well. Bleedin' hell, Livvie . . . you don't look it neither. You're white as a sheet. Not about to throw up, are you?' Ruby ushered her cousin inside, looking concerned.

Olivia returned Ruby's embrace then followed her into the parlour.

'I'm fine. Tired, that's all.' She hadn't realised that her run in with Harry Wicks had affected her so badly. She could still feel her heart hammering. 'I had a fall and ended up with stitches in me arm so they've let me come home to convalesce. But I'm going back soon.' She didn't feel as confident about that as she had yesterday. There were problems to sort out and they seemed to be increasing all the time.

But already she yearned to be back in France close to Lucas. He might have turned up injured. He could be one of the next casualties to arrive at St Omer and she desperately wanted to be there for him. She wanted to see him, tell him she loved him and that the moment they both could get together for an hour or two, they should find a vicar because she'd marry him without delay, in France if necessary. Yet she wasn't even sure if he'd had a chance to read her last letter and knew she was in England.

She'd planned to stop with Ruby for an hour or so, to swap news and reminisce about old times at Barratt's factory. Yet she was already itching to catch the bus home and interrogate Nancy. Much as Olivia despised Harry Wicks, she believed his jibes about her youngest sister. There was something unusual and worryingly secretive about Nancy.

'Rather you than me going back over there.' Ruby shook the kettle then put it on the hob. 'Tottenham got bombed a few weeks back.' She gazed at her visitor with a mixture of admiration and revulsion. 'Bet you see some horrible sights in the hospital, don't yer, Livvie?'

'Where's Mickey? Out with friends?' Olivia asked, hoping to avert Ruby's ghoulish curiosity. She certainly did see some dreadful things and she didn't want them playing on her mind as well. She sat down in the same scratchy old armchair that had been in the house when her family had lived here. In fact, nothing much had changed, apart from it all looking dingier and shabbier.

'Didn't the girls tell you? Me dad's taken Mickey to live with him in Edmonton. Don't think that's gone down too well with the woman he's shacked up with. It's all been a right palaver. Mickey still goes over and has a kick about with Alfie at the weekend in the Bunk.' Ruby raised her eyebrows. 'He wanted to know how Ed could be his dad, if Alfie was his brother. I told him to ask his father to explain. That confused him.'

'I'll bet,' Olivia muttered ironically. 'You've accepted Ed's your dad then, have you?' Ruby had seemed dead set against him at their reunion.

Ruby upended the kettle into the teapot. 'Thing is, Alfie needs a father and if Ed's the only one left then he'll have to do. It affected Mickey, finding our mum dead like that. Poor lad had bad nightmares about it. Ed's been a comfort to him. He's been good to me too, helping out with a few bob when I was short.' She shrugged. 'I won't cut off me nose to spite me face if Ed's making up for lost time. I don't reckon he'd bother with us if he didn't honestly believe we was his kids. The rest of 'em are all pushing up daisies so what's the harm in being friends with him?'

'None at all. For what it's worth, I think Ed is your dad.'

'You think me mum was lying about Tommy fathering us all?'

'If she wasn't sure perhaps she settled on the man who was around at the time,' Olivia replied diplomatically. 'So you've got this place to yourself?'

Ruby nodded. 'Not for long though. Can't afford it unless I get another lodger. I did what you said and took in a woman. She told me she was a widow with no kids.' Ruby snorted in disgust. 'Then next day when I got back from Barratt's, she had two in the room with her. I told her she'd have to go. Never got no sleep with the little 'un bawling all night long.' Ruby stirred the tea. 'Riley would have gone nuts when he come home on leave and found that lot camped here.'

'How is he? Does he write to you?' Olivia asked. She never knew with Ruby and Riley whether they were currently happy together or at loggerheads.

'Had a couple of letters. Not heard from him for weeks though,' Ruby said shortly. 'He's not a letter writer.'

Olivia was surprised that Ruby hadn't asked her whether she'd come into contact with Riley in France as other women did about their menfolk. Instead she seemed keen to change the subject and Olivia guessed that while Riley was away her cousin was keeping company with other admirers to boost her earnings.

'How's your lot at home then?' Ruby blurted. 'I've not seen much of the girls.'

'Neither have I since I've been back. Maggie and Nancy are always on shift at the munitions factory. I'm still getting to grips with things.' Olivia had been home nearly a fortnight and was already feeling restless. Physically she was well enough to be back at work. All that stopped her writing to St John Ambulance headquarters for a return date were the worries circling in her head. Yet women with husbands and sons abroad had far more reason to fret than she did.

Ruby asked slyly, 'Right what I heard, is it?'

'What have you heard?' Olivia hoped there wasn't another nasty surprise in store for her. She'd had more than enough of those lately. When she'd left home and caught the bus to Wood Green she'd been in high spirits, intending to call on Ruby and Cath who lived around the corner. She'd no time to spare to visit her old friend now though.

'I heard that me neighbour Harry Wicks is getting married to your Maggie. Case of having to.'

'Who told you that?' Olivia took the cup of tea Ruby held out to her.

'So it is true then.' Ruby plonked herself down in the chair opposite, looking astonished. 'If it wasn't you would have marked me card straight off.' She gulped at her tea. 'I didn't think Maggie'd be daft enough to get caught twice.' She jerked her head at the street. 'Harry's the one been telling the world. Anybody'd think he's pleased he's knocked her up.'

'He is. I've just bumped into him.' Nothing in Olivia's tone hinted at the acrimony she felt.

'Thought your Maggie was well and truly over him.'

'Yeah . . . me too.' Olivia couldn't hold back a sigh when she answered. She'd no intention of chewing the fat with Ruby on that particular subject though. She needed to come to terms with it herself before discussing with others being landed with Harry Wicks as a brother-in-law. 'Just paying a flying visit, Ruby. Popped by to say hello before I go back to France.' She drained her cup and stood up. 'Sorry to leave so soon but I want to call on Cath as well while I'm this way. I might not get another chance to see her.'

'She's not there,' Ruby said. 'They moved away last month. Not that she told me herself 'cos as you know she don't speak to me. A neighbour told me they've gone down Kent way, close to a sanatorium. Trevor's taken a bad turn again and needs more treatment.' Ruby shook her head. 'Mrs Cook reckons that Cath couldn't stand the shame of him acting nutty and being talked about. So she's upped sticks and gone where nobody knows 'em.'

That news brought a spontaneous lump to Olivia's throat. 'Oh, no. Poor Cath . . . '

'Got time for another cuppa then?' Ruby asked brightly.

'No . . . thanks, all the same. Best get back. Got a letter to write about booking a passage to return to work.'

At the door they embraced and Ruby nudged Olivia in the ribs. 'Hope you're throwing a party before you leave. We all need cheering up. We've got something to celebrate if Maggie's getting married with a little 'un on the way.'

'We'll see,' Olivia said with a smile. She glanced up the road, relieved that there was no sign of Harry hanging about. She waved before closing the gate and hurrying off towards the bus stop.

* * *

169

'Where've you been?'

A chorus of voices greeted Olivia as she closed the front door. Alfie and Nancy stood on the kitchen threshold, gazing at her.

'Thought you might have got home in time to do tea. I'm on shift soon.' Nancy looked annoyed as she turned about and resumed spreading bread. 'Maggie's upstairs. She'll be late if she don't stop heaving and move herself,' was thrown over her shoulder.

Olivia put her bag on the kitchen table and Nancy gave her an old-fashioned look to let her know she was aware what was up with Maggie.

'Who'll be doing meals for you lot when I'm back in France?' Olivia had been doing more than her fair share of the cooking and cleaning since her return. She'd accepted that she was well enough to help out while the girls were at work. But there was no point in them falling into old habits and relying on her to do everything for them.

Alfie poured the teas and put them on the table.

'I'd like a word before you go to work, Nancy,' said Olivia.

Her sister started buttering faster. 'Ain't got time right now . . . '

'Upstairs,' Olivia said, with a significant glance at Alfie. 'It's important and it won't wait.'

Nancy let the knife drop and with a heavy sigh stomped out of the kitchen. Olivia could tell she knew exactly what this was about.

'Finish the sandwiches, Alfie, there's a good lad.'

Her brother didn't seem curious to discover what business he couldn't be part of. He stuck a knife in the pot of fishpaste and started to make their supper.

'I'm glad I've got the two of you together. We need to have a serious talk,' Olivia started to say the moment the door was shut and she was in her sisters' bedroom. 'I would've given you a hand getting tea ready but I'm late back because I missed me bus from Wood Green. I bumped into some old colleagues from Barratt's and stopped for a chat.'

Olivia had felt guilty about trying to edge away from the women. She'd worked with Sal Shaw and some of the others for years so had promised them that she'd come back another time and catch up properly, for old times' sake.

'Why've you been over Wood Green?' Maggie interrogated her.

'I went to see Ruby. I planned to call on Cath too, but she's moved away.'

'That's all you've been up to?' Still Maggie sounded suspicious.

'I did bump into Harry in Ranelagh Road, if that's what you're after knowing.'

'And?' Maggie set her hands on her hips. 'Did you argue with him?'

'Not really,' Olivia replied. 'I didn't say I objected to you two getting married, if that's what you mean.'

'More fool you then,' Nancy muttered. ''Cos he thinks he's moving in here, and if he does you'll be stuck with him for ever.'

'He's not moving in; I made that clear to him.'

171

Olivia ignored Maggie's scowl, concentrating on Nancy. 'He told me that you've been doing what you shouldn't. Not that he needed to, 'cos I'd already guessed that for meself.'

'You can tell him he's got a big mouth.' Nancy turned on Maggie, face red with fury. For a moment it seemed slaps might ensue but instead Nancy wound in her neck and shrugged. 'I'm moving out soon so you don't need to worry about what I get up to.'

'I know you've been stealing, you stupid girl.' Olivia shook her by the shoulders. 'D'you fancy a stay in prison?'

'I know what I'm doing.' Nancy shrugged free from her sister's hold. 'I'm a good hoister. I haven't got caught so far, have I?'

Olivia laughed sourly. 'The prisons are full of people who thought they'd never get caught.' She was shocked by her sister's brazenness. 'If Harry Wicks knows, it won't be long before the police come knocking.'

'Oi, Harry ain't a grass,' Maggie snapped.

'He won't grass,' Nancy echoed. Seemingly unconcerned, she put on her ankle boots and started doing them up with the button hook. 'He knows if he does he'll have to buy stuff for the baby instead of getting it free.' She shrugged into her coat and sauntered to the door. 'Not only that, if he opens his mouth again, he'll get his head knocked clean off his shoulders.' She turned about, still smiling, and pointed a finger at Maggie. 'And you can tell him that 'n' all.' She straightened her hat. 'I'm off to work. Forget tea for me.'

172

Olivia ran down the stairs after her sister, shocked by how callous she seemed. 'What's got into you? You were never like this, Nance . . . '

'Surprised you noticed what I was like. You never had no time for me before, what with Maggie and Alfie being yer pets.' She opened the front door but Olivia shoved it shut with the palm of her hand.

'You're not going anywhere, young lady, until I say you can. If I've left you alone it's 'cos I trusted you . . . thought you were sensible enough not to need me checking up on you, like I've had to with the others. Seems I was wrong though. And for that I'm sorry.' Nancy looked bored by her explanation so Olivia shook her arm to gain her attention. 'Insolence won't help. What did you mean about Harry getting beaten if he opens his mouth? Who are you involved with?'

'I've got somebody looking out for me. And he's good at it.'

Olivia's hand fell away from her sister. 'Looking out for you . . . how?' she demanded, while dreading hearing the answer.

'I'm not a brass, and he's not a ponce,' Nancy said. 'And even if he was, you'd be a fine one to talk when your Joe used to be a pimp before he met you!'

'That was different,' Olivia cried hoarsely. 'I told you what he had to do to protect his mother from violent men. He never could live the life he wanted.' She had turned ashen with dismay, not only at her sister's conduct but at this painful reminder of what Joe had lost. He'd cherished

their plans for married life . . . for a family
. . . for a fresh start. None of it had come true.
The war had denied them a future together.

'I don't need to act like a tart to get what I
want,' Nancy said coarsely. 'He wants me to be
his girlfriend. I do like him. But right now I'm
gonna bide me time, 'cos he's just got his call-up
papers. We can't make plans so we've agreed to
wait and see what comes next.'

'Who is he?' Olivia demanded, but Nancy
again made to open the door. 'You've got to stop
this!' Olivia pleaded, though she could barely
speak she was so upset. She enclosed her sister in
her arms and for a moment Nancy allowed the
embrace before elbowing herself free.

'Don't worry about me, Livvie,' she said, quite
kindly. 'You won't need to bring Lou round here
on my account . . . I'm far too cute for that. I am
gonna stop shoplifting soon though. Not 'cos
you've told me to. He has. After he goes, he
wants me to pack it in till he's home and can
watch out for me. He cares about me, y'see,
Livvie.' Again she seemed about to leave but
instead said, 'I *am* moving out soon. I've almost
saved enough now from me wages and extras to
get a nice room of me own.' She pulled open the
door and Olivia didn't attempt to stop her. 'I'll
get you some Lily-of-the-Valley next time,'
Nancy teased, and then she was gone.

Olivia stood staring at the door for a full
minute before turning around. She felt as though
she'd just been talking to a stranger, not her
lovely Nancy. Or perhaps the girl's jibe had been
merited: Olivia had not taken enough notice of

her youngest sister to *really* know her at all. As a young child Nancy had loved reading about ballerinas and would dress up as the Sugar Plum Fairy, complete with homemade wand. She'd always been the one to offer to help with washing or shopping while Maggie swanned off out with her friends. She'd never been callous. Olivia still believed she had a kind heart, but Nancy was hard as nails too. In an odd way, Olivia admired her for it. She believed that her youngest sister was far more capable of looking out for herself than Maggie would ever be.

'And you thought *I* was trouble,' Maggie said sarcastically, coming down the stairs.

'Who is it Nancy's knocking about with?'

'Nat Gunn, and I wouldn't bother him if I was you. He's only eighteen but he's *real* bad news.'

'So Harry said.' Olivia still felt in a daze.

'Don't go getting Harry into trouble over this. If he warned you about what Nancy's been up to, it was for your own good. But keep yer mouth shut! We don't want no trouble with gangsters. Now you're abroad most of the time we all manage well enough on our own. Even Alfie.'

'Tea's ready,' their brother said from the kitchen doorway.

'Don't want none . . . going to work.' Maggie unpegged her coat from the hallstand.

Olivia sat down opposite Alfie at the kitchen table, but she was in turmoil and knew she wasn't fooling her brother by trying to act normally. She was aware of him watching her while he ate so gave him a reassuring smile. He grinned back.

'How have you been while I've been away?' she asked and gulped at her lukewarm tea.

'Alright,' he said through a mouthful of sandwich. 'You don't need to worry about me neither, Livvie,' he said sweetly. 'Me 'n' Mickey are setting up in business soon as we can leave school. His dad's gonna help us.'

'Uncle Ed, you mean?'

'Yeah . . . that's Mickey's dad, so Mickey's me cousin again, I suppose, not me brother.'

Olivia took another gulp of tea, raking her fingers through her hair, beyond commenting on that. 'What business are you interested in?' she ploughed on, trying to make conversation although at the back of her mind she was wondering what on earth had happened to the family she'd known just a short while ago.

'Mending cars.' Alfie grinned. 'Mr Wright reckons that one day everybody'll have a car. So there'll be plenty of work keeping 'em all running.'

# 13

'I'm so pleased to meet you, Miss Bone. I know it's a cliche but I've heard a lot about you and it's good to put a face to a name.'

'It's nice to meet you too, Mrs Black.' Olivia knew that was a lie, just as she knew she shouldn't have come. Her mouth felt dry and her palms clammy but she was determined not to be intimidated by her surroundings or her hostess. What worried her was not that she'd make a fool of herself with clumsy manners but that Lucas would be furious when he found out she'd met his old flame behind his back.

She knew this was no friendly invitation. Caroline had lured her here for a reason. Olivia imagined that Mrs Black had something to say that she hoped would drive Lucas and his latest flame apart. If that was her game then she obviously still wanted him even if she had married his brother. Or was Olivia's elegant rival simply feeling resentful that she'd been thrown over for a factory girl? Whatever her motive, Olivia was puzzled that Lucas had mentioned her to Caroline in the first place. It wasn't the way he usually behaved. But Valerie had told her that Caroline already knew about her, and who else could have brought her name up?

Olivia's friend Hilda Weedon had once described Miss Caroline Venner, as she'd then been, as willowy and polished rather than pretty.

But Caroline was very pretty in Olivia's opinion. She understood why Lucas had been attracted to her. She reminded Olivia of the sharp-featured ballerinas Nancy used to admire in picture books, all angled cheekbones and sleek, brunette hair swept into a bun. Olivia reckoned Caroline would look younger without the powder and scarlet lipstick. But it suited her . . . made her look as glamorous as a film star.

Caroline was nothing at all like her, and Olivia imagined the woman had come to the same conclusion. From the moment she had risen languidly from the sofa to greet her guests, shown into the drawing room by a maid, Caroline's eyes had been minutely examining Olivia.

Mr and Mrs Henry Black lived in a huge white-stuccoed mansion on a quiet square. Railings similar to those edging the Bunk's tenements fronted the gracious exteriors of properties approached by wide stone steps. And there ended any likeness to Olivia's neighbourhood. In Campbell Road the railings guarded cracked brickwork and the tenants would use the spikes to display boots or items of clothing they wanted to sell, to raise a few bob to pay the rent.

'Do sit down, Miss Bone. You too, Val. I shouldn't need to tell you not to stand on ceremony.'

'Thank you,' Olivia said as she perched next to Valerie on a velvet sofa strewn with tasselled cushions. She'd picked up on a barb in that last remark. If her hostess believed her overawed . . . well, she was, but she damn' well wasn't going to show it. And she'd give as good as she got, just as she always did.

'You have a lovely house, Mrs Black,' Olivia said, clearly and confidently. Might as well get that out of the way, she thought.

'It's not as nice as Lucas's in Hampstead. Perhaps you know that though, if you've been there?' An expectant silence followed but a reply was not forthcoming.

Olivia settled back carefully into the sofa, glad that she'd taken considerable trouble to style her hair into waves. She wore a navy blue crepe skirt and lace-edged blouse, bought for the occasion off Chapel Street market. Not that she would ever admit to going to such trouble, or to buffing her ankle boots to a shine, the like of which they hadn't seen since the day she'd bought them off Billy the Totter. He'd told her a lady's maid in Chelsea had handed them over by the back door. Olivia had guessed they'd not been the servant's to sell but she'd paid Billy his five bob for them anyway because they were beauties.

Olivia wasn't vain but knew that in her own way she was a match for Caroline in looks, if not in breeding. And she had a few choice remarks ready, should they be needed. She'd never fought over a man in her life but she knew she'd stand up for Lucas.

'You'll stay for tea, I hope?'

'Of course since we've come for tea,' Valerie piped up before Olivia had a chance to reply. Valerie had been watching the interaction between her friend and her cousin, wondering what was causing the frosty atmosphere. Caroline had been sweetness and light when issuing the invitation. Valerie took out her cigarettes, handing them around. 'Livvie was saying on the way over that she's not eaten yet today.' She thought some chat might lift the tension.

'I've not had time to stop for a bite to eat,' Olivia hastily interjected. She didn't want Caroline thinking she couldn't afford to feed herself. 'Can't expect my sisters to do all the housework while I'm spare at home and they've got shifts to go to later.' This woman probably didn't know what housework was, she realised. Mrs Black certainly hadn't been pulling wet sheets around or washing dishes with those soft white hands and painted nails.

'Worn out with housework and not eaten . . . oh, what a shame,' Caroline murmured. 'I'll get Betty to bring extra cake.' She smiled and rang a small bell on a side table, giving the prompt servant an order.

The distraction allowed Olivia a few moments to study her hostess's classic profile without being observed. She realised that the veneer of politeness between them was already chipping away. They both had questions they'd like answered. She decided to get one of hers in first. It was driving her mad not knowing.

'Has your brother-in-law spoken to you about me, Mrs Black?'

'Lucas? Heavens, no!' she exclaimed. 'Lucas is far too prudent to talk about factory affairs.'

'You told Val you'd heard a lot about me.'

Olivia kept her tone even despite having picked up on another dig.

'Oh, but not from Lucas. Unsurprisingly, he's never mentioned you, even in his previous life as your boss at Barratt's.'

Olivia's hackles started to rise higher. The hint that she wasn't worthy of Lucas's time or attention hadn't gone unnoticed. 'How odd that you've heard a lot about me then. Who should I blame for gossiping?'

'Deborah Wallis is a friend of mine.' Caroline's voice had sharpened with impatience. She obviously wasn't used to being pressed to explain herself. 'Or perhaps I should say she's an acquaintance. We were at school together, though never bosom pals. Just as well since she seems to have rather let the side down.' She glanced at Olivia. 'She was your supervisor at the factory, I believe.'

'Actually . . . she wasn't,' Olivia replied airily. 'Nelly Smith was my supervisor when I was a sweet roller-out. Miss Wallis was the directors' secretary.'

'Fascinating,' Caroline drawled and settled back in her armchair, brushing imaginary flecks from her skirt with scarlet-painted fingernails.

'It is . . . fascinating . . . that Miss Wallis found anything much to say about me. I hardly knew the woman other than to say good morning.' Olivia had held an unlit cigarette in her hand while speaking. She quickly placed it between her lips and dipped her head to the match burning close to Val's fingers.

'Deborah kept a close eye on things, especially

where Lucas was concerned. The poor girl had a pash for him. Unrequited, of course.' Caroline smiled and blew out smoke.

'She should have kept a close eye on her job. I heard she got the sack for misconduct.' Olivia blew out smoke too, feeling furious that Miss Wallis had seen fit to chinwag about her and Lucas.

'Deborah left by mutual agreement with the management. They didn't want bad publicity, I expect.' Caroline rose from her chair and extinguished her unfinished cigarette in the ashtray on the mantel.

Olivia also went to the mantelpiece, collected the small crystal bowl and sat back down with it on her lap. 'Don't want the rug getting spoiled by ash,' she explained.

'Don't worry, my dear. Henry will buy a new one.'

Val reached across and bashed ash off her cigarette into the ashtray. Her tortured expression made it clear that she wanted to apologise for bringing Olivia here, to be ambushed by continual snide remarks.

'Why don't you go and chase up that tea, Val, while Miss Bone and I continue our chat?'

Olivia would have liked to tell Valerie to stay right where she was but she simply shrugged as her friend shot a startled glance her way.

Caroline barely waited for the door to close before demanding, 'Has Lucas asked you to be his mistress?' Her red lips tightened on the cigarette, dragging a fierce glow from it before she exhaled smoke that hid her expression.

'I'm not sure what Deborah Wallis has told you but I doubt much of it's true,' Olivia replied mildly. She'd stopped herself from blurting out the first phrase that entered her head. *Mind your own bloody business* was what a factory girl would have said, but Olivia was a VAD now, just as Caroline had been. They were equals in that, if nothing else. 'If Lucas wants you to know what's gone on between us, I expect he'll tell you.'

Caroline's scarlet lips twitched, but not in amusement. 'He told you that I was out in France with him?'

'I heard that you'd volunteered as a nurse. It's not easy over there, is it?' Olivia decided to find some neutral ground. She didn't want to continue this sniping. They had seen the dreadful human cost of the war and probably had more in common than they knew. If they forgot about both loving Lucas for a moment it shouldn't be too hard to have a cup of tea and a civilised chat with a fellow VAD.

'I've been at St Omer hospital for over a year now. Just before I came home it was chaos. We were constantly trying to find room for more beds for the stream of poor souls injured in the Somme offensive.' Olivia glanced again at the painting on the wall. It had caught her eye as soon as she'd entered the room. She got up to look at it. 'That reminds me of France . . . it's the poppies . . . did you paint it? I know your cousin Val loves art.'

Caroline snorted a laugh. 'It's by Monet, my dear. He's a French Impressionist,' she added with mocking amusement.

Olivia sat down feeling she'd just been put in her place as an ignoramus. But she kept her chin high. The snooty cow should've been flattered to be thought capable of producing something so pretty.

'Val said you were quite the heroine when the German escaped.'

'Any nurse would have done the same. I just happened to be the one on duty at the time. Val did her bit too and got hurt in the process. Anyway, I've had a good rest and feel well enough to return now.'

'I would have gone back,' Caroline said, her voice sounding distant. 'Ghastly as it was, I wanted to return to France.'

Olivia smiled, feeling they were tiptoeing closer to a truce. 'It's just being useful that counts, isn't it? That's why I joined. I wanted to do something to help even if it was just putting washing in a copper.' She realised that might have been a touch too truthful for her hostess. Caroline's eyebrows had shot up in disdain. 'Have you had any word of Lucas?' Olivia was desperate to find out about him before their momentary harmony dissolved. 'Val said you had received news he was missing.'

Caroline sighed and shook her head. 'He'll turn up, though, like the proverbial bad penny.' A wistful smile touched her lips. 'He has a way about him, hasn't he, that's hard to resist?'

'There's no denying he's handsome,' Olivia said carefully.

'I was told your fiancé perished there a while

ago. I'm very sorry he didn't come back.'

'So am I,' Olivia said quietly.

Caroline gestured with her cigarette. 'There's no need for us to beat about the bush or be coy about this, Miss Bone. Engaged or not, Lucas wouldn't have minded either way if he'd made up his mind to have you. He always gets what he wants. He wanted to bed you when you worked at the factory, didn't he? Deborah Wallis told me everybody there knew, even your father. I take it he didn't object — who could blame a man for wanting his daughter to better herself?'

*Me*, passed through Olivia's mind then but she didn't utter the word. She had hated her father for his hypocrisy. He'd not wanted her to have a boyfriend of her own choosing; he'd sneered at Joe, calling him a pimp. Yet Tommy Bone would have sold his daughter to Lucas Black in exchange for a second chance at a job in the factory. And if Lucas hadn't been the decent man he was, he'd have gone along with it.

'No need to feel ashamed. Lucas is rich and charming . . . so very persuasive. Any girl like you would've jumped at the chance to bag him.'

The edge was back in Caroline's voice. The ceasefire hadn't lasted long, Olivia realised wryly. 'I wouldn't say you were a girl like me,' she shot back.

Caroline lit another cigarette from a pack on the mantel then threw the lighter down. 'So he told you we were lovers. Did he tell you that I came home from France because I was pregnant? Unfortunately, I miscarried.'

'I'm sorry . . . for you and for your husband.'

185

'Yes, I think Henry's rather sorry for himself too.'

Caroline said sourly, contemplating the smoke ring hovering just above her head. 'Although he has no need to be. I chose him in the end, after all.'

Olivia finished her cigarette and remained quiet. She knew that her hostess was watching her, wanting her to ask if the child had been Lucas's. But she wouldn't. He'd said it wasn't . . . though in truth she doubted he could have been absolutely certain of that. Just as her father couldn't have been absolutely certain he hadn't fathered Sybil Wright's kids. And sometimes the pregnant mothers didn't know who was responsible either. Perhaps that was the case with Caroline. She'd been sleeping with both brothers and had told the one she wanted most that he was the father.

Now she'd satisfied her vulgar curiosity about Lucas's former mistress and discovered there was no good news about him from France, Olivia wanted to go home to her cosy house and her exasperating, if beloved, family. She didn't like Caroline yet in an odd way she felt pity for her. Mrs Black was beautiful, lived surrounded by luxury, and yet she wasn't as content as a factory girl.

'A man like Lucas is attractive to women and he knows it,' Caroline broke the quiet. 'He lacks self-discipline and isn't capable of remaining faithful to any woman. That mongrel blood running through his veins is to blame.' Caroline smiled sourly. 'Such men are like stray dogs

. . . you never know if they'll lick you or turn on you.' She abruptly sat down. Settling her chin on her fist, she gazed at Olivia. 'He's told you he's adopted, has he? A favoured son, though, where his father was concerned. Lucas ousted the rightful heir. Henry is older and legitimate.'

Olivia stood up. She knew if she stayed any longer she'd blurt out that actually Lucas had asked her to marry him, and she wasn't listening to anybody talk about her future husband in this disgusting way. 'I know Lucas has Romany blood. He's told me about his mother, and that he was adopted.'

She could tell that Caroline hadn't been expecting that. 'He's told you about his brother too, hasn't he?' She stubbed out the cigarette with savage jabs.

'Yes, I know Henry has some health problems . . .'

'Have I indeed? Who says so?'

A man bearing a striking resemblance to Lucas had entered the room behind Valerie, who'd returned carrying a tray of tea things.

Everybody started talking over one another.

'I didn't know you were back from your club, Henry . . .'

'I told the maid I'd bring the tea to save her legs . . .'

'So he told his bloody factory tart I'm an imbecile, did he?' Henry came further into the room and stood, hands on hips, boldly assessing Olivia. 'Did he tell you he's a bastard, literally and figuratively? There, see, I'm not quite as mad as he'd make out. He wanted everybody to think me off me rocker so the old man would give him all the loot.' He threw back his head and laughed.

Olivia could tell from Henry's flushed cheeks and the strong smell of alcohol that he was quite drunk. But that apart there was something not quite right about his manner. He was shorter and stockier than Lucas and his eyes were hazel rather than deepest blue like his brother's. And there was an unusual and disturbing look in them. Olivia had seen that sort of blazing yet vacant stare in the eyes of patients with head injuries at St Omer.

'Pretty, ain't she? Can tell what he sees in her.' Henry had turned to his wife to make that last remark. He curled his lip at Olivia. 'He won't marry you, though, sweetie, whatever he says. Ask my wife . . .'

Olivia signalled to a drop-jawed Val that she was ready to leave. Valerie dumped the tea tray, looking as relieved as Olivia felt to skedaddle.

'I'm glad we met,' Olivia said truthfully. 'Thank you for the offer of tea, but I have to get home. My sisters will be off to work soon and my brother needs an eye kept on him.'

'Sounds a bit like my brother,' Henry boomed out. 'Lucas needs an eye kept on him or he'll shag the factory gels. Ain't that right, Caro?'

Olivia was soon striding across the marble-flagged hallway with Henry Black's loud, strident laughter following her. A male servant pulled open the door and, as was her way, she thanked him. In return she received a surprised, rather disdainful look.

Valerie caught up with Olivia as she was turning the corner out of the square.

'What the hell was that all about? Why did she ask you for tea then act like a bitch?' Val shook her head. 'Sorry, Livvie. Wish I'd never told her now that I knew you from St Omer and that Lucas came to the hospital to see you and you seemed fond of one another and . . . '

'Never mind,' Olivia interrupted, and gave a weary chuckle. 'It's my own fault for being equally nosy and wanting to see *her*. Well, I've met her now, and Henry. Don't think I'll want to do it again though.'

'Don't blame you. Bloody family!' Val snorted, linking arms with Olivia. 'They're all completely bonkers on my mother's side.'

189

# 14

'There's a soldier on the front step, Livvie, and he wants to have a word with you.' Nancy had poked her head around the kitchen door to rattle that off before racing up the stairs to tell the others the interesting news.

Olivia dropped the potato peeler and whipped about. Her excitement wilted as she realised that Nancy would have introduced Lucas by name. She went into the hall, her heart in her mouth in case it was a visit from one of his comrades, bringing her bad news and a final letter. That's how she'd learned about Joe; Lucas had been brave enough to knock on her door to bring her back precious mementoes even though he'd known he'd break her heart.

She angled her head to see who was waiting outside and a sigh of relief escaped her. A smile on her face, she hurried forward. 'Well, you look to be in fine fettle, Private Carter.' She beckoned him in, wiping her damp hands on her pinafore.

Albert stepped over the threshold looking bashful. He removed his cap, securing it under one arm.

'I knew where you lived 'cos Wicksy talked about visiting your sister Maggie in Islington. Hope you don't mind me showing up out of the blue like this?'

''Course I don't!' Olivia squeezed his hands in welcome. 'What a smashing surprise.' She was delighted that he'd made it home safely on his Blighty pass.

'I wanted to say thank you for all you did for me in the 'ospital, Sister Bone. Never got a chance to speak to you again after all the commotion with those rotten Krauts.' He beamed at her. 'You look good as new, though, so that's put me mind at rest. Last time I clapped eyes on you, you and the other nurse was out sparko.'

'Sister Booth is back home and fighting fit, and so am I,' Olivia reassured him. She rolled back her sleeve to show him the scar and prove she'd suffered no lasting damage. 'I should thank *you* for being a marvel that night, Albert, so I'm glad you've come to find me.' Olivia hadn't had a chance afterwards to see the lad. While she'd been recovering from the ordeal in her dormitory bed, he'd been taken by ambulance to catch the hospital train, headed for the coast. At Calais he would have boarded the ship ferrying the casualties back to Dover, and onward from there by rail to the capital. 'How is that leg?' She'd noticed his slight limp as he'd come towards her.

'Set me back a bit, having that scrap with Fischer, but it's nothing to worry about.' He was dressed in baggy hospital blues and pulled up his trouser leg to display the injury.

'You'll be playing football soon,' Olivia ribbed him although she could see the trouble he'd caused himself in protecting her. The wound appeared to have been restitched and looked messier than before. 'Your mother must be overjoyed that you're back home, Albert.' Spontaneously she gave him a hug that made him blush.

'She is, but she did box me ears like you said she would.' He pulled a face.

Olivia chuckled then tutted an apology. 'Oh, what am I doing, leaving you out here in the hall?' They'd had so much to say to one another that she'd forgotten her manners. She quickly closed the front door and ushered him towards the kitchen. 'Come and sit down by the range. There's a nip in the air today, isn't there? I'll make a cup of tea and we can have a proper chat in the warm.'

The nights were fast drawing in. Fog had swirled about the road that morning and the threat of its return hung like musk in the air.

'D'you know if the Red Caps got that Hauptmann wot escaped St Omer?' Albert asked eagerly, settling on a kitchen chair. 'He and his pal need stringing up fer what they did to you nurses. After all you done for 'em too!' He made a sound of disgust.

'There was no word of his capture by the time I left.' Olivia set the kettle on the hob. She didn't really want to talk about that now. Her family didn't know the details of her accident, and she didn't want to go into it at this late stage. She was about to tell Albert that they'd keep it between themselves when her brother came in, followed by Maggie. They'd been in their bedrooms but had come down out of curiosity to meet the boy soldier who, according to Nancy, looked like Alfie.

Olivia introduced them and she noticed that Private Carter's eyes darted back to Maggie several times. Suddenly he blurted out: 'Just like to say that Ricky Wicks was the nicest bloke I knew and he thought you was the best gel ever. I'm real sorry about what happened to him.'

Maggie mumbled and blushed but held out her hand to be shaken when Albert suddenly offered her his.

'You don't look very old to be a soldier,' Alfie piped up. He'd recognised at once that the visitor did resemble him and seeing his double in uniform fascinated the younger boy.

'Sixteen soon,' Private Carter announced proudly. 'Been in the infantry since I was fourteen.'

Maggie sat down at the table. 'Ricky wasn't much older when he enlisted. Shouldn't be allowed, kids joining up.'

''T'ain't allowed,' Albert said ruefully. 'But 't'ain't allowed for you to come back neither when you tell 'em the truth and that you've made a mistake.' He looked earnestly at Maggie. 'Your fiancé had already been out there six months when I turned up in the platoon. He was a good pal. We had some larks when we was billeted in the villages. He never stopped speaking about you. Read yer letters over and over, he did.' He gazed at his clasped hands. 'He couldn't wait to come back on leave and see you. He'd been saving to buy you a ring. Had it all planned out for the future, did Ricky . . .'

'I'd better get meself tidied up for work,' Maggie said, then disappeared in a rush.

'Did I upset her?' Private Carter took the cup of tea Olivia held out to him and sent an anxious glance at the door. 'Wouldn't have spoken about him if I'd thought it might upset her.'

'Mags thinks she might upset *you*,' Alfie said with surprising insight. 'She's forgotten about Ricky. She's getting married to his brother.' He wrinkled his nose. 'He ain't very nice either.'

'That's enough, Alfie,' Olivia quietly warned. 'Maggie won't like you talking about her behind her back.'

Alfie look embarrassed at having been told off in front of their guest. 'Going to Ranelagh Road to see Mickey,' he mumbled.

'I thought Mickey was living with his dad now, in Edmonton?'

'He's gone home to Ruby. So's his dad. The woman there didn't want Mickey under her feet so they both got chucked out.'

'Oh.' Olivia raised her eyebrows in surprise. She remembered her uncle telling her months ago that he'd moved in with a widow and they got on alright. Obviously all that had changed when Ed brought his son to live with him. She wondered how Ruby liked having her long-absent father back beneath the same roof as her.

After her brother had left the room Olivia turned back to Albert with a smile. 'Would you like a sandwich or a piece of fruitcake with your tea?'

'Best not. Mum'll skin me if I spoil me dinner.' He grinned. ''Fore I went to France, I was lucky if I got a rasher of bacon fer me tea. Now it's mutton stew and dumplings. Told her

194

we got fed like princes in the 'ospital by all the lovely Poppy Angels.' He winked at Olivia. 'I knew she'd not like that and would cook me up some lovely grub. She don't like being outdone, me mother.'

'She's intent on looking after you,' Olivia said.

'She's doing that alright. She's told all the neighbours I'm a hero and shows 'em the letter the Brigadier wrote to me, thanking me for me part in the 'unfortunate incident', as the top brass call escaping prisoners. I've got a medal on its way.'

'You deserve it. You *are* a hero.' Olivia patted his arm.

'Shame about what happened to old Jones though.' Albert sniffed. 'I know the others didn't like him but I thought he was alright on the whole even if he was a self-inflicted. He taught us all a lesson. He didn't miss a trick where the Hun was concerned.'

Olivia grimaced her agreement to that and sipped tea.

'Can I ask you a favour, Sister Bone?'

Olivia took a seat opposite the boy, intrigued. 'Go ahead.'

'Private Jones give me a box of stuff . . . biscuits and cakes and pickles that his missus had been sending out. He didn't fancy it 'cos of his upset belly.'

'He mentioned it to me too. Asked me to write home and tell her not to send any more.'

'Well, he knew I'd got me Blighty pass and asked me to take it all back to his wife 'cos he knew they needed it more than he did. I said I would.' Albert looked appealingly at Olivia. 'Would you come with me, Sister Bone, when I go and see her? His wife's bound to be upset and I might not know what to say to her. But as you nursed him, you might have a bit of chit-chat to pass the time.'

''Course I'll come,' Olivia said. 'I'd be pleased to.'

'Thanks.' Albert looked relieved. 'Thought I might go tomorrow morning, if that's alright? Get it over with. She lives in Shoreditch, not far from me. I can meet you by the station, if you like, at ten o'clock and we can walk from there.' He gulped from his cup and stood up. 'Thanks for tea. Best get off now.'

'I don't suppose you've had any news of Lieutenant Black since you've been back?' Olivia asked at the door.

Albert shook his head. 'Not heard from any of 'em. Glad I'm home . . . bet they wish they was too.'

'I've heard he's been reported missing again with some others from his platoon,' she said hoarsely.

Albert flipped his cap onto his head on the step, keeping his face averted from hers. 'Me officer's got the luck of the devil, everybody says so. He won't let Fritz beat him. So he'll bring 'em back, sooner or later.' Albert ran his finger under his nose. 'See you tomorrow then, Sister Bone?'

'See you tomorrow,' Olivia echoed through the lump in her throat. Even the devil's luck would run out eventually. And Albert knew it too.

'Me husband was always a courageous sort. Never shied away from a fight, Bill Jones didn't.' The woman dabbed her eyes with a screwed-up hanky then tidied her straggling ginger hair behind her ears. She held a child of about two years old on her knee. Its twin was seated on the floor at her feet. Both of them were only half-dressed in a dirty nappy and nothing else. The room was chilly, with meagre heat coming from the smouldering ash in the grate.

'He certainly was brave that day,' Olivia said, and took another small sip of weak lukewarm tea. They'd arrived in Shoreditch about half an hour ago and had now almost run out of conversation about the late Private Jones's heroics.

Mrs Jones was the sort of woman Olivia met quite often in her Islington neighbourhood. A widowed mother of about thirty years old who looked a decade older, thin and tired but with a fierce pride in her family. Once Olivia and Private Carter had introduced themselves and their business with her, Mrs Jones's natural defensiveness had melted. She had immediately invited them in and made them a cup of tea while thanking them for taking time to come and see her and speak of her late husband. The children had stared curiously while the guests found some space to sit down on chairs strewn with odds and ends.

As Private Jones's wife turned her attention to Albert, thanking him for the umpteenth time for returning the box of food, Olivia looked at the children and her eyes stung with tears. Their father had desperately wanted to come home to provide for them and anybody could see why. As well as the twin toddlers there was a mewling infant in a pram in the corner of the room. A girl in a faded dress, who looked to be about five years old, was bouncing the pram up and down in an attempt to quieten the baby. Seated at the table was an older boy, perhaps eight, his expression sullen and embarrassed. Olivia caught his eye and smiled but he dropped his head and stared at the splintered pine table-top. Olivia knew he should have been at school. She guessed his mother had already told him she needed him more than the school did now his father had gone. From the moment Mr Jones had been called up his eldest son had doubtless been burdened with responsibility as he was then the man of the house . . . a mantle that was heavier to shake off now his father was dead. And what a house it was.

The parlour they were in was similar to the rooms in the Bunk's tenements. Olivia's aunt Sybil had lived there for some years and Olivia had visited her and the Keivers in their slums. She herself had briefly lived in a tiny box room in the same street, until Joe Hunter turned her life around for her. The same foul smell of mildew and boiled cabbage permeated the air here as there, and every surface and piece of battered furniture was cluttered with debris. The hard-backed chairs they sat on had washing draped over the backs, and above their heads was a string supporting more linen drooping from one side of the room to the other. No doubt the toddlers would be clothed as soon as their vests were dry enough for them to be put on again.

'Well . . . I've got to get to me job soon,' Mrs Jones apologetically let them know they had to go. 'I'm charring in some big houses over the other side of the High Street.' The baby's whimpers turned into a wail and she glanced at the pram. 'Needs feeding 'fore I go . . .' She sent an embarrassed look at Albert and adjusted her bodice over her leaking bosom.

'We'll be off now. Thanks for the tea, Mrs Jones.' Olivia quickly stood up and Albert followed suit, looking relieved.

When they were walking back up the road, Olivia spoke aloud the thought that had been circling her mind since the moment they'd met Mrs Jones and her brood. 'How on earth did she afford to buy him pickles and cakes?'

Albert tapped his nose and chuckled. 'She chars in big houses. She didn't buy 'em.' He gave Olivia a wink. 'Got two aunties who work as cleaners for posh people. Be surprised what falls in their bags when they're scrubbin' the pantry.'

At the corner they stopped as they had different directions to go in.

'Well, that wasn't so bad, after all,' Albert said. 'When I saw all them kids I wasn't 'arf glad you came with me, Sister Bone.'

'She's certainly got her hands full.'

'Can I stop by and see you another time?'

'I'd like that, Albert. But I'll be going back to

France soon. I've already written to my bosses to ask for a return passage.'

'You're a brave 'un, you are, going back for seconds.'

'Not as brave as some.' Olivia sighed. 'I want to find out what's happened to Lieutenant Black. I can't bear not knowing.' She wasn't sure why she told this young soldier her innermost thoughts when she bottled them up inside while with her own family. But Private Carter had guessed that she and Lucas were in love and wanted to get married.

This boy soldier had spent years, day in, day out, with Lucas, breathing cordite-fouled air and existing on army rations. Private Carter had spent more time with her future husband than Olivia had herself. He understood.

'Reckon you will find him too,' Albert said softly. 'He won't give up easily, that's fer sure. Could be you'll get a letter eventually . . . from a German camp. Still hope for him.' He rubbed one finger under his nose, a habit he had when feeling emotional. 'Yer sister Maggie's getting wed then? Hope she'll be happy. Tell her I said that, will you, Sister Bone?'

Olivia nodded and shook Private Carter's hand as he extended it, though she'd been tempted to hug him as she had yesterday. As she would've done if saying goodbye to Alfie. But Private Carter wasn't a child, no matter how youthful he looked. He was a soldier who'd earned a medal for bravery.

⋆ ⋆ ⋆

Olivia was almost home when she spotted a sight that gladdened her heart and sent her belting across the road.

'Oh! How lovely to see you back!' she announced breathlessly. 'Matilda said she'd not heard from you for a while. Are you home on leave?'

Jack Keiver had been talking to his brother-in-law but he left Jimmy Wild by the railings and hurried over to Olivia, to clasp her outstretched hands.

'Got back yesterday, Livvie.' He grinned. 'And never been gladder in me life to see this old place, I can tell yer. It got a bit hairy out there fer me this time.' He blew a whistle through his pursed lips.

Matilda emerged from the dim tenement hallway and immediately joined them, linking arms with her husband. 'Hello, Livvie. Jack tell you he's got a whole two weeks with us? We're gonna make the most of that! Party in ours this Saturday night, so make sure you and the kids come and join in.' She tickled her husband's chin. 'Oh, can't believe you're back home, love.'

Olivia began edging away. She could see Matilda wanted her husband to herself, and who could blame the woman? Olivia would be the same with Lucas. She'd not want to let him out of her sight, or out of her arms.

'See you Saturday then, Livvie?' Matilda called after her.

'I'll be there.' Olivia waved over her shoulder. 'Welcome home, Jack!'

She'd only gone a few yards when he escaped

his wife's clutches and came after her.

'Run into your friend out there — Lieutenant Black,' he explained. 'Fact is, Livvie, if I hadn't met him, I wouldn't be here. We all got into a spot of bother. It took a while, but he got us back to our side of the barbed wire. Then made sure we got leave granted us, 'n' all.'

Olivia blinked at Jack, her lips parting in wonder. 'You've seen *Lucas*?' she squeaked. 'You've *really* seen him?'

'I certainly have. And mighty glad I did. Don't know how he did it, but he and that ginger sergeant of his, they pulled us through.' Jack's eyes flooded with tears at the memory of falling, dodging, crawling over bomb holes and squelching mud in darkest night. And trying to do it silently with the enemy sometimes so close you could hear them pissing into bushes and striking matches for their pipes. 'Thought we were all goners at the tail end of it,' he croaked. 'Within spitting distance of our trenches . . . could see our boys . . . when some of Fritz's snipers spotted us in no-man's-land. Your Lucas gave 'em a blast, walked straight towards the buggers. Never seen a man shoot a Lewis from the hip before. But the lieutenant did. We'd only just come across ammo to feed the bleedin' thing, too. Luck o' the devil . . . oh, we *was* lucky . . . ' Jack couldn't go on. He turned his head and blinked back the tears and fearful memories until they quit his head.

Olivia couldn't stop her tears from streaming down her face; hearing that Lucas was still alive was making her shudder with relief. She cupped her wet cheeks with her hands and leaned into Jack as he embraced her.

'Tell me he's alright, Jack, please?'

'He's alright, love. Shot up a bit, but . . . ' He grasped her chin as she choked back a cry. 'Hush. He was shot in the arm but he was treated in a clearing station and 'fore I left I went to see him. He's doing fine.'

'Which clearing station?' Olivia demanded.

'Outside Thiepval. He remembered me, and us having a drink together in the Duke.' Jack beamed a smile, repeating proudly, 'Remembered me, he did! And he spoke about you. Said if I saw you when I got home, to tell you he'll see you soon, 'cos he keeps his promises. Said you'd know what he meant.'

'I do,' she croaked. 'Thank you, Jack.'

'What's up, love?' Matilda had come up behind them, looking concerned to see Olivia's shoulders jerking with silent sobs.

'Everything's fine,' she gurgled, and started to laugh.

'Oh, right then . . . good.' Matilda frowned. 'Thought Jack might have told you about Herbie Hunter and upset you. I thought better of saying anything to you about him meself. You've got enough on your plate as it is. *He* ain't important.'

Olivia wiped her eyes, composing herself. 'What about Herbie Hunter?' she asked. She'd not thought about Joe's father in a long while. And why should she when she'd never liked him? Despite his smarmy way she knew he'd never really liked her either. But learning about his sudden passing had come as a shock at the time.

'Herbie ain't dead after all.' Matilda shrugged. 'But like I said, alive, dead, he ain't important any more even if he is back dossin' too close fer comfort. So let's forget about him.'

# 15

There was standing room only in the Keivers' front room on Saturday night. The double bedstead that usually dominated the room had been stood on end to allow in more revellers. Those who couldn't elbow themselves a space had propped their backs against the wall on the landing or found a seat on the stairs.

Jack was at the piano, and the brown ale bottles ranged along its top were jingling an accompaniment as he bashed out song after song on the keys. Every so often he'd stop to wet his whistle only to receive bawled encouragement from his audience to 'give us another toon'. His wife was the one with the loudest voice and Jack would send her a bawdy wink. While he played he'd watch her and her sister Fran jigging about, roaring with laughter. He looked like a man content.

It seemed most of the neighbours in the street had crammed into the building to welcome Jack Keiver back home. He was well liked by all, whereas his wife was more of an acquired taste. But people had a healthy respect for the Bunk's hard-nosed rent collector. Matilda wasn't bothered about her lack of popularity anyhow. She tipped her cap to the man who paid her wages, and adored her family, and that was it. In her opinion it didn't do to let folk get too familiar or they'd put her in Queer Street with her guv'nor, wheedling for her to fiddle their rent books when they were short. They'd all come to her when times got tough though; if Matilda Keiver took up a cause and went knocking door to door, brandishing a pudding basin, nobody refused to drop a copper in it for a needy family.

Olivia had had first-hand experience of Matilda's help.

On the night Olivia's father had thrown her out she'd turned up on the woman's doorstep like a battered waif, begging a roof over her head. At the time it had seemed as though a calamity had befallen her and she'd never recover. Since then she'd accepted that a jolt had been necessary to yank her out from under her father's thumb.

It had been hard at first with nothing other than a change of clothes and a few shillings to call her own. But Matilda had had a whip-round to start Olivia off in her life as an independent woman. The neighbours in the street had donated bits and pieces to help her set up home in the tiny room. Threadbare sheets and dented saucepans; chipped crockery and mismatched cutlery, had all been treasured gifts. When she'd come to really appreciate how poor those people were, their generosity had humbled her.

Nowadays Olivia herself always put coins in the pudding-basin whip-rounds, organised when a family couldn't scrape together enough money for a birth or a funeral or a hasty wedding. The wheel of misfortune spun ceaselessly in the Bunk and nobody knew when it would turn for them and the collection would be tipped onto their table.

Olivia and Maggie had been stationed in the doorway of the room, singing along with everybody else to 'Pack Up Your Troubles'. They'd been glad of the draught coming up the stairs, cooling their flushed faces. The atmosphere was stifling despite the breezy evening. Olivia glanced about. Outsiders might brand these people the dregs, living as they did in a slum notorious for being the worst street in North London. But they were decent folk, as far as they could be. And then she spotted one who wasn't.

Herbie Hunter had just entered the hallway and glimpsed her on the landing. He was about to turn tail but thought better of it. He knew she'd seen him so he started up the stairs, soppy smile on his face.

He hadn't been invited to this do but the chance of a free drink and a bit of company had lured him in. He'd slowly been trying to worm himself back into life in the Bunk. He'd rented a box room up the other end of the street — the cheapest he could find — that wasn't owned by Mrs Keiver's guv'nor. Thankfully he'd avoided having to face her every rent day and receive a withering look. After Ed Wright had spotted him loitering by the fish shop, Herbie knew the game was up and he'd have to quickly tell his own tale before others made up their versions of his rebirth. He'd even stopped wearing his wig as he knew it made him a figure of fun. It had been a pretty paltry disguise; Sybil and Ed Wright had recognised him straight off. Herbie knew his gangly frame was more of a giveaway than his bald head.

'How you doin' then, Livvie?' Herbie gave her a tobacco-stained smile as he reached the landing. 'Heard you was nursing our lads out in France.'

'That's right. I'm just home on leave.' She kept her welcome cool.

'You look well, gel, despite what you must've been through out there.'

'So do you, Mr Hunter. We all heard you'd drowned.'

'Yeah . . . odd that,' Herbie muttered, and struck a match to the drooping dog end in his mouth. 'Feel sorry for whoever it was that they pulled out of the Carbuncle Ditch. I swear a Belgian pinched me hip flask out of me coat. It had me name engraved on it. That was found in the water so must've been him, I suppose, poor blighter.' He added that lie for good measure. The flask had been in his own pocket when he was dumped in the ditch and he'd not had it when he dragged himself out. But he believed that a tramp probably had tumbled in, or else done himself in.

'Did you go away to find work then?' Olivia wasn't really interested in knowing but she'd sooner make polite conversation than stand in silence for a few minutes before excusing herself.

Herbie jumped on that lead. 'I did do some farm labouring, love, but when that dried up I took meself off to see me sister in Southend.' He continued, 'Me 'n' yer aunt couldn't rub along so I thought it best to put some distance between us. Wasn't easy living under the same roof as her in Wood Green. She was a drinker, as I expect you know.' He shook his head dolefully. 'Shame what happened to old Sybil though.'

'Yes, it was,' Olivia said. She couldn't deny that her aunt had been an unpleasant woman and, according to Ruby, bloody hard to put up with. But neither was this man pleasant. Joe had told her he'd been a cruel, drunken father.

Maggie had been tapping her foot along to the music and peering over the banisters while her sister was talking. Spotting a newcomer, she gave an excited wave. 'There's Harry at last!' she burst out.

Another familiar face to make Olivia's heart sink was staring up the stairs at them. 'You invited him, did you, Maggie?'

''Course! He's me fiancé,' Maggie said over her shoulder, already on her way to greet him.

'So yer younger sister's getting wed before you, Livvie, is she? Never mind, you'll be next in line.' Herbie added slyly, 'Don't expect you to pine after me son for ever, luv, so don't fret about upsettin' me on that score.'

Olivia was tempted to tell him she didn't give a monkey's what he thought and the idea that he could be upset on Joe's behalf was laughable, considering he'd led his son a dog's life.

'I remember yer brother saying that the posh army officer seemed keen on you. Still around, is he?' Herbie hid his calculating look beneath the brim of his cap, fiddling with the lid of his tobacco tin. He wanted to know the whereabouts of the bastard who had knocked him out and dumped him in the ditch to drown.

'Lieutenant Black's still in France.' Olivia was surprised that Mr Hunter would have remembered him, or that her brother would have mentioned him in the first place. As always when Lucas's name cropped up her heart quickened. She'd not let this nasty man spoil her joy at knowing Lucas was alive and safe in hospital. Neither was she going to let Harry Wicks get under her skin. To prove that to him and to her sister, she said goodbye to Mr Hunter then picked a path through the people on the stairs to join the couple by the entrance leading onto Campbell Road. The door was missing but that wasn't unusual in this street.

Fixtures and fittings frequently disappeared from the tenements in the Bunk. They were removed and sold off by desperate tenants who would even prise the glass from their windows for cash. Wood that could be burned disappeared on cold winter evenings to warm up icy rooms. Stair spindles were few and far between in most of the houses and people had been known to come home on a dark night and fall on the stairs because treads had disappeared in the few hours since they went out.

Herbie squinted over the banister, watching Olivia go with a bitter twist to his lips. He'd been hoping to hear Lieutenant Black was in a cemetery somewhere, having copped a bullet in Flanders. It was obvious that Livvie Bone didn't know about the night Lucas Black had come looking for him in order to protect her and her family before he returned overseas. The lieutenant had worked out that Herbie had committed two murders. Or, as he liked to think of them, 'accidents', he'd been forced to get involved in, so as to protect his own interests. The lieutenant had been right to come after him; Herbie had been planning on finding a way to remove Livvie Bone so he could get his hands on what was rightfully his. And he hadn't given up on that ambition yet.

He'd taken Black by surprise that night, sneaking up on him in the mist with a blade, but the fellow had come back at him like a pro and knocked him senseless before dumping him in the ditch to drown. A nob like the lieutenant would be listened to and believed if he went to the police with his suspicions about Tommy Bone's murder and Freddie Weedon's 'suicide'. Herbie bucked himself up. The lieutenant was a thousand miles away fighting and probably had no idea that since their encounter Herbie Hunter had miraculously resurfaced. There was still a good chance the Boche would send the lieutenant to meet his Maker and save Herbie the job.

\* \* \*

'Shame Nancy didn't come along tonight. It's a good party,' Maggie said, hanging onto her fiancé's arm.

Harry was eyeing up Connie Whitton, made up to the nines and dressed in mink. She'd stationed herself outside by the railings, talking to Ruby. It had spread like wildfire in the street that Connie had found herself a rich old man who'd set her up in style in Mayfair. Matilda had stopped to chortle, midway through telling Olivia about it, that she reckoned Connie would be out on her arse in the gutter before long because she was two-timing her sugar daddy with a local copper she'd known for years. Connie looked still to be in Swell Street, though, and Olivia was surprised to see her back, hanging around in Campbell Road in a fur coat. Connie had her mother and sisters to visit up the other end but that apart the Bunk was like a drug to some people; best avoided yet impossible to resist despite its reputation.

Maggie muttered beneath her breath and tugged on her fiancé's arm to stop him ogling the glamorous blonde.

Harry tickled her under the chin but Olivia, observing the scene, knew that he liked winding Maggie up by paying attention to other women. That was how he was and she'd have to get used to it because he'd never change.

'So Nancy ain't coming along tonight.' Harry gave a foxy smile. 'Reckon we all know where she's got to instead, don't we?'

'Livvie knows she's sweet on Nat Gunn,' Maggie retorted, still in a strop. 'So no need to try and drop Nancy in it like that.'

'Ain't planning on stopping yer sister seeing that villain then?' he taunted Olivia. 'Can't say I blame you. Nat Gunn's a handful for a man to deal with, let alone a woman.'

'Nancy knows how I feel about her behaviour,

and I've told Maggie the same thing about what she gets up to.' Olivia bluntly replied. 'They're old enough to make up their own minds on things, then deal with any consequences.' She could tell he didn't like that unsubtle dig at Maggie for choosing him. Harry did his usual trick of wiping his thumb and forefinger around his moustache and squinting down his nose at her. Olivia knew he'd love to engineer some friction between them all. But he wasn't pushing her into rowing with her sisters. She loved her family too much to let Harry Wicks poison their relationship. Inside she was seething and knew it was best to walk away now.

'I'm going to have a word with Ruby . . . not seen her in a while.' Olivia slipped past the couple and out into the cool night air. Along the street a bonfire was burning, spitting sparks up to dance against the night sky. Some youths were capering around it, letting off bangers although the fifth of November was still weeks away.

'Riley's back!' was Ruby's breathlessly excited greeting to Olivia. She flashed her hand. 'Look! He asked me to marry him and bought me an engagement ring.'

'Oh, that's wonderful!' Olivia immediately hugged her then looked properly at the small diamond on her cousin's finger. 'It's lovely. I'm so pleased for you both.' She glanced about. 'Where is he then?'

'Propping up the bar in the Duke.' Connie acidly interjected and hiked a pencilled eyebrow at Olivia.

'I'm just going to fetch him. He's only seeing

his pals for a quick reunion then he's coming to the party.' Ruby scowled at Connie. 'He travelled home from France on the same boat as Jack Keiver.'

'No need to fetch him.' Olivia had spotted a large figure lumbering along in the dusk, swinging its arms in an unmistakable gait.

Ruby turned and dashed up the road to greet him, holding onto her hat.

'Weren't so long ago she was never letting him move back in again.' Connie fished a cigarette out of a chased silver case then offered one to Olivia before lighting them both with a match.

Olivia shrugged and drew on her cigarette. 'Jack Keiver told me they're all lucky to be alive and back home. P'raps that's made Ruby see things differently.'

'Yeah . . . ' Connie still sounded resentful and expelled a stream of smoke through a bow of crimson lips.

'Surprised to see you over this way.' Olivia cocked her head at Connie. For a girl supposed to be enjoying the good life she didn't look very content.

'Come to see me mum and give her a few bob. Never hear the end of it otherwise.'

Olivia chuckled. She knew that's how it was in most families round these parts. The kids who had managed to escape were expected to send money home to help out those left behind.

'Nice, is he? Your boyfriend?'

'He'll do fer now,' Connie said in a brittle voice, blocking out of her mind thoughts of an old man's sour breath and bony fingers mauling her skin.

She seemed to be in a funny mood so Olivia decided to leave her to stew. 'Well, I'm just off to check on Alfie. He's had a bad cold so stopped home in bed.' If her brother had been feeling well enough he'd have been sitting on the kerb with the other kids, drinking pop. She set off briskly but came to a halt close to the newly engaged couple, approaching her arm-in-arm.

'Glad to see you back, Riley, and good luck with this one.' She tipped her head at Ruby, grinning.

'Need it 'n' all, so I will.' He plonked a beery kiss on the side of his fiancée's head.

'Riley's just been saying that your Lieutenant Black got wounded out there.'

'Jack's already told me. He's alright though, isn't he?' Olivia immediately stared at Riley for confirmation.

'He's alright, so he is. Best officer in the whole fookin' army.' He grimaced an apology as Ruby dug him in the ribs for swearing.

'I doff me cap to him, so I do,' Riley said, and flipped it off and back onto his head, resettling it on his dark hair with a flourish.

'Not leavin' the party already, are you?' Ruby asked as Olivia started to go past them.

'Alfie's not been well. I'll be back if he's not taken a turn for the worse.' Olivia carried on up the road. She took a final drag on the cigarette then stepped on the stub before opening the gate.

The sound of muted conversation greeted her

as she let herself in. She wondered if her brother had invited a friend round. She'd left him lying in bed, blowing his nose and complaining of a thumping headache. But the voices seemed to be coming from the parlour.

She opened the door to find Alfie and Mickey setting out the train set on the floor and her uncle perching on the edge of an armchair, watching the boys.

Alfie had perked up and that made her smile, as did the sight of her visitors. 'What a nice surprise,' she exclaimed. 'Sorry I was out. The Keivers are having a shindig 'cos Jack's home.'

Ed had got to his feet, looking embarrassed. 'Didn't mean to barge in on yer, Livvie, but as we were this way Mickey wanted to call on Alfie.'

Olivia flicked her fingers, dismissing his apology as unnecessary. 'I've just seen Ruby and Riley. I've heard the exciting news about their engagement.'

Ed nodded, looking awkward. 'Me 'n' Riley don't get on. But not my business who she marries. She told me that.'

Olivia remembered the two men had got off to a bad start at Sybil's funeral. 'I'll make a cup of tea,' she said diplomatically.

'Don't stop home on my account, love, if there's a party round the corner.' Ed had followed her into the kitchen. 'We'll be off now. I only come over to Islington on a bit of business. Just looked at a room for me 'n' Mickey in Brand Street. It's a dump but it'll have to do fer now.'

'I heard that you'd moved in with Ruby.' Olivia sounded surprised to hear her uncle was

216

hunting for somewhere to live.

'When Riley got back things turned sour. Can't keep moving in and out when he's home on leave. Now they're getting wed, I'll need somewhere of me own. Mickey fancies moving back this way to be near his cousin and it suits me to be close to me job at Houndsditch warehouse.' Ed paused. 'Mickey and Alfie get on well. I'd like them to stay friends and go to the same school. Least I can do is try to make it up to one of me kids for not having been around all them years. Bit late in the day, I know but . . . ' Ed's voice trailed off and he grimaced.

'The boys do get on well,' Olivia agreed softly. She spooned tea into the pot but the idea buzzing in her head wouldn't be denied and tumbled off her tongue. 'Why don't you move in here? I'm going back to France so there'll be a spare room, if you and Mickey don't mind sharing.'

Ed gawped at her. 'How will yer sisters take to that?' he eventually spluttered.

Olivia shrugged. 'Maggie's getting married. She'll be setting up home with her husband in the New Year. As for Nancy . . . ' Olivia rolled her eyes. 'She tells me she's all grown up too and wants to move out. So eventually it would've just been Alfie and me here on our own. You'd be doing me a favour if you kept an eye on him and this place, Uncle Ed. I don't want to give up being a VAD. There aren't enough of us volunteers as it is.'

Olivia knew her work wasn't just a moral duty any more, or a gut reaction to her having lost Joe

217

to the war. She felt proud to be employed in something so vital. Gladys Bennett had praised her for being good at her job, and said she'd welcome her back with open arms. But Olivia knew she needed the VAD as much as it needed people like her. It had been the making of her as an adult even if it had put lines on her face and sorrow in her heart. And it took her close to Lucas.

It had been a spur-of-the-moment decision, offering her uncle accommodation. Olivia didn't regret it, though; in fact, the more she thought about it, the more it seemed to make perfect sense. She'd already been thinking about the problems that would arise when both her sisters flew the nest. She'd never leave Alfie on his own while he was still a schoolboy so had accepted she'd have to resign her nursing post. The pull of family duty still outweighed all else where her little brother was concerned. She'd also been worrying about returning to France and leaving her home at the mercy of predatory men. But if her uncle was taking care of things at Playford Road, she could relax. Harry Wicks wouldn't try forcing his way in with Ed Wright around. And neither would Herbert Hunter. She'd been astonished to learn that *he* was back on the scene.

She'd never trusted Joe's father; much as he tried to appear friendly to her and indifferent to the matter of his son's property, she knew he had always resented the fact Joe had left her his house.

Olivia liked her uncle; in fact, loyalty apart,

she knew Ed Wright was a nicer character than her own father had ever been. It seemed odd to her that Sybil had chosen Tommy Bone over her decent husband. The lovers had suited one another . . . been kindred spirits, she supposed, who'd recognised similar traits in one another. But her father had been better before his wife had died. Olivia remembered him as being quite fun in his own way, larking about with her in the street with a bat and ball when she'd been at primary school. Yet even then he'd been deceitful, carrying on with his sister-in-law behind her mother's back. When Olivia had grown older she'd still not suspected him capable of that sort of behaviour and the truth had been a horrible blow. Love had blinded her, she supposed. She *had* loved her father despite his many faults.

'Please say you *will* move in? I honestly want you to.'

'If you're sure, Livvie.' Ed had finally conquered his amazement and was glad to accept her offer. 'I'd jump at the chance for me 'n' Mickey to live here s'long as your sisters don't object. Wouldn't want to create bad feeling between all you gels. I won't make no bones about leaving when the time comes neither. Once you're back for good . . . and please God it ain't long 'cos this war's getting to us all . . . I'll pack up me bags and leave you in peace.' Ed looked as though he couldn't believe his luck. 'I know Mickey'll be over the moon when I tell him.'

'Don't say anything yet though,' Olivia

cautioned, stirring the brew in the teapot. 'It's only fair I speak to the girls first. But I've made my decision, so that's that.' She gave a contented sigh. 'I've had a letter offering me a passage to Boulogne. All I have to do is accept it. I'll do that in the morning.' She poured the tea and handed Ed his cup. 'Let's drink to it.'

★   ★   ★

'You've already made yer mind up so makes no difference if we do object.' Maggie plonked herself down on a chair, turning a sullen profile towards the room's occupants.

Alfie was jigging about excitedly, having heard the news that his uncle and cousin would be moving in when his big sister went back to work. His glee served to deepen Maggie's scowl.

'Well, I think it's a smashing idea.' Nancy had been buffing up her best boots but she dropped the rag to give Olivia a wide smile. 'I've found a nice place in Blackstock Road and they said they'll give me first refusal. But they won't wait for ever. I was hanging off making a decision 'cos of Alfie. Didn't want to leave him on his own if you're definitely going back to France.' She stood up. 'Looks like everything's turned out fer the best then.'

Olivia gave her a grateful smile then turned to Maggie. 'Don't sulk, Mags,' she coaxed. 'You know you'd sooner be mistress of your own home if you had the choice.' She crouched down by Maggie's chair, angling her head to look into her sister's evasive eyes. 'If you're worried over

220

Harry's reaction to the news then I'll speak to him again. Although I have already made it clear to him he can't set up home here, so it shouldn't bother him one bit that Uncle Ed's moving in.'

'I *do* want me own place,' Maggie admitted. 'He says we can't afford it though.'

'Well . . . fewer tins of baccy and pints in the pub and perhaps he'll find he can afford a couple of rooms to call his own after all.'

Olivia didn't want to sound as though she was preaching but she knew that Harry Wicks was no worse off than many men who managed to put a roof over their family's heads. In fact, he was luckier than most in that he was safe at home instead of being knee-deep in mud in a trench in Flanders.

'I'll sort out a few bits and pieces to help you start off married life,' she volunteered. 'I've more than enough pots and cutlery in the cupboards. And there are some lovely glass fruit dishes in the sideboard that you're welcome to . . . '

'Thanks, but Nancy'll get us all new stuff . . . ' Maggie started.

'She won't,' Olivia said, giving her youngest sister a stern look.

'No, I bleedin' won't!' Nancy agreed. 'I ain't walking out of Dickins and Jones with a saucepan up me skirt and that's final. Anyhow . . . I've already said I'm done with it fer now.' She glanced bashfully at Olivia. 'Nat's gone off doing his training then he's shipping out. I'm on me best behaviour . . . at least until he comes back,' she added saucily.

Maggie looked disappointed to be starting off

221

with hand-me-downs after all.

'You'll soon get into the swing of things, Mags.' Nancy gave her an encouraging hug. 'I can't wait to have me own space and come 'n' go as I please. First thing I'm doin' is arranging a house-warming party and having all me friends round.'

'Alright!' Olivia jokingly protested. 'You'll make me think I've been a right dragon to live with if you carry on like that.'

Nancy came and laid her head on Olivia's shoulder. 'You've been the best sister ever. Won't forget that you saved us all from Dad's temper and let us move in here with you.'

This impromptu display of gratitude and show of affection brought tears to Olivia's eyes. 'I've loved us all being here together,' she said huskily, cuddling Nancy to her. 'But I don't blame you for wanting to leave. You two girls . . . well, you're young women now, and I'm proud of you both. Mum and Dad would be too. We'll still be a family, just won't see each other so often.' They all looked quite emotional; even Alfie had glistening eyes. 'I would never have been able to put you all up but for Joe leaving me this house. God bless him,' Olivia added softly. 'I'd still be living in the Bunk if he hadn't and there was barely room for just me in that box room.'

'Can we look in the sideboard later then for stuff I can have?' Maggie asked.

'Do it now, if you like,' Olivia said cheerfully, and opened the doors of the heavy oak furniture.

She had been chary of bringing up the subject of their uncle moving in. But it had been received better than she'd hoped and she wanted to treat them all as a thank you. 'Why don't we have a night out before I leave for France?' she announced. 'How about we go to the theatre and see a show?'

'Can I come along?' Alfie immediately piped up.

''Course you can,' Olivia said. 'You can ask Mickey if he'd like to go too.'

'I've been asking Harry to take me to see *Chu Chin Chow* at His Majesty's Theatre.' Maggie had brightened up. 'People at work say it's really good.'

'Well, let's go and see it then,' Olivia said. 'You can ask Harry if he wants to come and I'll ask my friend Val Booth. I'd like to see her before I go back and wish her all the best.' Olivia hadn't had a chance to see Val again and ask her if she'd sorted out another VAD posting. It would be a crying shame if a nurse with her ability and enthusiasm was shunned because of one silly slip up.

She hadn't thought about that horrible incident for a while. But she did now, wondering if Ernst Fischer had been sent to a prisoner-of-war camp and whether his superior officer Karl Schmidt had been caught. Of the two, Olivia reckoned that Schmidt was the more dangerous. He'd played his part very well, fooling them all. Fischer had just been his sidekick.

# 16

'I wish I had fingernails as long as Chu Chin Chow's.' Maggie was giggling and making clawing motions with her hands.

'Me 'n' all,' Ruby chipped in. 'I'd scratch that cow's eyes out.'

'What cow?' Maggie and Nancy chorused as they walked along arm in arm.

'Widow up the road's been giving Riley the eye since he got back on leave. She's got a couple of kids and I reckon she's after finding 'em a new father. She knows we're getting married but I've caught her smiling at him. Ain't jealous,' Ruby said airily. 'I know I can trust him.'

'Can he trust you though?' Maggie ribbed her with a wink.

'Oi, you!' Ruby protested. 'I'm engaged. I'm a respectable woman now, I'll have yer know.'

'Blimey . . . that's a turn up,' Nancy snorted.

Ruby spun the diamond on her finger, unaffected by her cousins' drollery. She called out to Alice Keiver and Connie Whitton, bringing up the rear of the theatre party with their sisters.

'You lot coming to the caff with us for something to eat?'

'Dunno, ain't decided yet,' Connie shouted back after they'd put their heads together for a confab.

Olivia and Val had been up in front, leading the way. They'd been nattering non-stop about the show they'd just seen. *Chu Chin Chow* was based on the story of 'Ali Baba and the Forty Thieves' and they'd all been fascinated by the lavishly decorated Eastern costumes and the spectacular scenery, depicting far-flung places. Abu Hassan, or Chu Chin Chow as he presented himself during the production, had long curling fingernails like scimitars attached to the ends of his fingers. The songs had been catchy and they'd all joined in with the choruses, clapping along. Their exuberance had drawn frowns from some of the people in the expensive seats, who leaned over the balcony to gawp at them. At one time Olivia would probably have told her lot to pipe down, feeling embarrassed. But not this evening. It was their last chance to make merry as a family before she went back overseas and she was determined that they'd enjoy the very best outing they could. She'd sung and clapped along just as loudly as the rest of them. Folk having fun was a wonderful sound for somebody used to groans and cannon fire.

They'd emerged from the theatre into a dreary evening. But nobody wanted it to end yet. When getting up from their scratchy seats they'd shouted to and fro to one another to find out who fancied having something to eat before calling it a night.

In all, eleven of them had gone to the theatre. Harry had turned up his nose at the invitation, as Olivia had suspected he would. Secretly she'd been glad. She was gladder still that Maggie had come along without him and hoped it was a small sign that her sister wasn't completely under his thumb. Val had been delighted to join the group, as were Alice Keiver and her sister Beth. Then Connie had said she'd treat her two sisters to a night out, to stop them moaning jealously that she was lucky to have a sugar daddy.

Mickey had readily accepted the invitation and Ed Wright was so pleased his boy was being included that he'd insisted on sending his son along with money for Alfie's theatre ticket as well.

Nobody had moaned about paying the entrance money, and the consensus of opinion was that the show had been well worth the cost of a cheap seat.

'So you'll be off back to St Omer soon then?' Val said, striding at Olivia's side as they walked along.

'I'm sailing early next week. Did you get a new posting?'

Val nodded. 'I managed to sort something out, thank the Lord. It's unbearably boring being at home. There's a nursing home by the sea at Hythe for the poor blighters who've been shell-shocked. More of a God's waiting room from what I've been told. The Red Cross woman there said they don't get many volunteers because the work's a bit grim.' She pulled a face. 'Can't be any worse than what we saw at St Omer. Anyhow, doesn't bother me if the poor boys have got two heads. And Mummy's delighted to be rid of me.' She snorted. 'I said 'likewise', but not to her face. Can't upset the mater.'

Olivia gave her a smile. 'You're a good sort,

Valerie Booth. If anybody can cheer up those fellows, I reckon you can. I shall miss you over there in France though.'

Val blushed with pleasure. 'Miss you too.' She gave Olivia a fond nudge. 'You know that Caroline will be absolutely furious you heard about Lucas being wounded, and in hospital, before she did?'

'If my neighbour hadn't told me, I still wouldn't know. He's Alice and Beth's dad.' She tipped her head at the two girls walking a few yards away with Connie and her sisters. They were all in fits of giggles as they mimicked the Arabian accents they'd heard in the theatre. 'Anyhow, there's no reason Caroline should find out that I heard first.'

'She will. I'm going to tell her *and* I'll rub it in.' Val cackled with laughter. 'Rotten bitch she was to you that day. *And* she's had the cheek to ask me if I'll give you another invitation to tea. I said, not bloody likely!'

'I don't know why she'd want to see me again, unless it's to fire more insults at me.' Olivia shrugged. 'Anyway, it's all forgotten.' And it was. She hadn't seen her old roommate since that bizarre, unpleasant excursion and had barely thought about Caroline and Henry Black since. Olivia realised that Lucas's old flame was no longer of any importance to her. Neither was discovering more about his Romany birth family. Nothing mattered to her other than knowing he was safe and well. And when she got back to France she was going to find him, and tell him that.

'We having tea then? I'm starving.' Alfie had been running ahead with Mickey, the two of them re-enacting the sword fights they'd just seen on stage. 'There's a caff.' He pointed across the road. 'We could stop there.'

'Might be a bit pricey so close to the West End,' Olivia said. 'Why don't we go back to the Orange Caff in Blackstock Road? We can have a blow out for what he'll charge over there for a pot of tea.' She winked at Val. 'Game for slumming it?'

'Raath . . . err,' Val said, rubbing her palms together. 'Lead on. Any nice chaps likely to be in this caff of yours?'

'I wouldn't get yer hopes up,' Maggie said ruefully, trotting over to join them. 'Connie's off home. Don't reckon she wants to stump up for her sisters' grub. And Sarah and Louisa ain't got a penny on 'em. Alice and Beth are coming along with us though.'

Olivia knew that Connie's sisters were always broke because their alcoholic mother took all their earnings off them. 'Tell Sarah and Louisa that I'll buy them a cup of tea. The more the merrier.' Olivia linked arms with Val and they set off towards the bus that would take them back to Islington.

★   ★   ★

'Convoy's in! Shake a leg!'

Olivia blinked into pitch blackness. 'Convoy's in!' was a phrase that haunted her, night and day. She'd thought she'd dreamed it at first so had turned over, burrowing her head into the pillow. But when the call came again, louder, and accompanied by an unmistakable command to get up, she'd swung her legs over the edge of the scratchy mattress.

Sliding her toes over the cold floor she found her slippers. When they were on her feet, she dressed as all the staff did in the dark when still befuddled by sleep: as quickly as was possible with inflexible fingers and lungs heaving from blowing out long shivery breaths.

A hurricane lamp was set on the draughty window ledge behind the beds and as its flickering flame steadied she could just make out the silhouette of a colleague pulling on her uniform. Flora Thistle was her bunkmate now. They shared a small brick-built hut that'd once been used by the gardener but had been requisitioned as staff quarters during Olivia's absence. It was barely big enough to house two pallet beds and nightstands, plus the small stove that was used to heat the space and to boil a kettle. Since Olivia had got back to St Omer Flora had been much friendlier. Which was just as well; there was no time for pettiness now, or anything else for that matter.

'I swear I'd only just closed my eyes,' Olivia said through chattering teeth. But she had already donned her woollen stockings and pulled on her boots to protect her freezing feet. Then the rest of her nurse's uniform was grabbed from the end of the bed and quickly struggled into.

'We didn't finish shift until eleven o'clock and it's now . . . ' Flora fumbled with her alarm clock. 'It's not yet half past three. No wonder it's so bloody black.'

The bugle came again and was followed by somebody piping urgently on a whistle. Olivia speeded up, cursing beneath her breath as she dropped her belt on the floor in her clumsy haste. 'I'm turning in tonight fully dressed,' she vowed.

'Assuming we get a bedtime, you mean?' Flora ruefully enquired.

Olivia knew what she meant. The rota had gone out of the window and breaks and meals were snatched at random. Staff slept when they could and sometimes chose not to take a full quota even if it was available. Night staff stayed on shift until midday to support the day workers, who'd been up half the night helping them. And nobody was too precious to pitch in with whatever needed doing even if they were hungry and dog tired.

'Don't let Matron hear you say you're turning up on duty crumpled, Sister Bone.'

Olivia dredged up a smile. Flora was attempting to make light of things to buck her up, because Matron finding the time or inclination to tick her off about a creased dress, as she once would have, was unthinkable. Even the former stickler Gladys Bennett was different now. Everybody said so.

'Here.' Flora held out a mug. 'The kettle boiled while you were still asleep. It's Bovril. I've only drunk half of it. It's scalding hot.'

Olivia gratefully took the mug, curling her fingers about the warm china. 'Thanks. Don't know why I didn't hear the batman knocking.'

'He said everyone's to turn up for duty. It'll be a bad lot in again. God knows where we'll put them.' Flora hurried out, leaving Olivia to down her hot drink in desperate gulps, burning her mouth.

She briefly stared at her dim reflection in the spotted mirror: paper-white face and wispy hair curling on her sleep-dampened forehead. She pushed the strands under her cap and took two deep breaths. 'You've turned soft,' she berated herself as her eyes filled with tears. 'You can do this! You can!' With a sniff, she gritted her teeth and hurried out of the door in the direction of the wards, her mind fully alert now to what awaited her. She hurried over frozen inky ground, taking care to avoid skidding on patches of glittery frost as her mind pondered on the last few days.

She had been saddened to see the stranger who had welcomed her back to St Omer. Gladys Bennett, exhausted and gaunt, bore little resemblance to the tough capable woman of a month ago. She appeared to be succumbing to the mental and physical rigours of running St Omer while the big push along the Somme continued without let up. Food and equipment were in short supply and Matron felt her responsibilities weighing heavily on her. The hospital was heaving with soldiers, mostly in a very bad way with multiple wounds . . . some so badly injured it was a miracle they'd survived the ambulance train and van journey that'd brought them here.

Olivia felt privileged to be allowed to tend and comfort these men who clung so determinedly to what remained of their lives. Once they arrived at the hospital the surgeon-in-chief and his colleagues were likely to be too busy in theatre to prioritise cases. It often fell to Matron to make a decision that might condemn a man to death, who could have lived had he been treated sooner. Chest wounds were prioritised over head injuries; gas gangrene over mustard gas . . . the hundreds of casualties waited uncomplainingly to be seen despite their agonies. Matron's was of a different kind.

Olivia dashed into the assessment ward and straight into hell. It was a similar scene to yesterday's. Men were sitting, lying, being stepped over in the corridors where they lay groaning on the stretchers on which they'd arrived. And every one of them was caked in yellow mud that clung to their clothes and skin. It was up their nostrils and under their eyelids. Preparing them for diagnosis was so time-consuming that orderlies had been drafted in again this morning to assist in cutting off stiffly caked uniforms and boots. The orderlies' usual job of bearing stretchers had been filled by off-duty kitchen porters, who'd formed themselves into teams to carry more wounded men in from the ambulances. The nursing sisters were racing from ward to ward, washing and dressing wounds and dispensing morphine and assisting in theatre. Cleaning torn flesh then redressing men in pyjamas or long flannel hospital gowns, to prepare them for X-ray or surgery, was a delicate task when any movement could cause a patient dreadful pain. Yet the men bore it well . . . and in some instances apologised for causing trouble to the nursing sisters, who all looked so tired.

When a youth who was obviously dying said that to her, Olivia almost started weeping. She often did. But never when the patients could see or hear her. So she whisked herself away to the dressing store and cuffed her eyes on her sleeve before returning with lint and bandages. She gently removed the grimy field dressing from the gash on his head and began cleaning the wound with a solution of hydrogen peroxide. It was pointless, she knew that. The abdominal injury he had would be his downfall in a day or two. Flora knew it too. Her roommate stood a short distance away, shaking her head, wordlessly letting Olivia know things were hopeless with him. But she wouldn't leave him; she'd seen him close his eyes with a serene smile on his face as she gently smoothed the encrusted blood from his forehead. He wasn't with the mortuary corporal yet. But his whole body was aquiver as though it knew what was coming and would protest while it could at the idea of soon being sewn into a canvas shroud.

'When you've finished there, check for haemorrhaging of stumps, Sister Bone,' was Matron's urgent greeting on passing. She continued talking over her shoulder. 'Then the Radiographer would like someone with her as she's snowed under. If there's no problem with the amputees, go and find her and assist until I

233

call you back here. There's a staff meeting when time will allow.'

Olivia finished making the abdominal patient comfortable then headed off directly to the amputation ward. Tiredness was still lurking at the backs of her eyes and she tried to shake it off, forcing her lids wide.

She'd been back at St Omer camp hospital less than a week and the first setback she'd encountered had been seeing Matron a shadow of her former self. The second had been reading the letter awaiting her. It had been from Lucas. He'd written to her at St Omer, he'd said, because although he was hoping with all his heart to see her in London, he couldn't be sure she'd still be there when he got home. He was being sent back to convalesce but was doing well, he emphasised, and whether she were in England or France he would catch up with her as quickly as he could.

A bullet had passed clean through his arm, he said, with little damage sustained. Olivia had learned enough about the ways of soldiers to guess that was probably a great exaggeration on his part. She missed him so much yet felt selfish . . . wicked . . . for wishing him still in France. God knows, he deserved his rest. And what she'd encountered in just a few gruelling days back on the wards made her blessedly grateful that he was out of all this for a while.

The constant stream of casualties had been so great during her absence that even the church and refectory tents had been turned over to makeshift wards in an effort to cope. Trestle beds with straw-filled palliasses were all some of the lighter casualties could expect, laid on the floor between the regular bedsteads. 'A donkey's breakfast' those lads called them, the ones still able to laugh. And when even those had run out, the stretchers had been put on the floor, lifted clear of the wet when it rained, as it frequently did, and floodwater started creeping up the legs of the beds.

And all the time more men arrived and some . . . not nearly enough . . . were evacuated home, or else returned to the horrors that had brought them to St Omer in the first place. And still the dreadful weather continued, a biting cold giving way to rain that froze and then thawed, turning the ground boggy once again.

Everybody 'mucked-in' in a way that made Olivia feel proud of her fellow countrymen and women. No surgeon deemed himself too high-ranking to help butter bread or set cups or collect up clothing for delousing. The padre went about with his safety razor, shaving heads, legs, abdomens, to facilitate the cleaning and dressing of wounds.

Olivia felt ashamed for wishing she were back in London, waiting for Lucas to call. She felt guilty for having been at home at all. She should have returned sooner because none of her family's problems outweighed these. Might her pair of hands have saved a man or was that pure conceit on her part?

The stench of festering flesh reached her nostrils before she entered the ward. Within it a snaking line of patients — some sitting, some lying on the ground — stretched through the centre of a marquee that had beds lined close together to either side, some of them topped and tailed with patients. Fingers plucked at the hem of her skirt as she hurried along from one man to another, checking stained bandages, adjusting where necessary. Stopping, she crouched and comforted a boy of about eighteen who lay fidgeting on a stretcher. Some patients took the loss of a limb philosophically; others were devastated by an amputation even though it had been necessary to save their lives. A sweeping glance over him and she could see that he seemed to have been one of the lucky ones. His wound had been well dressed at a clearing station and there was no sign of fresh bleeding. She promised him she'd come back as she gently unfastened his fingers from her skirt. And she would do, even if it was midnight before she managed to do so.

★   ★   ★

'We have received word from the powers that be that some nurses in base hospitals should be encouraged to move down the line,' Gladys Bennett announced at the staff meeting late in the day. 'The clearing stations, ambulance barges and trains are desperately short-staffed. No doubt you've all heard about the bombing last week that destroyed Number Sixty-five. There were a lot of casualties, including a stretcher bearer and five medical staff.' She looked around at their intent expressions.

Only a dozen nurses had been called to this hastily arranged meeting. The majority were carrying on with their work and would be summoned another time. The sisters present had congregated in a store room-cum-office. Matron was standing behind her desk. She had surrendered her larger premises some while ago and they now housed beds. 'The clearing stations are critical to getting casualties treated as soon as possible and need to be fully functional,' she resumed in a clear voice. 'Men dressed and stabilised before journeying to a base hospital stand a greater chance of pulling through. Some stations have had to stop admitting new arrivals. They just don't have the resources to cope and are sending them onwards in a bad state.' She sighed. 'Saving a limb is often impossible if the boy's suffered a long journey and arrived with gangrene. Infection is *our* worst enemy, not the Hun.'

So far the assembled group had been quiet, listening intently, but a murmur of assent went up at that. Every nurse knew that infection led to a host of complications.

'I realise none of you are stupid and you already know this, and that moving closer to the front line would present a volunteer with a greater personal risk. Nonetheless I feel I *must* point it out,' Matron concluded.

Olivia looked about at the faces of her colleagues. All had been deeply interested in what had been said but none looked as though they were about to step forward. And neither did she relish putting herself in increased danger just behind the front line. Nevertheless she heard herself say, 'I'd like to volunteer to be transferred to a clearing station.'

'So would I,' another voice said.

Nobody else spoke. When the meeting dispersed Olivia was about to hasten away with the others, sure that Matron would talk to her later about her new posting. For now she had sunk down into a chair behind her desk.

'I've just remembered . . . you had a visitor while you were at home, Sister Bone,' she called after Olivia.

'Lieutenant Black?' she asked, turning back immediately.

'I'm afraid it wasn't. It was your ambulance driver friend. I hardly recognised her. She looked quite different with her hair cut short. I told her we were expecting you back in a week and she said she'd come again when she could. Rose is her name, isn't it?'

Olivia smiled. 'Yes, Rose Drew. I'd love to see her.'

'Well, I expect she'll find a few spare moments to pop in next time she's visiting Wimereux. As for us, no rest for the wicked. We must all have been *very* wicked,' Matron said with a glimmer of her old self. 'I'm off to theatre to assist with the ops.'

Matron was on her feet and Olivia noticed the blood stains down her apron.

'Would you write some 'break the news' letters for me, my dear? I have so many to do now. I usually send condolences in the same way so if I give you one, you could copy it for me to sign.

You have a nice hand; several of our boys have told me they like the way you write home for them.'

'Of course. I'll do it as soon as I can,' Olivia said.

'I'm glad you volunteered for a transfer, Sister Bone. Not that I want to lose you. But you have a backbone that would be hard to break, I think. You'll need it. I'd offer to go too, but my own backbone seems to be softening and I'm not proud of that.'

'You've been here since the beginning,' Olivia said kindly. 'I'm still newish by comparison.'

Matron smiled. 'Newish maybe but you're a tough nut. God bless you, wherever you end up.'

'I saw Valerie Booth last week.' Olivia wanted to find something to say to cheer them both up before they parted. 'We saw a show and had a lovely tea in a caff afterwards. A big group of us went out.'

Gladys gave her a smile. 'I'm glad you've kept in touch with Valerie. It was nothing personal, my sending her home. She was a good nurse.'

'She's found another post in Hythe. A nursing home by the sea.'

'Good luck to her . . . and to them,' Matron quickly tacked on.

Olivia suppressed a smile. 'Was the escaped German ever caught?' she asked.

'Not to my knowledge. It was the other man, Fischer, to whom I took a great dislike. Karl Schmidt did his duty as he saw it, I suppose. The one left behind had no need to use such violence against you nurses. But he's in custody now and will get what's coming to him.' Matron sounded satisfied about that. A moment later Olivia was heading in one direction and Matron in the other, to pick up where they'd left off.

# 17

'Is Miss Bone home?'

'She's not. Who wants her?'

'I do.'

Ed Wright pursed his mouth, cocking his head defiantly at the stranger on the doorstep. The fellow was dressed in smart hospital blues, not the baggy ill-fitting suit most rank-and-file wore. He spoke like a toff but he was a bit too sure of himself, in Ed's opinion.

'It's Lieutenant Black,' Alfie said. He'd come up behind his uncle and poked his head around the edge of the door.

'How've you been, Alfie?' Lucas asked him.

'Better'n you by the looks of it,' the boy said cheekily, nodding at the sling on Lucas's left arm. 'You can let him in,' he told his uncle. 'He's Livvie's boyfriend. He always comes in for tea.'

Ed looked at Lucas apologetically. 'Oh . . . well, come in if you like. Didn't realise, sir,' he mumbled.

Lucas hadn't taken offence. He knew how suspicious the folk round here could be towards strangers in their midst. He stepped into the hallway but didn't go any further when Ed opened the parlour door. 'I won't stop. I'd hoped to see Olivia before she returned to France. Am I too late?'

'Afraid so, sir,' Ed said. 'She left last week.'

Lucas felt disappointment churning his guts

but he kept his deep blue gaze fixed on the older man, wordlessly demanding an explanation of his presence here. And Ed felt obliged to give it.

'I'm the kid's uncle. Ed Wright's me name.' He tilted his head at Alfie, who'd sat down on the bottom stair to listen. A moment later Mickey came from his bedroom and perched on the stair above. 'Those two are cousins,' Ed added, unnecessarily as Lucas had recognised the lad with the limp from a previous encounter with the boys in Wood Green.

'Are you visiting?' Lucas recalled that Olivia had said her uncle had disappeared after discovering his wife's affair with Tommy Bone.

'I've moved in here; Livvie asked me to keep an eye on things for her while she's away. Her sisters are working shifts and the youngest, Nancy, is getting her own place next week. Maggie'll be leaving after Christmas when she gets wed. So I'm minding Alfie, making sure he behaves and gets to school.' He winked at his nephew's hangdog expression.

'Sounds like a sensible arrangement,' Lucas said. 'Thanks for telling me about Olivia. I'll see myself out.' He turned back after a few paces and said, 'I heard she had an accident?'

'She had stitches in her arm,' Alfie piped up.

'What happened to her?'

'Fell over, I think,' he said.

'She seemed right as rain, sir, when she left,' Ed reassured him.

'Good.' Lucas smiled and turned back towards the door.

'You still got me dad's cigarette case?' Alfie

jumped off the step and raced along the hall after him.

Lucas half-smiled and pulled the thing out of his pocket, displaying its battered appearance to a drop-jawed Alfie.

'You should've chucked it away. It's jinxed. That's why you got injured.'

'No, I'm one of the lucky ones.' Lucas gingerly eased his shoulder. 'The wound's healing well and I'll be going back soon. This has taken a bullet for me. Look ... ' He pointed to some dents in the pewter. 'Must be my talisman ... lucky charm,' he amended with a private smile, remembering Olivia ribbing him for using big words. Even that small memory of her made him ache to see her again.

Lucas pocketed the case. It brought back bad memories as well as good. A convalescing comrade had found it before it came into his possession. Freddie Weedon had been a decent man but he'd lost his life, not on a battlefield, but because he'd stumbled across Tommy Bone's cigarette case and knew too much. It had been stolen when Olivia's father was murdered and when the culprit discovered Freddie was on his trail he'd silenced him. Lucas didn't feel a shred of guilt about having avenged Freddie and Tommy by beating Herbie Hunter unconscious then dumping him in Carbuncle Ditch to drown. But the main reason Lucas had gone after Hunter before returning to his platoon was to protect Olivia and her family from a murderer while he was away in France. Despite its evil connections Lucas knew he'd always keep the case. But he'd never tell Olivia what he knew or what he'd done. She believed her father had been killed by an unknown assailant and that Freddie had committed suicide. Better that than tear apart her world by telling her the father of the man she'd loved had been responsible. Olivia cherished Joe Hunter's memory and the house he'd given her. But she wouldn't if she knew the truth. Even Lucas's twinges of jealousy wouldn't allow him to destroy what she still felt for Joe by telling her Herbie had murdered two men in his quest to get his hands on his dead son's property.

Besides, the case was a tangible connection to the woman he loved while they were apart. He'd put his lips to it at times when nobody was about to see him acting soft. Before he met her, he never would have acted like that. She'd found his soul . . . the one he'd not realised he had . . . and for her he didn't mind acting like a fool. He knew he'd die for her. Just as Joe had. Her fiancé had told him in ragged breaths, torn from his dying lungs, that it was better this way. Olivia deserved more than a war cripple, he'd said. Yet given the chance, she'd have loved him in whatever state he came home. That was how she was. But Lucas knew what Joe had meant.

'Best be off now.' Lucas reached for the door latch.

Alfie liked this man. He'd given the boy a ride in his swanky car once and got Mr Hunter to return his dead mum's silver picture frame to her family. Thinking the exciting news about Joe's dad might make the lieutenant stay a few more minutes, Alfie blurted, 'Bet you didn't know that old man Hunter ain't dead after all?'

Lucas had been about to step outside but abruptly pushed the door to. He looked down at the boy and frowned. 'Are you sure about that? Hunter lived with your aunt Sybil, didn't he?' He glanced at her estranged husband but it seemed he had nothing to add.

Alfie nodded. 'D'you remember when you made him give back the picture frame he was gonna pawn?'

Lucas gave a nod. He was shocked, and frustrated, by the news but managed not to show it. 'I'd heard he'd drowned.'

'So did we. But he didn't — I've seen him. He lives round the corner now,' Alfie added with a grimace. 'Fancy a cup of tea?' he brightly suggested. He wanted to find out how the lieutenant had got shot up over there. He liked listening to stories about the war. His future brother-in-law often came out with them but Alfie reckoned they were all hot air. Harry was a coward, so had probably hidden most of the time. 'Got some Bourbon biscuits . . . ' he added persuasively.

Lucas smiled. 'Thanks for the offer, but I've got to go and see a doctor about getting myself back into proper uniform.' He patted the boy's shoulder, and with a nod for Ed who'd been watching them, went out and quietly closed the door.

When the boys hared back up the stairs to play with the train set, Ed let himself out of the house.

'Hold up, sir.'

Lucas turned about by the corner of Playford Road.

'Heard you 'n' Alfie mention Herbert Hunter.' Ed chose his next words carefully. 'Could tell from your face you're no keener on that one than I am. He's a wrong 'un and not just because he shacked up with me wife and treated her bad. No . . . ' Ed shook his head. 'Herbie Hunter was bad news *long* before that.'

'I'm glad we're of the same opinion. I hope you intend keeping an eye on him if he's living nearby. He'll use Alfie to cause trouble if he can.'

'That's what I've come to tell yer. If you bump into Livvie when you get back over there, don't let her fret over what's occurring back home. Alfie's fine . . . we all are. I've got Hunter's number alright.' Ed tapped his temple.

Lucas held out his hand for Livvie's uncle to shake. 'I can see that. Pleased to meet you, Ed Wright.'

★   ★   ★

Herbert Hunter had been coming out of the corner shop, stuffing a sausage roll into his mouth, when he clocked that scene. A burst of rage almost made him choke. Two men he hated were looking very pally together and the common denominator there was Livvie Bone.

The tall dark handsome one was an individual Herbie would never forget. The fact that Lieutenant Black had one arm in a sling cheered him up, although he'd have preferred to see the

246

bastard crawling along on bloody stumps. The tough lieutenant wouldn't be giving anybody a battering and leaving them to drown in *that* state, Herbie told himself happily. Now that Ed Wright had disappeared back where he didn't belong — Joe's house! — Herbie reckoned he'd go and say hello to Lieutenant bloody Black. Gobbling up the pastry, he quickly swallowed it then set off, brushing away crumbs.

'Remember me, do yer?' he asked, coming up behind Lucas with the intention of scaring him witless. It'd worked with Sybil; she'd dropped dead, giving Herbie almost as much of a shock in his turn as he'd given her.

'Yeah . . . I remember you,' Lucas drawled. It'd been in his mind that he might bump into the creep; he'd recognised those tobacco tones even before turning to look down at Herbie from his superior height. 'Seems I didn't do a good enough job on you. Never mind, there's always next time.'

'I was thinking the same thing about you.' Herbie felt in his pocket for his knife. He still carried one with him wherever he went. But for the fact that it was broad daylight, he would have used it too. He was annoyed that slinking up on Black hadn't had more of an impact. Somebody — probably Ed Wright — must've already broken the news that Herbie Hunter had ducked the Grim Reaper's scythe. 'So what brings you here? Slumming it, are yer?' he taunted. 'If you're sniffing around after that tart who got her hooks into me son, you're wasting yer time. She's gone back nursing overseas.'

247

'Fuck off.' Lucas wasn't rising to the bait, or wasting any more time talking to this weasel. He was going straight away to see his doctor. He wanted to be signed on for active service and to return to France and Olivia. As he strode on he thanked the Lord that she'd had the foresight to put a sensible adult in charge of her house now Hunter was back hanging around. Ed Wright appeared to be a decent fellow. It seemed great changes had taken place in Olivia's family while he'd been fighting in Flanders. Just as they had in Lucas's.

His new sister-in-law hadn't told him about Olivia's visit to Belgravia, his brother had — in the usual coarse, provocative manner that always put Lucas's teeth on edge. But he made allowances for Henry from familial duty. It wasn't his fault he'd been born afflicted with the mental illness that ran down his mother's line. Lucas couldn't help but dislike his brother though. From when they were small boys Henry had made it clear that he resented the cuckoo in the family nest and intended to eject it. Their father had always favoured his able-bodied bastard over his legitimate son and that had infuriated his wife. Between them Lucas's stepmother and half-brother had tried all sorts of tricks to discredit him in his father's eyes. Often their ploys had worked and he'd been unjustly punished for misdeeds he hadn't committed; in the end he'd decided he might as well immerse himself in the vices he'd been accused of wallowing in.

Drinking, gambling and womanising had been

a way of life for him from his teens on. Despite that, he'd managed to graduate from university and keep alive his father's faith in him until the end. If he could turn back the clock, he'd thank his father for being so wise in the way he'd handled his Prodigal Son. Black Senior had been determined to make Lucas worthy of taking over the family fortune so he'd cut his heir's allowance and made him find gainful employment. Through his father's initiative rather than his own, Lucas had been brought into contact with the working class. He'd met Livvie Bone, and felt a contentment in her company he'd never before experienced. He found himself at ease with her and her slum-dwelling friends. If he'd been born a generation or two earlier he might've been in their midst, selling pegs and lucky heather, door to door, with his beautiful black-eyed Romany mother. He was no longer upset at the thought of his own lowly roots . . . the idea made him smile.

As for Caroline, there wasn't really any excuse for the way she'd behaved. It was his fault she felt scorned, but it wasn't his fault that she'd married a man she didn't love simply to spite Lucas and to gain a foothold in his affluent family. He had to own up to his own culpability in allowing them to remain lovers for too long. But he'd never promised her anything and she'd always known she wasn't his only girlfriend. Lucas knew her marriage to Henry was a sham and doubted it would last long. He suspected Caroline had aborted rather than miscarried the child she was carrying . . . if indeed there had been a child in the first place. At no time had she appeared to be pregnant.

Whatever the truth about Olivia's visit to his brother and sister-in-law that day, he'd only believe her version of it. She was honest and sincere. His remaining family members were neither.

Herbie watched the lieutenant disappearing into the distance, envying him his strong, lithe pace. Even from the back you could see this man was somebody to be reckoned with. But he was wounded, at a disadvantage, and Herbie wanted to capitalise on that while he could. Black had almost succeeded in killing him and Herbie wanted revenge. After that, with any luck, Fritz would finish the lieutenant off.

He trotted up behind Lucas, puffing as he reached his quarry's side. 'Me son was too good fer the likes of that little gold digger, so you're welcome to her, mate. She'll clean you out. Reckon you've got a few bob too, ain't yer?'

Lucas simply looked bored while shaking a cigarette out of a packet, one-handed. He drew it free with his lips.

'Want me to light it for yer now you're down to one arm?' Craftily Herbie snaked out his hand and fastened it on the lieutenant's injured bicep, squeezing beneath the sling with all his might.

Lucas had been expecting something as soon as he caught sight of a shadow moving up on him out of the corner of one eye. He swung up his right fist and punched Herbie in the side of the head, sending himself off balance in the process. He staggered back against the wall, instinctively bouncing off again with his foot raised. Slowly, he replaced it on the pavement. In France, you'd kick and stamp on the enemy when they went down. You'd do anything to save your own skin even when their eyes pleaded with you for mercy. But he wasn't in France, he reminded himself, and the man sprawling at his feet wasn't worthy of the title 'enemy'. Straightening his jacket, Lucas proceeded up the road, flexing his red right hand. He was grimacing from the pain in his shoulder, cursing the little rat to hell because already he could feel a trickle of warm blood beneath his armpit.

'Could see that coming a mile off,' Matilda said with a smirk. She'd been watching the fracas from across the street but crossed over to speak to Herbie, now laboriously dragging himself to his knees. 'Punching way too far above yer weight there. Lieutenant's well-liked round here. Hero he is, to Jack and McGoogan and all the others he brought back from enemy lines. You'd better watch yerself now or you'll have every one of 'em down on you like a ton o' bricks.'

'Piss off, you nosy old cow.' Herbie was incensed to have been knocked down by a one-armed man in front of a woman. Especially this woman.

'You should've stayed under yer stone, Herbie.' Matilda wagged her finger at him. 'You're not wanted round here.'

'I ain't going nowhere, not with my son's house just round the corner and some other man living in it.' Immediately Herbie regretted letting that slip and stalked off, looking furtively to and

251

fro in the hope nobody else had seen him laid out on the cobbles by a cripple.

'It ain't Joe's house no more,' Matilda bawled after him.

She watched him go, ruminating on things. She was fond of Olivia and knew Hunter was trouble for the girl and her family. She set off to warn Ed Wright. She knew he loathed Herbie as much as she did. Ed had more reason though. Ed and Sybil might have broken up but he still wouldn't have wanted his wife beaten for asking Hunter to chip in his rent money. Things were coming to a head between the two men. Herbie Hunter was finding it impossible to conceal the fact that he was livid Ed Wright was getting to do what Herbie himself longed for: to call Joe's old house home.

★ ★ ★

'What *have* you done to yourself?' Olivia examined her friend's shaggy short locks from different angles. 'Oh, why did you cut off all your lovely chestnut hair, Rose?'

'Had to, Livvie. Too much livestock nesting in it.'

Over the hand she'd clapped to her mouth, Olivia's eyes were bright with scandalised amusement. 'Oh, no! You weren't lousy?'

'Oh, yes, I was! Never seen so many of the little perishers. Me 'n' the other girls were itching like mad so . . . vanity be damned. We decided to grin and bear it and shear one another like sheep.' She shrugged, running her fingers through her cropped hair. 'It looks better now than it did. It'll grow back. We get the crawlies off the poor buggers we carry in the van. If they're well enough to sit up, they cram next to us in the front so we can wedge more stretcher cases in the back. I'll have three sitters and six stretchers in on a bad night. They come straight from the field dressing stations or trenches and are all alive, alive-o.'

Olivia was no stranger to the nit comb. All the nurses had one. So far she'd not suffered an infestation herself, but a handful of ward maids had come out in sympathy with some tunnellers who'd been brought in. The unlucky fellows had dodged the Hun but been injured in a cave-in, suffering broken bones and bad concussion. Every one of them had arrived looking like Robinson Crusoe, stick-thin with ragged clothing and bushy beard.

Rose had turned up at St Omer a short while ago and a delighted Olivia had immediately taken her to her dormitory so they could brew a pot of tea and have a good natter.

Spontaneously, Olivia turned around from the teapot she was stirring to give her friend a hug. Rose returned it with equal affection, joking, 'What's a few nits between friends?'

'Eek!' Olivia let her go, but she was grinning. What *were* a few nits between friends? She'd rather not catch them but the idea of not giving Rose a hug was worse.

It was Olivia's first afternoon off since she'd arrived back in France, three long weeks ago. The battles along the Somme had finally petered out. They'd had a lull; no new admissions for a few days now. Slowly things were getting back to normal at the hospital: rotas were reinstated and mealtimes observed. But once both sides had licked their wounds what then? Nobody was under any illusion that the guns would be quiet for long. And still the awful weather persisted.

A knock on the door heralded Matron's arrival. 'I thought I saw you arrive, Miss Drew.' She clasped her hands behind her back. 'I wanted to ask you a favour actually.'

Olivia and Rose exchanged surprised glances.

'Go on then,' Rose invited in her blunt way.

'We need some shopping brought back. We're dreadfully short of potatoes and the nice farmer in the next village has said we can have some at a very good price.'

'And you want me to dig 'em up?' Rose suggested with a chuckle. 'I drive an ambulance, not a tractor . . . though I could drive a tractor if I wanted,' she boasted airily.

'No, my dear, I want you to collect them for us. All our vehicles are out and it'd be a great help if you'd get them here, so Cook can start on the evening meal.' Matron rolled her eyes. 'He is a good chap but a bit of an old nag. He's threatening us all with macaroni cheese again if we don't get him his spuds.'

' 'Course I'll fetch 'em. Can't stand macaroni myself.' Rose turned to Olivia. 'Or I could finish me tea while Livvie runs the errand,' she teased.

Matron gawped at Olivia. 'You can drive?'

'I can . . . not as well as Rose though.'

'But why have you never said?' Matron wailed.

'There've been times I've needed a driver and there's been nobody available to take out the spare car.'

'You never asked,' Olivia said, sounding apologetic. 'Anyway I'm a bit rusty 'cos I've not had a practice in months.'

'Like riding a bike though,' Rose said with a twinkling smile. 'You never forget, do you, Livvie?'

'As I've got the afternoon off, we'll both go, if that's alright?' Olivia said. 'And we'll get as many spuds as we can from our *fermier amical*.'

'Get him to fill the back of me van right up if you like,' Rose said. 'It's clean. I scrubbed it out just this morning.' She pulled a face to indicate it had been no pleasant task. But Rose, even at her most brazen, wouldn't say what she'd found, or how every time she climbed aboard with a scrubbing brush and bucket, the stench of fleshy debris made her retch. She couldn't joke about that. Although some of them back at the base did because it was the only way to cope with loading up night after night with human wreckage.

'I'll whizz off and get you some petty cash,' Matron said with a beaming smile. 'And I'll let Cook know you're on your way so he can get his peeler out and his pots on the boil.'

As Matron walked away Olivia realised this was the first time she had heard her hum in a long while.

'If you drive back, Rose, I'll drive there,' Olivia said. 'By the way, I've got some news. I'm getting transferred in a week.'

Rose looked alarmed. 'Not off to the Eastern Front, are you?'

Olivia shook her head. 'Coming down the line, closer to you. A clearing station.'

Rose frowned. 'Are you sure about that, Livvie? Those places ain't a pretty sight.'

'Neither's what's gone on here,' Olivia returned. 'It's been dreadful since the big push began, even this far back from the line.'

'Yeah . . . 's'pect it's been just as bad.' Rose took the tea her friend was holding out to her. She loved Olivia too much to tell her different.

# 18

Olivia had taken the wheel on the outward journey to the farm. It would be good practice for her to do all of the driving today, Rose had said. They'd been motoring for about twenty minutes and so far had sailed along; the only hiccough had been when encountering a few goats that had straggled onto the road. Two local lads, aged about ten, had supposedly been in charge of them and seemed incapable of herding the stubborn things onto the verge.

The smallholding was a good seven kilometres from the hospital but its low whitewashed cluster of buildings was already within sight on the horizon.

'You should join us in the ambulance service. You're a better driver than a couple of girls in our team.' Rose was impressed by Olivia's skill, but that apart she'd adore it if they could see each other more often. 'The jitters get to 'em. Enid follows too close in a convoy and ends up colliding with the van in front. Margie can't see in the dark and last week ended up in a ditch. Luckily that was before she'd loaded up or she'd have finished the poor buggers off.'

'D'you reckon I'd get taken on?' Olivia asked.

'Never a day goes by but somebody throws in the towel. We're so short of personnel they'd take on a monkey if his feet could reach the pedals.'

'Thanks very much!' Olivia said with a

chuckle. Being with Rose always bucked her up, even if the weather was miserable and she'd learned just yesterday that her request for a fortnight's Christmas leave had been turned down. She had taken it philosophically; she'd been given more than her fair share of time off already.

But it meant she'd miss Maggie's wedding and must write and break the news. It was a bitter-sweet pain, knowing that she'd not be there to see the first of her sisters married. Yet she was glad to be spared seeing Maggie tie herself to a man like Harry Wicks. She would've felt awkward, smiling and saying things she didn't really mean. But she hoped to be back in England in time to see the new arrival in the spring.

It would be their first Christmas apart. The girls would enjoy themselves with their friends and workmates, but Alfie was a different matter. He *would* miss Olivia. She'd send a letter to her uncle Ed, asking him to make Christmas a nice time for her brother. At least they'd have their lovely theatre outing to reminisce about when she saw them all next year.

Her mind was jolted back to the present as the van sploshed though a deep puddle. The smallholding was up a slight incline and set a good way back from the road. She hoped she'd manage to negotiate the narrow track and wouldn't slither backwards on the slippery mud. She had Rose to get her out of trouble if need be, she reminded herself.

'Almost there.' Rose was pointing to a turning on the right.

'When we eventually get back home for good, d'you fancy coming to see *Chu Chin Chow* with me? If it's still showing, that is,' Olivia tacked on, finely balancing the pressure between the clutch and accelerator pedals. The tyres spun then slowly started to roll uphill. 'A group of us went to see it on my last leave,' Olivia resumed. 'We had a smashing time.' She turned to Rose with a grin. 'I'd love to go again. Coming?'

'Not 'arf,' Rose trumpeted.

Olivia pulled onto the churned up patch of mud and shingle that served as the driveway. A pig was snuffling around in the muck but it trotted off, squealing, when they inched past.

About fifty yards away a woman was pegging out washing, two small girls playing chase around her legs. She waved and called out in French for her husband. Beyond her, Olivia could see some labourers scything hedges.

'Leave the engine running,' Rose instructed as they opened the van doors to get out. 'She can be a temperamental so and so.' She patted the dashboard. 'But not a bad old stick.'

'*Bonjour!*' Monsieur Thierry called out then jogged over to join them. 'I have them ready for you,' he said in accented English, wagging a finger at a stack of hessian sacks by the barn.

'Good-o,' Rose said, jumping down. 'I'll open the back doors.'

Olivia yanked on the handbrake then got down too.

'What's up with him?' she asked. She'd glimpsed a fellow sitting facing away from them inside the shadowy barn. He had one arm raised above his head as though to stop it bleeding.

'Oh, Jacques was hurt while cutting the hedges. Clumsy fool. *Là-bas*.' The farmer jerked his bristly chin at the workers in the distance. 'Jacques stopped *le vieux* falling into the ditch, and the sickle . . . ' He smacked his own forearm with the side of his hand then gave a Gallic shrug.

'I can have a look at his wound while I'm here, if you like?'

'Ah, *bien . . . merci*.' Monsieur Thierry nodded his agreement. 'Jacques — *ici*,' he called the labourer to join them.

'There are some bandages in the van if you need them . . . ' Rose started to say.

The injured man suddenly leaped to his feet and disappeared from sight.

'Charming!' Rose snorted. 'Patch yourself up then, mate.'

Olivia had briefly glimpsed his profile as he'd half-turned towards them. The barn door was barely ajar, the interior dim, yet he'd seemed familiar somehow. Very few French civilians were treated at St Omer, other than as emergencies. But he could have been in the French military and been brought in. He'd looked fit enough for active service and about the right age to be fighting for the Allies . . .

'Is Jacques home on leave?' She knew soldiers sometimes helped out in a family business when they were home.

'Non . . . non.' The farmer tapped his head. '*Imbécile*.' He made a pitying sound at the back of his throat. 'You have the money for the spuds?' He grinned, pleased to have remembered the English Tommies' word for potatoes.

Olivia couldn't answer. Her tongue had stopped functioning, it felt so dry. The farmer's description of Jacques had helped her remember where she'd seen that thin face before. It *had* been in a hospital bed, and he had been a patient. But then the Hauptmann's hair had been longer and obviously fair. Now it was closely cropped and the colour appeared darker. But what was really convincing her she was right was his past trick of pretending to be a half-wit so as to dupe people. Still she hesitated to voice her fears. 'Jacques is French . . . he *speaks* French?' she interrogated the farmer.

'He can speak . . . *bien sûr.*' The farmer seemed confused. 'He is not dumb but *stupide.*' He tapped his own temple. 'Jacques is good strong worker. No trouble from him . . . sleeps in barn.' He pointed up to the hayloft.

'Has he worked for you for a long while? Years?' She longed to hear that he had.

'*Non!*' The farmer flapped his hands, becoming impatient with her questions.

'What's up, Livvie? You look like you've seen a ghost.' Rose shook her friend's arm.

'That labourer . . . Jacques . . . he looks like the escaped prisoner. Karl Schmidt. If it is him, he's a German.'

The farmer could understand enough of the girls' conversation to snort: '*Non! Pas possible!* He is French . . . how you say? . . . tramp. I have speak to him in French.'

'Speaks English, too, I'll bet,' Olivia said

261

pithily. Although she'd never heard him utter a single word of it. But his pal, Fischer, had been fluent in English and she reckoned Schmidt had been as well. He'd listened to, and understood, everything that had gone on around him during his stay at St Omer while craftily pretending otherwise. She was slowly conquering her shock, but the realisation that they might all be in dreadful danger was making her skin crawl. She believed what the farmer had said. He wasn't a collaborator; he had no idea he might have a German escapee in his barn. Or had the suspect fled while they'd been talking?

He had recognised her too! That thought hit her like a punch in the guts. It was Schmidt. He'd bolted so she couldn't get a good look at him and raise the alarm. 'Where's he gone?' She raced towards the barn and flung wide the half-open door.

Monsieur Thierry hurried after her, muttering soothingly, 'Du calme, s'il vous plaît, ma'mselle.'

Olivia hesitated on the threshold, uncertain whether to enter. The barn appeared to be empty and she guessed he wouldn't hang around. 'You must fetch the gendarmes, Monsieur,' she croaked, turning to face Thierry. 'We should go back quickly and tell Matron. She'll know what to do.'

'What? You sure about this, Livvie?' Rose sounded doubtful. 'We taking the spuds with us then?' She had scooted after Olivia and further into the shadowy barn. Her eyes had still not adjusted to the dark when she collapsed to the floor with a soft grunt.

262

Olivia spun around to see Schmidt lurking behind the planked door, holding a shotgun.

Beside her the farmer gasped in disbelief then started crossing himself. '*Donnez-moi le fusil!*' He beckoned as though believing Jacques might have had a brainstorm but would still obligingly hand over the firearm.

'Come here, Fräulein.' Schmidt beckoned Olivia with the barrel of the gun then levelled it on his employer. The farmer tottered back, clutching at his chest as though he might swoon now he understood the danger they were in.

'I *knew* I was right!' Olivia took a few paces forward, incensed at what the German had done to Rose. She dropped to her knees, feeling immediately for her friend's pulse. There was a large contusion on Rose's forehead where the gun butt had struck it.

'Get up! She's fine. You too will be fine if you do as you're told. Take off your belt,' Schmidt addressed the wobbly-legged farmer in French. '*Fermez la bouche!*' he snarled as the man appeared about to succumb to hysterics. When the belt was off Schmidt put the gun down on the straw at his feet. Monsieur Thierry was attempting to keep his trousers up and was mortified when his hands were tied and the garment slid to his knees. Schmidt lashed him to a sturdy timber in the barn so that he was immobilised.

'Stay still!' he snapped at Olivia as her eyes darted again to the weapon.

She was desperately trying to decide if she had the time to pounce on it and fire. She'd never

263

before handled a gun but knew she would pull the trigger if pushed to it.

'I can reach that before you,' Schmidt purred. 'It will be your fault if you all three perish, Sister Bone. And that would be bad for a Poppy Angel's conscience,' he mocked the Tommies' term for the hospital sisters.

Olivia stood shaking from head to toe while he pulled a handkerchief from the farmer's pocket and gagged him with it.

Then Schmidt grabbed the shotgun. 'Now, Fräulein, you come with me.'

'What?' Olivia whispered.

'The ambulance . . . you can drive, I saw you. It will arouse less suspicion if a nurse is seen at the wheel rather than a man with no uniform. Besides,' he raised his cut arm, dripping blood onto the straw, 'you can look at this for me. And then I have another job for you.' He gave her a hard smile. 'I remember how good a nurse you are.'

'And I remember how good a conman you are, Hauptmann Schmidt.'

'All is fair in love and war, as you say.' He smiled thinly. 'I'm flattered you remember me.' He gripped her arm and pushed her in front of him out of the barn, the shotgun pointing innocently at the ground.

The woman had finished doing her washing and was looking over, no doubt wondering where everybody had disappeared to. She seemed about to come to investigate but her daughters were clinging to her skirts.

'Sweet little children . . . don't want to hurt

264

them,' Schmidt muttered in Olivia's ear. 'I'll sit beside you. Don't forget, you'll all suffer if you try any tricks.'

'Drive where?' she mumbled through parched lips.

'You don't need to know . . . just go.'

Possible tactics were filling her head. She could jump into the vehicle and try to run him over. Or stamp on the accelerator and speed off on her own, to raise the alarm. But she couldn't leave Rose, defenceless and at his mercy. He might murder them all in revenge. Olivia scrambled into the ambulance, her mind mired in agonising indecision. And then it was too late to act in any case. He'd leaped in beside her.

'Go.'

She made a bungled attempt to turn the vehicle in a circle.

'Speed up!' he snarled when she crawled off towards the lane.

'Ground's boggy,' she retorted, giving him a hate-filled look. 'I'm a novice driver. You should have let my friend drive, she's an expert. You shouldn't have hurt her. That was a big mistake.'

'Maybe she is the better driver, but you're prettier. Besides, I told you, I have a job for you.'

'What job?' Olivia demanded. She sensed he wasn't just talking about patching up his arm. From what she'd seen of that, the bleeding was making the cut look worse than it actually was.

'We can talk about it later. Get going.'

She hoped if she left slowly it might give the farmer a chance to get free, rally his workers and come to the rescue. Unfortunately, there wasn't time for all of that, and besides the man didn't look like a hero. He would be more concerned with protecting his wife and children. And who could blame him?

From the corner of her eye Olivia had seen, not Monsieur Thierry but Rose, staggering out of the barn, holding a hand to her bleeding head. Olivia slowed down as her friend made a stumbling run for the van. 'The pig . . . ' she explained as the Hauptmann spat something threatening beneath his breath. 'Not you . . . that one.' She jerked her head at the animal that was trotting about in front of the van. 'Don't want to run the bloody thing over.'

She heard the back door of the ambulance click and guessed that Rose had attempted to climb inside.

Schmidt had heard it too and was momentarily distracted. Olivia braked hard and made a grab for the gun as he thumped one hand on the dashboard to steady himself. But he beat her to it and fastened a punishing hand about her throat then brought up the gun with the other. She had no doubt that he'd pull the trigger if she pushed him to it.

'You really want them all to die, Sister Bone?' he enquired politely. A moment later he'd jumped out and closed the back doors of the ambulance, gesturing Rose away with the shotgun.

Olivia's eyes met those of the farmer's wife. The poor woman looked terrified. She'd discovered her husband tied up in the barn and had freed him. But she was gripping his arm to prevent him from getting further involved while sheltering her two children in her skirts.

'You alright, Rose?' Olivia called out of the ambulance window as her friend sank to her haunches, looking defeated.

Olivia received a nod but she could see that Rose was weeping and that the gash on her head was bleeding down her face. Olivia felt like crying too. But she wouldn't let Schmidt think he'd cowed her. She'd washed him, changed his dressings, fetched him cups of water to drink. She knew he'd kill her, though, if he had to. Just as she'd do whatever she had to in order to escape. But they'd a relationship of sorts. That's why he'd not hit her . . . yet. Rose and Olivia exchanged a final bleak look before losing sight of one another as Olivia drove away.

'There was no need to strike a woman,' she said contemptuously. 'You had a gun to threaten us with after all.'

'I believed her to be a young man, with her short hair and trousers. I didn't want him trying to impress you with heroics.' Schmidt shrugged, darting glances to and fro at the surrounding countryside. Olivia knew he was checking for possible dangers but wasn't distracted enough for her to risk lunging for the gun again.

'You might as well take the vehicle and let me go,' she reasoned desperately. 'You'll *really* be in for it once it's known you've kidnapped an Englishwoman. If you let me go, I'll give you time to get away. I won't report this for an hour or so.'

The Hauptmann threw back his head and

barked a laugh. 'My dear Sister Bone, I am already *in for it* with your people. I'll be shot whatever I do to you.'

His eyes slid downwards from her face and Olivia felt a frisson of alarm shudder through her. Again she wondered what the job was that he had in mind for her. If he intended trying to force himself on her, she'd go down fighting. 'You didn't get very far. It's been months.' She quickly resumed their conversation, to distract him from looking her over. 'I'm surprised the Red Caps didn't catch up with you.'

'You know the best way for a spy to hide, Fräulein? It's not to hide. Your Red Caps didn't think I'd be in plain sight any more than you did. It wasn't my intention to get far. I could have reached home had I wanted to. But the war is not yet won.'

'You're a German spy?' Olivia demanded. He had a very faint accent, but it wasn't German; it reminded her of the Kilts she'd nursed at St Omer.

'What difference does it make . . . soldier, spy? We're on different sides. That's all.'

'We're both human beings. I've helped you . . . treated you with respect. Will you treat me equally well, Hauptmann Schmidt?'

'I have been lenient to you . . . and to your lover. I let him live when I could easily have killed him.'

Olivia turned sideways to gawp at him while driving along. Suddenly she recalled the night of Schmidt's escape. It had been the last time she'd seen Lucas. They'd been embracing when they'd heard a noise. Lucas had drawn his pistol, immediately suspicious. She'd thought him just on edge from the battlefield. When the padre had emerged from the church tent they'd relaxed ... laughed about it. But it hadn't been the clergyman spying on them after all. Lucas had sensed an enemy's presence.

'Were you watching us?' She felt furious rather than embarrassed to think he'd acted as a Peeping Tom.

'Not for long. I thought him lucky to be loved by you. So, will you thank me for saving your lieutenant? I wanted his revolver. I could have overpowered him and shot him with it. I remember the guns had started up in the distance. Nobody would have heard the commotion or come to your rescue.' Schmidt smiled thinly. 'But I'm not without a heart. He was proposing to you; it would have been churlish to spoil the moment.'

'You'd never have got the better of Lucas,' Olivia said staunchly. 'But I do thank you for leaving us be that night and going quietly. In return, will you thank me and my colleagues for saving your life?' she demanded. 'We could have left you to starve and your leg to rot and poison you with gangrene.' She glanced at his injured limb beneath its rough twill covering. His limp had been barely noticeable in the barn and certainly hadn't slowed him down. Bitterly, she realised they'd done too good a job on him. The head wound he'd sustained had healed well and was now just a whitish scar close to his spiky hairline.

'Yes, I thank you. Now . . . no more questions. Just drive,' he ordered tersely.

'Where to?' she snapped. 'I'm not a bloody mind reader.'

They were approaching the bottom of the muddy farm track, and she slowed at the crossroads.

'Away from St Omer. I'll tell you which lanes to take. If anybody stops us, you say I'm a shell-shock patient. Don't forget, I can use this gun on you before they suspect anything. So be convincing, my Poppy Angel.'

'You act the *dummkopf* a bit too well,' Olivia said sarcastically. 'Not all acting, I reckon.' She muttered the last bit beneath her breath. She'd not spoken quietly enough and saw she'd amused him when his lips twitched. With a grimace, she turned the wheel in the direction he'd said.

Half an hour later the dusk was drawing in fast and none of the vehicles they'd passed on the road had taken the blindest bit of notice of Olivia and the man beside her. She'd hoped the fierce glare she'd given to those few oncoming drivers might have alerted them, but they'd blithely sailed past with a toot or a wave. They were heading now into isolated countryside and twilight was almost upon them. She squinted at the dashboard. Rose had taught her enough about the instruments to know they were nearly out of fuel. She told Schmidt so and he leaned over to take a look as though he didn't believe her.

'We left the engine running when we got to the farm. We ought to have been loaded up with spuds and back at St Omer by now. They'll send out a search party for me.' Olivia looked at a dark forest looming ahead on the horizon. He could kill her and dump her in there and she wouldn't be found for months, if ever. Wild animals might devour her . . . 'We can't go much further in this,' she burst out. 'Why don't you let me go now? By the time I'm found you'll be miles away.' She hadn't managed to conceal her fright, she realised, seeing his smirk.

'Left here,' was all Schmidt said in reply.

He seemed to know where he was going. As she entered a tunnel of overhanging trees, bare branches clipped the windows of the ambulance to either side. He gestured her to continue as she slowed to a snail's pace along the narrow rutted track. Then up ahead she saw a faint pinprick of light.

'Stop here. I told you I have a job for you and you will do it. A comrade has been badly wounded. You are a nurse and will help him.'

Olivia stared at her captor. She hadn't been expecting this. 'How badly wounded?'

'He's been shot. The bullet must be removed before it poisons him.'

'That's a doctor's job. You should take him to a hospital. My people treated you . . . they'll see to him.'

'Ah, but he cannot go to an Allied hospital, Sister Bone, any more than I could return to one for treatment. Our faces are known now. No kindly Poppy Angels for us next time. A firing squad instead.' He looked at her with blazing eyes.

Olivia felt a wave of fear then. She and her colleagues had treated Schmidt well but that obviously counted for nothing with him. They were enemies, he couldn't have made that plainer. She jammed her foot on the brake, making the vehicle jump like a kangaroo. 'Like I said, I'm a learner,' she said defiantly.

'So I see, Fräulein.' Schmidt replied dryly. 'Stay exactly where you are. I shall soon be back to take you to my friend. Don't be foolish enough to try and escape or I will tie you up and throw you in the back.'

Olivia heard a whistle given as a signal then silence for a while before a mixture of French and German was being spoken, too rapidly for her to understand any of it. She peered into the ambulance's side mirror to find out how many of them there were. But it was too dark for her to glimpse more than a few shadowy figures and the voices were kept low and indistinct. Depressingly, she realised Schmidt had met up with more of his own kind and she was now in the midst of a gang of French collaborators and German spies. Schmidt might decide to be lenient to her, for old times' sake, but his pals wouldn't give a hoot what happened to her if they thought she might endanger their safety.

She squinted into the mirror again, to try and see which one of them was wounded. She could just make out the silhouette of a fellow with a drooping head. He was being supported by another man. She surreptitiously wound down the driver's window to try and make sense of what was being said. She'd learned a few words of French and German. She poked her head outside and heard in amongst the fast-flowing dialogue the hissed words '*schiessen*' and '*schwester*'. Olivia squeezed shut her eyes and tried to steady her racing heart. They'd been talking about shooting her, no doubt after she'd served her purpose.

She turned the handle and leaned against the door, dismay furrowing her brow as it emitted a squeak. She sat back in her seat, trying to appear innocent, and waited, barely breathing. But Schmidt didn't come. The men's conversation continued, growing louder and more guttural, and she realised an argument was taking place. She guessed they were rowing over her. Perhaps Schmidt had stuck up for her and wanted to let her live. But she couldn't stick around and take that chance. She shouldered the door and it opened quietly this time. Olivia slid out of her seat and landed soundlessly. Gathering her skirts away from her boots, she walked fast then broke into a run, the breath she dragged in tearing at her lungs. She knew she'd make a noise sooner or later and she did, stepping on a twig that snapped with a crack like gunshot. She heard a shout and knew they were onto her. Then she heard Schmidt bark her name in a threatening tone.

She bolted, dodging bushes and trees and leaping over undergrowth until she was defeated by a thicket of brambles that brought her crashing to her knees. She felt as though her chest were about to burst and knew she couldn't have gone much further. On hands and knees, she scrambled behind the bole of a tree. She covered her head with her arms, making a small tight ball of herself. But her ears were straining to hear them coming for her, through the deafening thud of blood in her ears.

No hands grabbed her. Slowly her breathing settled. Every rustle in the undergrowth made her stiffen but still nobody came. Woodland creatures pattered past. Carefully she drew one then the other of her feet beneath her hem, wondering if those long-tailed scurriers were rats.

She prayed Schmidt and his accomplices had given up bothering with her. She was no immediate threat to them; no search party would come for her yet. And it was unlikely she'd have been able to save their comrade if his wound were badly infected. They might have realised that dragging her along with them as they tried to escape could be a hindrance, not a help. She peeped around the tree. There was no glimmer of light visible. She knew it would be best to wait for dawn before looking for a way out of the forest. She'd lost her bearings and might stumble around in a circle in the blackness, taking herself straight back into danger.

A cramp was niggling in her calf and she tried to ease her foot forward. It encountered a fallen stump. Her boot travelled on, investigating. Beneath the log was a hollow . . . her heel fell a long way down, into a soft cushion of rotting leaves that crackled softly as she disturbed them. Slowly she shuffled forward on her bottom, slithering into the woody chamber. She thanked the Lord she'd put on her big coat over her uniform before leaving the hospital. Even with its protection she felt damp and frozen. She wrapped it about her, sinking her chin onto her knees. Then she tried to rest.

# 19

'I'm so sorry, Lieutenant. Sister Bone isn't here,' Matron said hoarsely. 'You haven't heard the news then?'

'What news?' Lucas felt a weight like a stone settle in his belly. Something here wasn't right. This woman sounded distressed and several nurses had stared at him in an odd way as he'd arrived. 'What news?' he demanded. 'I've just disembarked at Boulogne. I've been on convalescent leave.'

'An escaped prisoner-of-war is on the loose, and Sister Bone and another young woman were unlucky enough to be involved in . . .'

'I heard a rumour about that,' Lucas interrupted. 'Surely the incident was some while ago though?'

'The initial incident . . .' Matron began to say.

'I didn't know for certain that Olivia had been caught up in it. I heard from her family she'd had a fall but was fine and had returned to duty.' Lucas abruptly stopped talking. He could see that there was something else. Something awful he'd yet to find out. Matron looked ashen-faced and guilty as hell.

'It's all my fault,' she croaked. 'I asked them to run an errand. Had I known what I was sending them into . . .'

'What's your fault? Where did you send them?' Lucas blasted at her as panic took over. He bit his tongue to prevent himself from swearing at the woman. He wished she'd hurry up and spit out what she knew.

'We needed potatoes so I sent Olivia and her driver friend Rose Drew to Ferme Thierry. They set off in the ambulance and . . . '

'Did they have an accident?' Lucas stopped prowling and stared at her.

'They reached the farm safely. The escapee was there, masquerading as a labourer. He recognised Olivia from his time here at the hospital when she'd tended him. She recognised him too . . . ' Matron's voice tailed off into a sob. 'He attacked Rose and then . . . '

Lucas put one hand over his face. For a full minute he stayed silent. Then he asked: 'Is she dead? Did he kill Olivia?'

'I don't know. He made her drive him off in the ambulance. He-He kidnapped her,' Matron quavered.

'*Kidnapped her?*' Lucas parroted in disbelief. 'How long ago?' He was amazed to hear that he sounded to be in control of himself. He felt as though somebody had ripped a hole in his chest.

'Two days,' Matron said.

'What's being done? Are the Red Caps out searching for her? What's happened since?' Lucas rattled off his questions.

'Rose was gun-butted by the monster. But she's on the mend. The ambulance hasn't been recovered yet. The farmer was taken into custody but I believe he was released. Rose backed up his story. He didn't appear to be a collaborator. He was distraught, poor fellow, as was his wife.'

'What else? What about Olivia?' Lucas demanded. He had a feeling he was being given the run around. This woman was holding something back. He took a step closer to her. 'What's being done to find her? Or have they found her?' His next words were barely audible. 'Has a body been discovered?' He started prowling again. He knew if he stayed in one place he'd either put his fist through the wall of the hut, or start shaking this woman to make her tell him everything.

'She's not been found,' Matron whispered. 'Relying on the French to organise anything is hopeless. If it had been one of their own countrywomen it might have been different. An Allied search party is supposed to be arriving from Calais in a day or two.' She paused, twisting her fingers in her agitation.

'What else?' Lucas growled at her. 'There's something more, isn't there?'

'A Brigadier Saville came straight away to see me . . . just hours after I'd reported it.' Matron's attitude had changed from one of caginess to outright alarm. 'He told me I must keep our conversation top secret.' She pursed her lips. 'But damn him! I'm going to tell you it all because I know how you feel about Olivia. You've a right to know.

'The dratted pipsqueak was in a tizz. He was more concerned for the men's morale than he was for my nurse. The way the top brass see it, this incident must all be hushed up . . . 'dealt with delicately', was the expression he used.

They're worried they might have a mass exodus of nursing staff if word of this atrocity gets out. He said the business with Edith Cavell a couple of years ago affected everyone badly, especially the folk back home. They don't want something similar coming to a war reporter's attention and appearing in English newspapers at this crucial time.

'It's true we're struggling for staff since the big push went horribly wrong,' Matron carried on. 'But I found his attitude abominable . . . unforgivable . . . and I told him so!'

She was visibly shaking, flushed with fury at the memory of the encounter. She turned away to compose herself. She wouldn't reveal all that Saville had said about being unable to send infantry on a wild goose chase that was likely to be a lost cause. Soldiers were in short supply after recent battles, he'd said, and in his opinion, Sister Bone was probably already dead. But she didn't have the courage to tell that to the man who loved Olivia. Matron refused to believe it herself. Despite hating the brigadier's plain speaking, she understood that everybody was becoming desensitised to death. She was too. It was the only way to carry on.

Lucas said hoarsely, 'The German's a spy, isn't he?'

'I think so,' Matron agreed quietly, 'although I've not mentioned a word of my suspicions to a soul. I dared not tell the brigadier. And I would advise you to keep your ideas to yourself too. God knows, these are ruthless people.'

'Indeed,' Lucas muttered bitterly. 'I'd say

they're already onto Schmidt and don't want this incident upsetting the apple cart as they close in on his likely accomplices.'

Matron nodded, biting her lip to stop it from wobbling.

'Have you got any spare horses here?'

'I think so . . . or the dairy farmer has stables just down the road.' Matron frowned at him, coming forward with a gleam of anticipation in her eyes. 'Will you go and search for Olivia?'

'If anybody comes here looking for me, I came in as walking wounded. My injury needed treatment but I discharged myself just before they turned up.'

'Are you going AWOL?' Matron blinked at him.

'It's probably better you don't know what I'm doing.'

'Take off your jacket, lieutenant, and your shirt.'

He obliged, impatiently ripping off his clothing, allowing her to assess the deep hole at the top of his arm. She found a bit of gauze and dabbed the inflammation with ointment. 'There . . . no lies, you see. I recall examining you and thinking your wound needed more time to heal. As it does; you've come back too soon, that's the truth. Unbelievably brave chap that you are, you wanted to get back to the fray so you disappeared from my hospital. Nevertheless I dutifully made you a record chart.'

'If the brigadier or anybody else comes back, you've no idea of my whereabouts or my intentions.' Lucas dragged on his jacket over his unbuttoned shirt.

'Deaf, dumb and blind.' Matron gave a slight smile.

'Can you describe Schmidt to me?'

'Yes, of course.' Matron hastily obliged. 'He is a man of about your age, early- to mid-thirties. Fair hair and thin-faced. Wiry build and an inch or so shorter than you, I'd judge. He came here with a bad leg wound and a head injury. Shrapnel. He might still have a limp and a scar on his forehead. He spoke only a few words of German to the nurses. The cunning wretch was faking shell shock. It is hard for a doctor to disprove such mental affliction. Doctors don't have the time to make a detailed psychiatric assessment of prisoners-of-war.' She stuck up for her colleagues. 'Our boys must take priority.'

Lucas was about to say something scathing but swallowed it. Matron was right, however unpalatable a truth that was to him right now.

Gladys Bennett put out a quivering hand for him to shake then clung to his fingers. 'I put my trust in you to bring Olivia back.'

*So will Olivia*, Lucas said in his mind. She'd pin her hopes on him coming for her. And he would, or else die trying. He knew there was no point in returning without her when she meant more to him than life itself.

'Goodbye, lieutenant. Good luck and God bless,' Matron whispered, but he'd already gone from the room.

★ ★ ★

Olivia knew Schmidt was still out there. She'd watched his boots pass by quite close to her hiding place. They *were* his too because she'd noticed one drag slightly as he limped. But she knew she would have to emerge from her hidey hole soon or perish within it. She'd scrambled out a few times during the night, confident the dark provided sufficient cover. Her limbs were cramped and she knew she must keep them supple in case she had a chance to flee. But she was getting weaker and the effort to draw herself up and out into the open was growing more arduous. The gnawing ache in her belly drove her to search for dried berries and a puddle to lap at like an animal. Despite her constant hunger, she'd always save the berries she found by touch until morning. She'd open her scratched palms and squint at them in the daylight to see if they resembled blackberries. She knew she could accidentally poison herself in her desperation to eat.

She'd also needed to relieve herself. The idea that Schmidt might come upon her while she was squatting down had made her rush to tidy her dress.

She was furious that he hadn't just abandoned the area and saved his own skin. *Why* hadn't he when people were bound to be out searching for her? She needed to help any rescuers locate her before she was too weak to do so, but so far Schmidt seemed to be the only one looking for her; his able-bodied colleagues must have fled. At least that was a relief. He often called to her, promising he'd not harm her if she came out.

But she believed the only reason he'd stayed behind was to silence her.

'Sister Bone . . . ' His voice reached her now from some distance away. 'Come out . . . my friend is dying. He is in pain. You are a good nurse. Your conscience will trouble you if you do not help a mortally wounded man. I will not hurt you and will let you go afterwards. I have some bread and milk. I know you are hungry.'

Olivia pressed her forehead to her knees. Her stomach had growled and growled when she'd woken from fitful sleep, but seemed to have given up protesting. She was so tempted to believe him. Her conscience *was* bothering her. If Schmidt was telling the truth, she might be able to save a man's life and still keep her own. But could she trust him? He'd conned her before and might do so again. Yet still she abhorred the idea of a man close by, gasping in agony when she might have been able at least to ease his suffering. There might be morphine in the ambulance, but Karl Schmidt was too clued up not to have raided the vehicle already. He *was* attempting to trick her into revealing herself, she was sure of it, and instinctively curled up tighter in her shelter.

How many days and nights had she been here? She had seen three dawns . . . or was it four? It was hard to tell because sometimes the gloomy day merged with the night before. The rain that spattered down through the overhanging canopy of branches soaked her, made her shiver, yet was welcomed like manna from heaven. It filled her drinking puddles and as it fell she turned her face up so it trickled into her mouth. It tasted as sweet as the sherbet she used to make when she was still a girl at the factory. Long, long ago. And then she'd think of her brother and sisters. They would be desolate to know she'd been reported missing and her body might never be found. And then she thought of Lucas . . . wondering how he was, and struggling to bring his beautiful face to mind. She was distressed every time his features eluded her but concentrating for too long was becoming painful. And then she wished . . . wished he'd come and find her so that they could have the life together that she yearned for.

She knew she was ill. Her throat was sore, her lungs tight. Her forehead was damp, not from the rain but from fever. She craved sleep and was tempted to give in to it. She wished she was in blissful ignorance of where she was heading but she was a nurse now and had tended to men with pneumonia. She knew she might die. Soon she would have to make a decision: leave her shelter before she was too weak to crawl out of it or allow it to become her final resting place.

Olivia jerked her forehead away from her knees, frowning and blinking. An odd silence was as noteworthy as an unexpected noise. Usually Schmidt would call to her for longer than this. It was a different pattern and that forced the numbness out and made her more alert. She was a creature of habit now. Ten minutes out of the hollow at night for the lavatory, ten minutes to forage and drink . . . she'd count off the seconds in her mind.

Something was telling her to take a chance.

But emerging now would go against her self-imposed rules. He was just playing games with her. She huddled down in her nest of leaves. And listened and waited.

★   ★   ★

'You speak English?'

'I do, sir. I am British . . . Scottish actually although I've not been home in a long while.'

'What are you doing out here?'

The fellow did have a slight Caledonian twang and had approached with a limp in his stride that he'd attempted to disguise. It was a colourless December day but there was enough light to see that he had a thin face and wiry build. And he was carrying a shotgun.

Lucas looked around at the dank woodland with red-rimmed, gritty eyes. He'd been riding for two days almost without a break, stopping just to save the horse and fill his water bottle. He'd been traversing the countryside to and fro, guessing the wooded areas would be the best places to look. No spy would abandon a purloined vehicle out in the open or conduct his business there. Moments ago he'd spotted somebody moving on the fringes of the woodland nearby and had shouted to him to show himself. A tramp-like figure with a shotgun dangling from one hand had sauntered into view.

'I've been shooting game,' he said to Lucas. 'I'm a Presbyterian minister. More used to grouse moors than rough shooting, but I can bag a brace of hare. I always shoot the fellows something for the pot when I'm off duty from the chapel.'

'No luck then?' Lucas jerked a nod at his empty hands.

'I was just beginning the search when you stopped me. I'll take something back for the Kilts. Always do. Can't let the troops down.' He moved the shotgun, cradling it over one arm. 'Light's fading. How about you, lieutenant? On your own?'

'I'm on my way to St Omer, hospital visiting.' Lucas spurred his horse on but he knew, as did Schmidt, what came next. Lucas wheeled about and leaped down, hand at the holster on his hip, firing fast from beneath the mare's belly before the German could properly cock and aim the long barrels at him. The shotgun jerked up, firing at the sky as Schmidt crashed to his knees. Crows erupted from their nests, raucously protesting at being disturbed. Lucas was praying he'd only winged the German or he might never find out what had happened to Olivia. He raced over, seeing blood darkening Schmidt's jacket close to his heart.

'Don't you dare die, you fucking cunt!' Lucas fastened one hand over the man's face, hauling him up by the hollows in his cheeks and shaking him like a rat.

Schmidt smiled as his eyes rolled in their sockets. 'She's nearby somewhere . . . brave little soul. I couldn't fool her and get her to show herself.' His lungs bubbled blood and, as Lucas released him, Schmidt turned his head and spat a mouthful to the ground. 'Guessed you'd come if you could.' He gasped for breath. 'Should have killed you while I had the chance. You're lucky, lieutenant . . . she's worth fighting for. What men do for women, eh?' Bitterness stretched his features. 'Ask Mrs MacLeod. Risked it all for her . . . wish I'd never met the conniving bitch . . . her husband felt the same . . . better for me this way . . . can't let your lot get to me.' His chest heaved as he forced a bitter laugh. 'Won't betray her now . . . even though she cheated me.'

He clutched at Lucas. 'My comrade . . . ' He rolled his eyes towards the fringe of the woods. 'Put him out of his misery before the Red Caps get to him. Do that for me. You owe me. I could've harmed your girl . . . given her to the others to play with . . . ' As his voice became softer, words spaced out between gasps, Lucas bent his head. He listened to the man's final words for a few seconds more until Schmidt's throat rattled and he went limp.

'Olivia! Livviiie! Livviiie!' Lucas grabbed the shotgun and started to sprint into the woods, bawling her name over and over again as loud as he could until he felt his chest might burst. He spotted the German propped against a tree, head drooping onto his chest. Lucas approached, pointing his revolver, and the man lifted his head and smiled, bringing up his own pistol in a slow, shaking hand. Lucas fired on the run, again bawling out Olivia's name.

Olivia's head jerked up. She'd heard the gunfire, peered upwards to see the cawing crows clog the sky, and had immediately burrowed as deeply as she could into her shelter. As quiet once more descended her heartbeat settled. She wondered who or what had been shot. Had Schmidt been hunting? He must be hungry too. He'd been lying about the bread and milk she was sure. Where would he get them out here? Or had he learned enough about her routine to go off to a farmhouse and leave her, safe in the knowledge she'd still be hiding when he returned?

He might have shot a rabbit; she'd seen them at a distance. Lively creatures . . . she'd never have managed to catch one with her bare hands even had she known what to do with it after that.

The sound of somebody bursting through bushes and undergrowth made her gasp and shrink into herself. Schmidt stalked her stealthily, never like a bull in a china shop. The rough male voice became more distinct, urgent with anguish as it called her name. And Schmidt didn't know her as Livvie.

'Lucas?'

The magical word unstuck her tongue from the roof of her mouth. Her heartbeat, already erratic, became more frantic. She tried to shout but couldn't do more than mouth the words. She'd only spoken aloud to herself in days. And had given up on that lately, carrying on conversations in her head instead.

In a sudden panic to get out, she clawed her way to the top of the burrow, slithering over the edge and out on her belly. She kept going on her elbows for a yard or two before pulling herself upright against a tree trunk. Her lungs were pumping painfully and she knew that wasn't wholly due to the exertion.

'Lucas . . . oh, Lucas. I'm here . . . ' She stumbled forward, lurching from tree to tree to steady herself. She felt her eyes clouding over, blackening, and shook her head to clear them. She'd not faint . . . not now!

'Lucas!' she cried with all her might. And then she saw him burst into view, though her eyes were filled with tears and dazzled by shards of light. With a thumping pain in her head, she swayed to a blessed standstill and held out her arms to him.

# 20

'Lieutenant Black to see Brigadier Saville.'

'Is he expecting you, lieutenant?'

'Yes,' Lucas lied, stepping past the saluting captain. Too late the fellow jumped up from his paperwork in an attempt to block the way.

'What in damnation . . . ' The brigadier dropped his pen on his desk then stood upright as Lucas barged into his office.

'Who are you?' the senior officer demanded.

'Lieutenant Black, at your service, sir.' He saluted and thrust his cap beneath his arm.

Saville jerked a nod of dismissal at his minion. 'Ordinarily an appointment would be made but I know these aren't ordinary times. You've done a capital job, bringing back the nurse that went missing.'

'She wasn't missing, she was abducted by Karl Schmidt.'

The men's eyes met. 'Quite so,' the brigadier enunciated. 'Now I know you've been briefed by your superior on the need for strict confidentiality regarding this episode . . . '

'I thought you'd be interested to know what Schmidt said to me before he died.'

The brigadier looked startled then barked, 'I thought he was killed outright? A single shot to the chest. We would rather have had him alive for questioning, y'know, Black.'

'Me too, sir, I would have liked to question

him some more,' Lucas said, in a way that made the brigadier squint at him suspiciously.

'Haven't you disclosed everything in your report?'

'There was something else I saved to tell you personally.'

Saville strode out from behind his desk. 'I'm not sure I like your tone, lieutenant. What *did* Schmidt say to you?'

'I'll get to that in a moment. First, I want leave granted. Two weeks.'

'You *are* being bloody insubordinate, lieutenant!' The brigadier's eyes popped beneath their wiry brows. 'If you want *leave*, man, speak to your commanding officer about it and he'll put it through the proper channels.' He took a deep breath before composing himself. 'Now, what information have you been withholding? This is a matter of the highest importance.'

'And Olivia Bone? What's she a matter of? The truth is, she doesn't matter to you, does she?' Lucas said through gritted teeth. He knew he was treading dangerously close to a court martial, but right now he didn't care. All that mattered to him was Olivia and confronting this man over the disgraceful way she'd been abandoned to her fate at the hands of a German spy.

Their eyes locked and, grudgingly, the brigadier relented.

'Look . . . I realise the young lady's an acquaintance of yours and has been through an ordeal. There's the bigger picture to consider here though. There's a war to be won. Keeping tabs on Schmidt was our priority. Our intelligence was that he'd head to Paris to meet his collaborators. You put the brakes on that when you shot him, y'know.'

'Are you expecting me to apologise for saving my own life? He had a shotgun and he used it.'

Saville paced to and fro, darting brooding glances at his visitor while hoping for a conciliatory sign. 'Sister Bone used to be a factory girl, I gather, and an orphaned one at that, so nobody back home's going to kick up a stink over her. I've seen your records . . . managing director of Barratt's sweet factory. You were her employer, weren't you, and you've kept in touch with her out here? Commendable.'

Saville eyed the handsome lieutenant. He'd heard all about him and his dissolute ways, as had most people in good society. But Black had turned into a damn' fine officer so the brigadier was prepared to overlook his temper. Hotheaded chaps made recklessly brave soldiers, in Saville's opinion. And, God only knew, such men were in short supply after the Somme offensive. 'Pretty gel, I've been told.' The brigadier looked for a moment as though he might wink but then thought better of it.

Lucas could have punched the bastard in the mouth just for thinking Olivia might be his part-time tart. At one time he'd contemplated the possibility himself. And that's why he hated this man and all the others like him: they reminded Lucas of himself a few years back, when he'd been that sort of bastard as well.

Saville cleared his throat. 'Well, you've done a

292

splendid job with your platoon, lieutenant. I've read through your service record. Mentioned in dispatches on numerous occasions. Military Medal and DSM. Better to come, I promise you.' This rousing speech seemed to have little effect on Lucas though. 'Come, man, you must take the promotion you've been offered. I see you've turned down a captaincy on two occasions . . . how does Major Black sound to you then?'

'I've no interest in rising through the ranks. I'd sooner get out than deeper in.'

Lucas didn't care how the brigadier took that. It was the truth, and he was by no means the only officer unmoved by the honours and glory conferred on them by pompous gits sitting safely in their dugouts. Lucas knew these anarchist views could get him into trouble. His own father would have been horrified to witness him behave with such blatant insubordination. Though he had taken full advantage of the wealth and privilege that his father's name brought with it, Lucas had often felt uncomfortable about his own lifestyle. Money had paid for the excesses that filled the emptiness inside him. Loving Livvie completed him now. And even if the worst happened, and he lost her, he knew he'd never go back to being the person he'd once been.

'Had Sister Bone been searched for straight away she would not have contracted pneumonia.' Lucas kept his tone even, though loathing blazed from his eyes.

'No need for you to inform me that she's ill.

I've been kept up-to-date on her progress.' The brigadier sat down and sorted through some papers on his desk. 'I have her file right here. I'll try to get the girl some proper recognition for her bravery if . . . ' He cleared his throat. 'Bad business. But these things happen in wartime. The lass was in the wrong place at the wrong time.' He shook his head in a momentary show of regret before his face brightened again. 'But we mustn't forget, it might have been very much worse. The daughters of some of the highest in our land are now serving on the Western Front as VADs, you know. Imagine the uproar in drawing rooms up and down England if one of those young ladies had been captured by a German spy!'

When Lucas failed to express a suitable level of horror at this prospect, the brigadier frowned and told him, 'I knew your father, lieutenant. A man of your background must understand how the world works.'

'I'm nothing like my father. And Schmidt wasn't a German, he was Scottish . . . or perhaps a bit of both.' Lucas turned away in disgust. The more he considered this man who'd refused Livvie help, the more he wanted to haul Saville across the desk and batter him mercilessly. 'But I imagine you already know that. You know who he is, don't you?'

'Scottish mother and German father. Obviously preferred his papa's side,' Saville said contemptuously. 'Now carry on with what you have to tell me, lieutenant.'

'I assume you'll sanction my leave so I can

visit Miss Bone while she's gravely ill.'

'Mmm . . . yes . . . carry on,' the brigadier muttered.

'Schmidt, or whatever his real name was, spoke to me about a woman as he was dying. Someone he called Mrs MacLeod.'

'MacLeod . . . MacLeod . . . ' The brigadier was up on his feet again. 'That name sounds familiar,' he said animatedly.

'Perhaps from a blue light,' Lucas suggested sourly.

Soldiers often sought female company when billeted back from the line: a blue-light brothel for the officers and a red-light one for the rank and file. These establishments often had a queue of men waiting outside and were used by both Allied and German soldiers in turn, as they lost then reclaimed the same territory. Usually the women were locals trying to survive in a war zone and not bothered which side they serviced. But some had a clear allegiance if they'd fallen for a particular man.

'You believe MacLeod's a British prostitute, working in France?'

Lucas shrugged. 'I've no idea. Schmidt called her a whore and a bitch and said he understood now why her husband had divorced her. Just before he died, he said, 'Mata Hari thinks she's become a big star in Paris and is too good for me now, so fuck her.'' Lucas felt he couldn't stomach much more of his superior's company. He walked over to the door then turned to look back at the brigadier. 'For what it's worth, I don't think he was going to Paris to meet other

295

conspirators. He could have left Sister Bone and his dying pal at any time. I just thank the Lord he didn't and stuck around or I'd never have located her. I think Schmidt had had enough and was intending to make his way home.'

The brigadier pounced on these words. 'The dying man . . . Was he still alive when you got to him?'

'Not for long . . . he said nothing . . . was too far gone,' Lucas replied.

'Have you told anybody else about this?' Saville demanded.

'Nobody.'

'We'll forget about your impertinence just this once. Your father was a friend. That apart, you're a credit to the army, Black, if not to yourself. Rein in that temper of yours, won't you?' The brigadier looked back at the papers stacked high on his desk, a clear hint that Lucas should leave him.

'Yes, sir. Thank you, sir,' he said with studied politeness. 'One more thing you should know, though.' He waited until Saville glanced up at him. 'There *is* somebody to kick up a stink on Sister Bone's behalf . . . I will, because that former factory girl's my future wife.' He pointed at the papers before the brigadier. 'Be sure to put that in her file, won't you? If she doesn't pull through, I'll make sure what happened to her is reported in every newspaper in England. You threw my fiancée to the wolves to please your masters in the War Office.' Lucas paused then added, 'I take it you recovered the ambulance and Schmidt's body?'

The brigadier gave a curt nod, his face tightening.

'So an enemy spy will get a burial of sorts while you would've left a British nurse out there to rot, wouldn't you?' Lucas didn't expect a reply. He turned and went out, barging the captain out of his path.

The brigadier pursed his lips, wishing he could deny that damning accusation. But there was no point. They both knew it was true. 'Keep me informed on the girl's progress, Black. Convey my best wishes . . . ' he called.

Lucas kept walking. With heroic restraint he refrained from sticking two fingers up over his shoulder.

*  *  *

'Lieutenant Black! She's awake!'

Lucas was groggily aware of somebody shaking his shoulder. He jerked his head off the steering wheel, licked his dry lips and blinked himself conscious. He'd felt like this before . . . many times, in his misspent youth, when a night of debauchery shared with a willing woman had left him with a drumming head and aching limbs. But he'd not touched a drop in days, and as for a woman . . . it'd been a long, long time. Even the phantom lover in his head was now out of bounds to him.

And it was because of her that he was stupefied with exhaustion and anxiety.

He remembered that a convoy had turned up during the early evening. Wanting to do something useful, he'd helped carry stretchers into the hospital for about an hour. There had been pitiable cases amongst the casualties and he'd done what he could to reassure them. He didn't want to lie to those wild-eyed boys pressing him to say a leg or an arm could be saved. Instead he'd taken the coward's way out, clamming up and leaving the nurses and doctors to take over, as brave in their own way as their patients.

As he'd rushed to and fro, his mind had constantly returned to thoughts of Olivia, lost in her own mad world. As the ambulances emptied out and pulled away and the orderlies and medical staff worked together like a many-cogged machine, he'd gratefully sought rest in his car, parked on the road. He didn't remember dozing off. He guessed it to be the early hours of the morning now. He'd made Matron promise to let him know if Olivia's condition changed, whatever time it was.

'She's opened her eyes. The fever's abating . . . the worst is over,' Matron rattled off, her voice tremulous with relief. 'Olivia said your name . . . lucidly this time.'

She stepped smartly aside as Lucas threw off the greatcoat he'd draped over himself in an effort to keep warm. He scrambled from the driver's seat, clumsy with haste, and broke into a run, vaulting tent ropes. Matron hurried after him in the direction of the staff dormitories.

He'd been about to burst in, but halted outside the door. Like a boy on a first date, he thrust his fingers through his hair to neaten it and straightened his collar.

Earlier, he'd sat by Olivia's bedside for hour after long hour, listening to her rapid breathing and watching for a flicker of something to give him hope she was beating the infection. She'd been mumbling nonsense, interspersed with names he recognised as her fingers clutched his. Her brother and sisters, her dad, even Mr and Mrs Keiver in Campbell Road, had featured in her delirium. But she'd not mentioned Schmidt or Rose Drew. The memory of that day had been with her though. She breathed 'Lucas' in a way that tore at his guts and made his eyes swim. He'd never forget the way she'd called to him as she'd sunk to the forest floor like a wounded creature.

Lucas entered quietly, barely registering the beam that Sister Thistle gave him. His eyes were fixed on an oval face almost as white as the pillow beneath. She'd been watching for him. Their eyes met. Swiftly, he crouched down beside Olivia and took hold of one restless hand, holding it gently between both of his. She sighed, and a smile tugged at her lips. Then, as though she'd seen what she needed to, her eyelids drooped again.

'How do you feel?' he croaked, desperate to talk to her . . . stay with her. 'Sorry — stupid question.'

Olivia cupped his unshaven cheek in her free hand. 'Thumping head. Bones feel like they've been put through a mangle. Seeing you has bucked me up though,' she murmured. 'Have you been here a while?'

'Only a few days,' Lucas said, although he'd been hanging around the hospital now for almost a week, barely eating or sleeping. He'd got himself a billet in the village but had rarely used it, preferring to be closer to her and take naps in his car. His days had become a familiar round of sitting with Olivia or walking the perimeter of the hospital compound, staring into space and begging any god who was out there to save her.

'I won't be far away if you need me,' Flora Thistle said, and tactfully withdrew from the room.

'You gave me quite a fright,' Lucas said hoarsely. He leaned over to cradle Olivia in his arms and tenderly embrace her before lowering her back onto the pillows.

'Now you know what it feels like.' She wasn't wholly joking. She caught his hands in hers, smoothing her thumbs over his rough skin. She breathed air carefully into her battered lungs. 'Every time you go missing I'm frantic. There's nothing I could ever do to help you. But you saved me.' Her green eyes glowed impishly. 'You *are* my knight in shining armour, Lucas Black, whether you like it or not,' she murmured.

Long ago, before the war, she'd jokingly asked him to be her knight in shining armour. He'd refused her an answer then because he'd wanted his factory girl in his bed, not in his heart. She could tell from his wry expression that he remembered that afternoon at Alexandra Palace, when no matter what their ages or stations in life, they'd both been children, larking about.

He smoothed her lank fair hair back from her

forehead. 'Don't put me through that again, will you?' He nuzzled his lips against her cheek. 'It wasn't easy, and I couldn't find a white horse.'

She started to laugh but coughed instead, waving him away when he immediately jumped up to summon her nurse back. 'I'm fine . . . a sip of water.'

He gave her the beaker, helping her hold it to her lips.

'Do I look a fright?' Olivia pulled a face. 'I asked my roommate for a mirror but she hasn't brought me one yet.'

Lucas cocked his head, adopting a critical expression. Her usual English rose complexion was greyish, eyes huge and dark green above sharp cheekbones. 'It is hard to know what I see in you,' he told her gravely, dipping his head to kiss her in a gentle loving way that answered her question better than any fraudulent words might have done.

'You need a shave.' She giggled softly, lifting arms that felt like dead weights to hold him against her.

'I'd like to get in with you, you know, pull up the covers and just hide away until it's all over and we can come out and go home,' Lucas said, his breath warm against her cheek.

'I know . . . I want the same thing.' Olivia felt tears burn in her eyes but he wiped them away with his fingertips.

'I meant it. I want you to get into bed with me. I want you, Lucas, and I don't want to wait any longer . . . '

'Hush!' He dropped to his knees by the

bedside. 'No more of that talk or, weakling that I am, I won't be able to act like a gentleman and refuse you.' He gave her a crooked smile. 'In which case, I hope your Sister Thistle has her smelling salts handy.'

Olivia pressed her lips to the callused palm of his hand. She knew she looked a wreck and he looked different too . . . older . . . made haggard by what he'd been through over two long, embattled years. But the sight of him still melted her heart, and the love and desire she felt for him made her feverish in a good way that kept the bad memories from her head.

'I met your brother and sister-in-law, you know, last time I was home.'

'Yes, I know.' He sat on the floor by her bed, holding her hand.

'They told you about it?'

He nodded. 'It's not important, Livvie. They're not important.'

'I thought at first it was kind of your sister-in-law to invite me to tea.'

'Did she?' he asked mildly.

'Yes . . . didn't you know? She sent me an invitation through Val Booth.'

Lucas muttered something beneath his breath. Caroline's version had been that his factory girl had invited herself along with Cousin Valerie.

'Did they treat you well?'

'It was an odd experience and I wouldn't want to repeat it,' Olivia said. She brought their clasped hands to her lips. 'But, as you said, it isn't important. None of it really matters, Lucas.' She sighed. 'I remember Rose being hurt by

Schmidt.' It was the first time she had mentioned that dreadful day and she found that she barely winced. 'Has she been sent home to get over it?'

Lucas nodded. 'Matron told me she came to see you just before she sailed from Boulogne. You were still feverish then. I expect your friend'll be relieved to know you're on the mend.'

'Olivia needs to rest now, lieutenant,' Matron said, poking her head discreetly around the door before coming further in. 'And she must eat. Soup to start, to build up your strength, Olivia, then doctor can sign you off as fit to travel. It's back to Blighty for you soon.'

Olivia frowned, and started to say she'd prefer her visitor to stay. Being with Lucas made her feel better, more alive than she'd dared hope. She wanted him with her, although it was hard to keep her eyes open, even to look at his beloved face.

Lucas gently wriggled his fingers free from hers and stood up. When Matron left he drew from an inner pocket a bar of chocolate. 'Have it later,' he told Olivia. 'As a treat for eating up your gruel.' He'd seen her grimace when the soup was mentioned. He leaned over and kissed her on the lips, stroking her cheek before he stepped away. 'You'll go home for good now, won't you? Promise you won't come back here? I couldn't bear to see you hurt again. I love you too much.'

Olivia gazed into his deep blue eyes for a long moment. 'I'll take leave . . . and I'll get better, I promise I will. But . . . ' She paused for breath.

'I'm coming back to St Omer. I'm not leaving you here. I can't . . . not now because I love *you*, Lucas, and without you . . . ' Her voice tailed off and tears sparkled in her eyes. 'So . . . when it's finally done . . . we go home together, or not at all.'

# 21

'He looks just like his pa, don't he?' The proud father puffed out his chest while tickling his infant son under the chin.

'He certainly does.' Olivia managed to smile and to keep the disappointment from her voice. She'd have much preferred little Ricky to resemble his mum.

The boy was two months old now and a bonny little chap. He'd arrived early, in mid-March, but had nevertheless been a fair weight. Maggie had wanted Olivia to be with her for the birth but in the end the local midwife had got her through a speedy night delivery without a single stitch being needed. At that time Olivia had still been feeling weak and when the baby made an unexpected appearance she'd felt relieved to be spared the responsibility of bringing her nephew into the world. In the event, though, Maggie had just been glad to be in capable hands and get the labour over with.

Olivia hadn't seen her nephew Ricky for a week and even in that short time he'd grown plumper and more alert. He had a thick mop of auburn hair and brown eyes that were definitely inherited from the Wicks side of the family. Harry was dandling the child on his forearm like a doting father. Apart from that *he* hadn't changed much at all. Olivia had noticed him giving Ruby the eye earlier, at the church. Her cousin hadn't appeared displeased either. Their sly behaviour had niggled at Olivia and she'd decided to have a word with her cousin later. Ruby had said she'd changed her ways but perhaps she couldn't control her bad habits for long.

Maggie was kept busy, rushing to and fro, handing out cups of tea to the guests following her son's Christening. It was the first time the new Mrs Wicks had entertained at her own place. When the couple had gone ahead as planned and tied the knot a few days after Christmas, Olivia had still been in France. Following a short stay with Harry's aunt in Yarmouth, the newlyweds had moved into a ground-floor flat in Wood Green. Olivia had enquired how Maggie had enjoyed her seaside honeymoon with Harry's aunt. Her sister's scowl and rolling eyes had been answer enough.

'Here, let me help with those.' Olivia took some cups and saucers. Maggie was looking hot and bothered while her husband stood lording it with a pal from the butcher's rather than lending a hand. Harry had propped his son in one corner of an armchair the moment the boy started to whimper.

'Thanks, Livvie. Would you make another pot of tea?' Maggie leaned in to whisper, 'Use the grouts again though 'cos I'm running short on tea and Harry'll moan if we've got none left for tomorrow.'

Tea and wheat especially were getting scarce and the government was urging people to be economical with butter and sugar as well. The merchant ships bringing in supplies to Britain were being targeted by enemy submarines. Food queues were becoming a common sight on the High Streets and the kids playing out in Campbell Road would often chant the poster slogan, 'Save the wheat, help the fleet,' in time with their skipping ropes. Rationing couldn't be far away now that even parks and open spaces were being turned over to allotments, to encourage folk to grow their own food. Farm labourers' jobs were being filled by young women since the young men had joined up and a new army of Land Girls was emerging throughout the country.

Olivia set the kettle to boil on the hob then turned to Maggie, who was pouring milk into cups. 'You look lovely. Where did you get your new costume?' The bottle green two-piece her sister had worn for the Christening had a peplum skirt under a nipped-in waist, with pretty frogging around the buttons. She'd topped off the outfit with a neat pillbox hat.

'Where d'you think?' Maggie grinned.

'Chapel Street market?' Olivia guessed.

Maggie nodded. 'Got the fellow down to a guinea for it, hat included, 'cos it's second hand. But you can tell it's hardly been worn. Had enough left to buy me boots 'n' all.' She displayed a foot neatly encased in supple, shiny leather. 'Bought it all months ago, out of me last pay packet. But I'm hoping to go back to Turner's soon.' She darted a look her husband's way, adding in a whisper, 'Harry ain't keen on me working there. Says it's his job to provide for us. But the money's so good it'd be mad to turn it down. Ricky's nearly old enough to take a bottle and be left for a while with me mother-in-law.' She jerked a nod at a sour-faced woman sitting in the corner with her fingers clasped together on top of her handbag. Olivia thought Mrs Wicks didn't look as though she'd volunteer to do anybody a favour.

'Nance got herself a fur coat from Selfridges out of her wages on nights,' Maggie continued. 'She was doing shifts back to back to earn enough for it. She actually paid for it 'n' all instead of lifting it.' Maggie smirked. 'Anyhow . . . we've all got to do our bit while this rotten war drags on.' With that parting shot, she set off to hand round more cups of weak tea.

Olivia did likewise, collecting crockery and bringing people refills. She used the same leaves for a third time when refilling the pot. While giving the brew a vigorous shake and stir she realised she had to hand it to Maggie . . . her sister had developed into a capable young woman. Maggie had known what was best for her future and Olivia was glad now that she'd not interfered. Being a wife and mother suited her sister. And perhaps, in an odd way that Olivia couldn't fathom, Harry Wicks suited her too.

Maggie had blossomed in her looks. Motherhood had helped her face and figure fill out nicely, making her look like a young woman rather than an adolescent. Harry often praised his attractive wife, grabbing her rump in company, and making her blush while crowing,

'You're getting a nice arse on yer, gel.'

And Maggie was a natural with her baby. She never grew flustered when he was fractious.

As he was now. Olivia handed a cup of tea to Maggie's old factory pal then picked up her whimpering nephew.

'He's getting his teeth,' the older woman said with a sage nod. 'My eldest started teething almost as soon as his cord was cut.' She hoisted herself to her feet, hanky in hand. 'Come on, feller me lad, let's wipe that chin.'

'Thanks, Livvie,' Maggie said, coming over to them. She took her wriggling son. 'There's plates of sausage rolls and seedcake in the kitchenette. If you don't mind handing those round, I'll have a look at this little one. He might need his nappy changed.' She nuzzled her son's soft pink cheek.

Nancy turned up then with the baby's dummy, taken from his pram in the hall.

'Don't give it to him, Nance!' Maggie waved it away. 'I'm trying to stop him having it so much. He'll get buck teeth.'

'Right 'n' all, gel,' the factory hand said. 'Ain't easy to break 'em of that habit. My youngest . . . he was a bleeder for his dummy. Had gnashers like a rabbit, did Ronnie.' She wagged a cautionary finger.

Olivia gave Nancy a private smile. That was an old wives' tale if ever she'd heard one! Nancy had only been trying to help. Her youngest sister rolled her eyes and took the dummy away while Maggie disappeared to change Ricky's wet nappy.

'You're looking a sight fer sore eyes today.'

Harry had noticed his wife leave the room and had sidled up to whisper in Olivia's ear. 'Was worried about you, y'know.' He squeezed her waist in a way that might have been meant to be comforting but Olivia knew wasn't. 'When you first come back from France you looked like death warmed up, gel.'

'Felt like it too,' she replied bluntly. 'Pneumonia takes it out of you.' She moved away from him, gesturing to the sunshine outside the window. 'Warm weather helps, of course.' It was May and blossom could be seen on the trees in the street; its scent wafted in through the open sashes.

'Going back for another stint, are yer?' Harry had shunned his wife's tea in favour of a bottle of brown ale to celebrate his son's Christening. He swigged from it, eyes still wandering over Olivia's curvaceous figure.

'I've got a return passage at the beginning of June.'

She'd travelled home in late-January, when Matron judged she'd be well enough to brave the Channel's choppy winter seas. Fortunately, the gods had been smiling on her. It had been an unusual start to the year: mild with very little wind. She'd made no protest about leaving France, accepting she needed time to build up her strength away from the hospital.

Memories of those terrifying four days lost in the forest still gave her nightmares, but they were less frequent now she was home. Matron had filled in some of the gaps for her, telling her that wonderful man Lieutenant Black had brought her back, unconscious and with a raging fever. She hadn't needed to add that Olivia had been lucky to be alive when he'd galloped up with her on his horse, bawling out for assistance. He'd run inside with her hanging as limp as a rag doll in his arms. Luckily he was young and strong, Matron had said. Then added with a wink that she'd never doubted Olivia would pull through because what woman wouldn't be determined to get better with a man like that waiting for her?

Olivia had missed seeing Rose in London by a week. Her friend had returned to the Western Front, so they hadn't managed to make their trip together to His Majesty's Theatre. Rose had written to her saying she hadn't forgotten about it, though, and was still looking forward to seeing *Chu Chin Chow* with her when they next met up back home.

'Let's hope it'll all be over soon now the Americans have joined in.' Nancy had noticed Olivia edging away from Harry and had come to help her out. Their brother-in-law gave her the creeps too, always ogling and touching. When he did it to her Nancy would quickly elbow him in the ribs, accidentally on purpose.

'Our lads don't need the Americans.' Harry made a disparaging noise. 'The French and Russians are letting the side down. That's the problem.'

'How's your leg then, Harry?' Olivia asked pointedly. She knew speaking about that was sure to get rid of him.

'Yeah . . . not bad,' he mumbled, shaking his trouser leg. 'Considering the amount of shrapnel it took. Some still in there 'n' all.' He moved off, with a pronounced limp, to talk to his pal.

'Bloody shirker,' Nancy muttered beneath her breath.

Olivia thought the same but decided not to pursue it. He was Maggie's husband now and she'd never want her sister to receive notification that her husband had perished. So let him stay where he was. Besides, it was a happy day . . . a day for celebration. 'Maggie's a good mum, isn't she?' Olivia glanced proudly at their sister, swaying her son to and fro on her hip.

'Yeah,' Nancy said. 'Shame the kid's old man ain't up to much.'

'Perhaps Maggie'll bring something better out of him . . . eventually.'

'Perhaps pigs might fly,' Nancy responded dryly. 'We're Ricky's godmothers so reckon that means we get to have a say if Harry don't shape up.'

'I'll always have me eye on Harry Wicks,' Olivia said pithily, reckoning their brother-in-law had taken up enough of their conversation. 'Heard from Nat lately?' She'd never met Nancy's gangster boyfriend so wouldn't make up her mind about him before she had. When she'd been with Joe, people had judged him by his reputation and family without ever getting to know the truth behind the myth.

'He's coming back on leave in June. Can't wait,' Nancy said wistfully.

'That's a shame. I'll be back in France by then.'

'When we're all together in one place I'm

going to have a party round at mine,' Nancy said. 'You can meet Nat then.' She gave Olivia a hug. 'You've got to take care of yourself out there. You frightened the life out of me when you came home this time — you looked so thin and pale. You won't get pneumonia again, will you?'

'I'll be fine,' Olivia said, returning the hug. Her family had been shocked by her appearance and knowing about the kidnap would have worried them even more. So she'd not told them the whole story.

'We're getting off home now, Livvie. Just gonna say goodbye to Maggie.' Uncle Ed had come up with Alfie and Mickey either side of him. 'I expect you'll stay a while longer with your sisters so we'll see you back there, if that's alright?'

'I'll be following on quite soon.' Olivia gave the boys a smile. They could have been twins. Just months separated them in age and their looks were almost identical too.

With a bittersweet pang she realised that her brother had got used to life without her. He had grown fond of his uncle and she could see that Ed liked him right back. The man treated the boys equally, as though they were both his kids. Alfie had found a father to care for him at last.

Her uncle had offered to move out when Olivia had said she'd be convalescing at home for a few months. But there had been no need for that. There was enough room for all of them. Ed had taken a step back, allowing her the run of the place. In the end Olivia had to tell him he didn't have to stay in his bedroom or ask to use the parlour while she was around. Nevertheless she appreciated his courtesy.

'I'm heading off home as well,' Nancy said. 'I'm meeting some friends later.' She glanced at Harry. 'I can only stand him in small doses.'

Olivia grimaced her understanding; yet it was a shame the party would break up prematurely because of Harry Wicks. 'I won't be late leaving myself. I want to have a word with Ruby first though.'

'She's in a right mood,' Nancy said darkly. 'Don't know why she's come along with her face on her boots. Free feed, I suppose.' She glanced at their cousin, busy filling her plate with sausage rolls and seedcake. 'I noticed she ain't wearing her engagement ring,' Maggie hissed. 'When I mentioned it she got snappy, said it was at home in the drawer. Knowing her, she's pawned it to pay the rent.'

★   ★   ★

'How's things at Barratt's?' Olivia asked brightly, cheekily helping herself to a sausage roll off Ruby's plate.

'Same old stuff,' the girl said glumly, picking at cake crumbs. 'Time I looked for something else, I reckon.'

'Is Riley coming home on leave soon?'

'Don't know . . . don't care.' Ruby's top lip curled at the mention of her fiancé.

'Have you had a tiff?' Olivia glanced at her cousin's bare fingers. 'You've not broken up, have you?' she asked gently.

'Ain't talking about it. Ain't talking about *him*. The pig!' Ruby put down her plate on the window ledge. 'I'm getting off home. Somebody's coming round about renting one of me rooms.'

'Hold up, Ruby, I'll walk with you to the corner.' Olivia could see tears in her cousin's eyes. She didn't want Ruby to go off feeling upset, without at least offering to lend an ear.

Ruby sniffed in a conciliatory way. 'I wanted to ask you about something actually, Livvie. A Christening's probably not the right time though.'

'I'll just tell Maggie I'll be back later to help her clear up then we can have a chat outside. You going to say goodbye to her and that dear little chap of hers?'

'Who, Harry?' Ruby joked weakly.

'That'll be the day,' Olivia breathed. But she wasn't going to bring up the matter of Ruby and Harry exchanging that look until the problem with Riley was out of the way.

By the time they got outside Ruby seemed more amenable. The girls linked arms as they walked along. They loitered at the corner while Ruby plucked up the courage to blurt out in a whisper, 'D'you know how to get rid of French VD, Livvie? The bastard has only gone and given me the clap.'

'What?' Olivia gasped.

'You're a nurse so I thought you might know what they give the men over there. I know Riley ain't the only one. Me friend at Barratt's chucked her old man out because he gave her it.'

She's pregnant 'n' all, the poor cow. She reckons the army's riddled with pox on account of all the men using those dirty French tarts. Last time Riley come back he must've given me a dose. I've written and told him we're finished. He never even let on he was infected, the rotten swine.'

Some men didn't realise they had venereal disease until it was quite advanced. Hospital staff were aware it was becoming an epidemic but saving lives took priority over treating the clap. Even if a serviceman contracted syphilis, what was the point of worrying if he was probably going to die anyway? Infected men with little else troubling them were sent to the VD hospital, segregating them from the more 'respectable' patients.

Olivia could see her cousin was waiting for her to comment so said, 'It's possible he didn't know he'd caught it.'

'Well, I bloody know I've got it!' Ruby winced. 'Been itching like mad and leaking stuff . . . ' Her face was a mask of disgust.

'Go and see a doctor,' Olivia said quietly.

'No, I ain't doing that! He'll think I'm a right old trollop. I've been faithful to Riley ever since he asked me to marry him.' Ruby sounded incensed. 'I've always kept meself clean down there.' She used the back of her hand on her wet eyes. 'I've douched meself with Eusol. If that don't clear it, any other ideas what might work?'

'You could try black salve or potassium permanganate,' Olivia told her quietly. 'I've heard about those but I don't get involved in that side of nursing. The senior sisters or the doctors get the job. It saves red faces all round. We all know about it though.'

'Thanks, Livvie,' Ruby sniffed.

Olivia realised now why she had preened when Harry had leered at her. Her cousin was hedging her bets. But not with Maggie's husband, she wasn't! Olivia was just about to tell her so when Ruby interrupted her. ''Ere, look . . . ain't that Cath over there, pushing that pram? She must be back from Kent.'

Olivia whipped her head around. It certainly did look like her friend Cath. A delighted smile transformed her worried expression. 'Bloody hell, I think you're right. Coming to say hello to her?' Olivia asked.

Ruby shook her head. 'Ain't in the right mood. We never got on anyway. Thanks for the advice about . . . you know what. I'll try the chemist on the High Street.'

Before Olivia could bring up the subject of Harry, Ruby had set off. Not wanting to lose sight of her friend, Olivia dashed across the road, calling out, 'Cath! Wait up!'

The young woman glanced over her shoulder and seemed to hesitate. But instead of stopping and smiling as Olivia had expected her to do, she started pushing the pram away faster than before.

Olivia slowed down feeling confused, then with a determined spurt she started after Cath again. They'd not seen one another in a good while and it was possible that her friend hadn't recognised her. Olivia had not regained all the weight she'd lost and still looked drawn in the face.

'It's me . . . Livvie. Didn't you recognise me, Cath?' she burst out breathlessly as she came alongside her friend. 'I know I look a bit of a state.'

Still Cath kept going, turning her head away.

Olivia caught her arm. 'What is it? What have I done?' she asked, feeling hurt.

Cath slowed to a halt with a sigh. 'Nothing. You've done nothing. I just don't want to talk to you, or to anybody.' She turned to face Olivia then with a watery sniff. 'Ain't you, it's me,' she croaked. 'Sorry, it's just the way I feel. So leave me alone.'

'No, I bloody won't!' Olivia retorted indignantly. 'After all we went through together when we worked at Barratt's? I thought we were friends. *Real* friends.'

'We were,' Cath said huskily. 'But things change . . . '

A silence fell in which the two women locked eyes then Cath's chin dropped. Olivia relented and put a comforting arm round her.

'Oh, Cath,' she sighed. 'Don't cry. It's Trevor worrying you, isn't it?'

'Yeah . . . it's always him worrying me,' Cath said bitterly, cuffing her eyes.

'I heard you'd moved down Kent way,' Olivia pressed on, keen to keep the conversation going. 'I wanted to write but didn't know your address.'

'Didn't want anybody knowing it. Didn't want visitors. Want to be left alone.'

'Come and sit down with me . . . just for a

318

minute,' Olivia coaxed, pointing to a low brick wall fronting a small green. 'I'd love to get to know your little 'un. I haven't seen Rob since he was tiny.' She bent over to smile at the toddler sitting in his pram.

Cath let Olivia steer her son towards a patch of wall that was bathed in sunlight. She too trudged over and sat down in the warm.

'Remember when we used to do this dinnertimes at Barratt's?' Olivia nudged her friend. 'We'd sunbathe on the front wall with our sandwiches and flasks and get whistled at by the blokes from the stables. Then off we'd go for a walk down the High Street and look at all the stuff in the shop windows that we couldn't afford.'

'Yeah.' Cath smiled faintly. 'Seems ages ago now.'

'I remember you being sick that day your mum mixed up your sandwiches with your dad's and you ended up with fishpaste instead of cheese.'

Cath chuckled. 'I was up the duff then, that's why I threw up.'

As quiet settled on them Olivia knew they were both remembering taking that trip to Lorenco Road so Cath could have an abortion. 'How's Trevor?' Olivia asked gently but received no reply. 'How's your husband doing, Cath?'

'Ain't got a husband,' she said flatly. 'Just some bloke I go and visit in the sanatorium once a week. Sometimes he's so bad he don't even know who I am.'

'I thought he was getting better? Last time I

saw you he was back working down the railway yard.'

'The loud noise got to him. Doctor warned it could bring back bad memories. But he wanted to get out of the house and try to be normal again. And, God knows, that's what I wanted too.' Cath rocked the pram but when her son continued to whine she lifted him out. The sturdy little lad wanted to be on his feet but his mother kept him close by on his reins.

'Have you moved back this way?' Olivia asked. 'It'd be smashing to see you more often.'

Cath shook her head. 'Visiting Mum and Dad, that's all. I only come out for a walk to tire this one out with some fresh air. He's been playing up and driving me mum crackers. I keep to meself while I'm here. Can't stand all the gossips . . . ' She broke off abruptly. 'I know you ain't like that, Livvie. But some of 'em never give it a rest. I don't want people to keep asking how I am, how Trevor is, then feeling sorry for me when I tell them.' She turned away, blinking red-rimmed eyes. 'I feel wicked for wishing he'd died over there. But I do. And so does he. And sooner or later, I'm gonna shout it out and really give everybody something to chew over.'

Olivia squeezed her friend's hands. 'I do understand, Cath, honestly,' she said through a lump in her throat. And she did. There had been nights when she'd walked the wards, wishing a tormented soul a speedy end, knowing it was what he wanted too.

'Didn't expect to see you Wood Green way.'

Cath tried to sound brighter than she was feeling.

'I'm on a visit as well. Maggie lives round the corner. She's married now with a baby. Ricky was christened this afternoon at St Michael's and Maggie put on a tea for us.' Olivia paused then continued, 'I'm going back nursing in France soon though. It'd be smashing if we could meet up again before I sail.'

'I've got an appointment in Lorenco Road. That's what really brought me back this way,' Cath blurted out. 'I'd've got rid of it down in Kent but didn't have a clue where to go there.'

Now her friend had mentioned it, Olivia could detect a little tell-tale sign; Cath's dress buttons were gaping across her abdomen.

'Mum 'n' Dad don't know. Ain't telling them neither.'

'And Trevor?' Olivia asked, conquering her shock.

'No point telling *him*. He wouldn't remember. Anyway, ain't his.' Cath jutted her chin defiantly. 'It's the same bloke as before. He found out where Trevor was and paid him a visit in the sanatorium. I was there at the time and we got talking on the way out. I said he could stay overnight as he'd missed his train. He stopped five days in all. He knows about Rob being his now. I told him.'

'Does he know you're carrying again?' Olivia asked.

'Not told anyone about that, only you.' Cath hung her head. 'He's said he'll leave his wife for me, but he was back on leave from the navy.' She paused. 'So, we'll see what happens when this war's done. No point swapping one war cripple for another. Not sure I believe him anyway. And perhaps I won't break up his family even if he does mean it. Ain't decided yet.' She pursed her lips. 'Sound like a real hard-nosed cow, don't I? But I don't care. Me son comes first now. It'd be better if he believed his dad had passed away than know the truth about either of them.'

Olivia put an arm around her friend's shoulders, trying to comfort her.

' 'Nuff about me,' Cath said gruffly. 'How have you been, Livvie?' She cocked her head and frowned. 'You don't look as good as usual, if you don't mind me saying?'

'You should have seen me before,' Olivia replied ruefully. 'I had a bout of pneumonia in France. I came back to convalesce.'

'I didn't think you'd still be a VAD.'

'Reckon I'll see it through till the bitter end now. Please God, that won't be long.'

'Have you kept in touch with Lucas Black?'

'I had a letter from him just the other day. His platoon's stationed around Passchendaele. He says he's fine . . . but they all say that,' Olivia added wistfully.

'Sounds as though things could get serious between you two.' Cath smiled archly.

Olivia shrugged and chuckled. She couldn't talk about being loved by Lucas and loving him in return. Her happiness would just rub salt into her friend's wounds. 'We'll see what happens when this war's done.' She used Cath's words of a moment ago. She lifted the little boy onto her lap but he soon wriggled to get down again. 'We had some good times together, didn't we, Cath?'

'Yeah, I often think about those days at Barratt's. Especially you putting Nelly Smith in her place.' Cath got to her feet, picking up her son and putting him in the pram. 'I'd better be off. Mum'll wonder where I am.'

'What day is your appointment? I'm at a loose end all next week.'

'You'd come with me?'

'I won't let you go on your own,' Olivia said flatly. 'You felt faint last time.' She clearly remembered holding Cath up as she stumbled in pain on the way home.

'That's not why I told you, Livvie. I wasn't dropping a hint.'

'I know. I want to go with you,' Olivia said stoutly. 'I'm your friend ... always will be wherever we end up. I won't ever stop thinking of you as me friend Cath Mason even if I live to be a hundred and never see you again.'

'I'll say to Mum we're going out somewhere, like I did before, shall I?' Cath was blinking back tears.

'I'll tell you all about *Chu Chin Chow*; you can make out we saw that, if you like,' Olivia replied.

'Meet you outside Barratt's then? Friday at six o'clock if that's alright.'

'Fine by me,' Olivia said.

They parted with a hug and Olivia headed back towards Maggie's place in an odd mood. She hesitated at the gate and looked over her shoulder at Cath, wanting to give her a final wave. But Cath had her head down and pushed the pram around the corner without looking back.

# 22

Everything had looked the same, as though the house in Lorenco Road had been mothballed since their last visit. The unpleasant odour, the jumbled assortment of ornaments and clocks in the parlour where she'd waited while Cath had her operation, had all been as Olivia remembered them. As had the sly-eyed woman who'd palmed Cath's money into her pinafore then ushered her into the back room with the promise of a whisky to settle her down.

Thankfully Cath's experience was different from the last time. When it was all finished the abortionist had patted her client's arm, saying she could tell she had pushed a kid out since they'd last met. That apparently made things easier.

The weather was better too. Their last trip to this seedy neighbourhood in Edmonton had taken place on a dreary autumn night. Now, as they ambled arm in arm towards the bus stop, evening sunshine warmed their shoulders through the cotton blouses they wore.

Cath winced as they climbed aboard. 'Thanks for coming with me, Livvie. It's good of you, especially after the way I snubbed you. Sorry for being a rude cow.'

'You've got a lot on your plate; I'm not surprised you've been feeling crabby.' Olivia gave her a cuddle as they sat down together on a hard

325

seat. 'I'm just glad I bumped into you so we can keep in touch again.' She searched Cath's strained features. 'How do you feel? Any bad pain?' Her friend was putting on a brave face but she guessed Cath was suffering more than she was letting on.

'A bit uncomfortable. More worried about making a mess before I get indoors.' Cath fidgeted on the seat. The abortionist had given her wadding to stuff in her bloomers but it already felt sodden. 'Mum's bound to notice me stained underwear when she does the washing. I'll have to tell her I've got a heavy monthly.' She glanced at Olivia. 'She won't suspect a miscarriage anyhow. She knows me 'n' Trevor ain't shared a bed in ages.' Cath understood her friend's quizzical expression. 'They wouldn't think I've got it in me to have an affair. Come to that, neither did I,' she added wryly.

'I never thought I had it in me to leave home and go abroad on me own and learn to be a nurse. Surprising where life leads us,' Olivia remarked.

'D'you regret it?' Cath asked.

'Sometimes I do when the suffering gets to me. And I know I'll never again be as close to Alfie and the girls as I was. They've learned to do without me. Perhaps that's a good thing. For me as well as for them.' Olivia glanced through the bus window at the street scene. 'On a lovely evening like this it's hard to believe that such bloody rotten things are going on in the world.' She shook off her melancholy suggesting brightly. 'Here . . . why don't we go and see the old timers at Barratt's before you return to Kent? I bet Sal Shaw's still there. It'd be nice to see her and Nelly and some of the others.'

'Oh . . . I don't know . . . ' Cath didn't sound keen.

'Oh, come on, let's!' Olivia urged. 'I feel nostalgic about the place and I reckon you do too. I bet you a tanner that Nelly Smith's still there, cracking the whip on the roller-out girls.'

Cath gave a bashful smile. 'Alright, if you promise to slap 'em down when they start asking awkward questions about Trevor.'

'You don't need me for that! I know you can stick up for yourself, Cath.'

'Not any more, I can't,' she replied glumly. 'I've had the stuffing knocked out of me, Livvie. I'd rather avoid people now 'cos I start blubbing too easily.'

'I'll be in your corner then, till you buck yourself up. And you will, Cath. I know it,' Olivia encouraged her.

She might be Cath's knight in shining armour but she was thinking of the man who was *her* saviour. Lucas was always in her mind and in her heart. She said a prayer for him every night and wished him safe again every morning. Since she'd been home she'd written to him dozens of times, and had letters back telling her he loved her and longed for them to be together in England. But he didn't say he missed her. He'd never imply that he wanted her back in France with him. But that's where she was going. She was counting off the days until she could see Lucas again.

'What's it like in France?' Cath asked as the bus turned into White Hart Lane, heading towards Wood Green. 'I've tried talking to Trevor about it. I thought it might help to bring it out into the open instead of him bottling it up.' Cath wanted to understand the nature of the conflict that had destroyed her husband.

'St Omer's not far from the Channel ports and the weather's not that different from here,' Olivia began. 'When I left in January, though, I was lucky enough to travel on a good day. Just a week before it had been bloody freezing with snow on the ground. The winters can be hard to bear.' She gave Cath a wide-eyed look. 'Sometimes we wear two pairs of socks over our stockings, to keep the chilblains at bay, then can't get our boots on over 'em. Or if we can, they pinch so badly it's a toss-up between chilblains or crippled toes. The huts and tents we sleep in are draughty as hell and the heaters stink the place out with fumes. Then we're always running out of stuff. It's beg, steal or borrow most of the time. But we always return equipment as soon as we can. It's just not fair otherwise. And food's getting scarce, same as it is here. We grow vegetables . . . not enough, though, to keep us all going, especially when we've had in convoys of wounded. So many mouths to feed.'

The thought of vegetables had brought with it the memory of being sent with Rose to fetch potatoes. But that terrible day would remain unmentioned. Cath was a close friend and they'd shared secrets before, but the last thing she needed to hear now was a depressing story. The silence lengthened and Olivia realised Cath wanted to hear more about France.

'The battlefields get churned up, as you can imagine, and the patients arrive at the hospital caked in mud. It's not like the dirt round here. It's yellowy. And don't matter if the weather's been wet or dry, it's on 'em.' Olivia paused, then added dreamily, 'But there are still some spots that haven't been bombed and look pretty and peaceful. Like lovely paintings.' She recalled the one at Caroline Black's house that had reminded her of the fields behind St Omer. 'Lots of flowers out there, Cath . . . snowdrops after Christmas then later the bluebells take over in the woods. At this time of the year the meadows are packed with poppies blowing in the breeze. It's a wonderful sight, seeing them swaying about. We pick them and put them in the wards to cheer the place up. The patients call us Poppy Angels when we walk round with the vases.' Her voice had grown husky. She coughed to clear her throat. 'Then the guns start up again, and you forget about gazing at the scenery.' Olivia stood up. 'Come on, it's our stop next. Don't want to miss it.'

When they were on the pavement she suggested, 'Shall we meet up on Monday dinnertime and nip into Barratt's, to surprise them? Don't have to stay long if you don't want to.'

Cath nodded. 'I'm travelling back to Kent on Wednesday. Dad's borrowing his pal's Austin to save me the train fare and all the palaver of carrying luggage and folding up Rob's pram. It'll all go in the boot.'

Olivia gave her a hug, planting an affectionate kiss on her brow. 'See you on Monday then. Hope you get a good night's sleep.' She watched Cath walk away from her with small, careful steps but she gave a cheery wave over a shoulder.

Olivia got off the bus in Islington feeling in a better frame of mind than she had on setting out to accompany Cath to Lorenco Road. It was a relief that the operation was over with but it hadn't just been Cath's predicament worrying her. She'd had Ruby on her mind, too, and was wondering how on earth things would end up with Riley.

On turning the corner into Campbell Road she spied Herbert Hunter having a chinwag over the railings with Matilda's brother-in-law. Jimmy Wild started leering at Olivia and Herbie spun around to discover who'd caught his pal's eye. She cursed beneath her breath as he stepped away from Jimmy and into her path. She would sooner have slipped past unseen. But if things had turned out differently this man would have been her father-in-law. Whatever she thought of him, he *was* Joe's flesh and blood. Her uncle had told her that Herbie hadn't caused any trouble in her absence and had been keeping himself to himself.

'You're looking a bit better, love. Last time I spotted you up the road you was white as a ghost.' Herbie adopted a caring expression. 'Heard on the grapevine you've been proper poorly.'

'I'm much better now, thanks.' Olivia began edging past.

'Been back months, ain't yer, yet I've hardly seen you. Don't suppose you've been able to get out much, though, you poor old soul.'

'I've managed, thanks,' Olivia said shortly.

'Well, that's good to hear,' Herbie smarmed. ''S'pect yer back to stay now. Don't want to go catching nuthin' else nasty out there, do you?'

Olivia gave him a sharp look, wondering if he was hinting at 'something nasty' being Ruby's ailment. News of men giving VD to their wives and girlfriends back home would soon spread even if the women were like Ruby and ashamed to admit to it.

'I'm heading back over there in a couple of weeks actually, Mr Hunter.'

'Take me hat off to you. Brave lass, you are.' Herbie swung his head in a show of disbelieving admiration. 'Not seen much of your brother. Alfie still at home, is he? Wondered if he'd gone back Wood Green way with your uncle.' Herbie was probing. He knew very well that Alfie Bone was still living round the corner with Ed Wright. He'd seen him and the other blond lad just the other day, kicking a ball around in the Bunk. He knew too that the boys had been told to have nothing to do with him. In his innocence, Alfie had blurted out as much while sidling away. Herbie knew the SP with the posh lieutenant and this young woman. They'd get married and live in Swell Street, leaving Ed Wright in possession of Joe's old house.

Herbie would sooner see the place in ashes

than allow Sybil's old man to get his thieving mitts on Joe's property. Once Olivia Bone had moved off with her boyfriend Herbie was making his move. That house was his.

But for now he'd keep his teeth gritted and play a waiting game. As Olivia stepped past with a polite goodbye, he returned it then called out, 'Take care of yourself, ducks, won't yer now?'

★   ★   ★

'Oi! Nelly Smith! Got any jobs going?'

Olivia needn't have worried about Cath feeling too timid to speak up for herself with her old colleagues. As soon as they'd strolled in through the factory gates and spotted their old sparring partner her friend had let rip with a brash greeting. Olivia knew Cath was putting on a front, but liked to see it and murmured encouragingly, 'That's the way, Cath.'

Nelly's thin figure detached itself from the crowd and she gawped at them both before breaking into a grin. 'Well, I never! If it ain't Tommy Bone's daughter. And there's Cath Mason who was always giving Miss Wallis lip.'

' 'Ere, watch it, you,' Cath carried on in the same vein. 'I'm a married woman now, you know. It's Mrs Williams to you.'

Nelly trotted over to engulf the two visitors in a double-armed hug. 'Well, how you two gels been then?' she asked. 'You ain't really after your jobs back, are yer?' A gleam of anticipation lit her eyes. 'I could start you both this afternoon, if you like. We're that short of staff, I've roped me old

332

man into doing a couple of afternoons a week on the boilers after he finishes down the market.'

'Don't want jobs. We've just come to see how you're all doing . . . those of you that're still here, that is.' Olivia gave a wave to some of the women Nelly had been talking to. It was dinnertime for the workers and some of them were putting flasks and food wrappers back in their bags. She gazed up at the chimneys, spurting pungent vapour into the atmosphere. 'You've been making aniseed balls this morning.' Olivia wrinkled her nose. 'We knew that the moment we turned into Mayes Road.' The tell-tale smell had hit them in the back of the throat long before they came in through the factory gates.

'We have at that,' Nelly chortled. 'Dunno fer how much longer we'll be making anything at all though.' She crossed her arms over her skinny midriff. 'Production's down and not just 'cos we're losing staff to the war and the munitions factories.' She paused dramatically. 'Can't get the sugar, see. The delivery boys didn't bring nearly enough back from the docks last time. If it gets rationed . . . ' She shrugged. 'Don't think anybody's found a way to make sweets without it.'

The idea of the factory having to shut down shocked Olivia. For the whole of her lifetime Barratt's had been chugging along nicely. She realised that she felt sentimental about the place and, looking at Cath's expression, could see that she did too. But Nelly had a point: no sugar, no sweets.

'I've been working here nigh on twenty years,' Nelly boasted. 'Only Tommy Bone started at Barratt's before I did.' Her expression turned nostalgic. 'I do miss your dad, y'know, Livvie. And I never thought I'd say that. They was good old days before this damn' war went and ruined every thing.'

'I miss him too,' Olivia said simply.

Her father and Nelly Smith had fought like cat and dog, vying to get top spot and gain the most influence over the workers. But it was all water under the bridge. Now even old foes held a certain charm because they were reminders of better times.

'Heard about Miss Wallis, did you?' Nelly sucked her teeth. 'Who'd've thought it?'

'Miss Butter Wouldn't Melt turns out to be worse than the rest of us. Miss Sticky Fingers more like . . . ' Cath crowed.

Olivia and Cath exchanged a glance. Neither of them had forgotten the time when Cath herself had been involved in pinching sweets. Tommy Bone had been part of the racket too, with his pal. Olivia had been distraught to find out he'd stooped to thieving. The memory made her smile now. It had at least been a time when they'd all been together at the factory and everybody had been safe and well.

'I thought the guv'nors would go after her and have her in court,' Nelly said. 'Reckon she must've had someone rooting for her upstairs in the boardroom.' She raised her eyebrows. 'Loose drawers that one, that's all I'm sayin'.'

'Did they replace Lucas?'

Nelly shook her head. 'Didn't replace Miss Wallis neither. Just an office typist took over. Cutting back, see.'

Just then Sal Shaw pushed through the crowd of women standing around, listening to the reminiscences. 'Bleedin' hell, you've lost weight, Livvie.' She gave Olivia a hug. 'They're working you too hard over there.'

'That's what I keep telling 'em, Sal,' Olivia answered gamely. She'd always liked this woman who'd been an ally to her in the early days at Barratt's when Olivia had constantly been at loggerheads with Nelly.

'Shame you didn't fetch along your little lad so we could see him,' Sal said to Cath. 'Bet he's a handful, ain't he, now he's up on his feet?'

'He's that alright! That's why I left him with his nan,' Cath replied.

'Trevor better now, is he?' a sly voice called out from the back of the crowd.

'Wouldn't be here if he weren't, would she?' Olivia shot back, but in a light inconsequential tone.

'Don't suppose you kept in touch with Mr Black, did yer, Livvie?' Nelly asked, a shade too inquisitively.

'I've seen him quite a few times. Thankfully he's not been brought into my hospital as a patient.'

Nelly crossed herself. 'God bless him and keep him. Yer dad didn't take to him, but I did. I thought he was alright.'

'We all did,' shouted a lewd voice.

The bell for afternoon shift pealed out,

sounding as deafeningly urgent as Olivia remembered.

'Come inside for a little while,' Nelly urged. 'Won't make you do no work, promise.'

'Better not stop any longer. Mum's waiting to go out and she won't want to take me son with her.' Cath indicated she'd had enough and was ready to go.

The girls both waved as their old colleagues started filing into the factory. They turned to go but before they'd reached the gates Sal came up behind them with a bag filled with sherbet and liquorice dabs. 'There . . . for your lad.' She patted Cath's arm. 'Keep yer chin up, gel.' She'd guessed how things were but, unlike the others, took no delight in gossiping about Cath's woes.

They strolled into Mayes Road and Cath snorted, 'Well . . . look who it is.'

Olivia had noticed Ruby heading towards them. She was late back after her break and was half-running.

'Alright, Cath?' Ruby said stiltedly.

'Not bad. You?' Cath snapped back.

Ruby grabbed her cousin's arm, pulling Olivia aside to hiss, 'You ain't told *her* about . . . '

''Course not,' Olivia said with a frown. 'How are things?'

'Better.'

'With Riley as well?'

'Ain't heard from him and don't want to.' With that, Ruby hurried off into the factory.

'What was all that about?' Cath said as they set off home.

'Oh, just Ruby and her problems. You know how she is.'

'Yeah, I do,' Cath said sourly. She'd not forgotten her husband having a fling with the cow.

'Rob'll like his sherbets.' Olivia changed the subject.

'It's good of Sal to think of him but I don't let him have sweets. He's too young and they'll rot his teeth.' Cath handed over the bag. 'There, give it to your Alfie, if you like.'

'Safe journey to Kent,' Olivia said when they parted on the corner.

'Safe journey to you, too,' Cath said, wiping away a tear. 'Write to me, won't you, Livvie?'

''Course I will, now I've got your address. And I want some letters from you when you get a spare minute.'

They hugged then parted quickly. Olivia let the breeze dry her damp eyes as she walked away. But she was smiling and feeling more content than she had in a while. She hoped that Cath was too.

# 23

'You'll soon be on the mend, Dawson. I need you to fall in, man, so no swinging the lead.'

'Right-ho, sir, be back in line in a jiffy.' Sergeant Dawson managed to execute a mocking salute from his supine position. At one time he'd never have dared to be so familiar with his commanding officer. He and his lieutenant were of a similar age and had come through unimaginable horrors shoulder to shoulder. They were all that was left of their original platoon and in a different life, where birth and class didn't matter, might have been pals. The others: Joe Hunter, Freddie Weedon, and numerous other young faces that Dawson would never forget in his lifetime, had perished. Their more fortunate former comrades had been invalided home. A few hadn't thought themselves lucky, though, as they'd boarded the ambulance train taking them to the ports, trouser legs or sleeves pinned up. Dawson understood how they felt.

He knew he wasn't going to lose a limb or die . . . not this time. But he'd never again be able to salute his lieutenant properly with his right hand. Not without the part of it he'd lost in the mud. He'd return to the platoon once the gash in his back healed; he knew that was the most serious of his injuries. He'd been thinking things through while being bumped along a duckboard with Lieutenant Black jogging alongside the stretcher bearers. Making plans had helped him block out some of the agony. He'd come back as a private, if need be, and carry a machine-gun pannier in his left hand. He might even be able to aim a rifle after he'd got used to being cack-handed with the bloody thing.

They were up and out of the trench and on rough ground. He could feel every jolt through his spine. He knew when they reached the track and their boots were on blessed firmer terrain. He heard his lieutenant shout that the convoy of ambulances was now in sight. The stretcher bearers slowed down as they joined a press of people. They put him down on the ground beside other casualties. The closest ambulance was having its back doors slammed shut before moving off. Even though they'd taken care about easing him onto the earth, the pressure on Dawson's back made him groan and fidget. The next ambulance in line reversed towards the queue of injured and some stretchers were lifted and pushed inside.

Lucas squatted down and stuck a lit Woodbine between his sergeant's trembling lips. 'You make sure the doctor notes down everything on your docket.' He tapped Dawson's breast pocket where a patient's records would be pinned. 'You've got a Blighty One so make the most of it, you lucky sod.'

'Ain't much wrong with me, sir,' Dawson protested in a gasp. 'Be back in no time after they've bandaged me up.' He coughed, accidentally spitting out his cigarette.

Lucas wedged it back between his lips. 'Swap

places in that case. I could do with going back home to see my girl.'

Dawson winked a mud-encrusted eyelid. He knew the lieutenant was in love. Not that the man spoke about personal things. In fact, it'd been the first time Dawson had heard him hint at a romance. But he'd seen him with his letters. All the courting men were the same: soppy smile as they read, breast pocket when they'd finished. The poor sods like him who were married with kids wore worried frowns when reading news from home.

The lieutenant was on his tod now with more raw recruits in the platoon than they'd ever had before. Dawson felt bad about letting him down. As the stretcher bearers lifted him and helped the orderlies get him in position in the back of the van, he turned on his side to ease the pain.

Lucas took out his cigarettes and struck a match with jittery fingers. He'd miss his sergeant, not least because he knew he himself was next. There was nobody else left from 1914. He'd been lucky again. Just a hole in his thigh from a bit of shell casing. It had missed his vitals by a few inches and for some reason, as he thought about the devastation that would have caused him, he started to shake with silent laughter.

He was aware that one of the ambulance drivers had detached herself from her colleagues and was staring at him. He was used to women staring at him even when he was rain-sodden and hysterical. But he gave her a friendly smile.

God bless every one of 'em for turning up under heavy shelling and prowling Fokkers. Just last week a convoy of ambulances had come under attack. All had been lost.

'Got a spare gasper?'

She'd come over while he'd been propped against the wall of the dressing station, puffing away for all he was worth. He wanted to see Dawson safely on his way before he went back to the billet in the village.

Lucas offered the girl his packet of Woodbines. 'Keep them,' he said, and started to move off.

'Are you Lieutenant Black?'

Lucas swivelled on the spot.

'Thought it was you! We've never met but I've heard about you. I'm Rose Drew — Olivia's friend. Don't suppose you've heard of me though . . . '

'I have!' Lucas grinned. 'Of course I have,' he said. 'She speaks about you a lot.'

Rose beamed. 'I had to come over and say hello. You rescued her after that bad business with the German and I wanted to say thanks.' Rose's voice was breathless with emotion as she added, 'I know you love her. But I do too. She's the best friend I ever had. So while I've got the chance, I just wanted to tell you that I think you're bloody marvellous.' She thumped him clumsily on the arm then looked bashful for having done so.

'Are you over it now?' Lucas asked. 'I know you didn't get off lightly.'

'Yeah.' Rose pulled a face. 'No sense, no feeling.' She tapped her head where Schmidt had

341

rifle-butted her. 'What happened to him? Should've strung him up.'

Lucas shrugged and mimed innocence.

'Ah! Hush-hush, eh?' Rose tapped her nose, making him chuckle. She glanced over one shoulder to where her van was being loaded up. 'Better go. You should get that looked at, lieutenant.' She pointed at a dark stain on his uniform.

'Will do.'

'She's coming back, y'know,' Rose added, turning about before she'd made a yard. It had just occurred to her that as he'd been on the front line for a while, he might not know Olivia was due in France. 'I had a letter. Bet you've got one waiting for you too when you get back to base.' Rose noticed her commandant glowering at her. 'That's me guv'nor. Got to go.' She stuck out her hand. 'Glad I've met you, lieutenant. Stay out of trouble.'

'You too, Rose,' he said, gripping her fingers. He'd not wanted the reminder of Karl Schmidt. The thought of that bastard having Olivia in his clutches still made Lucas wake up at night in a cold sweat.

'The bigger picture' Saville had called the possible sacrifice of Olivia. The memory of that meeting made Lucas grind his teeth. He understood the brigadier's predicament. He didn't have one himself. His conscience was clear. He'd do the same again . . . kill anybody he had to . . . to keep her safe. And thinking that didn't make him a traitor, it made him human. Tommy Bone's daughter's life was no less important than a brigadier's. The rotten establishment, determined to protect its own and bugger the rest, would've despatched a platoon to bring back a girl from Mayfair. Lucas stopped his thoughts there, smiling to himself as he savoured the first drag on a new cigarette. Perhaps he should go into politics when he got back. That'd shock them . . . a Black standing for the Socialists.

In the distance the Verey lights were popping into the sky, one after the other like Roman candles, shedding their lime-bright light over the weary faces of the walking wounded. They were congregating around the door to the dressing station, sucking on cigarettes and patiently waiting their turn. Every one of them was grateful not to have been rushed straight in as an emergency.

Lucas noticed Rose was helping load up a van with stretchers and on impulse he jogged closer, calling out a question: 'Olivia's going back to St Omer, I take it?' Oddly, he wished she was in France now, despite the curdling of his guts that signalled he was already fretting over her being once again in the thick of it.

'End of next week she's due in,' Rose yelled back. 'And I shouldn't tell you this, but she said she can't wait to see you.' Rose gave him a farewell wave before nimbly climbing into the ambulance to take the wheel.

'I can't wait to see her either,' he muttered to himself. But he knew that any meeting would be some way off still. By the end of next week he wasn't sure where he'd be. In hell quite possibly.

The darkness was getting thicker and she couldn't breathe. She couldn't bear to suffocate. Her fingers tried to claw open a hole in the wall of blackness to let in light and air. She was desperate to fill her lungs and to see. But she could hear somebody close by. She must open her eyes and find him. Then run before the footsteps stopped. Too late . . . he'd found her . . . he had her now . . . pinning her down . . .

'Livvie . . . Livvie, wake up, dear! You're having a nightmare.' Flora Thistle was leaning over Olivia's bed, holding her by the shoulders to calm her thrashing. 'It's alright. Hush! You were crying out in your sleep so I've woken you. You sounded so frightened.'

Olivia heaved herself up into a seated position, still panting. She cupped her face in her hands, sucking in some ragged breaths. After a moment of calm she whispered, 'Sorry . . . didn't mean to wake you again, Flora.' She felt guilty. It was the second time in a week her roommate had had to comfort her in the middle of the night. Olivia knew how desperately they all needed their sleep.

'It doesn't matter,' Flora said kindly. 'How about some cocoa? I'll put the kettle on. If I rinse out the tin there should be enough for half a cup each.'

'No, I'm fine, thanks. You should get back to bed. We're on early shift.'

Flora patted her shoulder and started back towards her bunk.

'You won't tell Matron, will you?'

'No . . . not this time.' Flora returned to her side. 'But if it goes on, I will. So perhaps you should tell her yourself, Livvie.' She paused. 'I'm not complaining, I'm worried about you. You must have some dreadful memories tormenting you. After what you've been through nobody would blame you for saying enough's enough.'

Olivia pressed her fingers to her eyes to drive out the demons lurking behind them. 'When it's over for everybody then it'll be time enough for me to leave,' she murmured.

Flora sat down on the edge of the mattress beside her, squeezing her hands. 'I know you think you'll be letting us down if you leave, but you won't. You deserve to be well as much as any patient does. I know you're physically better, but it wasn't just pneumonia making you poorly, was it? Perhaps you've come back too soon and needed a longer rest.'

'I can cope with it,' Olivia said earnestly. 'Please don't tell Matron or she'll send me home. We need every pair of hands, you know we do.' She managed a wry smile. 'I can bribe you with sherbet.'

Flora chuckled as she stood up. 'I'll hold you to that. One sherbet dab is the price of my silence.'

Olivia had brought some of the Barratt's sherbet dabs with her and still had a few left. She had been saving some for when she saw Lucas. A reminder for him of their good old times at the factory.

She'd been back at St Omer for over two months and the nightmares had started almost at once. Sometimes she'd have days free from torment; at others she'd have several consecutive sleepless nights. She wasn't sure what triggered them: perhaps the smell of the hospital, or the sight of soldiers ... some of them in grey uniform. There had been prisoners-of-war among the first convoy she'd encountered once back on the wards. Olivia had been grateful that Matron hadn't allowed her to see to them. She'd said it was too soon. But even after a disturbed night, Olivia would rise in the morning and carry out her duties cheerfully. If she felt tired then she wouldn't show it. Everybody was tired. And hungry. Lack of sleep and food was their way of life now.

'Sure you don't want a hot drink? Or to talk?' Flora offered.

Olivia shook her head. 'Get yourself tucked up again. I'm going to read my letters for a few minutes before I settle down. Do you mind if I have the lamp on? I'll keep it low.'

'No, help yourself.' Flora snuggled back under the covers.

Olivia lit the lamp then took the handful of letters from her nightstand. She opened the first envelope, angling the paper towards the glow. She smiled while rereading that Cath had decided to move back home with her parents. There was no point in being miserable and alone in Kent when Trevor wasn't aware of her most of the time, she'd written. She'd got a part-time job in packing at Barratt's, and every other Sunday her father borrowed the Austin and took her to Kent to see her husband. The next bit had made

Olivia exclaim in delight the first time she'd read it. Trevor seemed brighter the last time Cath had visited him. There was a new nurse he'd taken a shine to. He called her 'Poppy Angel' though her name was Valerie Booth. Cath had met her and described her as looking a bit like a man, but definitely a good sort and very jolly and patient. She'd added that she wished she had the Poppy Angel's qualities but feared being jolly and patient had been wrung out of her.

Olivia slipped the letter away then took out Maggie's note with news of home. She knew that all off by heart, she'd read it so many times. Alfie had been chosen to be in the school football team and was now confident he'd play for Arsenal! Her little nephew had cut three teeth in a week and Nancy had been promoted to Section Leader at Turner's. Olivia felt proud every time she read about her family, and how well they were doing. She folded the paper and reached for the next letter. It was from Rose. Her friend had told her wonderful news about bumping into Lucas and finding him well. He's gorgeous, she had underlined, and said he knew Olivia was back in France because Rose herself had told him. Olivia rolled onto her back then, having saved the best till last. Slipping the letter from its envelope, she placed her lips to it before reading it. She didn't need to strain her eyes to see the sloping black writing. She knew all of it word for word. Lucas loved her . . . he was coming to see her as soon as he could . . . he wished the war was over with . . . she must take good care of herself. Olivia placed that envelope under her pillow. She laid her cheek against it, cuddling into it, willing him to know she was thinking of him, loving him, wanting him in this bed with her. She closed her eyes, imagining his arms about her, his mouth on hers. No nightmares now . . . she turned out the lamp.

She could hear Flora's steady breathing and was glad her roommate had got back to sleep quickly. A nurse on night duty had gone past, swinging a hurricane lamp, and Olivia listened to her tramping feet and watched the shadows moving on the wall. She strained her ears but there was no other sound . . . just the distant rumble of the guns. Her eyelids felt weighty and she wriggled down further in the bed, hugging her happy memories about her like another blanket.

# 24

'As you're all aware there's been no let-up in the business around Passchendaele.' Matron's all-encompassing gaze roamed over her nursing team. 'I expect you know what I am about to say next. The centres and trains down the line are again struggling with the influx of casualties. Base hospitals are being pressed to send people. Are any of you willing to be transferred?' She glanced around for a sign of volunteers. 'This matter will doubtless keep cropping up. Would that we could bring an end to the whole confounded war and rejoice in the next move being back home,' she ended on a heartfelt sigh.

'Amen to that!' Olivia breathed amidst similar mutters from her colleagues. Nevertheless she put her hand in the air.

'Sister Bone,' Matron quietly acknowledged her, but looked elsewhere, counting other hands that had been elevated.

'Come to my office after supper to deal with the forms and so on,' she addressed the Queen Alexandra nurses who'd volunteered. 'Sister Bone, I'd like a quick word with you now.'

The group began to disperse back to their duties on the wards. A convoy had turned up last night with more serious cases than walking wounded. Staff meetings were brief and rare at such busy times.

Olivia approached Matron to find out why her

services hadn't been as welcome as those of others. She knew she was the only VAD to have put up her hand. She might not be as experienced as the regulars, but she was hard-working. Matron had often praised her for being conscientious. VADs were always needed to work in tandem with the ward sisters, to relieve them of routine tasks. She imagined that the clearing stations were no different in that respect.

But perhaps her superior feared she wasn't up to the increased challenge after her recent woes. She hadn't had a nightmare for weeks, though, and Matron wasn't aware she'd had any at all. Olivia trusted that Flora had kept her word on that.

'I am well enough to go down the line, ma'am,' Olivia started to say without preamble. 'I want to. I've been here for years and feel ready to move on.'

'I don't think you should go,' Matron answered bluntly. 'Selfish indeed I am, to want your capable hands here at St Omer, but it's not that keeping me from agreeing to a transfer. It's not even the other business with the German prisoners. You've been back here a while and seem to be working to your usual high standard. It appears you've pluck and resilience in abundance, Sister Bone.'

'Thank you, ma'am. So, what's the problem then?'

'The risks to your personal safety will increase dreadfully. You're young . . . so much life still to live . . . but even that's not the crux of it.'

Matron paused. 'You want to go to be close to *him*, don't you? Be on the spot in case you can save him, if the worst happens and he's brought in to your station, badly wounded?'

Olivia nodded. Tears were glistening in her eyes but she pressed her trembling lips together in an attempt to appear stoic and efficient.

'That hope of making a difference took me to the front line too, so I understand how you feel,' Matron said gently. 'I thought, if I could just be on the spot for my brother, I could save him. The arrogance of it . . . ' She cleared her throat. 'We weren't well prepared in those early days of the war. I saw things in that dungeon of a hospital that will always haunt me. A string of broken men carried straight from the battlefield into a church cellar to be operated on. Basic tools and little morphine . . . ' Her voice tailed away. 'You don't need me to elaborate. Suffice to say that we are far better placed here at St Omer.'

'I know we are,' Olivia said hoarsely. 'But at least you had a chance to care for your brother and do all you could for him.' She bit her lip, ashamed of what she was about to confess. 'My friend Rose met Lucas some months ago. He was bringing in his injured men from the trenches. I feel stupidly jealous of her. I wanted that precious time with him to be mine. Every morning I wake not knowing whether I've already seen him for the last time.'

'Does he want you to go into Flanders?'

'God, no!' Olivia barked out. 'He wanted me to stay in England where it's safe.'

351

'He's a good man, Olivia. I wish you had listened to him.'

'I know, and thank you for wanting to protect me. But I must go after him so we can be together if an opportunity arises. Please don't deny me what you had yourself. I want *my* chance to do what I can for somebody I love. Or to say goodbye, if that's what it comes to.'

Matron gave a wan smile. 'I'd rather you didn't go. I'd spare you the hellish ordeal, for make no mistake about it — that is what it is. In comparison this place is a Sunday afternoon in the park. You know that Brandhoek was shelled, don't you?'

Olivia nodded. They'd all heard that a nurse had been killed and others wounded at a clearing station set close to Ypres.

'I won't be a hypocrite. If my brother Ralph were still alive and in the thick of it, then the front line is where I'd still be. He was a smashing boy. Broke my mother's heart to lose him. And mine too. I'm glad my father never knew what happened to him. He passed away just before the war and Ralph was man of the house then.'

Matron had rarely spoken about that time, or about her family. But barriers were being ground down by the war. People had started to open up about their feelings. At one time virtuous daughters would only have discussed men and sex with their friends in self-conscious whispers. Now off-duty nurses from stately homes swore like troopers and talked without a blush about what it would be like . . . or *had* been like . . . to sit astride a fellow. And Olivia joined in with it, and not just to fit in. They weren't degenerates and hadn't developed barnyard morals. They just wanted to snatch at life and do those things their elders and betters had been fortunate enough to do already. And they promised one another, as they smoked and drank, that they'd never be as stupid as to start another war like this — as their elders and betters had done before they'd retired to the comfort of their clubs and drawing rooms to sit it out.

Matron started to walk away down the corridor and Olivia snapped herself to attention and trotted after her. 'I'm so sorry about your brother. It must have been an awful time for you all, ma'am.'

'It was, but thankfully he's at peace now.'

Olivia thought of Joe, also done with all the horror and resting in a Flanders graveyard.

'I'll see to the paperwork.' Matron clasped Olivia's shoulder. 'I'll expect you to write occasionally.'

'I will, I promise. Thanks very much.' Olivia smiled wryly at her. 'Lucas has asked me to marry him. I know in my heart that it might never be. One or other of us might be unlucky. But I refuse to think about that and pray we will at least have some time together first as a couple.'

Matron was about to say something encouraging but instead patted the girl's arm rather than tempt fate. 'If it gets too much and you want to come back, you have only to let me know and I'll do what I can to arrange it. But promise me one thing?'

Olivia nodded eagerly.

'Don't start smoking again. Your lungs are still delicate after the pneumonia.'

'I'll try not to . . . promise.' Olivia hadn't had a cigarette for months and hadn't wanted to either. It was still difficult enough drawing fresh air into her lungs.

★　★　★

It was mid-October and the poppy fields had died back to patchy brown grass. But even were it high summer there'd be no flowers here. For the past half an hour the train had rattled on through a terrain that was bleak and littered with broken buildings and skeletal tree stumps. But it was the carcasses of the dead horses, left where they'd fallen, that really upset her. Those innocent beasts had been led from quiet English meadows, unaware what horror awaited them on churned foreign soil. The battle must have passed close by at some time. Olivia hoped it never returned, as she knew it could. Lines were redrawn back and forth as both sides pushed then retreated over the same cratered ground.

Olivia and a colleague were well on their way towards their destination at Poperinghe. The other volunteers from St Omer were setting off tomorrow. Her companion was a single woman in her late-twenties. She had a sallow face set with lively blue eyes and framed by curly brown hair. Morag was a regular nurse from Scotland and used to a nip in the air, she'd said as the sleet had started to batter the train windows. 'Be hard pushed to find a wee bluebell in a wood round here,' she declared, wrinkling her nose at the scenery.

'Or a café selling coffee and eclairs,' Olivia lamented. She had enjoyed her trips to the villages surrounding St Omer to have lunch with Rose. The evening before they'd left, Matron had thrown a little party for the girls being transferred. Egg sandwiches, jelly, Madeira cake, even a few bottles of champagne had been purloined from a place Matron refused to reveal, to give them a send-off. The nurses had eaten a little then made sure that the boys on C Ward all got a look in. Especially with a beaker of champagne as that seemed to be favourite with those who were well enough to be allowed the treat.

Olivia sank back against the hard seat, smiling to herself at the memory. She tucked her woolly scarf, knitted by Alfie, more firmly about her neck and pulled her cap lower over her thick fair hair. Their long gabardine coats gave them scant protection from the draught whistling around their feet. Stamping their boots up and down at intervals on the carriage floorboards kept the chilled blood moving. Gazing out of the window over the spoiled ground once more, Olivia wondered how it had looked years ago before the war ravaged it. Away in the distance dark jagged cliffs rose against the horizon.

'Och . . . put a sock in it.' Morag clucked her tongue as the noise from the next carriage built to a crescendo.

Olivia simply chuckled. She loved the sound of

the soldiers singing lustily and a mouth organ being tooted. A troop of new recruits had climbed aboard about an hour ago. Olivia and Morag had hung out of the window to wave to them. By that time the girls had already been well into their own journey. The soldiers had waved back and whistled their appreciation. They'd all looked young and fresh-faced, probably just eighteen after receiving their call-up papers. The constant banging of the guns, under ten kilometres distant now, didn't seem to bother them as they broke out into a rendition of 'It's a Long Way to Tipperary'. They had the brash swagger of young men on their first time away from home.

Once the train had again jerked into motion Olivia had closed the window and sat down, whispering a prayer for them all. They had brought to mind young Albert Carter and she'd implored God to end this wicked war before he was of an age to be summoned back.

A whistle sounded and Olivia fought with the window to open it and poke her head out. But not for long; icy drizzle was driven into her eyes, making them sting. They were coming into a station, if you could call a stretch of concrete and a solitary bench crammed with people by such a name.

Their trunks and personal paraphernalia had been packed up and deposited in the goods wagon, leaving them to manage just their carpet bags filled with essentials. Having gathered those up Olivia peered out into the drizzle. She noticed at once the man she suspected was their chauffeur. An RAMC corporal with a luxuriant moustache was striding to and fro, looking impatient. As they disembarked, he spotted them and approached, thrusting out a tin hat in each hand.

Having noticed their surprise, he smirked. 'No nice cosy base hospital for you now, ladies.' He had a Scottish burr to rival Morag's. 'You'll need those beauties where you're off to. And your gas masks. Keep everything handy at all times.' He marched off, beckoning them to follow him. 'Come on then. Your stuff will be sent on. No time to dither. A convoy's due to arrive. We've had a runner up from the line bearing the good news.'

★ ★ ★

'This is quite a home from home,' Olivia exclaimed, casting a glance over the tents and marquees stretching off into the distance.

'Aye . . . that it is,' Morag agreed with a grin.

They'd sat alongside the corporal driving the ambulance to Nine Elms casualty clearing station. On arrival they'd been bemused to see that most of it consisted of marquees. Of course it had to be like that . . . they'd mocked their own surprise. Clearing stations had to be packed up and moved. Ground was won or lost and proximity to the shelling meant that often the dangers of being so close to the front line outweighed the benefits. But a station couldn't be shifted too far from the trenches. Badly injured men had little chance of surviving a

357

lengthy journey so needed to be operated on locally.

The compound was obviously unfinished in places; planking rested against half-built huts along the perimeter. It certainly wasn't the grim cellar of Matron's description, and for that Olivia was thankful.

But, as the sardonic corporal had warned on the short drive, there'd be no time for lassies to be star-gazing. As they were gathering their bags from the vehicle a convoy of ambulances began to arrive.

Immediately a hubbub broke out. The summons of bugles and whistles was interspersed with urgent calls from staff as they began streaming out of the rows of canvas tents to assist the casualties. A mass of white, blue and khaki uniforms mingled together as stretcher bearers, orderlies, nurses and medical officers bore down on the vehicles. The sitters were helped out of the front seats of the vans, to totter on crutches. Those gassed, with bandaged eyes, clung to whoever or whatever was available, but all so heartbreakingly patient and grateful for this sanctuary at last. Olivia and Morag exchanged a look then dumped down their belongings in the ambulance footwell and pitched in.

'Welcome to the mad house.' A VAD sporting the Red Cross insignia addressed Olivia with a bleak smile while sinking to her knees and soothing a boy with a gaping wound in his abdomen. 'Come far?' she asked Olivia without looking up from the lad on the stretcher.

'St Omer . . . ' Olivia replied, joining her on her knees and helping to restrain him as gently as possible. He seemed determined to try and get up and every movement made him haemorrhage.

'Here . . . put your fist on that while I fetch some wadding.' The nurse grabbed Olivia's hand and rammed it against a puddle of blood in the boy's ragged uniform. 'Be back in a mo' . . . won't get him in the door yet anyway.' She jerked a nod at the crush of stretcher bearers lining the entrance to the surgical ward then leaped to her feet and dashed off.

Olivia looked at the boy, her heart lodged in her throat. She felt determined not to let him die and yet she wondered how he was still alive. Her fist had fallen a long way into his abdomen and was now scarlet. She wanted to talk to him but all she could think was that Matron was right. Being a VAD at St Omer had been a picnic compared to this and she'd been here not one hour yet. 'It's stopped raining at last, so that's a good start,' she burst out.

He nodded, wanting to be friendly despite the pain making it impossible for him to unclench his jaw and talk to her.

Against her wrist she could feel the pulse of his life blood, sickeningly regular. And then the nurse was back and a thick pad of folded bandage was stuffed against the wound. The next moment some orderlies had run up and borne him away.

'Will he pull through?' Olivia gratefully wiped gore from her hands onto the pinafore being held out for her to use.

'Should think he might at that,' the nurse said. 'If a doctor gets to him in time. I've seen them brought in with multiple wounds and sitting up eating bacon for breakfast a few days later. Never can tell.'

Olivia had been aware of the barrage of mortar fire increasing in volume and frequency. A sudden explosion made her gasp and instinctively crouch down, flinging her arms up over her head in self-protection. A moment later she looked about to see that everybody else apart from Morag, who'd also taken cover, was carrying on. Nothing had been blown up but Olivia's head was pounding like a drum. She guessed she and Morag weren't alone in having ears that hurt even if they had been the only ones badly spooked.

Olivia shot upright and, dodging hot metal fragments dropping to the ground, caught up with her new colleague.

'Bit too close for comfort,' the nurse said. 'You'll get used to it, though. I'm Nurse Archer. Lucy, you can call me.'

Olivia introduced herself, feeling a bit foolish now for acting the Nine Elms novice. She dropped down before a patient when Lucy did, helping her to ease a boot from a foot so swollen that its owner panted out between groans that he'd not been able to get it off for a week. He was crying in pain from his mangled toes rather than from his fresh scalp wound.

'If you give me a pair of scissors, I'll carry on here and let you move on to another patient,' Olivia offered.

Nurse Archer handed over her scissors, and a length of wadding pulled from her apron pocket, then sprang to her feet.

'What's your name then?' Olivia asked the middle-aged fellow while peeling two sides of stiff cracked leather from his frozen blue-black flesh. She winced at the stench and beckoned frantically as she saw two orderlies emerge from a nearby tent. She continued talking to her gangrenous patient until he too was borne away on his stretcher. Then, still crouching down, she turned to the next man, and the next, and the next . . . until the civilised ways of St Omer hospital were forgotten and her routine was damp ground scratching at her knees and broken flesh held together by her hands until the orderlies came back.

When all the patients had finally been removed to the wards Olivia pushed herself to her feet in stages, trying to straighten her stiff back as painlessly as possible. She and Morag recovered their luggage from the ambulance then dropped it at their feet, taking a breather after their baptism of fire. They looked at one another but didn't speak. They didn't need to express what was clear to see in their eyes. They glanced about, wondering where their accommodation was, guessing it would be in one of the smaller bell tents. They'd seen a number of nurses emerge from those.

'Make the most of this, lassies. Ye'll be doing it all again soon enough.' The RAMC corporal who had brought them from the station gave them an ironic salute as he got into the ambulance and drove it away.

'Och . . . wee wretch that one is.' Morag appeared to have perked up. Her blue eyes were twinkling as they followed the departing vehicle.

'If I had a fag, I'd smoke it,' Olivia said ruefully, thinking of the promise she'd made to Matron and knowing it would soon be broken. With a weary exhalation, she reached down for her bags.

# 25

'D'you think we'll ever be able to explain what went on here to those back home?' Rose was looking philosophical, leaning against her ambulance's bonnet and staring up at the starless sky.

'I'm not even gonna try,' Olivia replied, taking another drag on her cigarette. 'We're in an exclusive club now, Rose Drew,' she announced. 'But at least we're in it together. When we finally break camp and sail into the sunset we'll keep schtum.' She put the toe of her boot on the dog end, savouring the nicotine tang on her lips and in her nostrils as she exhaled. 'We love 'em too much to tell the whole truth. So you and me'll have to keep meeting up until we're old and grey, just to let off steam about what happened when it wasn't all over by Christmas.'

It was now close to midnight. Verey lights were tracing stripes across the clouds and occasional bursts of fire could be heard. But after the recent bombardment it was comparatively peaceful. It seemed Fritz had retreated to lick his wounds. And they were deep, judging by the horde of wounded prisoners who'd been brought to Nine Elms.

The convoys had started to arrive at midday and had petered out about an hour ago. The stragglers with lesser wounds had been the last to arrive, a few of them German.

363

When Olivia had glimpsed Rose amongst the ambulance drivers pulling in that afternoon it had been the single joyous moment for her in hours of gruelling activity. Yet they had been unable to do more than beam at one another across a sea of heads then carry on with their work. Rose had returned three times; on each trip her vehicle and those of her colleagues were crammed to the gunwales.

'You didn't tell your lot about being kidnapped, did you?' Rose said.

Olivia grimaced at her. 'Did you tell your family about what Schmidt did to you?'

'Nope . . . just said I'd had an accident.' Rose shrugged. 'Was going to, but Mum's turned odd. She's got it into her head that Dad's deserted and is living in a Tunis pub or whatever they call it over there. He's been gone nearly two years now.' Rose paused. 'I didn't have the heart to complicate things for her by saying, he's dead — and, by the way, an escaped German brained me with a rifle.' She rubbed the faint scar beneath her fringe.

'I told mine I'd fallen over. It's partly true, I did, after Fischer clumped me.' Olivia's fingers ran over the place beneath her sleeve where her stitches had been. 'I certainly couldn't tell them about the kidnap. Hysterics all round that would have been.'

'Pair of clumsy cows, us two.' Rose stretched, sighing a cloud of warm breath into the frosty air. ''S'pose I'd better get going before me Commandant notices I've not clocked back in. She's a right bitch.'

Olivia gave Rose a farewell hug. 'I'm so glad we've met up. If you see Lucas on your travels, tell him where I am, won't you? I have written to him but Heaven knows when he'll get the letter.' She gazed up at the dull November sky, wrapping her arms about herself for warmth. 'Daft thing is, he might be billeted just down the road.'

'I will keep a watch out for him,' Rose vowed and crossed her heart.

'He wrote and told me that he's hoping to get some leave at Christmas. Matron sent on my letters for me. I've put in for leave. Don't know if I'll be lucky.'

Rose shook her head. 'Talking about Christmas already! How time flies when you're having fun.'

The girls embraced again before Rose climbed into the ambulance and set off at quite a crack despite the headlights being on low.

The chief nursing sister had insisted the day staff take a rest after the mad rush. Olivia was off duty until eight in the morning. She set off towards her dormitory just as a plane flew overhead. It was a German being chased by an Allied craft. She stood and watched as their deadly acrobatics took them further away then saw a thin trail of smoke and heard an engine whine. She couldn't tell who'd survived. As she quickly got undressed, she wondered if an airman might be brought in tomorrow.

★ ★ ★

'Sister Bone!'

Olivia had been on her way to her dormitory after night shift when she heard someone call her name and turned about to see who it was. Her jaw slackened and she blinked, sure her eyes were deceiving her. It was a misty grey December morning with poor visibility, but, yes, that was Albert Carter, shoving back his helmet and rushing over to her.

'Cor blimey! It is you!' He sounded astonished but stuck out his hand to shake hers. 'I thought I must be seeing things. But there ain't many nurses as pretty as you, Sister Bone.' He blushed following this off-the-cuff compliment.

'Private Carter!' Olivia clasped his fingers although she'd been tempted to give him a great big hug. His likeness to Alfie always made her heart leap. But this time her happiness at seeing him soon faded. 'What on earth are you doing back here?' she wailed. 'Why aren't you at home with your mother?'

He looked sheepish. 'Couldn't stay, Sister Bone. Had to come back and do me bit. Wish I didn't have to be here, of course, but we all think that, don't we?' He shrugged. 'Anyhow, me lieutenant got me transferred so I ain't going over the top like I was before. He promised he'd get me took on as a stretcher bearer and runner, and he did. I'm nippy on me pins.' Albert chuckled. 'Always won me races at school. I leg it from the line to the ambulances and get 'em to move up and take away our wounded lads.'

He looked very pleased with himself. And rightly so, Olivia thought, patting his shoulder, but what really preoccupied her was the need to hear more about Lucas.

'You've seen Lieutenant Black?' Olivia felt dizzy with excitement as she waited for an answer.

'Just last week,' the boy said. 'I told him I'd met up with you in London.' Albert winked. 'He was pleased to know I found you looking well.'

'How is *he*? Is *he* well?' Olivia grasped him by the shoulders in her eagerness to know.

'Lieutenant's always chipper,' Albert said proudly. 'Luck o' the devil, him. All of us say so.' He paused. 'Sergeant Dawson took one in the back. But he got his Blighty pass so he'll be alright.'

'I remember hearing talk about the sergeant,' Olivia said. 'I hope he makes a good recovery.' Dawson was a name from way back when Joe and his pal Freddie Weedon had been in the platoon in 1914. 'Copper' they'd called their strict, ginger-haired sergeant.

'Where is the lieutenant now?'

'The platoon was on the move towards Cambrai. It's kicking off that way.' Albert grinned. 'We'll give them Hun what for now we've got tanks. Might be all over by Christmas.' He showed her two sets of crossed fingers.

Olivia smiled, matching his gesture, though she'd felt her heart sink. She'd moved east and Lucas had moved in the opposite direction. But at least she'd had news of him. He was well. That was what mattered.

'I pray you're right, Albert,' she said. 'I'm not sure any of us can stand much more of this.'

'Right 'nuff, Sister Bone.' He dolefully swung his head then glanced over his shoulder. His fellow stretcher bearers were having a smoke while waiting for an ambulance to transport them back to the aid post. They'd been watching enviously as their young colleague carried on an animated conversation with the lovely nurse.

'Did you tell your mother you were off to war again?' Olivia asked.

Albert looked sheepish. 'Sort of . . . left her a note.'

'Oh, Albert, that wasn't fair.' Olivia sighed. 'You must make sure you write to her regularly and let her know how you're doing and where you're billeted.'

He nodded. 'I will.' He quickly changed the subject in case he got another ticking off. 'Before I come back, I went round your house in Islington. I wanted to have a chat with you before making up me mind about what to do. Your sister told me you'd gone back already to France. So I thought . . . right . . . you've been real brave so I ought to be 'n' all.'

'You *are* brave, without a doubt, but still too young to be here, Albert, and a worry to your mother.'

He blurted out a reply designed to stop her being cross with him. 'I soon realised your family didn't know nuthin' about you getting involved with those Germans. I clammed up and didn't let on that's how you got hurt. She made me a cup of tea, did Maggie. Thought that was nice of her. Had a chat with your brother too. And your uncle seemed a proper gent.'

'Thanks for not saying anything.' Olivia was relieved that her secret hadn't slipped out. 'You're absolutely right in thinking I didn't want to worry them.' She was wondering why Maggie had been round at hers at all. Now that Nancy had moved into her own place, Maggie didn't really have much of a reason to visit Playford Road other than to say hello to her uncle and the boys once in a while. 'Did you meet Maggie's husband that day?'

Albert shook his head. 'I saw her little lad, though, before she took him upstairs for his nap. I had him on me lap. He's a corker. She told me his name was Ricky.' He beamed with pleasure. 'Ricky would have been pleased about her choosing his name.' Albert continued huskily, 'Still miss him, I do. Your sister said she'd like it if I wrote to her, to let her know more about Ricky and the larks we had in France.'

Olivia felt confused. At one time the idea that Maggie had left Harry and moved back home would have pleased her. But now, with a baby to consider, things were more complicated. She had thought her sister too busy with her own little family to write as often as she once had. On reflection, Maggie's letters had become infrequent before this when she'd had personal woes she'd rather not share. Her uncle and Nancy had sent Olivia letters recently and there had been no mention of anything amiss at home . . . But she knew they'd avoid worrying her if they could.

'Best be off.' Albert raised a hand in acknowledgement to his colleagues as they called out, letting him know their transport had arrived.

'Take care of yourself, Albert,' Olivia said earnestly. 'And if you see the lieutenant, please tell him where I am and that I'm thinking of him.'

'Will do. Reckon he already knows the last part though.' The lad dashed off to join his pals and Olivia watched him hanging out of the window, and waved to him until the ambulance was out of sight.

# 26

'I should've listened to you, Livvie. You told me enough times that Harry was no good.'

'Hush. You were entitled to want to get married and have your baby.' Olivia cuddled her weeping sister. 'I'm proud of you, Maggie. You're a wonderful mum to Ricky. It's not your fault you fell in love with a man not fit to tie your bootlaces. You trusted him and gave him a second chance to change and come up to scratch. The fool's thrown it back in your face and lost the best thing he's ever likely to have in his life. Serves him damn' well right.'

'He said he wants his son and he's taking Ricky to live with him.' Maggie's wails increased in volume.

'He's doing no such thing!' Olivia attempted to soothe her sister by stroking her hair.

Inwardly she was seething at what she'd learned about Harry's mistreatment of his wife. From Maggie's tearful account it seemed that things had come to a head when he had discovered she intended to start work again. Olivia wasn't surprised that he'd not allowed Maggie to return to her munitions factory job, and her own independence. Harry had wanted her earning . . . but on *his* terms. He'd been using his fists to force his wife into taking in washing at home where he could keep her under his thumb. He'd expected her to skivvy to pay the rent so that more of his own wages stayed in his pocket. But that, of course, wouldn't be the half of it where the nasty swine was concerned. Olivia had no doubt of that and she was determined to find out the rest.

'Have you been to Turner's to ask for your old job back now you're settled here?'

Maggie gave a doleful shake of the head. 'I want to go back more'n anything so I can pay me way. I don't expect a free ride, Livvie. I was planning on asking his mother to mind her grandson while I did me shifts. I won't go near any of 'em now though. She'd hand Ricky straight over to her bloody son and then I'd never see my baby again.' She wiped her eyes. 'Uncle Ed offered to mind him if I can get night work. But Ricky's grizzly with his teeth; Ed might be up all night and too tired to get up for work himself in the morning.' Maggie stuffed her hanky back up her sleeve. 'Sorry to be such a pain, Livvie. You've come home to have a nice Christmas, not to listen to me moaning about how I've made a mess of things.'

'That's what big sisters are for: to help sort things out, if we can.' Olivia squeezed Maggie's fingers, feeling chapped skin abrade her palms. Maggie had told her that her hands had bled following the constant washing she'd been expected to do, to keep Harry off her back. But the fading bruises on her arms were what had really worried Olivia. Her sister had obviously been taking beatings for a while. She felt like storming off to Wood Green and having it out with the brute. But that wouldn't be wise.

Besides, it was likely the coward had run straight home to his mother, to get his meals and washing done by her.

'You and little Ricky can stay here for as long as you want. Don't worry about chipping in for now. You'll be safe here. Uncle Ed'll make sure that Harry Wicks doesn't set one foot inside this door.'

'Weren't even married a full year,' Maggie choked. 'I'm a bloody laughing stock.'

'Better to get things put right now than later.' Olivia gave her arm an encouraging little shake. 'You've still got your life ahead of you, Mags. And you've got your son, that's the main thing.'

'Harry seemed more concerned about his pals finding out his wife had ditched him than he was about losing me. I reckon he's been messing around behind me back with someone.' Maggie narrowed her eyes. 'When I said something about him having a fancy woman he looked shifty and said I was imagining things. But I know him! He's always randy yet he ain't touched me in months. Said he didn't fancy me after I got saggy and fat with the baby.'

'Think yourself lucky then,' Olivia muttered. 'You might have fallen pregnant again.' There were other reasons too why she felt it was a godsend that Harry had left Maggie alone. She still couldn't get out of her head that sly look Ruby and he had exchanged at the Christening. Olivia was hoping she was wrong and Ruby wouldn't sink that low. If she was right, though, and her cousin and Harry had been sleeping together for a while, then he might have picked up something nasty from Ruby and passed it on to Maggie. Thank heavens he had not.

'I'd better wake Ricky up. That baby would kip the clock round if I'd let him,' Maggie said fondly. She hesitated by the door. 'I'm so glad you're back, Livvie. Wish you could stay home now, y'know. D'you *have* to go back?' she asked wistfully.

'Yes, I do. I'm sailing just after New Year.' Olivia stared at the closed door, feeling wrung out. Maggie wanted her at home to pick up the pieces of her broken marriage, and to mind her son so she could go back to work. Olivia would willingly help out with Ricky while she was on leave but ultimately the boy was his mother's responsibility.

She sank down into a chair, staring blankly into space. She'd been back just one day. She'd turned up yesterday evening and her excitement at being home in time for Christmas had soon been dampened. Although Maggie had confirmed straight away that she'd left Harry, she'd waited until this morning to fill in the gaps in the story. Olivia had been glad that they'd not burned the midnight oil while chewing things over. She'd felt exhausted after the voyage and had slept like the dead until eight o'clock in the morning. Maggie had already been up with Ricky. So had Alfie and Mickey who had risen with the lark, but they'd waited for her to join them so they could all have breakfast together. Their uncle Ed had already eaten and had gone shopping early. But he'd taught the boys well. Between them they'd fried bacon and made toast and pots of tea without needing to be asked. Olivia had been impressed, not only by their cooking but by how mature and capable they seemed. They'd both make good husbands, she'd thought, watching them kindly taking turns to nurse the grizzling baby so Maggie could enjoy her breakfast too. But it had been obvious that she was itching for the boys to finish clearing up and head off upstairs so the real business could be aired. The talking had started the moment after Maggie had put the baby in his cot for a nap.

There'd been no satisfaction for Olivia in knowing she'd been correct about Harry Wicks. Maggie insisted she wanted a divorce and Olivia believed she meant it. Little Ricky was her sister's only love now and Maggie was fearful of Harry taking him away from her.

'You alright, Livvie?' Uncle Ed had just come in, carrying a shopping bag. He entered the parlour, looking sheepish.

Olivia nodded, thrusting her fingers through her fair hair. 'I wish you'd written to warn me about this.'

'I wanted to,' Ed said earnestly. 'But Maggie made me promise not to. I didn't know the ins and outs at first. I thought they'd just had a tiff. Then *he* turned up, shouting the odds about how he was well rid of her and that he was taking his son back to Wood Green. Gave the neighbours summat to gossip about, I can tell you. After that Maggie opened up to me about it all.'

'Harry Wicks came round here causing a

scene?' Olivia hadn't known that and it fired her up to think he'd given her neighbours a field day.

'Bloody hell, did he! But I wouldn't let him in. Told him either he cleared off or I was fetching the coppers. Never took to him myself.' Ed grimaced his dislike. 'Shortly after that to-do we had your letter saying you was back for Christmas. I thought it'd be best to leave breaking the news until you got home. Let Maggie explain it all in her own way.'

'Luckily I bumped into Private Carter before I sailed so had an inkling something was up. He told me he'd paid a visit here and seen Maggie and Ricky but no sign of her husband.'

'I should've gone over to Wood Green and given that Wicks a piece of my mind. I feel responsible for all of you now your dad's not about to stick up for you. Tommy would've punched that rat's lights out.' Ed looked as though he felt he'd let them down.

'I'm glad you didn't confront him. He'd only want tit for tat so he could come over and shout the house down again.' Olivia gave her uncle a weak smile. 'It'll all come out in the wash eventually.' She stood up and twitched the net curtain. 'Has Alfie gone out?' She'd heard the door go while she'd been talking to Maggie earlier.

'The boys are always out kicking a ball about since Alfie got in the school football team.' Ed paused. 'They know something ain't right with Maggie and just want to keep out of the way, I expect.'

At one time Alfie would have dogged Olivia's footsteps when she was home. But his cousin Mickey was his best friend now. 'Thanks for looking after this place and Alfie,' she told her uncle. 'I can see how well he's doing and how happy he is.'

Ed waved the praise away, looking self-conscious. 'It's *me* should be thanking *you*,' he mumbled.

Olivia smiled. 'Well, let's not forget it's Christmas. The boys deserve to have a nice time. I'm off out for a while. I've got Christmas shopping to do.'

'Everything's ordered and paid for, for Christmas dinner, so you don't need to worry about that,' Ed said at once. 'I've invited Nancy to come over and eat with us. She's looking forward to seeing you. There's plenty to go round: turkey and lots of veg. I got a plum pudding off Matilda's neighbour. She boiled up a batch in her copper. And of course there'll be a few bottles on the table to wash it all down.' He gave a wink. 'Think we could do with a little tipple, don't you?'

Olivia rolled her eyes. 'I'll take a double, please.'

Although she had told her uncle Ed to keep away from Harry Wicks, Olivia found it hard to stick to her own advice. As she browsed the shops on the High Street for presents for her family she felt so exasperated that she couldn't concentrate properly. She decided eventually that she must go to Wood Green and speak out, if not to Harry then to Ruby. She returned to the

377

house with the gifts she'd bought and secreted them in a drawer for wrapping later. Then she set off to catch the bus to Wood Green.

If she was stewing for no reason, and Ruby was innocent of having an affair with Harry, Olivia would take this opportunity of wishing her cousin a merry Christmas. She might also have time to pop in and see Cath around the corner. She could then come home with a clear conscience, content that she wasn't withholding anything from Maggie.

As she turned into Ranelagh Road and proceeded towards Ruby's she instinctively glanced across at the Wickses' house. It all appeared quiet, curtains drawn against the early dusk. It seemed like a good omen.

★　★　★

'So, I guessed right.' Feeling wrathful, Olivia followed Ruby towards the parlour.

'What d'you mean by that?' her cousin asked, striking a match to a cigarette.

'You've been knocking about with Maggie's husband, haven't you?'

Ruby darted an astonished glance at Olivia then started nervously pushing strands of peroxide hair behind an ear. 'What makes yer say that?' she blustered, cigarette wagging between her lips.

'That damn' great bruise on your chin. He was knocking Maggie about as well. But I expect you know that.'

'I fell over.' Ruby started chewing the inside of

her cheek in between dragging on the Woodbine.

Olivia ignored the lie. 'How could you! With your own cousin's husband?' she spat contemptuously.

Ruby abandoned the sham. 'Runs in the family . . . like your father knocking about with my mother,' she sneered. 'Now if you ain't come for any more reason than to start trouble, you can piss off.'

For all her brashness, though, Ruby was close to tears. 'I'm not here to cause trouble,' Olivia said flatly. 'I'm here to thank you. You've come between them and done something I never could: you've shown Maggie just what a disgusting pig Harry Wicks is. You're welcome to him. She wants a divorce.'

Ruby took another drag on her cigarette, looking sullen. 'Well, I'm done with the bastard too. So she's welcome to him back.'

'She won't have him back,' Olivia scoffed. 'Especially not now. Once she finds out he's been knocking about with you, she'll hate him even more. She'll hate you too come to that.'

'I thought *she* told you about us! Who told you then?' Ruby looked flustered.

'Nobody had to tell me. I know you, and I know him. And I saw the way you looked at each other at the Christening.' Olivia paused and considered her cousin. 'Did you give him the clap? Is that why he whacked you?'

'No, I bleedin' didn't!' Ruby stormed, putting out her cigarette with angry stabs. 'That all cleared up ages ago!' Her shoulders slumped as the fight went out of her. 'Ain't talking about it,'

379

she said hoarsely, and lit up again with shaking fingers.

'Well, you might as well, 'cos you've got nobody else to confide in, have you?' Olivia said. She glanced about. 'Is he living here with you?'

'No, he ain't. I threw the mean bastard out.'

'Ah . . . didn't last long then, the romance. Not so much like my dad and your mum after all.'

'Yeah, go on, laugh.' Ruby jutted out her chin. 'He told me he made a mistake in marrying your Maggie. Said she got pregnant on purpose, to trap him. Probably the only truthful thing he ever said. Maggie was always chasing after him, you can't deny it.'

'So what?' Olivia replied coolly. 'They got married. And you got engaged to Riley McGoogan.'

'Yeah, and look how that turned out,' Ruby muttered bitterly.

'How did it turn out? Are you seeing him again? Is that why Harry hit you?'

'Ain't seen nothing of Riley. Harry punched me 'cos . . . ' Her voice faded away.

'What?' Olivia could see that Ruby was dreadfully upset about something. 'What's gone on?'

'He raped me.'

'*Harry raped you?*' Olivia whispered in shock.

'I told him to clear off 'cos he wouldn't put anything in the kitty. He'd spent it all in the pub, second week running.' Ruby crushed the empty cigarette pack between her shaking fingers. 'Told him I was letting out a room and he could get his stuff together and go. He tried to cosy up to me, win me round. But I'd had enough of him and shoved him off . . . told him to go to his mother's and leave me alone.' She sniffed and wiped her eyes. 'So he took a swing at me then dragged me by me hair into the bedroom . . .'

Olivia sank down on the old armchair, feeling winded. Yet she knew Wicks was capable of it. He'd done it before. He'd raped a nun years ago. And there had been times when he'd got her alone and Olivia had known, but for the time and opportunity not being right, he would've forced himself on her. 'What are you going to do? Have you reported him to the police?' she asked.

Ruby laughed mirthlessly. 'They'd believe him not me. I've been done for soliciting. You know what coppers are like.' She swiped her eyes with her cuff. 'After he'd finished, the only way I could get rid of him was by threatening to go over the road and tell his mother what he'd done to me.' She fumbled in a drawer for another packet of Woodbines, then threw it back, finding it empty. 'Ain't seen him since. Surprised he ain't weaselled himself back into Maggie's good books.'

'He'd be wasting his time trying.' Olivia got some cigarettes from her bag and handed them over. At that moment, watching Ruby tearing into the packet and then pocketing them without offering her one, Olivia felt so sorry for her pathetic cousin that she was about to ask her to spend Christmas Day with them in Islington. But she'd not pretend to her family that it was all happy days when it wasn't. If Maggie ever found out what Ruby had done she'd scratch her eyes out. Most of Ruby's misfortunes had been brought on herself . . . because of men. In that she certainly was like her mother.

'D'you want a cup of tea?' Olivia shook the kettle to find out if anything was in it.

'Nah.' Ruby sniffed and straightened her shoulders. She took a half bottle of gin from the drawer. 'Turning into me mother alright.' She swigged from the neck of the bottle then sucked on her fresh cigarette.

'I'd better get going. I said I wouldn't be out long.'

'You won't go knocking on his door, will you?' Ruby cuffed her wet mouth, grabbing Olivia's arm and powdering her sleeve with ash. 'I don't want no more trouble off him. Just want him to stay away.'

'No, I won't.' Olivia said, brushing herself clean. 'None of us want to have anything to do with Harry Wicks either.'

★ ★ ★

Olivia had reached the corner of the street when she heard rapid footsteps approaching. She whipped around.

'So you're back on shore, are yer?' Harry gave her the once over. 'Had a feeling you'd be round this way looking for me, so I've been looking out for you.' He backed her against the hedge, glancing to and fro to see if anybody else was witnessing his behaviour.

It was only four o'clock in the afternoon but already dark.

'Come to tell me that me wife's come to her senses, have yer, gel? Well, I'll take her back but she'd better learn . . .'

Olivia interrupted him with a harsh, 'You must be mad if you think Maggie would even give you the time of day. I've just been visiting Ruby. Wishing her Merry Christmas.' She barged past him, curbing the urge to yell at him that she knew what sort of foul individual he was. He wasn't worth the breath though. Instead she gave him a long, loathing look before carrying on towards the High Street.

He was soon behind her again and when she ignored him, muttering close to her shoulder, he yanked on her arm, spinning her around.

'What's that lying bitch told you about me?'

Olivia could see that he was genuinely worried that Ruby had let the cat out of the bag. 'She's told me everything. And none of it surprised me. I know what you're capable of. I haven't forgotten what you did to the sister at the convent.'

'That was Maggie's fault. Teasing me, leading me on in the dark then running off. I thought it was her back again, wanting me to finish what I'd started.'

The shock of hearing him finally admit to what he'd done to the nun caused Olivia actually to stand still and gawp at him. Quickly she gathered her wits and carried on walking. It was too late to right that wrong, or to bawl her disgust at him now she knew he would have

383

raped Maggie instead if the nun hadn't got in the way.

'And it's me wife's fault that I needed another woman. She shouldn't've left me. I'm Maggie's husband and I've got rights. As fer that cousin of yours . . . I paid Ruby Wright, like everyone else does, for knocking her on her back. Anyway, what's another slice off a cut loaf . . . and fuckin' stale at that,' he added to himself as Olivia began to trot towards the bus that was pulling in at the stop.

She felt her heart pounding as she joined the back of the queue. She was glad to be away from him yet still so filled with hatred for Harry Wicks that for a moment she didn't realise somebody had spoken to her.

'Oh, hello . . . ' she said to Riley. He looked a bit flustered, rubbing one finger beneath his nose and darting shamefaced glances at her. He'd obviously guessed that the reason for Ruby throwing him over had been revealed.

'Is Ruby at home, d'you know at all? I was going to wish her a Merry Christmas.' He was dressed in khaki and had a kitbag on his shoulder. 'I bought her a present . . . it's from France. Should I bother her with it, d'you tink?' He looked quite enderingly diffident.

'She is at home but . . . ' Olivia shrugged. 'She is at home, Riley. Merry Christmas.' She clambered aboard the bus, found a seat and sat down. 'Good luck,' she murmured as the bus pulled away.

# 27

'Sorry, love. I'm not very good company. But come in if you want to.'

Olivia entered Matilda's home, remaining unaffected by the clutter everywhere and the musty smell. She'd been in here lots of times before and was used to the general air of dilapidation. In fact, Matilda had one of the nicer places on the street, courtesy of her employment as a rent collector. She'd often swap her old furniture for better pieces when her guv'nor's properties became vacant and something caught her eye. Then Jack Keiver would be seen bowling up and down the street with a nice bit of mahogany lashed on top of his handcart. That was back in the good old days before the Bunk emptied of men of fighting age.

What *had* surprised Olivia this evening was Matilda's glum expression. At this time of the year the woman was usually the life and soul of the party. Olivia imagined that contemplating another Christmas without her husband was the problem.

'Jack didn't get leave then?'

Matilda shook her head. 'Alice's boyfriend Geoff's joined up too. So she's on her own for the holiday 'n' all.'

'Didn't think Geoff was eighteen yet.'

'He ain't.' Matilda filled her glass from the half-empty bottle on the table and took a long swallow of whiskey.

'Thought you'd be round the Duke on Christmas Eve,' Olivia remarked in a jolly tone. 'I called in to have a drink with you but the landlord said you'd not been in for a while.' It was rare indeed for Matilda to spend Christmas Eve at home, drinking alone. 'Feeling browned off?' Olivia sounded concerned.

'Yeah . . . life's getting me down,' Matilda replied. 'Don't suppose I'm the only one sufferin', though, in this wicked world.' She bucked herself up. 'I can't offer you more'n a glass of whiskey, but you're welcome to it.' She held out the bottle.

'Just a small one then, thanks.' Olivia didn't really want it. She didn't like whiskey, but she could see Matilda needed a drinking pal and a sympathetic ear. Usually it was the other way around and the older woman would listen to her woes. Matilda was a private person; she might give advice but she rarely sought it and Olivia knew to tread carefully. Besides she *had* come to ask Matilda something, but was uncertain now whether to broach the subject.

Matilda's youngest was crouching on the bed, chewing on a biscuit. Olivia picked up the pretty little thing and planted a kiss on her forehead. She'd looked after the child on occasions when Matilda had had rents to collect and nobody had been at home to mind Lucy. The little girl fondly laid her head on Olivia's shoulder.

'Come on, out with it.' Matilda gave her an old-fashioned look. 'Something's brought you here and it ain't my Irish whiskey . . . nice as it is.' She took a gulp of her favourite tipple then pushed Olivia's half-filled glass across the table.

'Don't miss a trick, you.' Olivia sat down opposite with Lucy on her lap.

'I've found it's best not to, round here,' Matilda said with a glimmer of a smile. 'Anyway, where's me manners? It's lovely to see you home and looking well, Livvie. And here's to a Merry Christmas and a Happy New Year!' Matilda raised her glass and Olivia clashed hers against it. Lucy joined in by sticking her biscuit in the air.

'She's a chip off the old block,' Olivia chuckled.

'Certainly is.' Matilda beamed proudly at her little daughter. 'All the others've gawn out with friends and left me on me own. But I've got me little Lucy fer company.'

Olivia could tell Matilda had already sunk quite a few, to sound so maudlin. 'Want to talk about it?'

'Ain't worth talkin' about,' Matilda returned and upended her glass.

Olivia knew not to probe further. She'd just been told to mind her own business. 'Is your sister coming upstairs to raise a glass with you?' Fran and Jimmy Wild and their family lived in the rooms below. When Jimmy was out the sisters would often spend time together in the evenings.

'Yeah . . . she'll be up a bit later when she's sorted her two boys' suppers out.'

'Jimmy come up too, will he, as it's Christmas Eve?'

Olivia saw straight away what the problem was. Matilda's expression had blackened at the mention of her brother-in-law.

'No! He ain't welcome. Besides, he's slung his hook. And good riddance. Fran's glad he's gone.' Then Matilda clammed up.

Olivia left it there. She knew that Matilda hated her brother-in-law just as much as Olivia hated Harry Wicks. Jimmy was known to have fancy women and to shack up with them from time to time despite having a wife and two kids.

'We'll forget about him then. Absent friends.' Olivia again touched the rim of her glass against Matilda's. They both drank to that.

'Not seeing your nice lieutenant then this Christmas?'

'I really hoped I might this year,' Olivia answered sadly. 'But before I left France I heard that his platoon was on the move again. I expect his leave's been cancelled.'

'Shame.' Matilda sighed. 'Still, you'll have a house full with your uncle and all the kids.' She leaned her elbows on the table, supporting her chin on her hands. 'I've seen your Maggie in the street a few times, pushing a pram. Thought she'd moved Wood Green way with her husband. Everything alright there, is it?'

'It is now!' Olivia replied pithily. 'She's left him and wants a divorce. She's back home for the time being while she sorts herself out.'

'How's she gonna manage on her own with the baby?' Matilda's frown suddenly smoothed out and she lounged against her chair-back. 'Ah . . . she's hoping to get back to work at Turner's, ain't she?' She wagged a finger at her friend.

Olivia grimaced. 'That obvious, is it, that I've got a favour to ask?'

'You're very welcome, love, and you tell Maggie that I'll have the little lad as often as I can. So will me neighbour, Beattie. She won't mind lending a hand. If Maggie bungs her a bottle of sherry once in a while, she'll be happy as Larry.'

'Oh, thanks ever so much!' Olivia sighed in relief. 'It'll be the best Christmas present for Maggie, knowing she's got a chance to get back to work.' Olivia took a sip of her whiskey and added, 'She'd not leave Ricky with just anybody. That little boy's her world.'

'All us women got to look out for one another, Livvie,' Matilda said soberly. 'That's what we got to do, more'n ever now our men aren't about.' She suddenly stood up, looking emotional. 'You don't want to be hanging around here with a miserable old cow like me,' she said huskily. 'You have a good Christmas with your family, love.'

'I will.' Olivia didn't want to outstay her welcome. She put Lucy back on the bed then approached Matilda. She gave her a quick hug then cheekily tapped her fingers beneath Matilda's chin . . . an encouragement she'd received from the other woman umpteen times in the past when she'd felt as though her world was falling apart. 'You keep this up,' said Olivia, ''cos that's what us women do round here.'

'Get off with yer.' Matilda gently elbowed her away, but she embraced Olivia before pushing her towards the door.

⋆　⋆　⋆

As she started homeward Olivia was in an odd mood. She wasn't sure whether Matilda's melancholy had rubbed off on her or whether something else was to blame. She felt glad that Maggie was safe indoors, and yet begrudged having spent almost every minute of her holiday so far embroiled in family problems. She'd not had time to think about Lucas and mourn the loss of their Christmas together. She'd been yearning to see him. She'd wanted to find him a special gift but couldn't decide what to get. In the end she hadn't bought him anything at all, having done her Christmas shopping in a rush. She was determined to buy something to take back to France with her, though, and give it to him when they met up. All he had of hers as a memento was a battered old cigarette case that had once belonged to her father. He didn't even have a photograph of her to carry in his wallet.

She chuckled. Now she knew what she'd get him. The morning after Boxing Day she'd put on her best clothes and visit a photographer's studio. Her pace had slowed while she'd been thinking of him. It slowed further until she came to a standstill. Before she returned to the bustle of Christmas Eve at home she wanted to think about him some more . . . quietly and without interruption.

She stopped by the wall at the junction with Paddington Street and leaned back against it, watching the stars glittering overhead. The street was alive, as it always was; day or night, the Bunk

390

never slept. But she was oblivious to other people, some calling out greetings and Merry Christmases as they weaved on their drunken way. Somewhere close by an argument was taking place. A woman was effing and blinding; pots and pans were crashing against walls. Life in the Bunk didn't alter but it had quietened, as it had in every street in the land since the men left to go to war. Before, there would have been barrel organs, chestnut sellers and people capering about. Olivia continued gazing up at the winter sky, her breath freezing in front of her. She knew she was getting cold but all she could think of was that Lucas was somewhere beneath these same stars. She was certain he'd be staring up at them, too, thinking of her. He was safe, she was sure of it.

And then she heard a whistle . . .

She'd come out of Barratt's factory once, at the end of her shift, and he'd been waiting for her by his car. He'd whistled at her. Like a rough sort, he'd said. A joke, of course. At that time he'd been handsome . . . debonair . . . every inch the rich playboy.

She turned her head and saw him, and though her racing heart was urging her to break into a run she couldn't. She watched him come towards her with his easy stride. Still handsome . . . but no similarity to a debonair playboy. He was in uniform and he looked tired.

By the time he reached her tears were streaming down her face and she clung to him. 'I thought you weren't coming back,' she hic-coughed.

'So did I for a while. But I got a late passage. Just been round to your house. Your uncle said you were at Mrs Keiver's.'

Olivia nodded. 'I was,' she said shakily, pressing her face into his shoulder.

'Don't cry, Livvie,' Lucas pleaded, gently drying her tears. 'We've got Christmas together, darling. Home at last . . . together.'

She raised her head from his shoulder, cupping his angular face between her hands. 'It doesn't seem real. What's going to come and steal this away?

'Nothing . . . promise you. I've got a week . . . a whole week for us to spend together. Are you home that long?'

She nodded, swallowing back more tears. 'Didn't buy you a present 'cos I couldn't decide what to get.' She kissed his cheek as though it were as delicate as her little nephew's. 'Sorry.'

'Never mind, I know just what I want,' he teased. 'Shall I tell you what that is?'

'Think I can guess,' she said, turning suddenly shy. 'And it's what I want too. More than anything.'

'So . . . are you coming home with me?'

'It's almost Christmas Day, Lucas. I must spend it with the family.' She gave him another kiss to compensate. 'Will you spend tomorrow with your family?'

'Not if I can help it!'

'Then would you come to us . . . please?' She patted his bristly chin. 'Come to us and have dinner and tea and supper. Then we can spend all of Boxing Day together at yours, if you like.

Just the two of us — if no disasters occur in the meantime, that is,' she tacked on, not wholly joking.

'I'd like to come, thank you. I'm glad you asked me. There's nothing much in the larder at home.' He paused briefly then added, 'I saw your sister and the baby just now. They looked well settled in, both in their nightclothes. Has something happened?'

'Something's always happening in my family, Lucas,' she replied ruefully. 'I'll tell you later. Not now. I'm so happy to see you!'

He slid his arms about her and gave her a long kiss. Olivia felt dreamy as the bone-melting embrace came to an end. She took his arm and they started slowly up the road together, savouring every precious private second. She wished they weren't so close to home and could keep walking and talking together for hours.

'I've so much to tell you. Not just about the usual Bone family troubles, but about France and what I've been doing. Did you get my letter about my transfer to a casualty clearing station at Nine Elms? I bumped into Private Carter and told him I wished he'd stayed with his mother . . . Lucas, where are we going?

He'd taken a turn at the top of the road in the opposite direction from her house. She felt herself being backed against a different wall. He dipped his head and kissed her again, a more leisurely seduction this time, and his hands slipped inside her coat to caress her.

'I know we can't stand outside kissing like kids for long . . . wish we could, though, especially as you taste of whiskey.' He smiled against her mouth. 'I imagine a couple of kisses will have to see me through until Boxing Day, so it was worth the risk of scandalising your neighbours.' He nuzzled behind her ear. 'I love you . . . missed you so much, Livvie. I've been worrying about you. All the time.'

'Me too,' she breathed, and slid her arms around his neck, holding him close. 'It's the not knowing that's the worst thing . . . ' She stopped herself from saying more. It was Christmas. They were together and for now that was all that mattered. 'Luckily the neighbours have all got their own scandals to occupy them.' She kissed his cheek, took his hand and pulled him towards her front door. 'Come on, let's have a glass of something. Matilda gave me a whiskey but I'd sooner have a port. My uncle put some bottles on the sideboard earlier. Let's drink in Christmas Day by toasting everyone we've left behind in France.'

★ ★ ★

The table was laid, the house filled with a wonderful savoury aroma of rich gravy and sausage meat stuffing. It was a Christmas like no other, Olivia realised as she watched her family bustling back and forth making everything ready for the year's big feast. She felt happier than she ever remembered being in her life.

Nancy had arrived early to help out and was now putting sprigs of ivy and holly into a vase to decorate the dinner table. Nat hadn't got leave so she was on her own, but seemed beautifully cheerful nevertheless. Little Ricky had the colic so Maggie had been marching up and down the hallway rocking him in her arms and singing 'Silent Night' in an attempt to soothe him. The boys and Uncle Ed were red-faced from standing over the hot kitchen range, pulling trays of potatoes and parsnips and baked onions in and out, to test their crispness. And resting on the top, ready to be taken to the table, was the plump bronzed turkey.

'Let me help . . . I can make the custard . . . '

Ed waved her away. 'You go and pour yourself a sherry, dear,' he said. 'You deserve a good rest after what you've been through all year. We've got this under control, ain't we, lads?'

Olivia received twin grins from the two fair-haired boys, busy boiling carrots and topping up the steaming pudding saucepan with water so it didn't dry out.

Feeling restless with excitement, Olivia dashed upstairs and sat down at the dressing table. She gazed into a pair of glowing green eyes while pressing her fair hair into waves. If only life could always be this good, and she could feel this happy. She tipped up her head to gaze at the ceiling and whisper a Merry Christmas to her mum and dad, then a whispered prayer of thanks for this gift of a wonderful day. She heard the gate click shut and jumped up, butterflies fluttering amok in her stomach.

She opened the door to find Lucas standing there laden with boxes of chocolates and bottles of champagne.

'Oh, Lucas, you didn't need to bring all that,' she said, ushering him in.

'Just a few things to help out and say thanks,' he said modestly.

'And very welcome you are, sir.'

Uncle Ed had come out of the kitchen to grin at their distinguished guest.

'Now that we're all here, I reckon we're just about ready for the off . . . if you are, that is?' Ed diplomatically withdrew into the kitchen to allow the couple to have a quick canoodle before they seated themselves at the dinner table.

'Merry Christmas, Lucas,' Olivia said huskily.

'Merry Christmas, Livvie,' he whispered back to her.

★　★　★

It all looked nice and cosy inside. Log fire blazing and fancy food spread out on a white cloth. It made his mouth water, just thinking about turkey and roast spuds on a plate smothered in gravy. He'd not had food like that in so long he'd forgotten what it tasted like. Paper hats, ruby red glasses raised, people laughing and singing through the candlelight. He could see it all from where he stood in the shadows.

And he hated them for it. Should be him sitting in front of that fire, eating off that table, pulling those curtains against the gathering, icy dusk.

Ed Wright got up then and, laughing into the blackness outside, drew the curtains and removed the cheerful scene from view. The man had no right! Joe hadn't even known Ed Wright existed, yet here he was, lording it in Herbie's son's house.

With nothing now to look at but the red glow behind the brocade curtains, Herbie Hunter shuffled off down the street. He only had a dirty room and his own company to go back to. Even the tarts had something better to do at Christmas. He decided to keep walking in the hope of finding a pub open. He hated Christmas. Everybody merry and bright . . . apart from him. Even when he'd been married and living in the Bunk with his wife and kids he'd never enjoyed Christmas. But he would now . . . if he could do it all again. He'd be different to his wife and his kids . . . But it was too late now for regrets. They'd all gone and all that was left of his family was his son's old home.

Herbie'd been right about Livvie Bone catching herself a rich man. He'd seen the posh lieutenant in there with them, popping corks. Next year she'd be gone, drinking champagne somewhere better.

And next year it'd be finished for the others too because Ed Wright wasn't having Herbie's house. Next year *he'd* be sitting in that house, warming his toes by the fire. *He'd* be raising a glass to his kin. All dead now, but he'd remember them in his own way. That's what was going to happen.

# 28

'You said you had nothing in.' Olivia watched Lucas put down a tray that held cut-crystal glasses and two bottles of champagne. There was also a dish filled with what looked a bit like jam.

'There's always something decent to drink in the cellar. I found some tins of caviar in the larder. Nothing else though.' Lucas approached the bed, leaned over her, and kissed her on her swollen scarlet lips. 'You alright?'

'Yes . . . I am,' she said, stretching herself against the silk sheets. She was aware of his eyes, moving over her naked shoulders and the swell of her breasts. Her fingers tightened on the sheet and a faint blush touched her cheekbones. It was a bit late for modesty now he'd seen every bare inch of her!

Like a true gentleman he'd allowed her time to undress and settle in bed before joining her, but then his raw passion had been long and slow as though he couldn't bear to finish with her. She'd begged him to when the exquisite new feelings spiralled from bliss to bittersweet pain and any further, feather-light touch from his mouth or fingers became too intense for her to bear. And then he had taken pity on her, cradling her in his arms as he plunged into her until he too was spent.

'What's caviar?'

'Fish eggs. Tastes better than it sounds.'

'I think I'd sooner have a cold turkey sandwich.' Olivia wrinkled her nose. 'So until you've been shopping, we'll be eating Christmas leftovers round at mine.'

'What do you fancy while you're here then?' He looked back at the tray on the floor holding the Bollinger.

'What we just had was quite nice,' she teased.

'Quite nice?' Lucas sat down beside her on the bed. 'I'd better try again. I was hoping for excellent.' He pressed her back against the pillow, tormenting her with nipping kisses.

'It *was* excellent, as well you know,' she said softly. 'Practice makes perfect . . . '

He groaned and sat them both up then bent to pour out two glasses of champagne.

It tasted cool and bitter to her; she still preferred a port. She told him so and he knocked his back in two swallows then took her half-empty glass from her and put it on the tray.

He'd pulled on just his trousers to go and find them something to drink after exhausting her with pleasure. She'd expected a cup of tea. Now she felt annoyed with herself for letting her imagination run riot while she'd waited for him to return. She'd spoiled things. Of course, other women had been here, and had drunk champagne with him in bed. And probably enjoyed it more than she did.

She was a novice to it all. When she'd still been at school he'd been a playboy surrounded by Mayfair totty, as Val had called the girls who chased after him. He'd never lied to her about his past.

She slipped a finger over the ridges of muscle in his naked back. He had a strong torso, almost devoid of hair, but seamed and holed by the battles he'd been in. She'd soothed the marks with her fingers as he'd rested above her, loving her. She'd seen far, far worse damage to a man and had prayed to God in that moment that he'd collect no more cruel badges in France.

'Sorry, didn't mean to sound jealous.' She pressed her lips to his ribs.

'You didn't. You sounded reproachful.'

'Well, I'm not.' She hugged him about the waist, resting her forehead against his broad back.

'I don't mind if you're annoyed, Livvie. I'd worry if you weren't. I'm ashamed myself of some of it.' He turned around and lay down beside her, pulling her into his arms so that her head was against his beating heart. 'I enjoyed seeing all your family yesterday.'

'Did you really?' Olivia raised herself on one elbow to look into his eyes. 'I expect it was a different sort of Christmas from what you're used to with your lot.'

Her long blonde hair had fallen forward and he used a hand to gather it back from her face so that he could see her beautiful smile. 'It was just right. Every moment of it,' he said softly. And meant it. The Christmases he'd known with his family had been lavish. But even as a child he'd been glad when the charade was over and he could get back to school and the people he'd sooner be with.

Yesterday, at her house, the conversation and

laughter had been genuine. The fare, if not the best he'd tasted, had been appreciated more than the lobster and beef at the family house that were always cooked to perfection, but often left untouched on their plates. His brother's snide comments and his stepmother's histrionics would ruin anyone's appetite. From when Lucas was fourteen, Christmas Day would usually end with him retreating to his room with a decanter of malt whisky and a box of cigars stolen from his father's study, while the man himself sought sanctuary at his club.

'You were a great hit with my uncle, bringing all that champagne, and the boys loved the chocolates. I bet there's not one left.' Olivia settled against him, rubbing her cheek against the firm flesh of his chest.

'I like them all too. But nowhere near as much as I like you,' he teased.

His fingers were tracing circles on her cheek, making her feel drowsy, and she snuggled down further, wanting to fall asleep in his arms.

'We didn't get much time to talk yesterday. Has your sister Maggie left her husband? I know you never liked him.'

'I've always hated him. The pig's been mistreating her. I'm not surprised, though I feel guilty now it's happened. Perhaps I should have tried to stop her marrying him after all.' Olivia sighed. 'But she was adamant and I hoped against hope that the baby might change him.'

She knew Lucas would wait for her to elaborate rather than question her further. He was too well mannered to pry. So she explained briefly that her vile brother-in-law was an adulterer and wife-beater. And also a rapist.

'Your cousin Ruby surely won't take him back after that?'

'She'd be a fool to. But Ruby's unpredictable. I hope she gives her former fiancé another chance. They broke up because . . . ' Olivia hesitated, unsure whether to mention that Riley had been infected with VD in a French brothel. But she was a nurse and Lucas was a man of the world who would know about such things. So she told him.

And he was quiet.

'I don't blame men for wanting such comfort,' she declared truthfully, wondering if she'd shocked him by speaking of it. It wasn't a pleasant subject for a couple to discuss when they'd just made love. But she'd lost her innocence long before she'd given him her virginity. He surely knew that. 'People at home don't really know what it's like out there . . . the constant fear and the loneliness. I feel so sorry for all you soldiers, trying to carry on and be brave although you know the next minute might be your last. And you daren't tell anyone how you feel, least of all the people you love, for fear of worrying the life out of them.' She pushed herself up again to look at him intently. 'We should talk about Caroline and get her out of the way. I don't want her stuck between us.'

He grimaced agreement, holding her eyes with his.

'I understand why you were lovers over there,' Olivia said softly. 'I understand that another person lying beside you would comfort you and help you to sleep. When I was hiding in that dark hole in the ground . . . '

He immediately enclosed her in his arms and hushed her.

'No, I want to talk about it. Poison shouldn't be allowed to fester. I've learned that as a nurse.' She smiled wryly. 'When I was in the forest, feeling ill and so lonely and frightened, I considered surrendering to him — just to have somebody to talk to. The idea of perishing without ever again being with another human being . . . and my body never properly buried . . . '

'Hush, enough of this now.' He rocked her in his arms, bringing their heads together and soothing her with little kisses. 'It's all finished now, Livvie.'

'I just want you to know that I don't blame you for needing someone breathing by your side at night. That's all.'

'Thank you. That's all it was: a need. I've never loved anyone else. Only you. And now I have you with me all the time. Up here.' He tapped his temple. 'And that's enough for me, I swear.'

'Have you made friends with some of the new men in your platoon?' She hoped he wasn't lonely. She still remembered Albert Carter telling her about the loneliness of the battlefield.

'No . . . not really,' Lucas said. 'When we're billeted there's some drinking and larking about in the villages, but I suppose my old sergeant was the one I was closest to. And now he's gone home. I'm glad for him though.'

She nodded, brushing her cheek against his warm musky skin. 'I hope Ruby will be lenient with Riley. It's obvious he still adores her. Perhaps he was just tempted to find a girl out of sheer loneliness.'

'I hope it works out for them too. We all know about the brothels, of course. I've never been in a blue light . . . even at the beginning. I'm no saint, as you know, but neither am I a fool, ignorant of the consequences. Those diseases are a scourge on any army. Thousands of men are hospitalised needlessly. Some actually go to red lights hoping to get infected. They think catching the clap is preferable to being blown up on the battlefield.' He added dryly, 'Understandably. There is more chance of a cure.'

'Hark at us.' Olivia stroked his face lovingly. 'Busman's holiday. It's still Christmas, let's forget about France for now.' She settled down again, asking saucily, 'Did you like your present, Lucas?'

'Yes, I did. So much so that I want to have it again. It was the best ever, and that's the truth.' He hauled her up so she hovered inches above him, her hair curtaining her laughing face. He smiled crookedly. 'Suppose you want a present, too?'

'You brought along lots of presents yesterday.'

'I got you something a bit more personal.' He sat up with her on his lap. 'I promised you a proper proposal with champagne and a diamond ring.' He felt for his jacket, discarded on the floor, then withdrew from a pocket a jeweller's ring box. Then another. 'Open that one first.' He tapped the larger box.

She flicked it up to reveal a magnificent emerald flanked by diamonds.

'D'you like it?' he asked with boyish eagerness when she stayed silent. 'It matches your eyes.'

'It's beautiful, Lucas. But so grand.' She looked at him anxiously. She felt unsure about touching something so obviously expensive.

He took the ring out of its velvet nest and slipped it onto her finger. She beamed when it fitted perfectly.

'Then soon, if you want, you can wear this one too.' He opened the box containing a platinum wedding band and watched for her reaction. 'I mean it, Livvie. We can get a special licence and be married . . . go back to France as husband and wife.'

'You know I want to marry you more than anything,' she said huskily, her eyes aglow. 'But not yet, Lucas.' The idea that this joy could be short-lived, that she might in a week's time be a widow . . . it would be tempting fate. The same fate that was never kind to her. She closed her eyes against the horror of it. She would not think of it. 'Not yet,' she repeated against his fingers, then brought his hand to her lips and kissed it.

'I know . . . I understand.'

He held her against him and they sat together quietly, breast to breast, lost in their own thoughts of what was real and what was fantasy. The flickering firelight cast their entwined silhouettes against the tall pale walls. In the big four-poster bed they closed their eyes and clung to the dream that this was real and could last.

'I know what I'd like to do tomorrow,' Olivia said.

'So do I.'

'Apart from that. I'd like us to get our photos taken in the High Street. We can keep them with us over there.'

'That's a good idea,' Lucas said, then tilted up her chin and kissed her. 'Promise me one thing, Livvie?'

She gazed into his deep blue eyes and nodded solemnly.

'If you find out that you're pregnant in a month's time, you'll come home at once?'

'Promise,' she said huskily, wondering why that possibility hadn't occurred to her instead of him.

★ ★ ★

Olivia shut Cath's gate, returning a wave, and the toddler in her friend's arms followed its mother's lead, waving his chubby arms. Olivia walked off with a spring in her step. She'd been overjoyed to find Cath in such good spirits. Her friend had said she'd enjoyed a smashing Christmas and felt happier than she'd done in a long while. She'd also said she reckoned Trevor was on the up as well and that was due to the fact he hadn't seen her miserable face so often.

Olivia hesitated at the end of the street, wondering whether to catch the bus home or to call on Ruby and wish her a Happy New Year. It was the only opportunity she'd have before returning overseas.

In for a penny . . . she thought, and shrugged, turning in the direction of Ranelagh Road.

She found Ruby at home . . . with Riley. They had been sitting at the parlour table with cups of tea and a plate of sandwiches and biscuits between them.

'Oh, sorry. I won't disturb your tea.' Olivia retreated to the door although the cosy domestic scene had made her smile. 'I was just round the corner visiting Cath so I thought I'd pop in and wish you Happy New Year. I'm off back to France tomorrow, you see.'

'Oh, don't go yet, Livvie.' Ruby grabbed her arm. She looked puffed up with excitement, as though wanting to say something but unable to get it out.

'You've made up then? I'm glad,' Olivia said.

'We got married on Boxing Day,' Ruby blurted.

Olivia's jaw dropped and she gave a squeal of surprise. She smiled then at the bashful bridegroom. 'Congratulations to both of you.'

'I'm back to France in a week, so I am,' Riley announced as though unsure what else to say.

'Well . . . enjoy your honeymoon.' Olivia looked at Ruby. She knew this news would come as a surprise to Ed and Mickey. 'Shall I tell the others when I get back?'

'If you like,' Ruby said. 'I'll come over soon and speak to Dad myself. Tell him that, would you?'

Olivia nodded. 'Happy New Year then.' She'd

hoped to enquire if her cousin had had any more trouble off Harry Wicks but the time certainly wasn't right.

Ruby shut the door on her husband and accompanied Olivia into the street. 'Riley's threatened to kill Harry,' she hissed. 'He went over the road after him but the weasel hid behind his mother.' She rolled her eyes. 'The whole street heard what was going on. I told Riley not to go back but he wasn't having that! He went after Harry again the next morning. Mrs Wicks was bawling her eyes out, saying Harry had done a moonlight flit and taken her savings. She ain't lying neither about him disappearing. He's run off, alright, the coward! Riley went round the butcher's and they ain't seen him either.'

Olivia listened wide-eyed. 'You told Riley you'd been having an affair with Harry Wicks?'

'I told him it all . . . everything that pig did to me. When Riley turned up on Christmas Eve we had a long talk and made things up. We both promised no more lies or cheating. I really mean it, and he'd better too.' Ruby paused, chewing her lip. 'Did you tell Maggie about me 'n' Harry having an affair?'

'No, and neither will you ever mention it,' Olivia warned her. 'She's picking up the pieces of her own life and doing a good job of it. So let sleeping dogs lie, especially now Harry's done a runner and can't throw the truth in her face.'

Ruby nodded, looking shamefaced. 'I *am* sorry, Livvie.'

'Yeah, I know. Let's forget about it.' She embraced her cousin. 'I'm pleased for you both.'

'I bumped into Mickey and Alfie having a kick about with some local kids. Mickey said that your Lieutenant Black spent Christmas round at yours and brought loads of chocolates with him.' Ruby elbowed her in the ribs. 'Getting serious there, eh?'

Olivia simply smiled and murmured, 'Yes.'

'You seeing him before you ship out?'

Olivia instinctively touched the emerald she was wearing on a chain next to her silver locket beneath her bodice. She was tempted to blurt out her wonderful news but wouldn't steal her honeymooning cousin's thunder. Besides she'd not yet had an opportunity to tell her sisters as they'd both been back on shift directly after Christmas. They should be the first to know.

'We had a lovely time together but he's going back before me. This evening, in fact.' Olivia was glad they wouldn't be saying last-minute goodbyes; glad too that he'd felt duty bound to see his mother and brother before returning to France. Family was family, no matter how obnoxious they sometimes were. She was proud of him for taking the time out of his precious leave to visit his old sergeant as well, to see how Copper was doing.

But how she missed him! Just eighteen hours apart and the hollow inside her ached, the pain of it bittersweet now that they were married too, in all but name.

# 29

'I saved you some cocoa.' Lucy Archer had propped herself up on one elbow in bed. 'It's keeping warm on top of the stove.'

'Oh, thanks.' Olivia felt she could just do with a hot drink. She found her beaker then poured in cocoa from the metal jug, wrapping her fingers about the warm china. She kept close to the coke stove, and started shedding garments in between taking gulps of cocoa. It was April yet the biting wind merited a nurse wrapping herself up in coat and scarf for the brisk walk between the dormitories and wards.

She'd been on shift for such long periods that she couldn't remember when she'd last slept for a decent length of time. Now it was her roommate's turn to get out of her fleapit, as they termed their bunks. The staff dormitories at Nine Elms weren't nearly as well appointed as those Olivia had been used to at St Omer. The beds were little more than sleeping bags on top of thin lumpy mattresses. Still they considered themselves blessed when they compared what they had to what their patients had recently endured.

Yesterday a few engineers who'd lain for days wounded and starving in shell holes had been brought in. Without any flicker of visible life and with grey complexions, they'd looked like corpses already. Hot water bottles had been piled around their blanketed bodies to try to resuscitate them. In the end one man had revived. The others would be buried later in the week in the cemetery close by.

'How's the young captain?' Lucy asked. She'd started getting dressed inside her snug cocoon and cursed when her gyrations caused her to clumsily pull on a stocking and put a toe right through the wool.

'His father's still sitting with him,' Olivia said. 'He hasn't improved, I'm afraid. I don't think he can struggle on for much longer either.' Her eyes stung with emotion. A colonel's son had been brought in a week ago with so many injuries it was a wonder he'd survived the X-rays that were taken to find how much lead he was carrying. He seemed comatose most of the time but possibly was aware that his father had been sitting at his bedside for hours on end. She imagined he didn't want to let his parent down by dying. At St Omer, when mothers visited their mortally wounded sons, Matron would ask them to go outside to give the boy some rest . . . often it was only then that he would let go and pass into his blessed everlasting sleep.

The captain was well thought of; some of his men had also come by to enquire about him. He reminded Olivia of Lucas and that was probably why she spent every moment she could keeping an eye on him. He was younger than Lucas by years, and fair-haired. He was engaged to be married, his father had said. The colonel dreaded writing to the boy's mother and fiancée with the news.

Olivia had finished her cocoa and had been in the process of undoing her bootlaces to wriggle her sore toes free. But whistles were shrilling and a hum of activity had already started outside. Lucy flung off the covers and jumped upright. Olivia did her laces back up then grabbed her coat and dashed out of the tent a second after her colleague.

★   ★   ★

'Did you manage to get home for Christmas?' Olivia used a finger to swipe a crumb of cream eclair from her plate. It had been a long, long time since she and Rose had relaxed together in a café and enjoyed coffee and pastries.

'Crikey, Christmas seems ages ago.' Rose sighed. 'I arrived home just in time for the New Year. We had a bit of a sing-song in the pub even though I felt shattered. My brother had just got back too, and was raring to go. So I thought: anything he can do, I can do. He's the blue-eyed boy, so Mum agreed to come along with us. She wouldn't have if I'd been the one to ask her,' Rose added wryly.

Although they'd exchanged letters, the girls hadn't seen one another since late last year. Rose had been seconded to another depot for a few months. Yesterday she'd turned up at Nine Elms with some casualties and they'd discovered there was an opportunity for them to spend the following day together. Some patients on the mend were to be transferred back to a base hospital and Rose had been given the job of driving them.

412

Olivia's superior had insisted she take a day off as she'd not had a break in almost a month. That had delighted her because it meant she'd be free to ride shotgun with Rose to Calais. Things had quietened around Ypres. There was talk about breaking camp to set up in another position, closer to the fighting.

'Come on, out with it. You must have plenty to tell me about your Christmas with Lieutenant Black. Something's happened. You've got a certain glow, Livvie.'

Olivia snorted with amusement. 'I'm surprised I have a *glow* of any sort. I feel dirty as hell! I'd sell my soul for a long hot bath with bath salts.' The last time she'd had a proper soak was when she'd visited Hornsey Baths just after Christmas. A strip wash with lukewarm water and service-issue soap was not the same thing at all.

'Oh, the bliss . . . ' Rose wailed theatrically at the memory of such luxuries as hot water and bath salts. She crossed her arms in front of her. 'No more side-tracking now. Spill the beans about your gorgeous man.'

In response Olivia fiddled with her buttons and brought forth from her bodice the dazzling ring she wore alongside her silver locket.

'Oh . . . my . . . word!' Rose gawped at the gem. 'Is it real, Livvie?'

'I think it definitely is,' she answered wryly. 'We're engaged but only a few special people know about it.' In fact, nobody but Rose did. Olivia had not had the heart to tell Maggie about her wonderful news when her sister's marriage had just ended badly. So there'd seemed no

413

point in telling the others either. There was plenty of time yet.

'Well done, gel!' Rose hugged her gleefully. 'Have you met up with him since you've been back?'

Olivia shook her head. 'I've had a couple of letters though.' The first one she'd received had asked her if she'd remembered her promise to him. She knew he was asking whether she'd fallen pregnant. But she hadn't. She'd had a monthly soon after returning to France. There would be no cherished reminder of the first Christmas they'd shared as a couple. It was for the best . . . a relief . . . yet still she'd felt sad. She'd written to let him know that there was no cause for concern and he mustn't worry about her but take care of himself.

Having dropped the patients off at the Calais hospital, Olivia and Rose had gone into Wimereux for something to eat in a café. Since they were within striking distance of St Omer, Olivia knew it would be a waste of a precious opportunity not to pay a brief visit to her old colleagues.

'Shall we take the scenic route back and stop by and see Matron?'

Rose beamed. Anything that gave them more time together was fine by her.

They paid the bill and exited into a mild May afternoon and to the sound of droning aircraft.

'Not ours,' Olivia said bleakly, pointing towards the coast. A pack of Gothas sporting German crosses was just visible heading out to sea.

It was a depressing sight. Since Germany had signed an Armistice with Russia they now had their Eastern Front troops available to redeploy. In early-spring they'd started using an increased force against the Allies on the Western Front.

The British had been taken by surprise by the enemy's hard and furious Spring Offensive. But they weren't beaten yet even if their backs were against the wall. More American and Commonwealth troops were arriving in good numbers to support their battle-weary comrades.

Rose crossed herself, watching the menacing dark specks disappear towards the English Channel. Olivia closed her eyes, murmuring a prayer for her family. By her side her friend was doing the same. They knew the bombers were heading for London.

★  ★  ★

'This is a very nice surprise.'

'We thought we'd pop in and see you as we were over this way.'

'Well, now you're here you can make yourself useful, Sister Bone.' Matron was beaming with pleasure as she handed over a bowl of dressings. 'Be a dear and nip over to C4 with those, would you? I'd ask an orderly but a few of them have come down with influenza and the others are taking up the slack, darting about like bluebottles. Flu at this time of the year!' She clucked her tongue. 'Heaven knows what the winter will bring.'

'I'll come with you,' Rose offered.

'No . . . I've a job for you, too.' Matron took a tin from a cupboard behind her. 'I've a rather nice fruitcake I was saving for a special occasion. I think this merits the description. So we'll need something to wash it down with.' Matron nodded at the kettle on the stove. 'If you'd do the honours with the tea, Miss Drew, I'll just pop off and tell Staff Sister I'll be on the missing list for fifteen minutes. That's all I can spare, I'm afraid.'

The first person Olivia saw on entering the ward was Flora Thistle. Her old roommate looked startled for a moment before breaking into a grin and hurrying over. She hugged Olivia to her.

'Well, look what the cat's dragged in,' she crowed jovially. 'My, you're looking well, Livvie.'

'So are you,' Olivia said. 'Here . . . present for you.' She handed over the large bowl filled with dressings. 'It's good to see you, Flora. How have things been at St Omer?'

'The fighting's creeping ever closer.' Flora grimaced her concern. 'I'm transferring to Etaples in the next day or two. They're expecting it'll be all hands on deck very shortly.'

'Well, good luck.' There was a huge St John Ambulance military hospital there, close to an army barracks and training grounds. It was where Olivia had expected to be posted when she'd been taken on as a VAD, years ago.

'How's Morag doing?' Flora asked. She'd got on well with the nurse from Edinburgh.

'Och . . . she's as fit as a flea.' Olivia gave a

passable impersonation of her Scottish colleague's accent. 'She's head over heels with a corporal in the RAMC. They took to one another straight away. Although you'd be hard pressed to know it, the way the two of them bicker.' Olivia sighed. 'It's got to be a short and sweet reunion, I'm afraid. Matron can only spare a few minutes to have a chat and we've got a drive in front of us before nightfall.' Having said farewell to Flora, she turned for the exit.

'Olivia? Olivia Bone, is that you? I'm sure it is. I recognised your voice. Please stop. Talk to me, Livvie . . . I beg of you.'

Olivia was on her way out of the ward when the wheezed out words brought her to a startled halt. The voice that had spoken, though weak, had a familiar cockney twang that sent a chill through her. She approached the row of beds and saw at once who'd addressed her. He was propped up on pillows. His eyes were bandaged and one hand was plucking in agitation at the covers. He held it out to her, beseechingly.

'Harry?' she whispered, bending closer to make sure she wasn't mistaken. The man in the bed had matted hair and yellowish skin pocked with sores. It was Harry Wicks and Olivia could see straight away he'd been gassed. Judging from the rattle in his chest he was also suffering from pneumonia. His hand twitched on the covers again as though he wanted to touch her. Though feeling shocked to the core, she put her fingers in his. He gripped them fiercely.

'I'm blind, Livvie. I'm done for. I know I won't make it home to say to folk what I should.'

He paused, gasping in breath. 'Would you tell me mum and Maggie I said I'm sorry?' His chest rose and fell rapidly as he fought to drag more air into his diseased lungs. 'There's others too I should mention, but it's me mum and Maggie on me mind. Please speak to them for me so I can rest easy,' he begged.

'I will, I swear,' Olivia said hoarsely, squeezing his fingers. She perched on the side of his bed, cradling his ragged-nailed hand between hers. At one time the idea of ever touching Harry Wicks with kindness and compassion would have been abhorrent to her. But not now. He was a mortally wounded soldier in need of comfort. Just like all the others. 'They'll be so proud of you, Harry, when they know you've been fighting to keep them safe. When he's bigger, your son will understand his daddy was a hero.' Olivia blurted out what came into her head, what she thought she should say, even though she feared she didn't believe all of it.

'I hope so. He's a good boy. I want him to be proud of me. 'S why I come back here, fer Ricky. I'm his dad and should keep him safe. And you, Livvie?' he gasped. 'Are you proud of me?'

'Yes, I am.'

'I wish I could've been more like my brother. He was a good lad. I miss him. Hope me Maker lets me upstairs so I can meet me brother again.' Harry swung his head. 'But I was me father's son, y'see. He was no good. It'll be damnation fer me . . . though I did me penance by coming back here.'

'Hush . . . you must rest now.' Harry was

upsetting himself so she stood up and gently eased her fingers away from his.

'You won't come back, will you?' he said dully.

'I can't, Harry. I have to go back to my base at Ypres. I'm on a visit today, that's all.'

'Would you kiss me goodbye, Livvie? A last kiss that I can pretend is from you and Maggie and me mum rolled into one? I always wanted one from you given freely, not one I stole.' He hung his head and snuffled as a tear trickled from his left eye.

Olivia found a hanky on the nightstand to dab it away then placed her lips on his sallow, scabbed cheek. 'Goodbye, Harry. God bless. When I get home I'll tell them that I've seen you and how brave you've been.'

She walked quickly away then broke into a run as she got outside the ward. She stopped for a breather, wanting to compose herself before joining the others. She didn't want to spoil the atmosphere by looking distressed. Had Harry finally reformed? Perhaps the end of his marriage and the bad business with Ruby *had* finally made him ashamed of the man he'd become. He'd sounded humble and regretful. Just this morning hating Harry would have been as natural to her as breathing. Now she felt overwhelmed with pity and sadness for him. Anticipating the hurt she must bring to Maggie's door when recounting this episode was an equally sharp pain.

Her sister had wanted a divorce but she'd not relish knowing how Harry had suffered. Soon Maggie would be a widow and her little son would have lost his father before he'd had his second birthday. Olivia knew she had a very difficult decision to make about how to break this news.

★ ★ ★

Two letters were waiting for her when she got back from St Omer. The post had turned up and put a smile on everybody's face. But though she hugged her letters to her breast, and placed her lips to the one bearing Lucas's writing, Olivia couldn't shake off the melancholy mood brought on by her encounter with Harry. Gone for ever was the swaggering brute she'd grown up with; briefly in his place would be a penitent blindman before the mortuary corporal claimed him.

She'd told Matron and Rose that she'd had quite a shock speaking to her gravely ill brother-in-law on the ward, unaware he'd even returned to the front after being invalided home. Matron had sighed sadly and promised to write in due course of Private Wicks's outcome. She knew of his condition, of course, and said she didn't expect to be relaying cheerful news in about a week's time.

The drive home had been more subdued than the outward journey. Rose was attuned to her friend's moods and had realised she wanted to reflect quietly on things. She had dropped Olivia off, promising to come back another time so they could have a happier meeting.

Olivia settled on her bunk with her legs curled under her and gazed at her post, savouring the prospect of opening it. Lucas's letter was unfolded first. As always when reading his messages, she took out the photograph of him that had been with her since Christmas and was kept wrapped in a lacy shawl. If only she could keep him as safe! In between reading his loving reassurances that he was fine she smiled at his strong handsome face, kissing it as she came to the end. Carefully she put the photograph and letter away in the drawer of her nightstand, to be read again later, over and over again.

Olivia opened up Maggie's letter then, feeling an ache of sadness beneath her ribs. Soon she would have to write back. But not yet. She'd wait until she heard from Matron before she did so. She didn't want to relay bad news twice.

★ ★ ★

It was less than a week later that Olivia received a letter from Matron. Private Harry Wicks had been buried at Wimereux Cemetery.

When his brother had been killed, Maggie had accused Olivia of letting her down. She'd expected her big sister to come home and support her through the grief of losing her fiancé.

This time it would be different. Olivia wouldn't let Maggie down again. She had asked for, and been granted, eight days' leave. She was looking forward to seeing all her family.

Apart from dealing with the news about Harry, she wanted to reassure them that she was fine after recent events in France.

421

A German air raid on the Étaples hospital and military bases had resulted in patients and medical staff being killed. In the same letter that told her of Harry's death, Matron had written that Flora had been amongst those lost at Étaples. Sister Thistle had been gone from the relative safety of St Omer just a matter of days when she'd perished. Olivia and Flora hadn't always seen eye to eye but they had become firm friends in the end. Olivia had wept for the nurse she'd wished good luck to such a short time ago.

The outrage had affected everybody at Nine Elms, as it surely had at every other hospital on the Western Front. It seemed the Germans were playing very dirty in their desperation to snatch victory. Nobody was out of bounds and talk of reprisals on similar German targets was doing the rounds. Olivia hoped that talk was all it was. Or they'd all dance with the devil.

Reports of the atrocities would have reached England by now and her family would again be worried for her safety. She was equally worried about theirs. At about the same time as Étaples was hit there had been pitiless bombing over South London, resulting in civilian deaths. Would North London be next? The memory of that pack of enemy aircraft she and Rose had watched heading out over the Channel made Olivia's skin prickle with dread.

Morale was low at home and abroad. Yet caving in to the enemy after almost five long years of war was unthinkable.

# 30

The last time Olivia had come here she'd brought Ricky Wicks bluebells from the woods behind St Omer. In the meantime the rows upon rows of new graves at Wimereux Cemetery had taken up a vast area, separating the brothers' resting places by quite a distance.

It was June and this time she'd picked some crimson poppies from the fields she walked past on her way up the hill to the graveyard. As she made her way between the lines of wooden crosses she stopped on occasion to look at the names. Some she remembered. Men she'd nursed at St Omer. Grizzled faces were brought to mind before she moved on. She divided her posy between Ricky and Harry, bending to place the delicate papery flowers on the soil. She spent longer at Harry's freshly dug plot with its bright pine cross. She told him she was on her way to England to keep her promise to him. Then she pushed herself to her feet and, without a backward glance, set off to continue on her journey home.

★　★　★

'I'm so glad you're here, Livvie. Thank you for coming back. I wouldn't have wanted to find out about this from a letter.'

'I know. I wanted to talk to you . . . let you

know I'd seen Harry and spoken to him.' She gave Maggie a hug before taking her nephew from his pram and sitting down in an armchair with the boy. 'It's so good to be home. I've missed you all. Especially this little one.' She bounced her nephew on her knee, glancing at intervals at her sister. Maggie looked pale and very thoughtful after their talk but she had taken the news about her husband better than Olivia had dared hope. She hadn't given her sister *all* the distressing details . . . just that Harry had been gassed and had contracted pneumonia. Once Maggie had finished sobbing, Olivia had stopped cuddling her, allowing her to dry her eyes. Then Maggie's concern had been for her mother-in-law.

Mrs Wicks was now quite alone. Her husband, her two sons . . . all gone. But she had a grandson and Olivia hoped that would give the woman some comfort. She hoped too that the child on her lap never knew the sort of brutal conflict that had taken his father and uncle.

'D'you think I ought to go and tell her, Livvie?' Maggie frowned. 'I'm officially Harry's next-of-kin now, so she might not be informed. She should know . . . it's only fair.' Maggie looked pensive. 'I'll get a letter, won't I?'

'A notification will be sent eventually. I'll come with you to Wood Green, if you like. But if you'd rather see your mother-in-law alone . . . '

'No, please come with me,' Maggie immediately interrupted her. 'I suppose I'll need some widow's weeds. I'd better put on the black dress I wore for Dad's funeral.' She sighed, rubbing her bloodshot eyes. 'Harry told me he'd go back to war if he was fit enough to make his boy proud. I thought it was just talk. I didn't want him to. Neither did his mother. She was dreading losing the only son she had left. That's why he wanted you to say sorry to her. He thinks he's let her down.' Maggie took the toddler from Olivia. 'Your daddy was a brave soldier.' She kissed Ricky's rosy cheek. 'He won't remember. Perhaps it's for the best. But when he's old enough I will tell him that he should be proud of his father.'

Olivia smiled. She'd soothed Harry with similar phrases. And she felt uncharitable about being sceptical of what he had said at their final meeting. Had her brother-in-law *really* become a changed man? At the back of her mind niggled the thought that the old Harry would simply have fled abroad to escape Riley McGoogan's wrath. Ruby's husband was reputed to have put men who'd done him less harm than Harry had in hospital. Olivia stopped pondering on it. What did any of it matter now?

She'd arrived home last night to a wonderful welcome and a celebration fish and chip supper. She'd felt like a fraud, pretending all was well when it wasn't. She had waited until this morning, after the boys went off to school and Uncle Ed set off for work, before breaking the news to her sister. She'd not wanted to ruin their lovely evening; that apart, it was only right to let Maggie know in private that she was a widow. The others would find out soon enough.

'Albert Carter's sent me a few letters.' Maggie held her son up, gazing into his impish face. 'He asked me if he could. I like him. He makes me laugh, telling me about what he and Ricky got up to over there in the early days.'

'Lucas told me that they were good friends.'

'I've written back. He knows I married Ricky's brother. So in my next letter I should tell him Harry won't be coming home.'

'All our boys over there love to receive letters. It's what keeps them going. That and the treats from home. They really appreciate biscuits and chocolate and cigarettes.'

'If I can find anything nice in the shops, I'll send it. Now rationing's started there are always queues stretching down the High Street.' Maggie put Ricky in his pram as he started to grizzle then fastened his reins as he tried to get out again. 'I'm bringing in thirty-five bob a week from Turner's so can afford a few luxuries. Matilda was always the one to get hold of a bit of hooky stuff. I wouldn't ask her to now though. She's turned very funny since Jack . . . ' Maggie broke off, exclaiming, 'Oh . . . you don't know about Jack!'

'Don't know what?' Olivia had gone cold because she'd guessed about Jack. But she listened intently as Maggie recounted that she'd bumped into a distraught Alice Keiver and been told that her dad had been killed. Not only that, Alice's boyfriend had also perished. Olivia covered her face with her hands and started to cry. She'd not known Geoff Lovat well but remembered him as a handsome young man, full of life. Jack Keiver had been a good friend to her. The first day she'd met him she'd been looking for Ruby in the Bunk and he'd kindly escorted her into the worst street in North London. A rough diamond, Jack had been, though he'd have chuckled to hear himself called such. So would his wife on hearing her husband being complimented. Matilda! How on earth would she go on without him? Fight and argue, indeed they had, but they had been devoted to one another, and their girls.

It was Maggie's turn to give comfort but Olivia quickly pulled herself together. She brushed the tears from her eyes. She didn't want to start Maggie off again. 'I was fond of Jack, he was a lovely man.' She found a handkerchief to use. 'I'll go and see Matilda.'

'She doesn't want sympathy. I tried that. You know how she is.' Maggie rolled her eyes. 'She slammed the door in my face. Alice says she's drunk most of the time.'

'Well, if she won't let me in today, I'll try again tomorrow.' Olivia's heart was breaking for her friend. Matilda had always been there for her.

'I don't ask her to have Ricky any more. Her neighbour Beattie still offers and Uncle Ed's helping out. Nancy too when we're on different shifts. Ain't easy, but we manage between us so I can keep on working. I'll get those munitions out even faster now I know what happened to Harry.'

When they arrived in Wood Green Olivia went in with Maggie to speak to Mrs Wicks. The woman seemed to take the news philosophically at first. Then as the shock started wearing off she became quite hysterical. She grabbed Ricky from his pram and was reluctant to let him go. She wanted to hold onto the little boy because he was the image of Harry. Maggie, in her wisdom, allowed the woman to embrace her grandson and went to put the kettle on again.

After she'd finished her tea Olivia withdrew, leaving Maggie with her mother-in-law, trying to calm her down. She loitered outside in the warmth of the sunshine dappling the hedge, feeling immensely proud of her sister. At eighteen years old Maggie had endured a lot in her life and had matured into a loyal and caring woman. Nobody would have blamed her for not giving Mrs Wicks a second thought, considering the way the woman's son had treated her.

After ten minutes Maggie emerged, pushing the pram, and they set off towards the top of the road.

'Shall we go and see Mum and Dad while we're this way?' Olivia suggested.

'Yeah, I'd like to,' Maggie said.

St Michael's Church in Wood Green had always been important in the Bone family's life. Their parents had got married and then been laid to rest there. Before her mother had died, Olivia had attended Sunday School at the church. Her father lost interest in sending her after his wife died though.

'We should have brought some flowers.'

'They won't mind,' Olivia said, crouching down. She kissed her fingertips then patted them on their parents' names cut into the granite headstone.

'I wish they could give us a sign of when it'll all stop.' Maggie sounded wistful, pushing the pram to and fro.

'Yeah, me too,' Olivia said.

They lingered only briefly as it had started pattering with rain.

'Come on, let's go home.' Olivia took a turn with the pram. 'This afternoon, I'm going round to see Matilda.'

'Best of luck,' Maggie said as they strolled back along the path. 'Oh, by the way, I didn't tell you that a letter turned up for you yesterday. I put it in the sideboard drawer.'

'I'll open it when I get back,' Olivia said.

'If you don't mind looking after Ricky this evening, I'll fit in an extra shift at work.'

Olivia bent towards the pram and tickled the boy's cheek with a finger, making him giggle and clap his hands. ''Course I don't mind.'

★ ★ ★

'Di'nt know you was back.'

'Yeah, I am. Not for very long though.' Olivia was aware that Matilda was quite tipsy and slurring her words. Nevertheless she cocked her head, looking past her into the dingy interior of her front room. 'Going to let me in?'

'No point. I'm pissed, and in a bad mood. And I ain't sharing me booze this time. Only got a drop left.'

429

Olivia brought her hands from behind her back, showing Matilda a full bottle of Irish whiskey.

Matilda's lips twitched in the ghost of a smile. 'I'll be even worse company if I sink that lot.'

'Start on it tomorrow then, eh?'

'Get off home . . . I need a kip.' Matilda started to shut the door.

'Let me in,' Olivia said with a catch to her voice. 'Please . . . I can only talk to you. Can't worry the others. Not with this.'

Matilda narrowed her eyes as though searching out trickery. She pursed her lips then allowed Olivia inside. The mess was dreadful, the smell worse than last time. And little Lucy, playing with a doll on the bare floorboards, looked as though she needed a good wash.

Matilda must've read her visitor's thoughts, or felt ashamed of the state of everything, because she said, 'Alice always sees to things when she gets in from work.'

'I'm so sorry about Jack.'

'I know you are,' Matilda croaked. 'But sorry ain't gonna put things right for me. So what is it that's worrying *you*?'

'He's missing. Opened a letter just now from a Brigadier Saville. Lucas told him we were getting married, so the brigadier thought he should write to advise me that Lieutenant Black's missing in action. He's been missing for a while, Matilda. I'm really frightened this time . . . it's too official . . . he won't come back now, I know it.' Olivia sank down on top of old newspapers heaped on a battered armchair. Her chin sank to

430

her chest and she started weeping, arms wrapped around her abdomen. The huge sobs seemed to be dredged up from her bowels. They rattled in her chest before escaping.

Matilda crouched in front of her then, with a grimace, sank down onto her aching knees. 'Missing ain't dead. Jack's dead. Your lieutenant ain't been written off yet. So think yourself lucky and don't give up on that luck till you have to.' She gripped Olivia's fingers in hers, giving them a shake until the girl looked up at her blearily. 'You hear me?' Matilda brushed strands of fair hair away from Olivia's wet cheeks, demanding an answer with her fierce glare.

Olivia nodded but her eyes and nose were still dripping and she had to use her sleeve to wipe her messy face.

'You don't give up on hoping until the moment that hope's ripped from yer.' Matilda got unsteadily to her feet. 'I'll swap yer missing for killed in action any day, Livvie,' she barked, then made a noise like an injured animal.

Olivia got to her feet and embraced her, trying to contain her own grief but it was impossible. They clung together, shaking and howling, and Olivia knew it wasn't only for Lucas and Jack she wept but for every one of the men she'd crossed paths with that would never come back.

'Sorry . . .' She swallowed repeatedly to clear her throat. 'Come round to be a comfort to you and look what I've done.'

'You are a comfort to me, love. Knowing I ain't alone grieving might be a selfish way of looking at it. But I never said I was nice.'

Olivia sniffed. 'You are nice. In your own way. I think so.'

'Ain't expecting me to make you tea now, are yer?' Matilda said gruffly. 'Can't hardly stand on me feet.'

'No . . . open the whiskey.' Olivia dug in her pocket and pulled out her cigarettes. She pushed the pack across the table to Matilda.

'I don't usually smoke, but I will today,' she said by way of thanks.

Olivia lit their cigarettes and Matilda poured a drink for each of them.

'Absent friends,' Olivia said hoarsely. 'Wherever they may be.'

'Absent friends,' Matilda echoed. 'You told Maggie about your letter?'

Olivia combed her messy hair off her forehead with her fingers. 'I couldn't. She's just found out her husband was gassed in France. They were separated but it's still knocked her for six, knowing he's dead.' She gulped at her whiskey, wincing as the alcohol burned her throat. 'Anyway, best get back. I'm babysitting Ricky so she can go to work.' Olivia took a final drag on her cigarette and looked around for an ashtray.

'Just drop it.' Matilda almost smiled. 'Ain't as if I'm house-proud.'

Olivia put the stub in her empty glass and picked up Lucy from the grimy floor, kissing her grubby face before depositing her on the bed. If the child had been affected by being around two bawling women she gave no sign of it but continued trying to plait her dolly's hair.

'Will it all be worth it one day? For the kids?'

Olivia didn't expect a reply and let herself out into the street. She allowed the early-evening breeze to dry her face. She didn't want to go back with bloodshot eyes so decided to walk the long way home. She set off towards Seven Sisters Road and spotted Mr Hunter ambling in her direction. She certainly wasn't talking to him so trotted over the road and kept going.

Matilda emerged from the door of her tenement with Lucy in her arms. She'd decided to make an effort and get some milk and a bag of broken biscuits for her little daughter.

She'd spotted Herbie as well but didn't avoid him. It was usually the other way round. But not this time. He kept walking in Matilda's direction. He'd seen Olivia Bone come out of the woman's house looking upset. He never let a bit of gossip pass him by, especially where the Bone family was concerned.

'How you doing then, Matilda? Not seen you out much. Heard about yer old man.' Herbie sucked his teeth. 'Real shame. Jack was one of life's good 'uns.'

'Yeah, he was,' Matilda said tersely, about to barge past.

'Just seen Livvie Bone. The lass weren't looking her usual cheery self.'

'Well, she wouldn't be, seeing as her fiancé's missing in action. Lovely feller he is too. Real gent.' The gaze she passed over Herbie then needed no explanation.

He stared after her as she continued unsteadily up the street, his mouth puckered in disappointment. At one time he would have liked the idea of the nob buying it out in France. Lately, though, he'd been banking on Olivia Bone and her lieutenant getting wed and moving off. He didn't want the girl to be a permanent fixture in his son's house.

He moseyed on, feeling more dejected than he had in a long while. Ejecting Ed Wright from Playford Road he reckoned he could manage. But shifting the whole damn' lot of them was another matter.

# 31

The port of Boulogne was always busy with troops and civilians embarking and disembarking. The shops, guest houses and cafés in the vicinity did a roaring trade catering to the travellers.

When their free afternoons coincided Olivia and Rose would spend that precious time together. They'd go to the harbour to sit in a café and watch the ships coming and going. The fishermen with their zinc buckets crammed with wriggling sardines would hail passers-by while displaying a particularly plump specimen by its tail. The girls loved to watch the French housewives haggling over the price of their suppers.

It was midsummer and the battles were still raging, the casualties still filling the clearing stations and hospitals. Everybody carried on as cheerfully as they could. Things weren't all going the Germans' way and some strategic ground had been regained by the Allies. But people were wary of being too optimistic in case their hopes were dashed once more.

Olivia was determined to look on the bright side even though she'd had no word of Lucas. Matilda's fierce voice reverberated in her mind whenever she felt like dropping to her knees and weeping.

'*You don't give up on hoping until the moment that hope's ripped from yer.*'

The words were in her head now as she observed a group of dashing young naval officers strolling in the sunshine. One of them turned to eye up a mademoiselle pushing a bicycle with a basket of bread on the handlebars.

'No news yet?' Rose asked gently, following the direction of Olivia's gaze. She rarely mentioned her friend's missing fiancé knowing the distress it would cause.

Olivia's throat had a lump in it and a shake of her head was the only answer she could manage. She sipped her coffee and ate her bread and cheese. 'This is very good.' She pointed to the Camembert and finished every scrap of it. 'Best get going in a minute. Matron wants to fit in a staff meeting before the evening meal.'

They drained their coffee cups and paid the hovering proprietress then made their way outside to the ambulance.

'Sometimes it's hard to believe anything bad is going on,' Olivia said as they passed two small children being accompanied towards the beach by their mother. They had buckets and spades in their hands and were squealing with laughter. There was the ever-present boom of guns in the distance but the war barely touched the lives of people in Boulogne on this particular sunny July day. Tomorrow, of course, could be a different matter.

Just as it would be a different matter when she got back to St Omer and started her night shift. They had some bad abdominal cases in and only yesterday three Australians had died of gas gangrene.

The clearing station at Nine Elms had broken camp and moved elsewhere. Olivia had asked to be transferred back to St Omer. With Matilda so far away, Matron was the next best thing to a mother figure to her. Olivia had never before realised how much she missed having a mum; she'd always been one to her lot and now was in need of a mother's comfort herself.

She'd arrived at the conclusion that she was as likely to come across Lucas at St Omer as anywhere else. With every day that passed, the probability of him returning slipped further away. *'You don't give up on hoping until the moment that hope's ripped from yer.'* The friend in her head helped her eyes dry before a single tear had fallen. Olivia linked arms with Rose as they proceeded towards the ambulance. There was never a day nor an hour nor a minute that Lucas wasn't in her thoughts. When she was tending patients she was thinking of him; when she was sleeping he was the ghost lying beside her. And now, on her afternoon off, she was searching for him.

They were heading along the esplanade in the ambulance. Olivia was whipping glances here and there in the vain hope of one landing on a tall, dark-haired man. Suddenly she jerked forward on the seat, shouting, 'Stop. Oh, stop!'

'Christ, Livvie. What's happened?' Rose exclaimed. 'Did I hit something?' Stray dogs often darted out, attempting to snatch scraps from the fishermen.

Olivia gave her an agonised glance but didn't tarry to explain. She flung open the door, jumped down and then ran, dodging bikes and army vehicles and people who stopped and stared at her as though she were a madwoman as she flew along.

'Lucas!' she bawled, doubled over, holding the painful stitch in her side. He was beside a vehicle, opening the door, about to drive off.

He turned and stared for no more than a second before sprinting towards her. He grabbed her into his arms, spinning her around.

A group of Bantams close by started to whistle as Olivia flung her arms around his neck and kissed him full on the lips. She didn't care about modesty; she wanted to taste him, feel him, know he was real.

It seemed he felt the same way. His mouth was welded to hers as was his battle-hardened body. His hands caressed her back, her hips, her buttocks.

When she finally relaxed her grip she felt dazed 'Sorry . . . did I embarrass you in front of them?'

'They're jealous as hell,' he said. 'And I don't blame them. Who wouldn't be jealous of a man with a girl like you?' He kissed her fiercely. 'I could easily devour you,' he whispered.

'I've been so worried.' She held his face away from hers for a moment. 'I had a letter telling me you were missing.'

'I'm not now.' He thumbed away the tears on her lashes. 'I'm not now,' he repeated, achingly softly. 'I sent a letter to Nine Elms about a month ago, telling you not to worry. I didn't know you'd moved back to St Omer. It doesn't matter . . . look, I'm right here. I've been searching for you. Your matron said you were resident again but had time off and had gone out with Rose Drew. I've been driving all over trying to find you.'

'Oh, Lucas . . . ' She could so easily have missed seeing him. But in the end fate *had* been kind.

A vehicle reversing at speed broke into their conversation. Rose brought the ambulance to a jerking halt and leapt from it, grinning.

'About bleedin' time you showed up. She's been a nightmare to deal with.' She gave Lucas a thump on the arm. 'Welcome back. I'm heading off now. You'll see her home, won't you?'

'Reckon I can manage that.' Lucas gave Rose a smile.

Before she could climb back into the ambulance Olivia hugged her, eyes sparkling. 'I'm so happy, Rose,' she whispered. 'You'll come back and see me as soon as you get another day off, won't you?'

'Soon as I can.' Rose landed a kiss on the side of her head then gave a toot on the horn as she pulled away.

'What time do you have to be back on duty?' Lucas asked Olivia.

'I'm on shift straight after tea. I can't let them down, Lucas,' she said, melting beneath the heat in his eyes. There were lots of rooms to be had in Boulogne and she was tempted to agree to go to one with him. That was why she didn't want him to ask the question that was vivid in his blue eyes. She wouldn't let her colleagues and patients down . . . even for him.

'I know you won't let them down, Livvie,' he said softly, eyes brimming with love for her.

She embraced him again, laying her head against his chest. She closed her eyes, her lips moving silently in a prayer of thankfulness.

⋆  ⋆  ⋆

'Oh, do come in, lieutenant. We can spare a few minutes to give you a cup of tea.' Matron had hurried outside, beaming, when she saw the saloon pull up. 'I knew you'd find her. Now I expect you two might like a few more minutes to yourselves. There's still a short while before you go on duty, Sister Bone. You can use my office. I've got a tin of ginger biscuits. Wonderful to see you back, lieutenant, and looking so well.'

Gladys Bennett had adored this man from the moment he'd told her he would bring home her abducted nurse. Even had he been unsuccessful, she would have thought him wonderful for trying. 'I sense a slight limp though.' Unceremoniously she yanked up his trouser leg and found a long scar. 'A break?'

'Yes, but not a bad one.'

'You had a broken leg?' Olivia sounded concerned. She'd noticed him limping too but he'd said his boots had had it and needed replacing.

'I'm fine . . . really.' He gently removed the material from Matron's fingers and smoothed down his trousers.

He'd keep to himself that this time he had

440

nearly died, along with all his men, pinned down by mortar fire on an exposed piece of land with just shell holes filled with stinking silt to use as cover. Luck had been with them though. Unexpectedly and without warning, the Germans had withdrawn from their position, allowing Lucas and his men to find better shelter. Then what remained of the platoon had started the long trail back to the line.

Lucas had broken a lump of wood from a tree and a young carpenter, on his first tour, had fashioned him a crude crutch. It had been a torturous time. But he'd had the good fortune to be taken to a hospital run by an orthopaedic surgeon who was ex-St Bartholomew's. He'd told Lucas he'd seen much worse and fixed him up. But along with his surviving men, Lucas had also suffered dysentery from fouled water. They'd all thanked their lucky stars they'd avoided getting smallpox as that had been diagnosed in a couple of French soldiers in the hospital. But his discharge had been delayed by quarantine.

'Well, I'll leave you in peace.' Matron approached the door. 'Ten minutes only, Sister Bone, until the staff meeting. Better put that kettle on sharpish.'

Gladys Bennett withdrew and walked away misty-eyed. She'd thought the lieutenant might have outrun his luck this time. She knew that Olivia had feared the worst too despite her stoic little spirit. Gladys had been overjoyed to see them reunited. The lieutenant wasn't only unbelievably brave and noble, he was wise

441

enough to have recognised a rare jewel in Olivia Bone. Gladys had had many probationers pass through her care but never found one she admired as much or was as fond of. Numerous more skilled nurses had been under her command in France but none matched Olivia's ability to show compassion and gain the trust of a wounded Tommy. And what might her factory girl have been capable of achieving had she been blessed with the privileges and education of a middle-class upbringing? Gladys sighed contentedly. Together, what a force to be reckoned with would that golden couple be!

'D'you want tea and ginger biscuits?' Olivia asked, turning to Lucas when they were alone in the office. She knew what he wanted, what she wanted, and it wasn't tea and biscuits! On the drive back to St Omer she'd longed to touch and be touched. Every movement of his long-fingered hands on the steering wheel or the gears had drawn her hungry eyes. She'd thought she would have so many questions to ask when this blessed day arrived but nothing seemed important. Drawing out every moment together to its fullest, and breathing the same charged air, was all that seemed to matter.

'I want you so much,' he said.

She turned, pressing her mouth to his palm in wordless agreement.

'Ten minutes. Not long,' he said hoarsely.

'It's long enough, if it's all we've got,' she said, moving closer. Her eyes locked with his until their lips touched and her fingers found his shirt buttons, undoing them.

# 32

France, 11 November 1918

'Is it true, Sister?' The patient struggled into a half-seated position so as to catch her eye.

'Yes, it is. Isn't it wonderful news?'

''Spose it is,' he mumbled, then turned again onto his front to allow Olivia to continue dressing the wound on his buttock.

The middle-aged gunner had given the impression that the declaration of peace was an anti-climax for him. His attitude had struck a chord with Olivia, and she was bewildered to feel like that. For what seemed an eternity she, and everybody else, had prayed for this day. Now, finally, it was here. There was a release of tension, certainly, as though an enormous sigh had just emptied her lungs, leaving her utterly limp. But the joy . . . the longing to celebrate? Perhaps they would come, in time.

For now there were still temperatures to take, bedpans to empty, battered bodies to bandage or to bury. The mortuary corporal wouldn't be getting his marching orders just yet.

They'd all been aware for weeks that the Allies had driven the enemy back towards Germany and that victory must eventually come. And now it had.

A short while ago the camp buglers had sounded the ceasefire. Work had stopped and the sisters had gone to every exit to investigate the din. A party of orderlies and kitchen porters had got together to form a procession, and bash out 'Rule, Britannia' on pots and pans using soup ladles. A good many of the recuperating patients had joined in the march, some on crutches, all singing with gusto. Perhaps it was the padre, watching from a distance, who best represented how everybody inwardly felt: torn in two by the news. He had dashed from the church to join in. He'd waved at the rag, tag and bobtail group as they passed him by on their lap of honour. Then he'd sunk to his haunches on the cinder path, hanging his head.

Olivia and the other nurses had given the impromptu band some hearty applause before returning to their patients. Triumphant whoops could still be heard coming from the other wards and a rendition of 'God Save the King'.

But it soon petered out. No explanation was really needed for the muted atmosphere: minds had been freed to roam over what had gone before rather than what would happen next. The dead couldn't come back to celebrate victory with them.

The gunner had started weeping softly, burying his head in the pillow in hopes that Olivia wouldn't notice his grief. She rearranged his pyjamas and pulled up his sheets then patted his shaking shoulder. 'All finished now,' she said brightly. She picked up the bowl containing Eusol and dressings and left him to his thoughts, blinking back her own tears.

'What's going on?' Alfie muttered to himself as he opened the front door and peered out into the street. He could hear a proper commotion. Church bells were ringing, not just at the local church; he could hear them pealing in the distance too.

Along the High Street vehicles were tooting their horns and the sound of tin whistles and voices singing was mounting in volume. He rushed to the gate, hanging over it to peer up and down the street. 'What's happened?' He addressed his question this time to the fellow who always seemed to be loitering about outside. His uncle had told him to have nothing to do with Mr Hunter. The man was bad news. But the boy usually mumbled a greeting when he saw Herbie just because he'd liked his son. Joe Hunter had been nice to him when he'd been Livvie's boyfriend. Alfie had been sad when he'd died.

'It's peace, son,' Herbie called back, having finished licking a Rizla. He stuck the smoke in his mouth and lit it before continuing, 'Bleedin' war's ended. And not a moment too soon.'

Alfie grinned in delight then caught sight of his cousin. Mickey was haring along with his uneven gait, yelling out, 'Alfie! Come on! Smithie's gone nuts. He's pissed as a noot and givin' kids free sweets. I've had mine. Come 'n' get yours, 'fore he sobers up.'

Alfie needed no second telling. He raced off and straight around the corner with his cousin.

Herbie licked his lips then crossed the road and loitered by the gate, darting looks at the half-open door to the house. The boy had forgotten to close it, he'd been in such a tearing rush. Herbie sidled up the path. He'd never been inside his own son's house. And he had more right than anybody to do so.

More people were coming into the street as the news of the Armistice spread. There was a growing hubbub of laughter and conversation. Few people took any notice of him. His neighbours in the Bunk needed little excuse for a shindig. They'd be at it for hours . . . days. Bonfires would be lit the length of the street and revellers would be capering about until the early hours of the morning. Then after a quick kip they'd re-light the bonfires and do it all again.

Herbie would rather warm his hands at his son's hearth. He slipped into the hallway, confident that the boys would be drawn into the Street's celebrations. Ed Wright wouldn't be back for hours yet, nor would Alfie's widowed sister. Herbie had seen her drop the nipper off to Beattie Evans earlier when going on shift at Turner's. Herbie reckoned he had some time yet before he was ejected. Or perhaps he should just barricade himself in.

Possession was nine-tenths of the law or so he'd heard.

He opened the parlour door and his bristly face creased into a contented smile. He approached the smouldering coal fire, holding out his hands to warm them. He rubbed his palms, looking about. It was a lovely place . . . as he'd known it would be. Cosy and clean. Even when he'd been married, he'd never lived in a place as good as this. His wife had been a slut.

He perched on the edge of the fireside chair, tentatively at first, then feeling bolder he sank back, settling in with a sigh. Bliss . . . they could keep their Armistice jollies. This was all he wanted. A fire, a smoke; if he had a drink too, he'd be in heaven.

He noticed the full bottle on the sideboard then. Ed Wright's brandy. He smirked. Yeah, he'd definitely tuck into that.

Herbie swigged from the bottle as he sat back down, then he got out his tobacco tin and started rolling himself another smoke. He sighed. If only life could always be this good, he'd die a happy man.

# 33

She knew he'd come for her so she waited patiently, busying herself assisting the remaining staff to gather up and clear away what had been her home for so long.

Most of the nurses had already left. Some had transferred with the patients to Calais or other base hospitals on the coast to carry on their work. There were still soldiers to care for and make well enough for the journey home to their families. Influenza and pneumonia epidemics had taken hold in a final brutal twist of the knife.

But many medical staff had already returned to try to pick up the threads of the lives they'd had in England. And Olivia was going home too.

She glanced at the bare area of field where the marquees had already been dismantled and cleared away. A few huts were still standing to house the carpenters and engineers occupied in removing all trace of St Omer hospital. Soon the French countryside would reclaim its meadow and the poppies would grow.

Matron had left yesterday with a large party of Olivia's colleagues, heading for Calais. They'd all promised to write to one another, but Olivia doubted they would. When they thought about it they wouldn't want to revisit these memories. But she'd write to Gladys Bennett. She loved the woman, as she had loved Rose.

Rose, the sister she'd always wanted for herself, because she'd always had to be a sister to others, with little given in return. Rose who would never have those good times in London that they'd planned to share when they got back. Rose who was buried at Nine Elms because she had come under fire driving the ambulance back to her depot on the day Olivia had last seen her in Boulogne. Rose whose grave she had visited and cried a thousand bitter tears over until her eyes burned when none were left to shed. The cruelty of it! The stupid waste of it! Rose had been alone, no wounded soldiers in the back to finish off. But the war had never shrunk from cruelty and stupidity.

Olivia wrapped up in her shawl her photos of Lucas and of her family and placed them in her trunk then closed the lid. She'd wanted to keep them on display until the last minute.

She heard a car scrunching on gravel and looked eagerly out of her dormitory window.

They walked towards one another, not as they once would have, urgently, but as people who'd stayed afloat in a stormy sea and were now exhausted. But their embrace was strong.

When finally they broke apart she said, 'There's something I want to do, Lucas, before we sail.'

'I know. I remembered.'

'I couldn't get much in the way of flowers . . . just a few Michaelmas daisies that were growing wild.'

'We might see something on the way. If we do we can stop and pick them.'

She cupped his cheek, loving his thoughtfulness.

★ ★ ★

Joe's resting place wasn't what she'd expected. In her romantic mind's eye Olivia had conjured up a quaint French church, whitewashed walls and clipped hedges round the graveyard. In five long years she'd never let go of that vision. But this was Ypres, and there was nothing romantic here.

The church had obviously been hit many times. Nothing was left other than jagged mortar sticking up like rotten teeth. The ground was studded with shrapnel and they picked a careful path through it into what Lucas assured her was a small cemetery.

'How will we find where he is?' She looked around in dismay. There were no crosses that she could see.

'I know where he is.' Lucas took her hand and led her on to a spot close to a mound of debris. He crouched down, started digging into rubble with his hands until he found what he was looking for.

He eased free a splintered wooden cross, rubbing his thumb on the covering of mud. Then he cleaned it with his handkerchief until the lettering was visible. He'd used his penknife to carve Joe's name back in 1914. He held it out to Olivia and she kissed its gritty surface before handing it back so he could skewer it upright again.

She caught Lucas's hand as he started to leave her to her private thoughts. 'He'd want you here with me.' She laid down her few Michaelmas daisies on the scrap of ground he'd cleared. They'd not found any more to pick. It was late-November and the earth barren.

'There's something I never told you about Joe. He wanted you to marry me if anything happened to him. He told me that in his last letter. The one you brought back.'

Lucas smiled crookedly. 'He knew how I felt about you alright.'

He found a boulder and perched on it, close by where she was kneeling. He leaned forward, patting the cross. 'He was a good man. The best.'

She sighed, looking around her at the wasteland. 'I can't wait for us to go home. Will you search for your mum when we get back?'

'No . . . I'll leave her be. She doesn't want to see me. One of her relatives answered the letter I sent to Ireland. I found out she'd gone home to be with her folks.' He gazed off into the distance, a smile quirking his lips. 'I also discovered I'm a distant cousin of Riley McGoogan.'

'No! Really?' Olivia started to chuckle. 'I like Riley. He's a bit of a bad boy but alright on the whole.'

'We're definitely kin then,' Lucas said ironically.

'Oh, you must visit your mum, Lucas. I'll come with you.'

He shook his head. 'I don't blame her for wanting nothing to do with me. She was treated badly by my father. I think he loved her but never had the courage to do the right thing by her. He did the right thing by me instead.'

'She might change her mind, you know, you shouldn't give up.'

He hung his head, frowning at the ground as though feeling emotional so Olivia changed the subject.

'When we get back home Alfie and Mickey will want to have all your stories of derring-do. Boys of that age will envy their older brothers and uncles for going to war and coming back heroes.'

'Yeah . . . they'll envy us the glory and we'll envy them the easy pickings.'

'Don't be bitter, Lucas,' she said softly although she knew he had every right to be. Every man who'd given himself or his youth to the war shared that right.

'Sorry, shouldn't have said that. Don't know why I did.' He stood up and walked away, leaving her alone with Joe.

But she knew why he'd said it. Devil's own luck had kept him alive and healed the wounds on his body. But scars would remain in his mind for the rest of his life, as they would in hers.

She whispered her farewell to Joe and pushed herself up with a sigh.

Lucas reached out to her as she drew close to him. 'Sorry, I didn't mean it.'

'I know,' said Olivia, telling a lie in return. Some truths would remain unsaid, those that were too painful to share even with a loved one . . . maybe especially with a loved one. And they wouldn't be alone in that. Husbands would polish their shoes and go off to work and bring home the bacon. Wives would raise families and pretend they didn't know any different when the kids asked Father what went on in the war and he told a tale that made them all laugh.

Lucas looked about at the land he'd fought on, crawled on, bled on. But he could go home now and leave it all behind him. He pressed thumb and forefinger to his smarting eyes.

'We can't let peace defeat us when the war didn't. We did it for the children, Lucas.' She wrapped her arms around his waist in the way she always did to comfort them both. 'Joe and Rose and Freddie and Ricky and all the others lost here . . . it was worth it for the children. We have to believe that, don't we?'

He nodded. 'How is your sister? Is she coping on her own with the boy?' He'd hung his head as though ashamed of himself.

'Yes, she is. But I meant these children too.' She took his hand and glided it across her belly. 'Child . . . children . . . in time, God willing.'

His stillness didn't last long. He eased her away from him, his questioning blue eyes searching her face.

'I know I promised to go home but by the time I knew for certain things were going our way. I couldn't write and tell you then, not with victory in sight.'

He was still staring at her when tears formed on his lashes then rolled down his cheeks. He composed himself only with difficulty, wiping his face with his sleeve. 'You're having a baby?'

'Yes, I am. And so are you, Lucas Black. And

so pleased am I that I even told Matron the truth when she asked why I'd been throwing up in the morning. I didn't let on that the happy event took place in her office though.'

He laughed silently before tenderly kissing her.

'So what I want is Joe for a boy or Rose for a girl. If that's alright with you?'

'That's fine by me,' he said huskily.

'And when the baby's born we'll go to Ireland and find your mum. I defy her not to want to meet her grandchild. Babies make everything better. They heal families. Start us afresh on new paths to happiness. Maggie's testament to that.' Olivia carefully pulled out her engagement ring from her bodice and slipped it onto her finger before extending her hand to him.

'Come on, let's go home. I think it's time you made an honest woman of me.'

# Epilogue

'I'm so sorry, Livvie. What a welcome home for you this has been.'

'Where is everybody, Matilda? Where's Maggie and little Ricky? What about my uncle and Alfie and Mickey?' Olivia babbled. 'Oh, what on earth happened? How did it start? Do you know?'

Only moments ago she had turned up at Matilda's door, white-faced and agitated, having arrived home to find her own house a burned-out shell. She'd banged on the doors of her immediate neighbours who'd reassured her that her family hadn't been home when it started and had now moved away. The elderly widow who lived next door had offered to make her tea and give her board and lodging until she found somewhere to live. The woman had hugged her with tears in her eyes. Olivia could tell that people hereabouts still hadn't got over the shock of a fire having destroyed her property on Armistice Day.

Thankfully Lucas had accompanied her all the way home. When she'd said she must speak to Mrs Keiver, he'd offered to go and find out what he could at the police station.

'Your family's fine, so put your mind at rest about that.'

Matilda drew Olivia towards a chair with one arm around her shoulders. 'Maggie and the baby have moved in with Nancy. Your uncle and the boys have gone back to Wood Green, to stop with Ruby until things are sorted out,' Matilda poured a glass of whiskey and put it in Olivia's unsteady fingers. 'Now get that down you, it'll calm your nerves.'

Olivia took a gulp. She closed her eyes in utter relief that all her family were safe with friends. Panic had struck her like a fist in the guts when they'd rounded the corner into Playford Road and seen the blackened brickwork and timbers. She took another swallow of whiskey and her rigidly held shoulders started to slump.

'It wasn't arson but an accident, so far as the police know.' Matilda took up the story as she saw Olivia begin to relax. 'I should tell you, though, that a body was found in the house,' she added cautiously.

Olivia's fearful eyes raked Matilda's face.

'Coppers believe a tramp might've got in when the Armistice celebrations were in full swing. Whoever it was had been sitting by the fire, smoking and drinking. They found a tobacco tin and a brandy bottle by the chair.' She frowned. 'Your Alfie was beside hisself, saying it was his fault. He remembered leaving the door open when he dashed off with his cousin to join in the fun.' Matilda paused. 'I asked him a few questions 'cos I could see he had something on his mind but was afraid to speak up. He told me that just before he ran off with Mickey, he spoke to Herbie Hunter who was hanging about outside.'

'You think the body was *his*?' Olivia turned cold.

'I reckon so, but couldn't say for sure and neither could the Coroner. Who'd want that job?' Matilda grimaced. 'Thing with Herbie was, he had a history of dying then turning up alive. And the other thing is, nobody's seen him since Armistice Day.'

Olivia listened intently, thinking things through. Herbie might have tried to conceal his resentment but she'd always known he hated her having his son's house. If he'd been presented with an opportunity to go inside, he would've taken it. 'It was him in there.' Olivia sounded convinced. 'Whether he meant to set the fire, we'll never know.'

'He could've drunk himself stupid and dropped a fag on the chair. Wouldn't be the first time a fire's started like that round here.' Matilda poured herself a whiskey. 'Don't reckon he'd've meant to kill himself.' She nodded at her friend's empty glass. 'Want another?'

'Thanks, but I'd best get going and catch up with the others.'

'Where you off to after that?'

'I'm getting married, Matilda. I'll be living Hampstead way.'

'Hampstead, eh?' Matilda looked delighted. 'Told you you was going up in the world, didn't I, Livvie?'

'Doesn't mean I won't be coming back to see you all.'

'I'll look forward to that,' Matilda said gruffly. 'And I'm pleased as punch for you, gel.'

Olivia knew that her friend's happiness at her good fortune was sincere. Matilda loved to see

457

people . . . women especially . . . pull themselves up by their bootstraps.

'You might've lost Joe's house but you're still on a winning streak.'

'How have you been, Matilda?' Olivia felt bad at not having enquired sooner. Bricks and mortar could be rebuilt, but people once lost were just shadows. 'Have you heard any more about where Jack's laid to rest in France?'

'Ain't laid to rest, nor's Geoff Lovat. They're just trampled in the ground somewhere round Hill 60.' Matilda turned away, stifling a sob. 'Didn't do much celebrating Armistice Day meself,' she said bitterly. 'I miss him so much, Livvie . . . '

Olivia embraced her, resting their foreheads together. 'You won't let this get the better of you, Matilda Keiver. You're too strong for that.'

'The gels at Turner's all got put off. No more munitions needed.' Matilda eased free from her friend's comforting arms, wiping her eyes. 'My Alice is moving Wood Green way. She's met a new man and got taken on at Barratt's sweet factory. I thought your Maggie and Nancy was going there as well to get jobs. But it seems Nancy reckons she's got an idea about something that'll pull in better money than sweet factory work.'

'Heaven help us, if it's what I think it is.' Olivia rolled her eyes.

Matilda pulled a rueful face. 'Now the men are home wanting their jobs back, the women gotta make their own luck. Those gels who've been wearing furs ain't settling for pinnies. I don't blame 'em for doing a bit of duckin' 'n' diving to keep the money rolling in.'

'Will you move away too, now Jack's gone?'

Matilda gave a fierce shake of the head. 'The Bunk's for me, cradle to grave. I'm staying here close to him.'

'If I wasn't getting married, I'd move back into the Bunk, y'know. There's something about the place . . .' Olivia felt too drained to find the words to explain why the road held such appeal for her. But she reckoned Matilda knew the answer anyway. It might be a crumbling slum but it had a heart, a community spirit, that was unbreakable. 'I'd better get going. Lucas will be waiting.'

At the same time they both raised one hand, tapped its fingers beneath the other's chin, then chuckled wryly.

Olivia was halfway up the street when she felt the baby move for the first time. She stopped, a hand pressed to the fluttering. She realised she'd not told Matilda she was expecting and was tempted to go back, but she didn't. There'd be another time for that. She carried on, aware of people sneaking her sympathetic glances as she passed them. A moment after she turned into Playford Road, Lucas pulled up in his car.

She knew he wouldn't want to tell her what he'd learned from the police about a body being inside the house so she said, 'I know somebody was in there during the fire. It was Herbie Hunter.'

'It wasn't possible to identify the body, Livvie.' Lucas drew her into a comforting embrace.

Olivia nodded. 'But Alfie saw him hanging around outside and now he's disappeared. I just know it was him. My family are all safe and well. That's all that matters.'

'They're welcome to live with us, you know.'

She thanked him with a smile. 'Plenty of time to sort it all out.' She was sure they'd love the idea of living in a big house in Hampstead, but the girls had tasted independence and it had made women of them. Her brother had found a father figure and had blossomed beneath Ed Wright's care. She didn't want to undo any of it with well-intentioned interfering.

'Joe wouldn't have wanted his father having his house,' Lucas said.

'Indeed he would not! He hated the man,' Olivia said passionately.

She gazed up at the house, the home that had once meant everything to her. It had given her shelter, freedom, the means to care for her family until they were able to care for themselves. She felt like weeping for the loss of it, for having let Joe down. The first floor looked quite intact and she wondered whether anything might be salvageable.

'Do you want me to go inside and see what sort of state it's in?' Lucas had read her wistful expression.

'I don't know . . . I *would* like my mum and dad's picture . . . and the photo of Joe . . . and there are other things in there . . . '

She squinted at her bedroom window. The December sun caught it and the glass flashed blindingly for a second before the light died. The house had seemed to wink at her. Olivia felt serenity settle over her.

'I'll go in and have a rummage around if you want,' Lucas said, turning her face up to his.

She glanced again at her window and the blaze was back. It faded away when a cloud was chased across the sun by a sudden breeze. It whipped Olivia's hair into her eyes. She brushed it back and blew a kiss to the heavens before gazing up at the man she loved.

'I've got my family and I've got you. There's no reason for us to go inside there again. It was Joe's house and I know he wouldn't want us to. Not now I have everything I'll ever need.'

# Acknowledgements

I owe my gratitude to the men and women who tended wounded servicemen during the Great War and wrote memoirs and diaries of what they went through at home and overseas. These reports were of great help in writing the Bittersweet Legacy series.

Anna Boatman and the editorial team at Piatkus, many thanks for your enthusiasm and support for the Bittersweet Legacy Series.

Lynn Curtis, your professional input has been much appreciated.

And thanks to Juliet Burton, my agent.

# Author Note

I have loved writing the Bittersweet Legacy Series trilogy and giving Olivia and Lucas their hard-fought happy ending. It was nice, too, to revisit Campbell Bunk and meet some infamous old faces.

In this, the last novel in the Bittersweet Legacy series, I have included a mention of another notorious character and taken some authorial licence!

Margaretha MacLeod, née Zelle, was executed in 1917 by the Allies for passing military information to the Germans during the Great War. Accounts differ as to whether she was in fact as bad as she was painted or whether she could have been a scapegoat duped into passing misinformation to the Germans, as well as spying for the French.

Her husband was Dutch although he sounds Scottish because his ancestors hailed from Skye. After she was divorced Margaretha started earning a living in various racy ways — circus performer and exotic dancer to name but two — using the stage name Mata Hari.

Although the following quote is attributed to her: 'A harlot, yes, but a traitor, never!' she had some influential and wealthy protectors so it's unlikely she would have worked in a blue-light officers' brothel close to the front line.

On another note, the Defence of the Realm

Act was in force during the Great War. Amongst other things, pub opening hours were reduced and it was an offence for people to treat others to drinks. Inhabitants of Campbell Road were often a law unto themselves and so I have taken a view that it was likely the rule was flouted more or less from the start, especially as the police were nervous about venturing into the Bunk to tackle bad behaviour. So throughout the trilogy it has been business as usual round at the Duke public house for Jack and Matilda Keiver and their pals.

And finally, thank you! I hope you've enjoyed reading the series and following Olivia's journey as she goes from being a Barratt's sweet factory worker to a nurse on the front line. If you have enjoyed the trilogy, please do consider leaving a review — there's nothing I like more than hearing from my readers! You can also find out more about the series and my inspiration for it at *www.kaybrellend.com*.

All my best,<br>
Kay

We do hope that you have enjoyed reading this large print book.

Did you know that all of our titles are available for purchase?

We publish a wide range of high quality large print books including:
**Romances, Mysteries, Classics**
**General Fiction**
**Non Fiction and Westerns**

Special interest titles available in large print are:
**The Little Oxford Dictionary**
**Music Book**
**Song Book**
**Hymn Book**
**Service Book**

Also available from us courtesy of Oxford University Press:
**Young Readers' Dictionary**
**(large print edition)**
**Young Readers' Thesaurus**
**(large print edition)**

For further information or a free brochure, please contact us at:
**Ulverscroft Large Print Books Ltd.,**
**The Green, Bradgate Road, Anstey,**
**Leicester, LE7 7FU, England.**
**Tel: (00 44) 0116 236 4325**
**Fax: (00 44) 0116 234 0205**

## A LONELY HEART

### Kay Brellend

Growing up in fear of their cruel, drunken father, Olivia Bone and her siblings haven't had an easy start in life. But when Livvie's fiancé Joe is killed at Ypres and he bequeaths her his house in Islington, it seems like the Bone family might finally escape the worst street in north London. At least Livvie has good friends, and perhaps more than a friend in Lieutenant Lucas Black, her old boss at the Barratt's Sweet Factory. As they grow closer, she decides to enlist as a war nurse, hoping to help brave men like him in fighting for their country. Should Livvie follow her heart, or her head?